Edisto Song

Books by Lin Stepp

Novels:
The Foster Girls
Tell Me About Orchard Hollow
For Six Good Reasons
Delia's Place
Second Hand Rose
Down by the River
Makin' Miracles
Saving Laurel Springs
Welcome Back
Daddy's Girl
Lost Inheritance
The Interlude
Happy Valley
Downsizing

The Edisto Trilogy:
Claire at Edisto
Return to Edisto
Edisto Song

Christmas Novella:
A Smoky Mountain Gift
In *When the Snow Falls*

Regional Guidebooks
Co-Authored with J.L. Stepp:
The Afternoon Hiker
Discovering Tennessee State Parks
Exploring South Carolina State Parks

Edisto Song

BOOK 3 OF THE EDISTO TRILOGY

LIN STEPP

MOUNTAIN HILL PRESS

Cover design: Katherine E. Stepp
Interior design: J. L. Stepp, Mountain Hill Press
Editor: Elizabeth S. James
Cover photo and map design: Lin M. Stepp

Library of Congress Cataloging-in-Publication Data

Stepp, Lin
Edisto Song: Third novel in the Edisto trilogy / Lin Stepp

ISBN: 978-1-7361643-6-5
First Mountain Hill Press Trade Paperback Printing: April 2021

eISBN: 978-1-7361643-7-2
First Mountain Hill Press Electronic Edition: April 2021

1. Women—Southern States—Fiction   2. South Carolina - Coastal - Fiction
3. Contemporary Romance—Inspirational—Fiction. I. Title

Library of Congress Control Number: 2020925340

DEDICATION

This book is dedicated to all the new fans and friends I made in South Carolina since my new books in the Edisto Trilogy began to publish. Thanks for welcoming the books with such enthusiasm. I'm so glad we met through books!

ACKNOWLEDGMENTS

"Be present in all things, and thankful for all things." – Maya Angelou

I am so grateful to all those who have helped to make my books in The Edisto Trilogy a beloved success. Wonderful thanks to all who have read our books, talked about them, and looked forward to each one with enthusiasm.

Thanks to everyone at Edisto who shared stories and memories with us, helping me to know the island better and making its people and history come alive for me.

Special thanks to the Edisto Library and the Edisto Bookstore where I found, bought, or studied many books about Edisto's history, and heartfelt appreciation to all those at the Edisto Museum, local shops, restaurants, marinas, and the Wyndham Resort, and to friends like Babe and Gerri Hutto and Cheryl and Mickey Van Metre who shared local stories with me and made me feel at home on the island.

Last but not least, many thanks to those who work so hard behind the scenes with expertise, dedication, and love to always make my books the best they can be:

___ Elizabeth S. James, copyeditor and editorial advisor
___ J.L. Stepp, production design and proofing
___ Katherine Stepp, cover design and graphics

And thanks always to God for His help and strength in all I do. As Erma Bombeck once said: *"When I stand before God at the end of my life, I would hope that I would not have a single bit of talent left, and could say, 'I used everything you gave me.'"*

A BRIEF EDISTO HISTORY

2000 BC	Archaic cultures inhabited the island
1550s	Edistow Indians lived on the island
1663	SC Colony founded by King of England
	Lord Proprietors granted lands from Charles II
1700-1770s	Plantations grew, importing rice and indigo
1775-1783	Rev War; planters fled; property destroyed
1780s-1860s	Plantations thrived growing cotton
1800s	Edingsville Beach formed for wealthy planters
1861-1865	Civil War years; slaves freed; property destroyed
1870s	Many families returned; cotton still a big crop
1893	Hurricane destroyed Edingsville Beach
1920s	Boll weevil ended cotton production
	Drawbridge to island replaced Dawhoo Ferry
	Intercoastal Waterway dredged, linking rivers
	Truck farming and fishing grew on the island
1925	Resort development on Edisto expanded
	Early cottages built, no electricity or water
1935	Edisto Beach State Park built with CCC help
	Palmetto Boulevard paved for cars
1940	Hurricane destroyed most all homes on Edisto
1941-1945	WWII slowed growth; military patrolled island
	Coast Guard patrolled park; reports of spies
	Edisto S.C. Hwy 174 straightened and paved
1950s	Development on Edisto Beach resumed
1954	Big pier built near park entrance; later burned
1959	Hurricane Gracie did heavy damage
	Groins built to hold sand, stop erosion
1970s	Edisto tourism grew and expanded
1973	Oristo resort and golf course opened
1976	Beach changed fr Charleston to Colleton Co
	Remaining Island stayed in Charleston Co
	Many businesses and beach homes built
1976	Fairfield Resorts bought Oristo Ridge
1993	McKinley Washington replaced drawbridge
2006	Fairfield Resort bought by Wyndham
2008	Botany Bay wildlife preserve opened
	Growth continued with beauty remaining

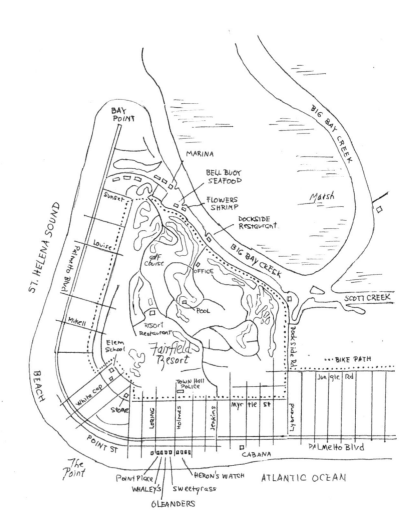

Map of
Edisto Beach

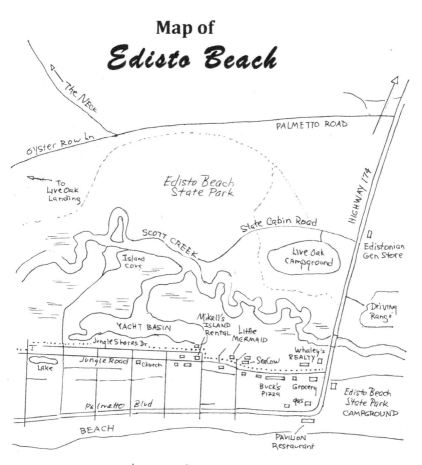

ATLANTIC OCEAN

CHAPTER 1

March 13, 2002

A tapping at the door startled Sarah, jerking her from sleep as the door creaked open. Panicked, her eyes flew to the clock on the wall before she even glanced toward the doorway to see the familiar face of her neighbor, peeking in with a polite smile.

"I didn't mean to startle you." Eito paused with diplomacy. "Julianne returned to say you'd fallen asleep."

Glancing toward the piano across the room, Sarah sighed. "I'm sorry. Julianne was practicing her scales and the song she learned for me. I didn't mean to fall asleep."

"It is perfectly all right. You have a performance tonight. You needed to rest." He hesitated. "I felt concern you might wake and worry at her absence though."

"Yes, I would have." Sarah remembered her manners, sitting up on the sofa. "Come in, Eito. I can make us some tea."

He paused to study her. "If you are sure. But you must let me fix it."

She watched as he moved to the small kitchenette in her apartment to fill a teakettle with water and to put it on the stove to heat. Her New York apartment was little, with a kitchenette, a combined living and dining area, and one bedroom and a bath off a short hallway. Eito knew the layout as well as she did since he often stayed here while Sarah was away on tour. As a concert pianist, she traveled a lot.

Eito Masako was a lovely, older Japanese gentleman with thick white hair and wise dark eyes behind black glasses. He always dressed neatly and moved with a gracious ease that relaxed her. He lived in the apartment across the hall with his daughter Marri, her husband Ken—Kenzou Takamura, and their five year-old daughter Julianne. When Sarah moved into the apartment, after graduating college and starting on tour less than two years ago, she and Marri formed a quick friendship—both new to the Terrace Court apartments on Riverside Drive. When off tour, Marri, Ken, and Eito were Sarah's family, watching out for her and sharing their lives with her.

Hearing Sarah cough, Eito turned to frown at her. "You are still not well. It concerns me—that deep cough. I do not like to think of you performing when you are ill."

She shook her head, glancing across the room at the small baby grand piano which dominated the space in the living area. "A concert pianist performs tired or not, well or not. Surely you know that. I've performed all winter since I got sick after the holidays. I'll be all right. I just can't seem to get rid of this cough and I often get so tired at the end of the day." She shivered, not wanting to mention how often a touch of fever flared in the afternoons, too, draining her strength.

He studied her for a moment and then turned back to the stove. "I am making Sencha Japanese tea. It is good for you." Eito put tea into the strainer in the teapot, added hot water and let it steam. "I keep tea here now since I stay here often. Sencha is a sweet green tea. Do not worry for the flecks in the liquid when I pour it out."

Sarah watched him hold the little teapot in just the right way and pour it out into a small white pitcher and then into two cups without handles. It was comforting to watch him perform the tea-making ritual.

"I hope you do not mind I brought my tea set over."

"Bring over anything you wish. I am happy you stay in the apartment so it doesn't sit empty so often."

"It gives my daughter and son-in-law some privacy. I have my own little bedroom in their apartment, but it is good for them to have time without me underfoot." He brought her a cup of tea and a few shortbread cookies he took from a box on the shelf.

Sarah straightened on the sofa to balance her plate on her knees, sipping at the hot tea. "You know Marri and Ken love having you live with them. You help them by keeping Julianne after school while Marri and Ken work." She smiled at him. "Julianne adores you. So do I."

"We honor you, as well, Sarah Katherine, and we are blessed to enjoy the beautiful music you play. We also thank you for the tickets to your concert at the Lincoln Center with the symphony tonight. We look forward to it very much."

She waved a hand. "I always get free tickets and I love to have someone to share them with."

"What will you play tonight?" Eito asked, settling into his favorite easy chair with his own cup of tea.

"The New York Philharmonic is spotlighting Tchaikovsky with a variety of the composer's pieces tonight. I'm playing *The Sleeping Beauty Waltz* in the first hour and after intermission *Waltz of the Flowers*, both expressive, lyrical numbers. It should be a lovely concert." She paused to cough at length after her words, finding it hard to catch her breath.

"What did the doctor say about your cough?" Eito gave her a worried look.

She shrugged. "I had a touch of flu back in winter. One of the doctors on tour said a little bronchitis developed. Later in Texas, another suggested walking pneumonia. They gave me some meds. I'll heal in time. It's hard to get the rest I need on tour."

Eito placed his teacup on a side table to reach over to put a hand on her forehead. "You are feverish and sweating, Sarah Katherine. You are not well." His kind eyes studied her face. "The good Lord gives you only one body to live in and take care of. I don't think you are caring well for yours right now."

She closed her eyes for a moment. "The tour schedule doesn't allow much time to rest. I'm glad to have a few days here at home in New York now, but then we're leaving for Philadelphia and after that Chicago. It means so much to Jonah that I do well on tour. It advances his career as my agent and manager and it advances my standing as an artist."

"You care for him, this Jonah, I think. Marri, Ken, and I have seen it."

"Yes." She smiled. "Jonah does so much for me and there is more than just affection." She glanced at her hands. "He talks of a future together."

Eito frowned.

Sarah saw the change in his expression. "I'm sorry you're not fond of Jonah."

He shrugged. "I told you before he is not a good match for you." Eito paused to sip his tea before continuing. "You know I was a *nakodo* in Japan as well as a counselor."

"A matchmaker. I've heard your and Marri's stories about that."

"Americans find the concept of matchmaking amusing but it is an old and honored tradition in Japan. Did you know an arranged marriage in Japan has a better chance of success than an American marriage based on falling in love? The divorce rate is very small, only six percent. That is because couples are matched sensibly, based on culture, families, and similarities. A *nakodo* does much research, spends much time with the couples, the families, to suggest a possible match. A good *nakodo* has a gift for knowing which couples will match well. It comes from many years of working with matching couples. My father was a *nakodo*. The gifting is often passed down in families." He finished his tea and set his plate aside. "Marri and Ken's marriage was arranged in Japan."

Sarah shifted, her head swimming a little as it often did in the late afternoon. "I have heard their story, Eito, and seen the photos of their lovely wedding in Japan before Marri came to live here with Ken."

"Well, you see?"

She tried to think what to say. "If you took time to come to know Jonah I think you would like him."

Eito got up to take their plates to the little kitchenette and began to wash the cups, plates, and teakettle, not replying.

A short time later he came back to sit beside her. "It is your health most of all that concerns me right now. You are pale. You have dark circles under your eyes. You are tired all the time, not yourself. You cough too much and often are feverish. I would ask of you, as a doting *otosan*, or father figure, that you ask this Jonah to let you out of the next performance, or maybe the next two or three, for a good rest and a time to recuperate. He can get another pianist to fill in, and a little rest will not destroy your career. Sometimes people grow ill. Performers, like all other professionals, must pause to care for themselves and heal. If he holds affection for you, as you say, he will understand this. Stay here in the city and rest a few weeks. Then return to the tour, well, in good health, and able to give it your best. This is wise counsel. If your mother and father were here and could see the condition of your health, they would say the same."

She bit her lip. "I hate to disappoint Jonah and cause him trouble."

"You say he cares for you and your future," Eito repeated. "He will understand. He may not even realize how ill you have been. You must tell him. It would not be good if you broke down at a performance."

"No." She frowned. "You're probably right."

She glanced at the clock. "Jonah planned to go early to the Lincoln Center for a meeting and to be sure everything is set up as it should be for tonight. If I go early I can talk with him." Her head swam as she stood up. "You have been kind to be so concerned about me Eito. You should go home now. I'm sure Marri is working on supper, so all of you can get ready to come to the performance tonight. I'll go and get dressed and go over to the Lincoln Center early to talk with Jonah."

He nodded and patted her cheek. "I am happy for you to do this."

An hour later, Sarah was nearly ready to head out the door to catch a cab to the Center, when her cell phone rang.

"It's Mary Helen," a familiar voice said as soon as she picked up. "I had to call and wish my little sister Suki a happy performance."

"You sweet thing." Sarah sat down on the sofa for a moment, loving the sound of the childhood nickname her family always called her. "How are you feeling?"

Mary Helen laughed. "Impatient for this baby to come. He's late, the little dickens. I'm sorry that meant Mother and Parker couldn't come to New York for your show tonight and to see you. They wanted to come. But Andrew is coming. Did you know that? He wanted to come and Parker and Mother liked the idea of someone being there for you. He flew in late today. I'm sure you'll see him after the show, and he's staying over, I think."

"It will be nice to see Andrew again." She glanced at the clock. "I need to head over to the Center for a meeting, Mary Helen. Be sure that you, J.T., or Mother call me as soon as the baby comes. I wish I could come home for a visit to see him, but I don't have another break in my schedule for quite some time."

"We understand. We'll send pictures, Suki. Don't worry, and have a great show tonight."

They hung up, and Sarah headed for the Lincoln Center, the cold bite of the March air in New York making her cough again as soon she stood on the street to hail a cab.

A short time later she threaded her way down a flight of stairs to the offices in the Lincoln Center where she hoped to find Jonah. She clung to the handrail, feeling dizzy from the trip over. Maybe I do need a break, she thought, and then worried again about disappointing Jonah. He stressed to her so often how important a large number of performances were to an emerging artist—and to him, building his career and hers. The first months on tour had been exciting. Sarah had always loved to perform, to share her gift and music with others. But traveling on tour had soon lost its excitement. It seemed she was always on the road, always waiting in an airport, making her way in a new city, staying alone in hotels with little to do and no one to talk with when Jonah was busy.

Her times with Jonah had been a joy though. Touring cities with him, visiting new places, eating in elegant restaurants. Walking holding hands in the dark. Learning about his life, his family, his hopes, and his dreams. Kissing sometimes. Talking about their future together. Sweet, sweet memories that kept her going.

She paused at the bottom of the stairs to catch her breath. Why was it so hard to breathe sometimes now?

Hearing voices down the dim hallway, Sarah made her way past several empty doorways to the office at the hall's end. She recognized Jonah's voice and pushed the door ajar just a little, but then stopped in her tracks. Jonah lay on the leather couch in the office with most of his clothes off on top of a young girl. Suki recognized her immediately. It was Nita Bianchi, the violinist traveling with them and performing with the Brooklyn Philharmonic later this week. Stunned and shocked, she backed away into the hallway, learning against the wall by the door, her knees shaking. She could hear their voices, their sounds, and felt the betrayal down to her bones. Quietly, she made her way back down the dark hallway and up the stairs, hoping to find a place where she could be alone to process this. To try to calm her rapid heartbeat. To quiet the barrage of thoughts swimming through her mind. To catch her breath.

"Oh, there you are Sarah Katherine." One of the Lincoln Center's marketing executives rounded a corner and spotted her. "Alfred said he thought he saw you here early. I'm so pleased. One of the reporters from the newspaper is here, wanting an interview. Follow me. He's in my office. You have plenty of time to talk with him before you go into make-up for the show."

Somehow Sarah pasted on her poised, professional smile and followed Jane Kiley to talk to the man from the press and then was shepherded on to make-up where a dresser fussed over her pale face and the dark circles under her eyes. Sarah changed into the dress she planned to wear tonight—a white one, a color she often wore. Around her waist she wrapped the red cummerbund that she always wore for her performances for luck, now also a trademark for her. She slipped the red shoes onto her feet she'd also become known for. "The angel in the red shoes and red cummerbund," they often called her—especially when she wore white. But even when she wore black, her fair, pale hair gave her an angelic appearance on stage in the spotlights.

Dressed now, waiting for her cue, Sarah looked at herself in the mirror, seeing a young woman, twenty-four now, tall like her mother and sister, with strong wide hands, slender in build. Her blond hair, carefully arranged, dropped to her shoulders. Shocked deep blue eyes stared back at her, and an artificial blush took the place of her usual rosy cheeks. She shook her head as the image swam before her eyes of Jonah with Nita and a coughing spell stole her breath until she could hardly breathe.

A few minutes later when her call came to head onto the stage, Sarah felt dizzy and unsteady on her feet. Detached from herself in an odd way. She kept experiencing disjointed thoughts, too. Seeing spots before her eyes. Struggling to breathe.

Somehow she walked out onto the stage to thundering applause. How kind people were. The conductor gave her a little bow, the members of the orchestra watched her, waiting, ready to accompany her. She found her way to the piano bench, sat down, arranged her dress, and reached toward the keys but found her eyes blurring again. Glancing up and across the piano, she saw Jonah in the wings, smiling at her as if nothing had happened. Behind him, Nita stood, a hand on his shoulder, her smile a smug one. Sarah realized she'd seen that smile before. *How had she been so blind?*

She heard the orchestra begin then, but the sound grew suddenly dim, her body felt peculiar and detached, her head dizzy and weightless. Then everything slipped away and she crumpled and slid off the piano bench to the floor.

CHAPTER 2

Andrew almost missed his flight to New York, and then it took nearly forty-five minutes in traffic to get to his hotel in Manhattan on the Upper West End, even after taking a cab instead of the shuttle. At the Riverside Tower, an older, more economical hotel where Andrew always stayed, he dumped his duffle on the bed and hung his garment bag, containing his dress clothes for the symphony, in the closet of the room he'd reserved earlier. There was nothing fancy about his room, or any room at the Riverside. It held a bare-bones twin bed with an outdated spread, a chest with a TV on it, and a small bath. But a small table and chairs, nestled in the room's corner, offered a great view out over the Hudson River. The room would do for a long weekend and it was within walking distance of Suki's apartment, also on Riverside. The hotel wasn't far from Central Park, an array of downtown attractions, and several relatively inexpensive restaurants, too.

With a little time to spare, Andrew stretched his legs by walking a couple of blocks to the New Wave Café on Broadway to grab a bite to eat. Back in his room, he showered, put on the black suit, the tucked white shirt, dress shoes, and the neat black bow tie he always wore to the symphony and then hailed another cab to get to the Lincoln Center. Parker had given Andrew one of the complimentary tickets Suki sent him, this one on the front row near the stage. He found his seat easily and had time to look over the program before the lights began to dim and the New York Philharmonic Orchestra began to tune up.

The orchestra led off with Tchaikovsky's *Serenade for Strings* followed by the more strident *1812 Overture* before Suki's softer, more lyrical piece, *The Sleeping Beauty Waltz* came in to change the pace. Andrew smiled as he saw her come out on stage to enthusiastic applause, dressed in a floating white dress with the red cummerbund and shoes she'd become known for, her fair hair shining like a halo in the stage lights. Seeing her move closer to the piano, he leaned forward, suddenly not smiling anymore. Something was wrong. She'd almost stumbled and her smile looked plastic, her face as white as a sheet. Andrew sat up straighter, his hands fisting, watching her. She looked disoriented. Always before, too, when she knew family or friends would be in the audience she sent special smiles their way, nodded at them, knowing where they'd be seated, but her eyes didn't even move to the front row seat where Andrew sat.

Would she be all right? he wondered. *Should he do something?* Ever since Suki had been a little girl, Andrew had always felt tuned in to her in a way not many were. He could feel her moods, her love for her music. He'd been her support through the years as her gift had grown, along with her family and her teachers like Morgan Dillon.

Suki sat down on the piano bench, shaking her head slightly as if dizzy. Not everyone would have noticed, but Andrew did. She took a moment a little too long to adjust her dress and her seat. Acting awkward in her movements, when usually so poised. When she put her hands toward the piano to prepare to play, she paused, looking across the piano into the wings. Andrew could see Jonah Dobrowski there, her agent and manager, a young woman behind him, a stagehand or two. As Andrew's eyes shifted back to Suki, he saw her head shift oddly, her hands drop from the piano, her body seem to go limp, and then she fell over toward the orchestra, sliding off the piano bench in a faint.

Without thinking, Andrew vaulted out of his seat and raced up on the stage, dropping down by Suki's side. Another man arrived at almost the same time, saying he was a doctor, gently shifting Suki over onto her back, checking her vital signs, giving directions for an ambulance to be called, taking charge.

Glancing at Andrew, he asked, "Are you family?"

"Yes," he answered, knowing it the only way to get into the ambulance to go with her to the hospital and to follow her medical care. When they sorted out the truth later, he'd explain, but for now he was her acting family, and he wasn't going anywhere.

He spoke to Suki, soothing a hand over her forehead. "It's Andrew. I'm here, Suki." He watched her eyes flutter open in recognition for a moment before closing again. He found her hand and squeezed it in comfort while the doctor checked her more thoroughly. The doctor looked up to the conductor and others gathered around in concern, including Jonah.

"She's fainted, not had a stroke or a heart attack," he assured them. "Fainting is caused when there's a drop in the amount of oxygen to the brain. I can't say why it occurred. It can be triggered by illness, emotional stress, or any number of other physical factors."

Since Jonah had already identified himself as her agent and manger, the doctor asked him, "Has she been sick? Are there reasons you know of for this to happen?"

"No." Jonah frowned. "She's dragged a cold or virus around for a month or two and hasn't fully shaken it, but nothing else I'm aware of." He glanced around, uncomfortable at the murmuring in the audience, the conductor hovering nearby with concern. Aware, as well, that the concert had come to a dead halt with the star pianist on the floor. "Would it be all right if we move her off stage?"

"She's breathing but she's very pale." The doctor lifted his head, his ear catching a sound. "I hear the ambulance coming. I'd rather they move and transport her. The concert can continue in a few moments, but this young woman needs medical help. I work with many artists in the symphony and I know they lead very disciplined lives. They don't faint on stage for no reason."

The next hour moved rapidly. With cars not readily available in New York, Andrew was allowed to ride in the back of the ambulance to the Mt. Sinai Hospital on Madison Avenue with

Suki, affirming he was her only family member in the city at this time. She was soon checked in and whisked off to an emergency area. Andrew went to fill out paperwork as best he could, getting the rest from Suki later when he was allowed to see her and to wait with her between tests and doctors. She cried and clung to him when one of the nurses suggested he shouldn't be there.

"You're not actually family," she said with a steely look at Andrew.

Suki grew frantic, jerking at her IV and then coughing, nearly losing her breath.

Hearing her, one of the ER doctors stepped in, trying to calm her, ordering a ventilator. When he learned why Suki was so upset, he wrote a note saying Andrew could stay with her, as a representative of the family, after Andrew explained why he was in New York in her parents' stead.

"A close family friend is acceptable at a time like this when the girl's family are across country." The doctor glanced at the nurse in censure. "The girl's obviously distraught, sick, and needs someone. What point is it for him to sit in the lobby or in a hotel room when she needs him?"

He pulled the note off he'd written and handed it to the nurse. "Put this on her chart and say Dr. Haggerty said this young man is her acting family."

"Thank you," Suki whispered around a sob, still crying and clinging to Andrew's hand. When the doctor and nurse left, she turned to him. "Don't call Mother and Parker. Mary Helen's baby is due any time. I want them to be there for her, and I don't want Mary Helen worrying about me when she's getting ready to have her first baby. I've just been sick and I fainted. I'll be all right. I don't want them upset." She squeezed his hand again. "Promise me, Andrew, you won't call them."

He hesitated. "I'll see what the doctor thinks and we'll see how you come along. I can't promise I won't call but we'll wait a bit. Then maybe you can call yourself."

She smiled. "It will be better when I call a little later and tell them I'm going to be all right. I only need a little extra rest."

Before midnight, Suki was put in a room. She called her parents then.

Andrew listened to her explain. "I fainted at my performance. I caught the flu after the holidays at home, didn't rest enough, kept relapsing into secondary infections. I'd seem a little better then get worse. It's hard to get a good long rest when you're on tour, when you're always seeing a different doctor, and when no one person is keeping tabs on your condition. The doctors here, and Dr. Haggerty, a really nice lung specialist, say I have a little pneumonia, that I'm run down and need to rest. That's all. But fortunately, I'm here in New York. After a day or two at the hospital and some more meds, I can go home and rest at my own apartment. I may have to miss my next show on tour, but it will be all right. You don't need to fly up. There's nothing you can do for me, and I want you both to be there for Mary Helen."

She glanced across at Andrew sitting in an easy chair in the hospital room. "Andrew's here with me. He says he'll stay with me until I'm feeling better if Parker will let him off of work a few days. Marri, Ken, Eito, and Julianne have already visited, fluttering over me. They'll watch out for me, too. You both know them and how nice they are."

After a little more discussion, Parker insisted on talking with Andrew. He affirmed Suki's story, assuring Parker he'd stay in New York until he knew Suki was better and keep them in touch with her condition. "I know you're torn with both daughters needing you, but Suki wants you to stay there. This is an emotional, rough time for her, fainting at a performance, realizing she's sick, knowing she's going to have to break her tour schedule to get well. She doesn't need to worry, too, that she's taking you guys from Mary Helen's side now with the baby due so soon. She didn't even want to tell you she was in the hospital, worried you might get on the first flight here."

He put Suki back on the phone again to speak with her mother before they could finally hang up. Suki sighed with relief when they got off the phone, then coughed at length from the effort, lying back to close her eyes for a while.

Parker and Claire had agreed to wait and not come if Andrew would call and give them frequent reports. Parker, who owned Westcott's Antiques in downtown Beaufort where Andrew worked, assured Andrew they'd cover for him at the store. He told Andrew he'd call Drake, the store manager, and Andrew's mother Nora, who also worked at Westcott's, to tell them he'd be delayed in getting back. They'd all rearrange their hours to cover for him. Parker insisted, too, he'd cover any of Andrew's expenses incurred in New York. They argued about that, but Andrew stopped arguing when he saw Suki crying again.

The thing he didn't tell Parker and Claire Avery was how much their daughter was crying, that her emotional state was borderline to a nervous breakdown—or so the doctors said. That she was broken down emotionally as well as physically, had spells of weeping and depression, refused to see her agent and manager Jonah Dobrowski, and said she didn't know if she ever wanted to play the piano again. With Suki so sick physically right now, Andrew didn't push her for more explanations about anything. When she felt better there would be time enough to talk.

"The body is heavily connected physically and emotionally," Dr. Haggerty explained to Andrew. "When someone has dragged along ill for as long as Sarah Katherine has, the emotions get frayed and rundown, too. She's probably carried pneumonia and relapsed with it more than once since this winter, never stopping to heal, always pushing herself on. Seeing various doctors here and there along tour didn't help either, and from what she told me, and from the records we've been able to retrieve, the doctors often differed on their diagnoses and treatment methods, not having all her story. It's likely she made light of her condition to continue on tour, to not be pulled off. Her agent seemed stunned she was this sick, so perhaps he never knew."

Andrew wasn't ready to be that gracious about Jonah. When Jonah pushed into Suki's room the next day, insisting on seeing her, Suki grew quiet and distant as Jonah worried out aloud about the tour and when she could get back to playing.

"Replace me," she said after a time when he grew silent. "I don't want to play."

"You know it's not that easy, even for one show." He paced the room. "You have a well-known name. You're a rising star. Our concerts ahead are almost sold out in anticipation of you coming. People want to hear The Angel play. That's what they call you. Sarah, you have the potential to go far, but timing is everything. This is our big opportunity. It's our future." He moved toward her bed to try to take her hand, but she pulled away.

Andrew wondered at this and at the change in how Suki looked at Jonah now. He'd seen the star struck, loving looks Suki sent his way in past, the affection they seemed to share. Suki had written him candidly about her feelings, too. It seemed likely the two might make a match for the future in more ways than just as agent and pianist. Or so it had seemed.

Jonah ran a hand through his dark, black hair, stopping to appeal to Suki again. He was a handsome man, about Suki's own height. Of Polish descent he had a somewhat full, square face with a short beard under his chin and a black mustache, dark brown eyes, always keen and sharp, a poised and easy bearing. Andrew had always seen him as a charismatic man, used to managing things and getting his way, but from the first Jonah had recognized Suki's potential and seemed to know intuitively how to best promote her. He'd taken Suki to incredible heights and recognition as a performer in the last two years, signing her even before her college graduation after seeing her perform at a national competition. In a negative sense, though, Andrew often felt Jonah pushed Suki too hard. He'd read enough to know that managing a talented performer could be a tricky balancing act between maximizing profit and creating the conditions that fostered art. It was tempting for a manager to push a newcomer with too many bookings. After all, they made a percentage off each booking scheduled and an artist was often more of a profitable product to promote than an individual to cherish.

He wondered now at what had changed in Suki and Jonah's relationship. Any time she looked at him, he saw pain in her eyes. And she winced, looking away, every time he talked about his concern for her, too.

"I don't understand why you didn't want to see me last night," Jonah said, moving closer to the bed now. "You know what you are to me." His voice dropped with those last words.

Suki turned her head away.

He sighed. "All right. I will talk with Greta at the agency," he said at last. "Get another pianist to cover the Philadelphia show coming up. The next one in Chicago isn't for another month. You'll be better then. I can reschedule that small solo performance at the college I set between the concerts with the Philadelphia Orchestra and the Chicago Symphony, too. How does that sound?"

She turned her eyes toward him, and Andrew could see the effort she extended to hold back the tears. "I don't want to play on the concert tour anymore. I think I said that earlier."

Jonah looked shocked. "You can't mean that. You're simply sick and worn out. When you feel better you'll be ready to play again." He paced across the room. "People will quickly forget about you fainting at the concert here. I can pitch it in such a way to the press that people's hearts will go out to the little angel who wanted so much to play that she tried, even when not well. We'll turn the negative publicity around to good. You're young. People are very forgiving and affectionate toward the young."

Suki turned to Andrew. "I want him to go away. I told you I didn't want to see him, and I don't want to talk to him anymore." She began to cough then.

"Let's step out of the room and let her rest," Andrew said, pulling Jonah somewhat reluctantly toward the door.

Outside the door, Jonah looked back toward Suki's room, his eyes alarmed. "What's wrong with her? Why is she saying these things? Is she crazy? This is her life, her career, what she's worked for since she was only a girl."

Andrew shook his head. "She seems upset with you. Has

something happened?"

"No. Nothing." He paced a short distance away and back. "We went to dinner and to the ballet the night before the show. Sarah likes the ballet; it's a break from seeing orchestras and concert artists perform. We had a good time." He shifted, considering his next words. "Sarah and I share more than a professional relationship now. Perhaps you know that, being a family friend. That makes this harder to understand."

"I imagine it does." Andrew didn't add more. There was some issue in all this he felt sure he didn't know. He offered Jonah a smile. "Why don't you let Suki rest and recover for a time? Seeing you, after all that's happened, might be putting pressure on her right now she doesn't need, making her feel guilty for being ill, as if she should be able to make it go away by her own will. You know how she is. She can overdramatize. I'm sure she's humiliated inside, even if she hasn't expressed it, about fainting on stage."

Jonah rubbed his neck, considering this. "You may be right. I have to fly out to San Francisco where one of my other artists is performing. I'll come to see Sarah when I get back in about a week. She should be home and rested then." He glanced back at the door to Suki's room. "Will you tell her that?"

"I will."

"When do you fly back to Beaufort, Andrew?"

"I flew up to come to this concert because Suki's parents are waiting for Mary Helen and J.T.'s baby to come any day. Parker gave me one of his tickets. You know I come to Suki's concerts when I can."

He nodded.

"This time I'll stay a few days longer before flying back to be sure Suki gets home to her place, is feeling better, and will be all right recovering on her own. My hotel is not far from Suki's apartment building, and her neighbors are eager to help with her recovery, as are several people in the church she attends. One of the ministers stopped by this morning, a kind man Suki seemed to know well."

Jonah interrupted. "When Sarah has time in her schedule, she often plays at the Riverside Church. They have a concert hall. A lot of performing artists attend there."

"I think the minister, Dr. Forbes, mentioned that."

Jonah stroked his short beard, thinking. "I can't stay in New York right now. I have meetings scheduled in San Francisco and a young performer's concert."

"Suki will be okay," Andrew reassured him.

"Can I have your number to call and check on her?"

"Sure." Andrew pulled a business card from his pocket with the store phone on it, not wanting to give the man his home phone.

Jonah left then, and Andrew slipped back into Suki's room.

"Is he gone?" she asked, without opening her eyes.

"Yes. He said to tell you he'd call and come to see you again after his trip to San Francisco. One of his artists is performing there." Andrew sat down in the chair again. "He worried about leaving, but I assured him you'd be fine, that you had people to look after you—me, your neighbors, your minister and perhaps some friends at the church."

She sighed. "I've never been here long enough to make many friends in the city. Friendships take time to develop. They need to be nurtured and built."

He picked up the bottle of water he'd left on the windowsill beside him to take a drink.

She giggled then, surprising him, but Andrew was glad to hear the sound. "What brought that on?"

"Jonah and I have been somewhat of an item. You know that. He wasn't worried about you staying or being here with me though because he thinks you're gay."

Andrew almost dropped his water bottle. "He said that?"

"Often. You come to many of my concerts but never bring anyone and you never link up with anyone when you stay over for a night or two. Often you go out with me and Jonah. And you never write or tell me about anyone special in your life." She smiled."It's okay if it's true, Andrew."

Angry, he stood up and paced over to the window to look out

across Central Park. "It's not true. And if I dated people, I didn't think I needed to share about it with anyone."

"I see." She giggled again. "Don't be mad at me. You've never been much of a ladies man like J.T. and Chuck always were. I always sort of liked that about you, and you're my very best friend in all the world. You know that, don't you?"

A little stung by her words, Andrew felt glad to see Eito Masako peek in at the door. "Would it be a good time to check on you, Sarah?" he asked.

She offered him a smile. "Yes. Come in Eito."

He walked in carrying a vase of mixed roses. "I brought you something pretty for your room," he said, taking the vase close to her so she could bury her face in the fragrance of the flowers before he put the vase on the windowsill nearby.

"They're lovely," she said.

"I thought I saw Jonah getting on the elevator as I arrived on your floor."

Suki looked away. "He pushed his way in. I didn't want to see him."

Eito's eyes widened. "So, you have finally realized he is not a good match for you. Good. I told you so."

Suki turned to Andrew. "You may not recall but Eito is a *nakodo*, a matchmaker, in a professional sense. Along with his counseling career in Japan, he worked as a matchmaker since he was a young man, linking many couples in marriage."

"I arranged one hundred and ten successful matches," he said with pride, offering a little bow with the words.

"That's a lot," Andrew said, sitting back down, glad for a change of subject. "I didn't realize arranged marriages were still so common."

Eito took the other chair in the room. "That is a western misconception. Sixty percent of marriages in the world are still arranged. For a time in Japan, fewer marriages were arranged, but now arranged marriages are making a comeback. The Japanese see, as Americans don't, that something as economically important as marriage shouldn't be based on only a fleeting emotion or attraction."

"I can see some sense in that." Andrew considered Eito's words, crossing his ankle over his knee. "How do you determine what a good match would be for someone?"

"In the *Omiai* System, the *nakodo* gathers information about the individuals, meets with their families, studies backgrounds, education, interests, and socio-economic situations to determine couples that would be compatible. A *nakodo* is known for his expertise in judging the compatibility of parties. Once he has decided on a good match, a meeting is arranged, usually with the parents present; then the couple may go out and get acquainted to decide on suitability. If they get along, they marry."

"Why would the families need to sit in when a couple meets?" Andrew asked, interested.

Eito looked shocked. "A couple must like each other's families. They interact often, impact each other, and elder parents may live with the couple when they grow older. These compatible relationships are very important."

Suki smiled. "I can see the sense in that."

"So can I," Andrew agreed. "If my mother had received counsel like that she might have been saved a lot of pain marrying my father and having to deal with his family."

"I remember you telling me your story. A *nakodo* would have learned of the problems your father had before a courtship began, his bad habits with alcohol and womanizing—is that the right American word?"

"Womanizing is exactly the right word," Suki said. "It means a man engages in numerous casual affairs. No woman wants a man with that trait."

"Mother never has married again either."

"One who is burned is shy of committing and trusting again," Eito added.

"Is there a right age for couples to meet and marry in Japan?" Andrew asked.

"There is much societal pressure in Japan for a couple to marry and have children in the late twenties and thirties. Perhaps the ideal age for men in the late twenties to thirty, for women by twenty-five. After that a woman is a Christmas cake."

"A what?" Suki asked.

"It is a Japanese term for an unmarried woman over twenty-five, like an unsold Christmas cake after Christmas is past. It is less wanted."

Suki laughed. "That's very sexist. I'm twenty-four, so I guess I'd better hurry and make a match."

"Would a man be a Christmas cake at thirty, too?" Andrew asked. "I'm twenty-six and getting close."

Eito looked offended. "You two laugh, but there is sense and wisdom in the old customs the young often don't see." He studied them both. "You two would make a very compatible match. You both have good educations, similar interests and appreciations. You are fond of each other's families and your families like both of you. Your socio-economic statuses are a good match." He let his eyes rove over them. "The two of you are attractive, too, of somewhat similar height and build. A nice-looking couple together."

"Andrew and I are *friends*," Suki said, looking a little embarrassed.

"Good friendship, with all the compatibility factors in place, is a fine base for a marriage. The rest grows. Love blooms well from good friendships. Many of the matches I made began with a rich, compatible friendship."

Suki waved a hand at him. "You're wasting your time, Eito. Andrew has never had what we call in America 'the hots' for me."

"You do not find Sarah attractive? "Eito asked him in surprise.

"Well, of course. She's very beautiful." Andrew felt himself flush with the man's scrutiny.

Eito grinned at Suki. "You see? It is there under the surface, the attraction. He has just not acted on it with respect for you and your family. That is an admirable trait. Restraint. America would do well to see more of it in their overly permissive society. Do you not wonder why the divorce rate is so high in this country?

Promiscuity, permissiveness, and lack of sense and restraint."

A nurse came in then, interrupting their conversation. "I will need to ask you gentlemen to leave as Suki needs a washing up and I want to change her bedding, too."

"Oh, but of course." Eito stood. "I am glad to see you a little better, Sarah. Marri and Ken said to tell you they will stop by tonight for a little visit and we all hope to see you back at your apartment soon."

Andrew pushed up from his chair, too, glancing at his watch. "Your dinner will be here shortly, Suki. I think I'll go back to the hotel, get a shower and something to eat myself before coming back later. Will you be all right on your own for a while?"

"Of course." She smiled at him. "I could probably use a long nap, too. Take your time. You can enjoy a walk in the park."

He laughed. "It's cold out. March or not, it's supposed to snow tonight. Just a light snow, but those of us with South Carolina coastal blood are hardly used to snow in mid March. The temperature was in the upper eighties in Beaufort today."

Suki closed her eyes. "I dream of warm places sometimes, and miss Beaufort, its quiet downtown streets, the moss hanging off the old oak trees, the lovely architecture, the blue skies, the green grass, flowers and trees—so much more beautiful than tall buildings and city sidewalks."

"I'm sure everyone in Beaufort—and down at Edisto—is thinking of you with much love and affection right now, concerned about you and missing you." Andrew followed Eito to the door. "Sweet dreams, Suki. See you later."

CHAPTER 3

Monday, March 15

Suki felt better the next day. The rest and medications helped, of course, but she knew, too, she felt greatly relieved Jonah wouldn't pop in again, pressuring her to go back on tour. As Mary Helen once told her: *When people show you who they are, believe them.* Jonah had certainly showed his true colors. Frankly, although it hurt to admit it, Suki realized he'd used her and if she never saw him again, it would be too soon.

Another stream of visitors from the symphony had stopped in earlier, including some members of the press Andrew got rid of. She looked across the dark room to see him sleeping in the leather recliner. He should have gone back to his hotel by now. It was late, dark outside, and as quiet as it ever got in a hospital room.

"What are you still doing here?" she asked quietly. "It's after midnight."

He stirred, opening an eye. "I thought you might need me." He glanced around the dim room and out the window. Her room looked out over Central Park, but the lights of New York City lit the night sky behind it. "Do you want me to turn on a light? Are you okay?"

"No. Let's keep it dark." She closed her eyes for a minute. "Do you remember when we used to play Secrets in the Dark when we were growing up? We'd sit on the sand or on an old bench in the dark at Edisto and tell each other secrets no one else knew."

He laughed a little. "I remember."

"You told me about your father there, how you hated staying

overnight with him sometimes because he got drunk and you were scared and didn't know what to do. You told me that was why you never drank, even a glass of wine or a beer socially. You never wanted to be like him. Never wanted to take the chance."

He shook his head. "He died drunk, you know. Running his boat full-throttle, he rammed into a channel marker. It flipped him out of the boat and broke his neck. His parents, his family, were still in denial when he died. Called it only a tragic accident. They still blame Mother for leaving him before I was born, too. Still refuse to acknowledge he had an alcohol problem and could be abusive when drunk. He wanted Mother to abort me."

"I remember you telling me that. But he left you his home and his money."

"I didn't even want his house, but Mom talked me into moving there. She wouldn't go with me though. I tried to talk her into it. She stayed in our old place, in the upstairs apartment above Ira Dean's big house. She and Ira Dean O'Connor bonded over the years and Mom didn't want to leave her or O'Connor House. Or so she said. She thought it was time for me to be on my own, too, at twenty-one. She all but pushed me out." He laughed. "She said regardless of all my dad hadn't done for me growing up, he did right by me in death, leaving me his home and money. And he had a lot. His will was a spit in the eye to his family. They were mad about it. Still are."

"It's a nice house, your dad's place in Beaufort. You wrote me that you bought a house at Edisto, too. I haven't seen it yet."

"Maybe not inside, but you know the house." He smiled. "It's The Sandpiper next door to J.T. and Mary Helen's place."

She searched her memory. "That older tan house with the red roof, the hexagonal screened porch on back, and all the palm trees?"

"That's the one, but it's white instead of tan now. I repainted it, and I've worked to renovate and decorate it over the last two years. It looks good now, although it's not as new as J.T. and Mary Helen's place next door or as large."

She plumped the pillow behind her. "I remember we could recite every one of the houses on the beach side of the Point from the house called The Beginning of Paradise at Murray Street to The Turnabout house after LaRoche. I still remember all the houses' names." She sighed, thinking of the island.

"So do I. I can still say them all backwards, too."

She laughed. "We shared a lot of Secrets in the Dark back then. Those are special memories to me."

"Me, too." Andrew shifted positions in the recliner. "You told me that no matter how many times you performed there was always that moment of uncertainty, even a touch of fear, before you walked out on a stage. But then as soon as you started playing, the fear and uncertainty left and you got swept up in the music." He reached for a bottle of water he'd put on the windowsill. "Do you still have those moments?"

She studied her hands. "Every time. But all the joy has gone out of playing for me right now. I hated being on tour this last year, and I feel sick inside when I even think about playing the piano now." She hesitated. "I'm going to walk away from it, Andrew, find another life. I mean that. Maybe I'll want to play again someday, but not now."

He stayed quiet.

"Sweet man. You're letting me find my own way in this. You always do that. Everyone else is always telling me what I should do, pushing me in one direction or another, but you've always let me find my own way."

"You've done the same for me, Suki. When I decided to go to college near home because I didn't want to leave mom alone, you didn't laugh at me. When I kept flip-flopping my major from business to history and back to business again, you didn't make fun of me when everyone else razzed me. You said you knew I'd find my way. When I decided at graduation I just wanted to work at Westcott's with your dad, Drake, and Mom, even when I had some job offers for more money, you didn't question me. You didn't even seem surprised at my choice. A lot of people called me a 'mama's boy,' continuing to live with my mom, going to work where my mother worked, too."

"It was right for you." Suki smiled. "You fit perfectly there. You always loved Westcott's. Your eyes shone whenever you were there working. Did you know that?"

"You would notice something like that. You see inner things others don't."

She snorted. "Not always. I'm overly trusting. Because I look for the best, I often get hurt, too. I forget to look deeper to discern the bad. To see the wrong, the evil under the surface. Maybe I don't want to see it. So I blind myself."

"Something happened with Jonah, didn't it?"

"If it did, I'd like to leave the memory behind me. It isn't something I want to talk about right now."

He stayed quiet. "You don't need to share anything you don't want to with me," he said at last.

"Thanks."

Suki looked out toward the darkness, thinking. "Did you stay away from getting too involved with girls because of your dad, too? You know, with what Eito called womanizing—thinking you might be like your dad in that way, too?"

"I guess. I always thought it might be one or those addictive things, too, like drinking, that once you got started, got a taste for it, you couldn't stay away from it. There is some research on that."

She shook her head. "No worries for me in that area. I've been so absorbed with the piano I've hardly had time for a serious relationship. My morals go pretty deep, too." She laughed. "We're a pair, aren't we?"

"I'm glad you're feeling better," he offered. "What did the doctor say this afternoon when I stepped out to get something to eat? I know I missed his visit."

"He said I still have pneumonia, that it will take time for it to get out of my lungs, for me to get all my strength and health back. Maybe months. That wasn't the best of news. He wants me to eat healthy, rest a lot, get more outdoor exercise and sunshine. Laugh and be happy more. It doesn't exactly sound like life on tour." She studied the IV still in her wrist. "My emotional health is kind of frayed, too. That's not like me. But Dr. Haggerty says everything will heal if I will give it time." Suki paused. "I guess the good news is that I can go back to my apartment tomorrow after the doctor stops by."

"That is good. Maybe after Mary Helen's baby comes, your mom can fly up and stay with you for a while."

Suki didn't answer for a long time. "Andrew," she said at last, "do you remember what Eito said about us being a good match?"

"Yeah." He didn't add more.

"Well, I've been thinking about that." She picked at the light blanket across her on the bed. "Do you think we could get married?"

He jerked upright in the recliner. "What?"

"You heard me," she said in a quiet voice. "I think we'd make a good match. I know there hasn't been any kissing and all that with us, but the friendship is there. Remember Eito said that was a good base and the rest would grow. I already love you in a strong way and have for all my life. I think we could figure out the rest as we went along, don't you?"

Andrew didn't say anything for a long time. "I think maybe you're tired, worn out, and sick. This might seem like a novel idea to you now but you might be sorry for it later."

"Why?"

"Because we haven't courted or anything like that. As you told Eito, we've been friends."

She squirmed a little at his words. "You don't think you could like me in another way even with time? … You know what I mean."

Suki saw him close his eyes and lean his head back.

"Any man would have to be crazy not to think about that with you."

She smiled then. "Well, see? We could learn together."

Even across the room in the dark she could see his eyes search for hers. "That idea offers a lot of scope for the imagination."

"It does, doesn't it?" She bit her lip. "I have a pretty good imagination, too."

"I'm well aware of that." A space of quiet fell again before Andrew added, "You've been seriously thinking about this, and knowing you as I do, I imagine you have some plan in mind. Want to fill me in on it?"

"I tend to be a little impulsive when I feel strongly I'm sensing the right way for my life. You've seen me be that way about my music and other things. Despite being artistic, I can be very focused and practical, too. I often know instinctively what's right for me. I think this is right for me, Andrew, and I think it's right for you. We get along. We like the same things. I think Eito is right that we make a good match. He's had one hundred and ten successes and told me none have divorced or had regrets. That's a pretty good track record. When Eito makes his matches, the couples spend a little time together—sometimes they only write letters—and then if it feels right, they get married. They don't wait around to let people talk them out of it. To introduce doubts. They move forward with certainty and just do it. That's what I'd like to do. I get out of the hospital tomorrow. We can get married the next day and I can fly home with you." She leaned forward. "I think I can make you happy Andrew. What we don't know about some physical things, we can read about in books and try things out until we find what we like."

Andrew got up to look out the window, turning his back on her.

"I hope I haven't offended you, but I think I could like you in a lot of other ways." Her voice dropped off as she watched him. *What was he thinking? Had she made him mad? Did he think she was crazy?*

"What if I said yes," he said then. "What would be the next part of your plan?"

"The Riverside Church has a lovely small chapel called Christ Chapel. I think Dr. Forbes or one of his associates would be happy to marry us there. During the week like this, and not on the weekend, I'm sure we could work something out. I think I'd like Eito to give me away and Marri and Ken would be honored to stand up with us. At this time in my life, I like the idea of something small and simple."

"You wouldn't invite our parents?"

"Parker and Mother are waiting on Mary Helen and J.T.'s late baby. And quite frankly they—your mother, my sister, and everyone at Edisto we know—would try to talk us out of this. You know they would. They'd think we should wait. They'd think we're acting impulsively."

"Wouldn't we be?"

She leaned forward. "We would be. Totally, and wouldn't that be fun for us? We always plan everything; we do everything so methodically and sensibly. Wouldn't you like, just for once, to do something impulsive because it feels right?"

He sighed. "Marriage is forever, Suki, and not like skinny-dipping in the ocean on a moonlit night when no one is around."

She giggled. "That memory is one of the wonderful ones I cherish. We had such an incredible time that night. If you're trying to use that example to try to talk me out of this, it isn't working. It makes me want to do this even more. If we'd asked anyone if we should have gone skinny-dipping that night, what would they have said?"

"They'd have said no and been shocked."

"But, see, we did it anyway." Her voice softened. "Come on, Andrew. Say yes. It's not like either of us has anyone else lined up. I'm tired of being sad and lonely. Aren't you lonely sometimes, too?"

"Often." He turned to look at her. "But marriage is forever, Suki. Not like skinny-dipping one night in the moonlight."

"Do you not think you might be happy spending your life with me?" she asked. "Sometimes I've thought about it. Imagined it. Haven't you?"

He groaned. "Yes, I have to admit I have."

Suki waited then.

Andrew came over to sit on the end of her bed. "I have a lot of thoughts running through my mind and a lot of questions. First, I think our parents may be hurt we didn't include them, that we didn't wait to marry when they could be with us."

She considered his words. "We could let Parker and Mother host a reception when we get back to Beaufort at Waterview. It's a big historic home; there's pleny of room there for a reception on the grounds. Parker and Mother could rent one of those big tents like they've used before. The weather is warm and pleasant this time of year in March for an outdoor event. It would be perfect." She smiled at him. "Your mom can help. Mary Helen's baby will surely be born by then and everyone can come—all our family and friends—to help us celebrate."

"That might help appease matters, but there's more to think about," he said. "What about all your things in New York? Eveything would need to be packed and moved. You have an apartment lease. You can't simply walk away from that."

"I've thought about those things. First, Eito wants to rent my place if I ever move. He already told me that. Second, it's a tiny apartment. I own a little couch, a chair, a table, a bookshelf, some kitchen things, a bed, chest, and not much more. There's nothing special about the furniture. I'd like Eito to have it. I can pack up my clothes and the personal belongings I want to keep in six or eight big boxes. I'm sure you know how to ship boxes, working at Westcott's. Parker has an account with one of those FedEx or UPS services. Honestly, we could box everything up, have it ready to ship in a day, and then fly home to Beaufort. You already have your return ticket. You only need to get one for me."

"And the piano?"

Suki shrugged. "It's an inexpensive baby grand. I'd like to leave it with Eito for Julianne. She's started to take lessons." She looked away. "The piano holds bad memories for me, and I won't need it. Besides, if I ever want to play again, you have a piano at the Beaufort house, a nice one."

"I admit I bought it at an auction with you in mind."

"Did you?" She reached out to tentatively put a hand on his.

"That was sweet."

"You visit me in Beaufort when you come home for holidays. I couldn't imagine you without a piano for very long."

"Things are different now, Andrew." She leaned back on the pillows. "Whenever I think about playing I get depressed and sad. Shaky. Panicked." She closed her eyes, tears slipping down her cheeks. "You won't push me to play, will you?"

"Of course not. How can you even imagine I would do that?"

"I've been pushed hard for a long time now. It's become a way of life, I guess."

"Well, it doesn't have to be your way of life anymore." His voice sounded angry. "Music should be your joy, to take pleasure in when your heart calls you to it. I hate that being on tour has taken that joy from you."

She leaned forward to put her head against his chest. "Can you not see why I care for you? You are so good to me. Do you think you might love me a little?"

He put a kiss on her forehead. "You have no concerns there, Sarah Katherine Avery. If we do this I will respect and honor you all our lives, always take care of you and cherish you. You can decide, too, when you want to move our relationship into more than friendship. You've been sick. My most important concern right now is that you get well."

"Then are you saying yes?" she asked, wishing she didn't have the IV still in her wrist so she could wrap her arms around him.

"I am." He put his hands on her cheeks. "I feel like you have just offered me the greatest gift I could ever imagine. I'm saying yes to everything—and to doing it quickly—because the images forming for my life are so good now, I think I'd be devastated if you changed your mind."

"I won't," she promised. And in her heart she thought, *I'm going home at last.* Andrew and home had always been synonymous to her but she simply hadn't noticed it before.

CHAPTER 4

Thusday, March 18

Andrew looked across at Suki asleep in the airline seat, her head tilted toward him, one hand tucked under her chin. So beautiful. The word "wife" slipped into his mind and he felt a jolt to realize once again it was true. He glanced at his watch. Almost eleven. The plane was starting its descent into Charleston.

"We're almost home, Mrs. Cavanaugh." Andrew traced a hand down Suki's cheek. "You might want to wake up."

Suki stretched and glanced out the window. "Your mother is meeting us, isn't she?"

She rolled her eyes at his nod in the affirmative. "I'd say our first afternoon home will certainly be eventful."

Andrew rubbed his neck, not eager to face his mother.

A short time later they landed and made their way from the plane into the waiting area. A tall man—Drake Jenkins—separated from the crowd to head toward them.

"Welcome back, Andrew. Your mother sent me to pick you up. She got tied up in the office," he explained. "I hope you don't mind." He hesitated, seeing Suki. "I didn't expect to see you here, Ms. Avery. Parker didn't mention you were coming when I left the store, either. Are you staging a surprise visit?"

"You might say so." Suki gave him a hug and a kiss on the cheek. "You look exactly the same as when I last saw you Drake Hartwell Jenkins, very handsome, suave, and sophisticated. Every inch the Southern gentleman." She pulled back to study him. "So sharp in your brown suit with that trademark handkerchief tucked in your suit pocket. I feel like I'm home again in the deep South simply seeing you and hearing that wonderful Southern accent of yours."

Drake's eyes scanned her. "You're talking pretty perky for someone who collapsed on stage with pneumonia only a few days ago. I see some dark circles under your eyes yet, and you look a little pale, but other than that you're as beautiful as ever. I imagine your parents will be tickled to see you and thrilled you could take a break from tour to visit with them. A little time in the South Carolina sunshine and you'll soon feel as right as rain."

He started out of the waiting area, Andrew and Suki following. Andrew gave Suki a little sign to wait about saying more.

In the parking area, Andrew and Drake loaded their bags into the trunk of Drake's car and then climbed in to head to Beaufort, about an hour's drive from the Charleston airport.

Suki insisted she wanted to sit in back in case she decided to nap again. "You sit in front, Andrew."

"Okay. Let me know if you want to change out," he said.

"Nice car," Suki commented, as Drake headed out of the airport onto the highway. "It looks new."

"It's a new Jaguar," Andrew told her. "Drake likes sporty cars—always keeps them looking spit-polished and sharp, too."

Drake slowed for the intersection ahead. "I talked Andrew into getting a decent car a year or so ago, too, pretty little red Pontiac Bonneville."

"I like red cars. Red has always been my favorite color," Suki said as Drake headed into the bypass that would lead them to Highway 17 toward Beaufort.

A small silence fell in the car then.

"Well, all this chitchat has been nice," Drake said finally. "But I wasn't raised a fool and something is going on. You two want to let me in on it?"

Andrew took a breath. "Suki and I got married in New York yesterday."

Drake swerved the car off into a parking area in front of an office building. "You what?" he said, turning to look at Andrew.

"Are you crazy? Parker may fire you for this. He sends you up to cover for him at his daughter's concert, trusts you to care for her after she's hospitalized, and you marry the girl while she's sick and vulnerable? And don't even call to invite the man up for his own daughter's wedding? What were you thinking?"

"Don't blame Andrew." Suki leaned forward from the back seat to get into the conversation. "It wasn't as though it was Andrew's idea. It was mine. I proposed to him, and I was the one who wanted to get married before we came home."

"I see. And you made this sterling decision between the two of you—with, I might add, no good sense—for what sound reason? As far as I've been informed the two of you have always been friends. Note the word *friends*." He focused on Suki. "Seems like I remember Parker and Claire telling me you were getting thick with that agent-manager that signed you. Jonah something."

"That's in the past," Suki replied. "And a loving friendship is a very good base for marriage. Eito Masako assured us of that."

"The Japanese guy that lives across the hall from you in New York?"

"Yes, he said …"

"Stop right now." Drake interrupted. "I *don't* want to hear more of this, and I *don't* want to be put in the middle of any of this because I had the bad fortune of picking you up on this particular occasion." He pulled out his phone and dialed a number.

"Nora," he said when he made connection. "I've just picked up Andrew—and also Suki. Are you sitting down? I hope so, because these two just informed me they got married yesterday."

Andrew could hear some of the shocked comments from his mother.

"Yeah, I hear you. Why don't you break the good news to Parker and then let him call Claire. Then I'd suggest all of you come over to Andrew's place where I'm headed with these two now. They can fill everyone in on this stellar event all at once."

Andrew heard his mother ask to speak to him.

"No." Drake shook his head. "I'm not putting him on now. I

need to drive in peace without listening to a bunch of arguments back and forth. Let's leave it for a bit, Nora. Being upset and slinging words around won't change anything. At least your son has married someone we all like, rather than coming home with a pole dancer from a New York nightclub we've never even met. It could be worse." He paused. "Just get everyone over to Andrew's place. Okay? Andrew and Suki can explain everything there."

He could hear his mom babbling on about something else.

"That's a good idea. I'm sure Ira Dean will come over to fill in at the store so you and Parker won't have to shut it down. She's worked a little part time for us before. She can take care of things on a weekday. Go talk to Parker. And Nora, pick up some food for everybody on your way over to the house. I doubt Andrew left anything much in the refrigerator. It will be lunch time by the time we all get there."

"I could have talked to her," Andrew said when Drake hung up. "I'd *planned* to talk to her when she picked us up."

"Well, things worked out differently." Drake swung back onto the highway. "You'll get to share with Mary Helen and J.T., too. Mary Helen started some false labor a day or two ago and came over to the hospital in Beaufort. Since the doctor said it couldn't be much longer now, Claire talked her into staying at their place at Waterview so they'd be closer to the hospital than down on the island at Edisto. Nora feels pretty sure Mary Helen and J.T. will want to come over, too."

Suki groaned. "I *so* didn't want to upset Mary Helen right now."

"Well, it will give her something else to think about besides waddling around like a tank—her words not mine." Drake chuckled. "Besides the hospital is closer to Andrew's place than Parker and Claire's. If the baby decides to make a debut, it's not far down the Ribault Road to get there."

They drove in silence for a time, Drake overly quiet. Andrew felt awful. He'd known everyone would be upset, but hadn't anticipated how difficult it might be. Drake had helped to raise him, been like a father figure, and Andrew hated he'd disappointed him.

They all made some effort to talk about mundane things on the drive back to Beaufort, but mostly they made the trip in silence. To fill in the awkwardness, Drake turned the radio on, popping back and forth between classical rock and genuine classic, whenever he liked the selections.

Back at the house, they unloaded their bags and then settled down in Andrew's comfortable great room to talk. His house on Lyford Place was a fine two-storied Southern home with double porches on the front and back. He felt glad today he'd taken his father's place those years ago so he could bring Suki home to a nice house now. The main level had a living and dining room on the front, an open great room and large kitchen on the back. Upstairs were four bedrooms, one a master, another made into a study. The house, on a quiet road off Bay Street, was only a mile from downtown Beaufort.

Andrew listened to Suki talking to her parents, assuring them she was all right, and to Mary Helen's incredulous words over her being married. He also endured Parker's and his own mother's disapproving looks often directed his way.

"Everyone come sit down," Drake said at last. "Let's allow these two to talk to all of us at once instead of drilling them separately and wearing them out. Suki still isn't well. I saw her wobble on her feet a few minutes ago."

They all settled on sofas and chairs around the sunny room that looked out over the back porch and yard. Andrew pulled in extra chairs from the nearby dining room to create enough seating for everyone.

He couldn't help glancing at Mary Helen several times in shock. Her large belly preceded her like a big masthead on a ship.

"Since I'm the only non-family member in this and got caught in the middle of this interesting situation, I think I'd like to take the lead to start things off," Drake said.

He studied Andrew and Suki, sitting together on a small sofa, leaning against each other for support. "Andrew and Suki, I've watched both of you grow up and always thought you were both sensible people," he said at last. "When Andrew was little and wanted to do something or buy something, I'd kid him and ask him to give me three good reasons why I should say yes. That's what I want to ask you both now. Each of you give us three good reasons why you've done this—and in the way you've chosen to do it."

"I get to start," Suki put in. "Because I told you this was *my* idea."

"Fine," Drake said. "Let's hear it."

"First, when I fainted at the Lincoln Center, it was Andrew I saw when I first opened my eyes. He's always been there for me, you know. He went to the hospital with me, took care of everything, watched over me. It opened my eyes to what a good man he is and to what he meant to me. Perhaps more than friends."

She paused. "Second, as some of these thoughts came to me, Eito visited me at the hospital and told me he thought Andrew and I would be a good match. In Japan, he was a counselor and a *nakodo,* a professional matchmaker." She lifted her chin. "He made one hundred and ten successful matches. I don't take his counsel lightly. This made me think some more."

Andrew felt Suki slip her hand into his then. "Last, and this is the hard part to say, I've been miserable on tour. I'm sorry, and I hope it doesn't disappoint you all terribly. I know you've been so proud of me." She heaved a big sigh. "I love to perform, but I hate traveling everywhere, staying in hotels and being in strange cities. Always being alone."

She hesitated. "Jonah made it better and I thought for a while there was more with him. But now I see that I simply fell into that way of thinking because I had no other family or friends around and was so unhappy. I pushed on and on, again and again, even when sick this winter. Now I don't even want to play the piano. I've told Jonah I don't want to be on tour anymore. I want another life. I realized all of this clearly in the hospital, and I realized, too, that what I wanted was a life with Andrew. He's always understood me. Loved me in a deep friends way. So I asked him if we couldn't make it more."

"Oh, Suki," Claire put in. "I'm so sorry you've been unhappy.

Surely you know Parker and I would have understood if you'd shared with us. Your joy is all we want." Her mother smiled. "But this sudden marriage seems impulsive to all of us. Are you and Andrew certain you've done the right thing?"

Nora leaned forward. "I personally think it's very selfish of the two of you to marry without considering how much we'd want to share in that moment with you." She directed her gaze to Andrew. "Surely you realize how hurt we all must feel to have been left out. Couldn't you have come home and let us be a part of this time?"

Suki interrupted. "I *told* you I pushed Andrew to marry in New York before we came home. He wanted to wait. I didn't. I felt you would all try to talk us out of it, fill us full of doubts, and question everything." She dropped her eyes to her lap, her voice growing quiet. "I worried, too, that you would push to make me go back on tour and talk Andrew out of marrying me at all. And I knew that wasn't what I wanted."

J.T. took the floor. "I think Andrew hasn't had much say here and that we ought to hear from him now. Personally, ever since we were kids, I think Andrew has carried a *thing* for Suki. I'm not too surprised, now that I think about it, that he said he'd marry her when she asked him to. When Mary Helen was finally ready to marry me, I jumped on the chance."

Mary Helen punched his arm. "That's hardly the same thing, J.T. You'd been asking me for months, but I just finally decided it was the time to say yes."

Parker cleared his throat. "Look, we don't mean to be unsupportive or negative. You two have chosen to marry and you *are* married. We want to stand with you in that decision, but we'd like to understand it better. It's caught us all off guard. Surely you realized it would." He ran a hand through his dark hair, slightly peppered with gray now.

Drake leaned forward. "Andrew, I think you need to give us your three reasons now."

"All right," Andrew said. "First, I was caught off guard when Eito said he thought we would be a good match, but his reasons were compelling. I saw the logic in his concepts about what aspects make a good marriage, and when Suki asked me, I thought more about it. I did agree we had the characteristics to make a good couple."

He rubbed his arm. "All those sensible thoughts aside, I couldn't believe my good fortune that a talented, beautiful woman like Suki, that I've cared about all my life, would want to spend her life with me. I didn't feel worthy, but neither did I want to miss the chance for the opportunity she offered to me. Especially when I realized how unhappy she'd been on tour. How misunderstood and unsupported. It hurt me to realize that, and I believe I have more love and support to offer her than she's been getting. I knew I could take care of her, cherish her, and protect her. It seemed to me she needed that."

Andrew saw Claire smile at that and lean against Parker's arm.

"Third, Suki said that we'd both always lived our lives too sensibly, always doing all the right things expected of us. She said wouldn't it be great once to do something impulsively just because we knew it was right, without waiting for someone's approval. She worried if we waited and came home to talk about it first, that many here might try to talk us out of it, try to get us to wait. In my mind, I saw that happening, and I didn't want to risk it. So we had a simple wedding right there in New York, took care of everything ourselves, packed up Suki's apartment, subleased it to her neighbor who wanted it if she ever moved. Made our own decisions. Made our own vows all on our own."

He stopped to catch his breath. "We'll make our way with the rest as we go along. Right now, the doctors say Suki needs a long rest time to get well physically and emotionally. I expect to help her with that every day. She needs support and love and someone to cherish her for the special woman she is, and I expect to do that every day, too."

He took another breath. "Parker and Claire, you know I've always loved Suki like a sister. I promise you I will be a good, faithful, and kind husband to her. I promise you I will support her in her dreams, care for her needs, share my life with her with great joy."

Andrew looked around at them one by one. "We didn't mean to disrespect you. We talked about how wonderful it would be if you might want to host a nice reception here in Beaufort to celebrate with us. Suki thought a big white tent behind Waterview would be fun. But we'd be happy to have it anywhere you'd like, whenever you want."

His eyes moved to Mary Helen. "Suki knew your baby was due any time. She didn't want your mom and dad to leave you to come to New York for a wedding, and she didn't want you to be upset that you couldn't come." He glanced at his mother. "We couldn't invite one parent without the others. The timing was bad for a family get together in New York. Suki hoped by the time a reception was planned, the new baby would be here. Then the event could be like a double one—to celebrate both things."

"Now I think you're making me cry," Mary Helen said, wiping at her face. Andrew could see tears on Claire's face and a softening in his mother's eyes now, too.

"Well, this has been a good conversation," Parker said. "Even if you acted a little impulsively, surely you know we all love you both very much and wish you the very best in your marriage. I'm sure Claire and Nora will be putting their heads together before the afternoon is out to start planning a reception, and I'm happy to host it at Waterview. Perhaps in another week, Mary Helen and J.T. can bring the new baby for everyone to see at at the same time we introduce the new bride and groom. That's a fine idea to have a double celebration, Andrew. I like it."

"So do I," Claire said, her eyes shining. She was still the same lovely woman Andrew remembered so fondly from his childhood, her dark hair pulled back in a bun at the base of her neck, her eyes still warm and full of life.

"Well, I don't know about the rest of you, but I'm starving," said Mary Helen. "I'm feeding two and this baby—who seems overly reluctant to make his entrance into the world—and I would like to have some of that lunch we picked up. I know Nora got a tray of deli sandwiches, sides, and desserts on her way over. Let's eat and then let Suki and Andrew tell us more about the wedding."

Over lunch, the strain in the room lessened, and their talk grew more congenial. Andrew, watching Suki, knew she felt relieved, and she sent him a smile now and then.

"I have some photos Ken Takamura developed quickly for us before we left," she said after lunch was put away. "A photographer friend of mine came and took others for us that I'll get later. They should be nicer, but I can show you these for now." She began to lay them out on the table, and those not already sitting there came to look, too.

"The idea was for Eito to give me away and Marri and Ken to stand up with us, but things grew a little," Suki explained. "The minister at Riverside let people know in the church, Marri told some of our other friends and neighbors in our apartment building. So we ended up having a small gathering at the lovely little Christ Chapel where we married."

"The minister, Dr. Forbes, even worked in a small counseling session with us," Andrew added, "and Suki and I quickly learned what an organizing woman Marri Takamura could be when she sets her mind to it. She helped Suki choose one of her long white performance dresses to marry in, came up with a veil and flowers, directed Eito, Ken, and I to wear our black symphony suits and found boutonnieres for us. She wore a deep rose-colored gown as matron of honor that coordinated in style with Suki's long dress and she let Julianne strew flowers and act as the flower girl."

Suki smiled. "Julianne is five and was so excited to walk down the aisle and sprinkle rose petals." She pointed to a picture of Julianne with a flower garland in her hair. "It really ended up being a nice ceremony, and some of the ladies in the church graciously ordered cake, and made a few light refreshments and punch for after the ceremony. So we even got to cut a wedding cake. Marri insisted we'd be happy for these small memories later on."

Claire held up a photo of Andrew and Suki together, with Suki holding a lush bouquet of flowers. "Look how sweet this is." She sighed. "Perhaps you and Andrew could wear these wedding outfits again at the reception. We could make a little slide show of some of the wedding pictures to show, too. What do you think?"

"Oh, That's a lovely idea!" Nora said, beginning to add some ideas of her own.

Mary Helen came back in to the room from the bathroom. "I hate to interrupt this nice little party, but my water just broke. Looks like Bailey Townsend Mikell has finally decided to make his grand entrance into the world." She winced and held a hand to her stomach. "J.T. and I are heading to the hospital. We've already called Dr. Werner."

Claire went over to give Mary Helen a hug. "I'll go with you, and Parker can drive back to the house to get the bag you've packed." She turned to Nora. "I hate to leave you to clean up here, but would you mind?"

"No, of course not."

Parker put a hand on Suki's shoulder and then leaned over to kiss her cheek. "Labor takes a couple of hours at the least. You lie down and rest for a while. I'll call Andrew when the baby comes so you two can drive over to see him and Mary Helen. You don't need to be sitting in a hospital waiting room for a long time as run down as you are."

"That's true," Andrew agreed. "I'll help Mother clean up and then take you down to the hospital as soon as there's news."

"Call me, too," Drake put in. "I'm going back to the store to close and to let Ira Dean go home. I'll take care of things there."

The house soon emptied out, and Andrew took Suki upstairs to the spare bedroom and found a quilt for her on the closet shelf. They'd both agreed she'd have her own room at first while she healed and while they made their way toward deeper feelings.

"Things didn't go too badly, did they?" she asked, slipping off her shoes and climbing up on the bed to settle down on the pillows.

"No, they didn't." He smiled at her. "Did you take your medicine?"

She put a hand to her mouth. "Whoops. I forgot with all that was going on."

"I'll get it," he said, returning with her pills and a glass of water in a few minutes.

She swallowed the needed meds, and then looked up at him. "You don't feel bad that I'm sleeping here for right now, do you?"

"No." He leaned over to kiss her forehead. "Like you said we'll find our way. Ira Dean once told me a person could learn everything they needed to know about sex by reading women's romance books. Maybe I'll check some out of the library for us."

She giggled."You be sure and wake me when the call from Parker comes, okay?"

"I will." He walked back downstairs and began to gather up the wedding photos still lying on the table. Stopping with one of the photos in his hand, it hit him again. He and Suki Avery were married, and she still had no idea he'd loved her, as far more than a friend, for years.

CHAPTER 5

Suki made her way downstairs to the kitchen the next day to find Andrew there, dressed for work, and cooking breakfast.

"Did I wake you?" he asked.

"I'm usually an early riser," she said, pausing in the doorway. "Like you, I put in long work days."

He turned to smile at her. "Well, for a while you get to be a lady of leisure." He frowned. "You had a rough night last night."

She came over to sit on a bar stool at the counter. "We had a somewhat eventful day yesterday. I think the stress of it caught up with me last night. I was so worn out and I ran up some fever again. I know I woke you coughing, too."

"Healing takes time and the last days haven't offered you much time to relax. I need to go in to the store to work today. Will you be all right here by yourself?"

"Of course. I'm used to being by myself, Andrew."

He turned back to the stove. "Pour us both a glass of juice from the carton in the refrigerator, if you don't mind, and a cup of coffee each. You'll find cream in the refrigerator, plus some butter and jellies. Get out what you like."

"I hope you're not cooking just for me," she said, noticing him stirring up several eggs in a side dish before turning them into a skillet.

"Breakfast is the most important meal of the day," he said, sounding like the practical Andrew she knew so well. "I always fix breakfast before work."

"Do you cook other meals? It would be nice to think I'd married a chef."

He sent a grin over his shoulder. "I don't cook at that level, but I know my way around a kitchen. Mother always worked, you know, and I learned to cook at an early age to help out. She was usually tired after work and I got home early from school. She was sweet to try all the recipes I experimented with—not all a success."

"You and your mother have always been so close."

He popped two pieces of thick bread into a toaster on the counter. "You and Mary Helen were close to your mother, too. We've both been lucky to have great moms." Andrew dished out scrambled eggs onto two plates, added a piece of toast to each, and put the plates on two placemats at the kitchen counter.

"Looks good," she said, realizing she was hungry. Breakfast for her usually consisted of a muffin and yogurt, sometimes a boiled egg. Often she ate it as she started to practice.

She watched Andrew put the skillet in the sink and swipe a sponge across the counter top by the toaster. He'd always been so orderly. His kitchen and entire house, for a man's place, was as neat as a pin and artfully decorated. She'd noticed new pieces of furniture and more paintings since she visited at the last holiday when home. She liked things neat, too, but between practice and travel she'd found little time to shop and make her apartment more than an occasional place to live. Andrew's house, however, was already a home, reflecting his personality—and surprisingly her own. They'd always liked so many of the same things.

He walked over to sit down beside her now, dressed in neat navy slacks, a blue checked shirt, light blue tie to coordinate with the shirt, and a navy vest. The vest hung open now, loose, but Suki remembered noticing this his usual attire for work.

"Do you always wear a shirt, tie, and a vest for the store?"

He dug into his eggs before answering. "Ann Westcott's father Vernon started a dressier tradition for work clothes; he always wore a suit. Drake picked it up. You always see him in a suit. Kind of goes with the image of an upper end antique store and it sets

Westcott's apart." He grinned. "When Parker came after marrying Ann, he hated suits and started wearing vests as a way around the custom. Ann's father and Drake were okay with it, so I picked up Parker's dress style when I started working in the store. I might wear a jacket now and then for a special event but I'm happier in a more casual look like your dad."

"We were so lucky Parker and Mother fell in love and married. You remember, my dad, Charles, was Parker's brother, and my dad and mom were close friends with Parker and his wife Ann. It was sad that both Ann and Daddy died so young, but I'm happy Parker and Mother's friendship turned into more."

Andrew spread butter and jam over his toast and then turned toward Suki. "Maybe seeing their friendship sweeten into love encouraged us to embrace the same idea."

She smiled at him, feeling a little shy sitting so close to him, sharing breakfast. "Well. Remember, too, that Eito felt sure we were a perfect match." She laughed. "With one hundred and ten successes, you have to give the idea credibility."

Andrew's cat ambled into the kitchen then, meowing and moving to rub against Andrew's leg. They'd gone by Nora's to pick him up last night after visiting Mary Helen and the new baby at the hospital.

"He's getting fur on your dark slacks." Suki glanced down at the big yellow tabby cat.

Andrew reached down to scratch his head. "Yeah, but I've got a roller that will take it off before I head out of the door. Can't expect a guy not to be affectionate. Melville's a lap cat, too. It's likely he'll try to settle on your lap or curl up beside you after he gets to know you. I always figure he must have had loving owners before he got lost—or maybe he's simply overly grateful I rescued him." He chuckled.

"Tell me again where you found him."

"I went down to get my boat at Drake's dock one day, planning to go out for a spin, maybe fish a little at a spot I know, and he was curled up in the boat in an old life jacket. He acted immediately glad to see me, obviously hungry. Drake and I both asked around for a month or two, hoping to find his owner. Put an ad in the paper." He laughed. "I suggested Drake keep him; his house was closer. But Drake insisted the cat had found me and marked me already. Drake's way of pushing him my way, of course."

Andrew got up to put some dry food in a dish for the cat, pouring himself another cup of coffee afterward and freshening Suki's cup.

"I named him Melville because I found him on the boat. Melville was a sailor you know, a smart educated man, too. He wrote *Moby Dick* and other works. I'd been reading one of his stories and had the name on my mind. It seemed to fit him."

She stirred cream into her coffee. "Melville reminds me of my old cat Ginger, that Daddy gave me. Remember the kittens Mary Helen and I brought to Edisto with us? They lived to be nearly sixteen. We both bawled when they died. We'd had them so long."

"I remember Ginger." He got up to take his dishes to the sink. "She had the same marmalade coloring as Melville, but with more white markings. She was a pretty cat."

"Well, Melville is handsome, too." She watched Andrew reach for her plate. "Leave the dishes for me to do. You need to go to work. And *don't* worry about me. Mother is coming to get me before lunch. We're going to get a bite to eat somewhere and then go to see Mary Helen and the baby again. Mary Helen gets to go home later this afternoon. Mother is going over in the morning to Edisto to stay for the first week to help her out." Suki pushed a strand of hair behind her ear. "I imagine Mother and Parker will be down at their house at the beach a lot for the next months with a new grandbaby to spoil."

Andrew glanced at the clock. "I guess I need to head out."

He hesitated for a moment, and Suki wondered if he was thinking about kissing her goodbye. She lowered her gaze and picked up her coffee cup so he wouldn't see the flush rise in her cheeks.

"I'll call to check on you later, and I'll be home a little after six." He leaned over to kiss her on the forehead and she felt both relieved and disappointed as he headed out.

Andrew had kissed her for the first time at the wedding—expected as a part of the ceremony. What she hadn't expected was the rush of feelings it brought. Andrew had looked into her eyes after that kiss, surprised, too. He kissed her again then, at length and rather nicely, pleasing everyone at the wedding. Afterward, he'd given her one of those smug looks that guys always seemed to offer when a kiss works out well. As if a great kiss was a personal triumph rather than a mix of good chemistry. Regardless, Suki felt sure she would remember that kiss and hold it in her heart for a long time to come.

"I never imagined it would be Andrew Cavanaugh to give me the most intimate, sensual, incredible kiss I've ever had," she told the cat. "But don't tell him I said so."

Thinking about it made her mind wonder about other intimacies, too, feeling a little embarrassed she was so inexperienced. Hadn't Andrew said he was, too? She hoped one of them could figure out what to do. Maybe picking up some romance books was a good idea.

Suki wandered around the house for a while after cleaning up the breakfast dishes, learning where Andrew kept things. Most of her clothes and personal items were in transit, expected to arrive in a few days. She hadn't shipped much, but she looked around the house now, imagining where she might put a few of her own things, where they might mix in without disrupting the harmony and style already in place.

At the living room door, Suki paused, seeing the Steinway grand piano, which dominated the room, both drawing and repelling her. She stepped forward, her fingers almost itching to reach for the keys but then she broke out in a sweat at the thought, fear rising up, bombarding her mind. Breathing hard, she backed away from the door.

She didn't want to get caught in the spell of playing again. What if she did and got pushed back on tour? What if she performed somewhere and Jonah came? Acting like everything was the same, telling her sweet things and lying to her. Pushing her in that charming way of his. She didn't want to see him again. Ever. Even Andrew and Mary Helen didn't know what he'd done. She wondered what Jonah would do when he got back from California this week, found her married and gone. Would he try to come after her? She felt panicked at the very idea and backed further out of the room.

Heading down the hallway, she let herself out through the back door and into the cozy screened porch looking across the lush lawn and garden pathways. She turned on the paddle fan to let it send a breeze drifting around the room. After taking a few deep breaths, she settled onto a wicker sofa at the end of the porch, tucking a pillow behind her back and putting her feet up on the table across from the sofa. She smiled at a small wooden sign on the wall that read: *Happiness is Relaxing on the Porch.*

"It will be okay," she assured herself. "Calm down. You can do this. You can make a new life." Looking for something to read, she spotted Andrew's Bible on a side table.

Perfect, she thought. She hadn't had much time for prayer or Bible study in a long time. What better time than now when she needed new direction? She opened randomly to the middle of the Bible and looked down to read these words in Psalm 32: "I will instruct thee and teach thee in the way which thou shalt go: I will guide thee with mine eye." Suki felt tears gather in her eyes as she read the words, knowing God was finding a way to speak to her. She relaxed some then, reading on.

The big yellow cat soon came out on the porch to join her, and after watching her thoughtfully for a few minutes, he jumped up on the sofa beside her.

"You knew I needed a friend right now, didn't you?" She stroked her hand down Melville's silky back, listening to his rumbley purr as she did.

After a quiet morning on the porch, Suki felt better and was pleased to welcome her mother shortly after noon. She'd put on a creamy white, lacy tunic to wear—one of her favorites—with a pair of leggings and black slides, and she'd brushed out her long, thick hair that hung below her shoulders, putting on a touch of blush and a little pink lipstick. She never wore much make-up except when on stage.

She and her mother ate lunch at a small out-of-the-way restaurant, Athenian Garden, on the Ribault Road across from the hospital. Suki had always liked the colorful painted mural of a Greek seaside scene on the wall. She ordered a Greek salad and spinach pie, her mother salad and eggplant Parmesan—and they traded out entrees as they often did.

"You look better today," her mother said, studying her across the table.

"And you look beautiful." Suki smiled at her mother, dressed in a striped dress, her dark hair tied back, her eyes bright and full of life. "Are you working on a new book?"

Her mother sipped at her iced tea before answering. "Fortunately, I just finished one. I worked hard to do that before Mary Helen's baby was due. I wanted some play time with my first grandchild." She eyed Suki. "I'm still adjusting to the idea of you being a married lady now. But I love the idea that you and Andrew might make Parker and I grandparents again in the future. With both of you blond and blue-eyed, we might get a little blond grandbaby this time. Can you believe how much dark hair Mary Helen and J.T.'s baby has? He's certainly a pretty thing."

Suki's mother chatted on, making their lunchtime easy, no longer trying to make Suki feel guilty for getting married. No longer upset with her. Suki felt glad for the change.

"Do you need anything before your boxes from New York arrive? We could run to one of the stores if you do before we drive over to the hospital."

"No." She shook her head. "I brought enough to see me through a few days. I won't be going much of anywhere for a while either. I still seem to need a lot of extra rest. I often run up a fever in the late afternoon or evening, still get some coughing spells." She sighed. "I feel tired much of the time. I read for a little while this morning after Andrew left for work and then fell asleep with the cat." She laughed.

"Your strength will come back." Claire reached across the table to put a hand over hers. "Parker and I noticed at Christmas you seemed tired and worn, with much of the joy drained out of you. We hated to intrude in your life to say anything about it. But Mary Helen told us you often confided in her that you didn't like your life on tour much." She patted Suki's hand. "Mary Helen always wanted to leave home, to do exciting things, and to travel but you always were so content at home, either at Waterview in Beaufort or at Oleanders at Edisto. Always more introverted than Mary Helen, too. Crowds and gatherings tired you, where they energized Mary Helen. I always saw how performing took so much out of you, but you loved it. After a show or performance, you wanted down time, quiet time to refuel. You'd take long walks, read or listen to music, practice by yourself for hours, making up your own songs, totally content to be by yourself, off in your own little world."

Suki laid her fork down, finishing off the last of her salad. "You're much the same way, Mother, off in your imaginary worlds writing your books. Often forgetting the time so that Parker, Mary Helen or I often started dinner for you."

Claire laughed. "I do get caught up, and I'm pleased at how well my readers have enjoyed the new Annabel books. They seem to love traveling to new places around the world with Annabel and reading about her adventures."

"You and Parker had fun traveling to many of those settings, too."

Her mother shrugged. "Somewhat, but we were both always glad to come back home again. Neither of us are eager travelers. When we want to travel we look for quiet, little out-of-the-way places to stay. Both of us dislike crowds and we like our privacy."

The waiter brought their ticket. Claire insisted on paying their lunch bill and then drove them over to the hospital. They found Mary Helen propped up in bed with the baby.

"You picked the perfect time to come," she said, blowing kisses at them. "I just finished feeding him, so he's quiet and satisfied right now, rather than red-faced and crying. He can sure pitch a fit, I'll tell you."

Claire went over to touch his cheek and to give Mary Helen a kiss. "Crying is his only way of communicating right now. You'll soon begin to learn what each little cry tells you as the days go by. Then he'll start to coo and goo. I can hardly wait."

Suki settled down in a chair across the room, still not wanting to get too close to either Mary Helen or Bailey, even though the doctor said she wasn't contagious any longer. There would be time enough later for her to hold her new nephew.

She listened to Mary Helen and her mother talk about going home later in the day, about feeding problems and baby questions. Claire, surprisingly, had all the answers. But, of course, as Suki often forgot, she and Mary Helen were once Claire's little babies. What a thought to realize she'd once been that tiny and vulnerable.

"How are you feeling now, Mary Helen?" Suki asked when Claire stepped out of the room for a few minutes.

"I'm sore and worn out but okay. Bailey was a pretty good-sized baby. Over nine and one half pounds, heading toward ten. That's one thing that slowed things down when labor started before and quit." She paused to study Suki. "How about you, little sister? You've been through a lot this last week. *And* you got married." She laughed. "I'm still working my mind around that one. It feels funny to think of you and Andrew as more than buddies. I guess it shouldn't. The two of you know each other better than most couples who marry."

She shifted the baby in her arms, who had drifted off to sleep. "I think it's special we both married friends from our childhood, don't you? Off we went to see the world and have a big career and now we're right back where we started from."

Mary Helen glanced toward the door and then leaned forward. "I didn't want to ask you while mother was here, Suki, but did you really mean it when you said you didn't want to play the piano anymore? That is *so* much who you are, who you've always been. I simply can't imagine it."

Suki rubbed her neck, trying to decide how to answer. "Right now I don't want to play, Mary Helen. Even looking at the piano at Andrew's this morning upset me, brought back unhappy memories. I can't bring myself to even sit down to play or practice. Maybe I will again some day. I don't know."

"You remember I went to work with Isabel at The Little Mermaid on the island when my career went belly up. I can't imagine you not wanting something to do besides sitting home after you get better." Mary Helen shifted the sleeping baby in her arms. "You, Mother, and I are simply not the types to simply be socialites or soap-opera watchers every day. You'll need something to do in time, something for all that creativity in you."

Suki looked down at her lap. "I've been praying about it, Mary Helen. There are a lot of transitions to think about right now. For the present, simply getting to where I can walk down the street—or the stairs—without getting short of breath and feeling tired will be nice. Healing takes a lot of energy. I never knew that, never having been sick for long at a time. So one thing at a time, I guess."

Claire came back in the room, a nurse behind her. "It looks like Dr. Werner is ready to let you go home soon. The nurse says he should be by to see you in a short while."

The nurse took the baby from Mary Helen to carry him back to the nursery. "We'll get him ready to go in the next hour or two, Mrs. Mikell," she said, leaving the room.

Claire went over to hug Mary Helen. "I think I'll take Suki on home and let you get a nap while you can." She glanced at her watch. "I know J.T. will be here soon to take you and Bailey back to Edisto. I'll drive down in the morning to arrive about the time J.T. goes to work. You'll be glad for some help for a few days. I'll probably stay at Oleanders though so you and J.T. can have some quiet time with Bailey and each other at night. I'll doodle on my new book while there. I'm getting it laid out in my mind."

Back at the house, tired again, Suki took another nap. She hoped by resting more today to be better company for Andrew this evening and to not wake him up coughing.

He called at about six to check in with her before leaving the store. "I think I'll pick up shrimp, scallops, and the makings for a salad for dinner before heading home. I have some yellow rice in the pantry we could fix to go with it. How does that sound?"

"Good," she said, and she suddenly felt *just the littlest bit married.* Her husband had called to see what she wanted for dinner. Like all the calls she'd heard Parker make to her mother through the years.

"Can you think of anything else I should pick up?'

She grinned. "Pick up one of those fancy non-alcoholic bottles of Sparkling Rose or a White Grape Juice."

"That's a good idea," he said. "It will make the evening special. If you feel well enough later, we'll take a walk down Bay Street and along the river at the waterfront park. We can sit on one of the benches and watch the sun go down."

"That sounds really nice," she said, and meant it. For the first time in a really long time, a sweet little sense of happiness and contentment crept over her. Wasn't that a nice feeling? Somehow everything would work out in time.

CHAPTER 6

The next morning about nine-thirty Andrew unlocked the front door of Westcott's Antiques to let himself in. He always liked coming to Westcott's early in the day when the store was empty, enjoyed walking around the two floors among the antiques, being quiet with his own thoughts. Drake had once told Andrew how much he felt at home at the store on Craven from the first day he discovered it on vacation, how the place drew him back again and again.

Andrew felt the same way and had since only a boy when he began to come to the store with his mother. He loved the times as a child when he got to go on buying trips with Drake or went fishing at Edisto with Parker. He loved listening to them talk about their work. He'd been blessed to have both these good men in his early life. Luckily, his childhood home stood only a short distance down Craven Street from the store, too. As a boy he could walk to Westcott's, and he often did.

When his mother Nora left his father, after a harsh drunken night, Al Brimmer at Brimmer's Antiques, where his mother worked then, introduced Nora to Ira Dean O'Connor and Nora moved into the upstairs apartment in her home on Craven. The apartment sprawled over the top floor of the old antebellum house, giving them plenty of space. Ira Dean helped Nora through childbirth and the early years of raising a child on her own and later Nora helped Ira Dean through the death of her husband. It was Ira Dean who kept Andrew in his younger years until he grew old enough to stay alone. She was like a part of their family now, and he understood why his mother stayed on at the big two-storied, brick home. She could walk to work from her apartment and walk home for lunch, if she liked.

Alone with his thoughts, Andrew made a pot of coffee in the back, looked through emails and circulars that had come in the mail, and then walked back to the front of the store to open the register and get ready for a new day.

"You're here early," Parker said a short time later as he let himself in the front door of the store.

"I thought you and Claire were going down to Oleanders to help with the new baby today." Andrew looked up from a box of antique jewelry he was sorting on an old table near the register.

Parker sat down across from him, putting a napkin on the antique table before he sat his travel mug of coffee on it. "Claire went down early this morning. I'll drive down later today and stay overnight with her at Oleanders since the store's closed tomorrow." He took a sip of hot coffee. "How is Suki?"

"A little better every day. She still sleeps a lot in the daytime but she isn't coughing as much now. We even took a walk along the riverfront last night, sat and watched the sunset. I'm seeing some color come back into her cheeks, too."

Parker picked up an ornate ring from the box to study it. "Thinking back, I can't remember you having many girlfriends in your life, although I remember quite a few girls hanging out around the store trying to get your attention. You've grown into a handsome man."

Andrew scowled. "I know I look like my father but I'm nothing like him, Parker."

He shook his head. "I wasn't implying that, son. Don't get overly sensitive at a compliment. I think what I was trying to ask is if your affections for my daughter might have started before we noticed them. Claire and I keep remembering how much time the two of you spent together growing up but we never saw it as more than friendship."

"It was always only friendship," Andrew assured him.

"You didn't feel more?" Parker's eyes studied his.

"I can't lie to you and say my feelings for Suki didn't change over time, but I never said anything to her about it. She had her music, her dreams, and plans. I knew her goals, and I knew mine."

Parker finished his coffee and set the cup aside. "That explains better why you said yes when Suki suggested marriage." He stood, looking at his watch, ready to open the store. "What if she wants to go back on tour when she gets better?"

"I won't stand in her way," he answered, putting the jewelry pieces back in the box to examine more later on. "I only want her happiness, Parker."

"If I didn't believe that, I might be more upset about all this than I have been." He clapped Andrew on the shoulder. "Drake and I were pleased when you decided you wanted to work at Westcott's after college. You've done a good job here, brought in new aspects of business to the store. You got interested in old jewelry and introduced that sales avenue into the business. Our sales have increased since you started working with us. Drake and I felt pleased to give you the title of Assistant Manager last year, too. He mentioned last night that it's nice to realize the business will not only pass to a good man one day—as we'd both decided—but to family. "

Andrew's eyes widened.

"Don't get that look." Parker cautioned him. "We know any interest you developed for Suki is unrelated to the business. Drake said he wasn't too surprised you and Suki married, remembering you'd mooned around after the girl for years. We should have all figured things out before."

Andrew tried to think what to say in reply while Parker walked over to unlock the door and flip the window sign from Closed to Open.

"Drake said to tell you that you'd better take care of Suki, too, or he'll come after you," Parker added, walking back and picking up his coffee cup from the table. "I'd add the same but I feel confident you will." He grinned then. "I'm going upstairs to Nora's office to do some paperwork. I'll keep a watch on the upper floor and leave you to meet and greet downstairs. With it Saturday, and with the weather warming and spring break kicking in, it might get busy at the store. Give me a holler if you need me. Drake will be in around noon."

He paused at the bottom of the stairs. "Oh, by the way, with Easter not until the end of the month this year, Claire and I decided to host the reception at Waterview next Saturday. That will give Suki another week to rest before needing to deal with a new event, and it will give little Bailey some time to settle in. Do you think that date will be okay with you two? Is it too soon?"

"I'm sure it will be fine, sir," Andrew answered. "I don't think it's too soon for Suki either. I'm sure she'll enjoy it."

"Good." He walked upstairs, leaving Andrew with a swirl of new thoughts to think about. He didn't have long to consider anything, though, before a string of customers began to come in the store.

An hour or so later, after Andrew had wrapped an antique bird cage for a couple visiting from Georgia and sent them out the door with it, Parker walked out of Nora's office to the upstairs landing to call down to him. "There's a phone call for you, Andrew. I've got a bad feeling about this one, too. I'll walk down in case you have a customer and I need to cover for you." He started down the stairs.

"Is it Suki?" Andrew asked, alarmed.

"No, but possibly trouble. Just a gut feeling. I think I recognize the voice."

Curious now, Andrew walked over to the landline phone by the register. He kept a cell phone in his pocket, but it fit the character of the store to still have old landlines around as well.

"Hello?" Andrew picked up the phone. "This is Andrew Cavanaugh. Can I help you?"

A string of expletives rang out before he heard Jonah Dobrowski holler, "What the heck is going on Andrew? I tried to call Sarah Katherine several times, didn't get an answer, then got a message her phone's been disconnected. I went by her place this morning and that old Japanese guy answered the door, said she got married and moved. After I got over the shock, he said she'd married you and he all but slammed the door in my face."

A few more unpleasant expletives flew out, and Parker rolled his eyes as he came to join Andrew. He'd obviously heard a bit of the conversation before hanging up the phone upstairs.

Jonah's voice was loud enough to carry as he continued. "Do you mind telling me what is going on?" he shouted.

Drawing on Parker's calm and the quirk of a smile on his face, Andrew answered, "Suki and I did get married, Jonah. She wasn't happy on tour and had decided to leave. I think she told you that. The timing seemed right for us to marry, too. Her health is still compromised so a long recovery time is needed right now."

"So she's moved in with you in Beaufort?"

Andrew almost grinned. "Generally, married couples live together, Jonah."

"Don't be a smart ass," he snapped back. "Besides I thought you were gay."

Andrew watched Parker's eyebrows lift. Jonah was talking so loud, Parker could hear every word.

"Evidently you were wrong about that," Andrew said, sitting down on a stool behind the register. "This breakdown in Suki's health, physically and emotionally, has taken its toll on her. I'm sure she meant to get in touch with you in time. But, again, if you recall, she already told you she didn't want to continue on tour."

"Well, get this." Jonah's voice turned mean. "Sarah Katherine has a contract with me and the Greenwood Agency and I mean for her to fulfill it. I rearranged her schedule so she could recover, cancelled her next two events, but she is scheduled to perform in a few weeks in Chicago and after that has a full calendar in place. Greenwood can sue her if she doesn't fulfill her contract without adequate reason."

At those words, Parker grabbed the phone from Andrew. "Jonah, this is Sarah's father, Parker Avery. We've met several times. I'm sorry you're upset about this change in Sarah's life, but I'd hoped you'd care more for her well-being and her health than a tour schedule. The pace of the tour these last two years has been too taxing for Sarah. As Andrew tried to explain, her health has broken down. Sarah's doctor in New York and her personal physician here can provide documentation for that. As for Sarah's contract, I know Andrew has not seen that contract to know how to respond to your threats to sue, but I have. Our attorney looked over the contract carefully before Sarah's mother and I let her sign. I know clearly that she has the option to step away from the contract if her health is in jeopardy."

Parker leaned against the counter, his fist tight around the receiver. "I also know she has the option in her contact to release herself from any obligation to her agent for the same reasons. I will have our attorney help Sarah sign any waivers to that effect that Greenwood would like her to officially submit." He hesitated."In fact, I'll have our attorney get in touch with Greenwood today if possible."

Jonah's voice dropped now, but Andrew could still hear him. "Surely Mr. Avery, after your daughter has worked to perfect her art all these years, you don't want to see her throw away her opportunities? She is just beginning to build her name as a concert pianist. She has an incredible talent. I believe Sarah could go far. But she has to seize the opportunity to do so."

Jonah's tone grew warm and persuasive now. "To walk away from the tour and from her ongoing concerts already scheduled will destroy her chances for continued acclaim. Do you realize that? You know I recognized Sarah's talent from the first time I heard her perform. I've worked hard to help her grow her career. Beyond my personal disappointment that I thought Sarah and I were developing a relationship, I assure you I will continue to help and support her career. Certainly you, her mother, and Andrew would want that for her."

Before Parker could answer, Andrew gestured to take the phone back. "What is most important right now, Jonah, is what Sarah wants, and for Sarah to recover her health." He felt his teeth clench. "Maybe if you hadn't pushed her so hard, over-scheduled her. Maybe if you'd seen that she got medical care and help before she collapsed, a different scenario might have occurred. Couldn't you see she was ill and unhappy?"

"Who do you think you are?" Jonah snapped back. "You don't understand anything about the demands of a concert tour. But I do. This is my life and my business. I believe I have a right to talk with Sarah about her career, too—without you or her father putting your oars in. Greenwood is her employer. I have been her agent and manager. Don't I deserve some respect for all I've done for her?"

Andrew winced. "I agree, you have been a strong support and advocate for Suki's career. Perhaps Suki hasn't handled this in the best way, not being totally up front with you about her plans or informing you herself about her wedding." He heard the bell ring on the front door of the store. "However, this is my place of business, Jonah. We have customers coming in the door now. Any further conversation will have to wait for a later time. As Parker said, his attorney will contact Greenwood. Sarah's wishes will be respected above all. It is her life, after all."

Jonah snapped off another crass comment and then hung up after saying, "You'll be hearing from me again. This isn't over. I have a right to talk to Sarah about this. When she is better, I will find a way to do that if she doesn't contact me sooner."

Andrew's eyes followed the two ladies who came into the store, waving at him and at Parker and then heading to a china cabinet to look at antique glassware.

"Well," Parker said after Andrew put the phone down. "That was certainly interesting. It also shows me a lot more about the man Claire and I thought Suki had formed an affection for." He thumped Andrew on the back. "Sure glad you rescued our girl from that one, son. That man sounds like a piece of work. I admit I never saw that side of him before."

Andrew studied the phone. "He certainly has a dual nature. I think Suki began to see that recently, too. She may be trusting, and she likes to see the best in others, but she isn't stupid. I'd say part of her unhappiness could be linked to her disappointment in seeing Jonah's true character revealed."

"Hmmm. Do you think that's the only reason she wanted to get off tour, to get away from Jonah?" Parker asked.

"No. She'd become genuinely unhappy on tour. I wish I'd seen it earlier before it led to her health being compromised and her love for the piano destroyed."

"Don't worry. A true love for music like Suki has will find a way back into her life. Claire and I feel sure of that."

"I hope so," Andrew said, glancing toward their customers.

He started toward one of the ladies in the store as she waved at him. For now he needed to put this unpleasantness with Jonah out of his mind.

"Could you tell me a little more about these lovely blue glasses?" the lady asked.

"Go wait on your customers," Parker said. "I'm going back to the office, and I will talk to our attorney today. So much has happened this week, I didn't even think about the necessity of Suki sending a formal letter of dissolution to her agency. We'll take care of it. Suki may need to get involved for signatures, but at least she wasn't the one to receive Jonah's angry call today."

I'm glad for that, too, Andrew thought, as he greeted the two ladies and began answering their questions.

At noon, Drake arrived for the afternoon, and talked to Parker for a few minutes in his office before Parker left to drive down to Edisto as planned.

"I picked up a couple of barbeque sandwiches, slaw, and some fries at Dukes Barbeque for us on my way in," Drake said, dropping his sack on the counter by the register. "We can eat around the customers. There's usually a lull around the lunch hour anyway."

Andrew and Drake perched on two stools behind the long counter at the register to eat while they could.

"Two ladies from over in Summerville just bought that entire set of blue Depression ware glasses and that matching pitcher you purchased at that estate sale in North Carolina last month," Andrew told him. "Parker helped me wrap and box it."

"That set was the Aurora pattern in cobalt blue. Pretty glassware. Only issued as a breakfast set so the number of pieces was limited." He grinned, giving Andrew a thumbs-up. "A rare pattern now and valuable—and a huge sale for the store today."

Andrew smiled. "Those women were tickled. A friend here in Beaufort, who also collects Depression ware, called to tell them she thought she'd seen some blue pieces at our store. She knew the McKenzie sisters collected it. Evidently, the friend here is a cousin or something."

Drake laughed. "You never know about these 'lookers' that come in and browse around—or who they may call afterward." He picked up his barbeque sandwich to take a large bite.

Andrew had always been fascinated with how Drake could eat food in a suit without getting a stain or spot on it. With that in mind Andrew wiped his hands carefully after eating a part of his sandwich, not wanting to wait on customers all afternoon with remnants of barbeque spattered over his clothes.

"Parker said you had an interesting call from Suki's old agent before I came in," Drake said, pausing when they'd almost finished wolfing down their lunch. "Wanna fill me in about it with the quick version?"

Andrew finished a big bite of his sandwich deciding what he wanted to say. One lesson Drake had wisely taught him was how to tell something concisely and well. It often made all the difference in whether you made a sale in the store. Drake was a master at drawing in and engaging customers at Westcott's. He knew exactly what to say to snag their interest, when and how to add more facts, and he intuitively sensed when to move in to close the sale.

They stopped to help a customer and then Andrew told Drake about Jonah's call when the store fell quiet again.

Drake shook his head afterward. "He sounds like a real sweetheart. Glad our baby girl didn't get hooked up with him." He stuffed all their lunch trash into a plastic bag and carried it out to the curb to toss in a trash receptacle on the corner. Coming back, he spritzed a jet of air freshener around the area, a spray he'd picked up with a light lemon smell. Drake was always conscientious about appearances—his and the store's.

"How's married life going?" he asked, sitting back down on his stool again and giving Andrew a suggestive look.

"We're working toward that," Andrew said in honesty, feeling his face flush. Drake was not a man you could lie to. He saw through everything.

"I see." He lifted an eyebrow. "Well, don't worry about it. With television, books, and social media not holding back any of the facts of life today it isn't the big mystery it once was. I've seen you watch Suki with more than a friend's eye over the years. In fact, after I thought about it I wasn't so shocked you said yes when she suggested marriage. A smart guy like you will find his way to the rest in time." He grinned. "Living with a pretty woman day in and day out will give a push to the issue soon enough."

Andrew laughed a little. "Yeah, I'm already feeling that push." He flipped through a pile of mail on the counter. "Why did you never marry, Drake? And don't give me one of those lines about all the beautiful woman out there you still need to discover."

Drake chuckled and then grew serious. "There was a woman I cared about enough to marry once. Got engaged to her back in Georgia when I finished college and started working in my dad's business. But when I walked away from the business to come here, she walked away from me. Seems she was more interested in the family money than in me. Left me some scars. Like your mother discovered, getting burned hard when you're young makes you leery of ever getting involved again. Sometimes it's easier to be alone than to risk another relationship."

"Do you think that's why Mother has never remarried?"

"It would be my guess. With a beautiful, smart woman like your mother, it would have to be her choice not to have men barking at her door. Have you looked at her lately?" He ran a hand over his eyebrows in a familiar gesture.

Drake paused then. "A woman that's interested in being courted or pursued gives off vibes a man can feel. I've met women I might have called, taken out, but I felt the door securely closed. Didn't sense a welcome mat out. Do you know what I'm saying?"

Andrew thought about it. "Yeah. I guess I can look back and see times I've felt that with some girl I met that interested me. I suppose I never thought about it in relation to my mother. I've always wished she could meet a good man, find love again and someone who would cherish her. She deserves it."

"I agree. And more than any woman I know." Drake looked out the window, watching people stroll by. "You may not know it, but I had it out with your father one time. Got mad when your mother let you stay overnight with him and he got drunk, didn't take care of you. I looked him up and gave him a piece of my mind."

Andrew's eyes widened.

"Don't look so shocked. You had a few run-ins of your own with him later on." Drake made a face. "I told him he didn't appreciate the gift life had given him with a beautiful, good wife and a fine, bright, and talented son. I also berated him because he hadn't done better by either one of you financially. He was loaded with family money, you know. I resented how little he did to help you and Nora."

"Does Mother know about this?"

"No, and I'd rather you didn't mention it. I feel guilty enough sometimes that I often wished the man dead. Went to church and sat for a while after his accident."

"You didn't cause his accident, Drake."

"Yeah, I know." He grinned then. "But I did grab him up by the collar at that visit and suggested he'd better put you in his will to make up for being such a sorry father. Considering his family is still mad about the will he later made, leaving you his money and house, I have to admit I don't regret that part of my visit. I also don't regret punching his face that day for Nora, either."

Andrew considered this. "As a kid, when mom cried sometimes

at night over my dad and over something he'd done or said, I always wished some guy would do that."

"Well, sometimes wishes come true, kid." He chuckled. "A fine woman is worth fighting for and sacrificing for. Women need a lot of love and sweet talk, too. Keep that thought in mind with your new wife, son. And if you need a conversation about the birds and bees, let me know, okay?"

CHAPTER 7

Saurday, March 27

In the next week, Suki's boxes from New York arrived. She began to strengthen and feel better, and she'd definitely bonded with Andrew's cat. Driving with Andrew to her parents' house for the wedding reception on Saturday, Suki found herself looking forward to seeing old friends.

"I can't wait to see Emma. I haven't even seen her since I got back and she was my best girlfriend growing up. I thought she'd have dropped by the house by now, but I guess she's busy at the college with her teaching." Suki glanced at Andrew, noticing how nice he looked in his dress clothes. The serious, blond-haired boy she remembered from their childhood had blossomed into a very good-looking man. She knew his father had been handsome, too, with a charismatic personality and a million dollar grin, but she knew Andrew hated to be told how much he resembled him.

As they turned down the familiar street to Parker and Claire's big antebellum home on the Edisto River, she saw that Parker had opened the gate to his side property, with an attendant directing cars to parking spots as they arrived.

"Looks like a crowd already." Andrew reached over to trace a hand over her arm. "Are you sure you feel well enough for a big event like this? If you get tired, tell me. We can always slip away. People will understand."

"I'll be fine Andrew, and if I get tired, I'll slip upstairs and rest for a few minutes." She looked up at the Spanish moss draped over the old Southern live oaks as they stepped out of their car. She'd missed the beauty of the old South.

Her mother came to greet them as they walked around to the green lawn sweeping from the house to the river behind Waterview. "Sarah Katherine, you look beautiful," she said, giving her a hug. "That's a lovely, graceful dress. I love it."

"Thanks." Suki gave her a kiss on the cheek. "You look beautiful yourself. That dress is so elegant and deep maroon is a perfect color for you."

Parker came over to greet them, also formally dressed.

As Claire and Parker had requested, Suki wore the simple, white, lacy dress she'd worn for her wedding, with the top embellished with small seed pearls, the skirt a drift of snowy white, swirling around her ankles. And Andrew wore his crisp black suit.

Suki's eyes moved around the yard with pleasure. "You and Parker have outdone yourselves to make everything look wonderful tonight."

A large white tent sat behind the house, tables scattered under it, twinkling lights draped inside. A small chamber orchestra played in one corner and a long buffet table filled with food and a tall wedding cake sat in another. A big crowd of guests already stood under the tent or around in the yard mingling and enjoying the perfect evening. At the end of the green lawn, marshy grasses made their way to the river, and the sky was already tinged with a touch of evening sunset.

"See that pretty arbor smothered in flowers over there by the tent?" Claire pointed toward it. "I want you two to go there first to meet the photographer for some photos, then you can socialize and enjoy yourselves before we open the buffet."

Suki and Andrew complied, posing for photos by themselves and then with their family, with Claire, Parker, and Nora, and then with Mary Helen, J.T., and the new baby. Afterward, friends came up eager to congratulate them. Old friends from Edisto had driven over from the island, the Whaleys, the Mikells, Isabel and Ezra Compton, and many others. In addition, friends from Beaufort had come to offer their best wishes, along with Parker and Claire's neighbors, friends in the community and the church, and old school friends of Suki's and Andrew's.

Suki almost cried when Morgan Dillon, her long time mentor and piano teacher, came to greet her and give her a warm hug. "I hear my favorite student has been both sick and unhappy. How are you now, my dear?"

Tears welled in Suki's eyes. "Better. Are you dreadfully disappointed in me?"

"Never. How could you not know I only want your happiness?"

Suki would have loved to talk with Morgan more but a crowd of friends from the symphony came up to greet them next, all chattering at once.

Morgan kissed her cheek. "We'll plan a long visit and a talk sometime soon. Tonight you just enjoy a lovely time." He shook Andrew's hand. "Congratulations to you, son. I couldn't have imagined a kinder and better husband for my Suki than you."

Suki watched him walk away with a small smile. She'd so dreaded seeing Morgan again, remembering all the years he'd spent teaching her the piano and preparing her for the concert stage. But he'd acted sweet tonight.

A little later Andrew introduced her to a tall dark haired young man. "Suki, this is Orin Jefferson. I think you met him on one of your holidays here when we went to the symphony. He plays the cello and also teaches at the college here in Beaufort."

Suki took his hand. "I'm pleased to meet you, Orin. Andrew says you are his best friend, so I hope you'll come over to the house soon so we can get better acquainted. Do you know Emma Whaley? She also teaches at The University of South Carolina at Beaufort."

He grinned. "I do know Emma and I know her well. She, Andrew, and I often go to the symphony or out to eat, and we hang out together—a congenial threesome."

"That's wonderful. We'll invite Emma to the house, too. I can't wait to see her again and I haven't even seen her yet tonight."

Orin glanced around. "She's over there beyond the tent. See?"

He pointed her out.

"Oh, good. I'll slip over to say hello." She left Andrew with Orin for a few moments to head Emma's way.

"I'll be there in a minute," Andrew called after her.

"Emma!" Suki called as she drew closer. "I came to find you. I couldn't wait to see you." She reached out to hug Emma, but felt her friend stiffen in her embrace. Overlooking it, Suki let her eyes drift over her old childhood playmate, Emma's hair still red and wavy—a little unruly, her skin a peachy tan, and her simple olive-green dress tonight a pretty match to her hazel eyes. "You look fabulous. I love your dress."

"Thank you," Emma said, sounding somewhat formal, and backing away from the group she'd been talking with, not saying more.

"Is anything the matter?" Suki asked, following her away from the others.

"Yes." Emma's eyes met hers now. "I can't believe you married Andrew. I heard that you actually asked *him* to marry you, too, not the other way around. I also heard you asked him while you were sick, after you collapsed at the concert. How could you do that? You know how kind he is. Don't you think you took advantage of that situation—talking him into doing something he probably didn't want to do?"

Suki felt stunned at her words. "What?"

She studied Emma's angry face, trying to figure out what was going on.

"It was so wrong of you," Emma went on, her voice rising. "Andrew deserved to make his own choice. Not to be pressured to rescue you."

"Whoa," Andrew said, coming up behind them, trailed by several of their friends, including Orin, Mary Helen and J.T., Emma's sister Jane, and her husband Barton. They'd all obviously heard Emma's words, spoken loud enough to carry.

"Emma Whaley, stop acting like a baby," her sister Jane admonished. "You're just taking it out on Suki because you've had a big crush on Andrew the last two years. Quit spoiling their nice evening by being ugly."

Suki saw tears start in Emma's eyes.

"You are so mean, Jane," Emma lashed back. "It's awful of you to say that right in front of Andrew, too." Emma glanced at him in embarrassment and then on a little sob, turned to rush quickly away.

"Should I go after her?" Mary Helen asked, watching Emma walk across the lawn to stop under an old oak tree, her back turned to them.

"No, let her calm down." Jane made a face. "I can't believe she verbally attacked Suki like that. What was she thinking?"

"This is simply awful." Suki turned to them, stunned. "Why didn't someone tell me about Emma. I I didn't even know she and Andrew were dating."

"They *weren't* dating. That's the whole point," Mary Helen answered, making a face. "In fact, Andrew was oblivious to the fact Emma even had a little crush on him. Don't worry about it. I don't know why Emma didn't drop her fantasy romance ideas long before now."

Jane smiled at Orin. "If she had, she might have noticed how much Orin likes her."

Orin blushed at her words, glancing toward Emma, worried she might have heard.

Suki shook her head. "I've been gone too long. I didn't know any of these things."

They all watched Emma, standing at a distance, obviously crying and upset.

"Let me go talk to Emma," Andrew said. "Come with me, Suki."

She followed him over to where Emma stood under the old tree, looking out toward the river.

"Emma, I'm so sorry you're upset," Andrew said.

"Just go away," she answered, not turning to look at them.

Andrew sighed. "Chuck and J.T. teased me once or twice in the past, suggesting you had a crush on me. I admit, I didn't take it seriously. We'd always been friends since childhood. I wish now maybe we'd talked about it."

She turned to him. "We spent so much time together here in Beaufort, went places together. I often rode down to the island with you either in your car or on the boat. We always had so much fun."

He ran a hand through his hair. "When we went places together in Beaufort, we went with others, Emma, usually with Orin. There was never anything but friendship in our times together. I don't want you to give Suki the idea there was anything else between us."

Emma rubbed her arm, looking down at the grass. "I guess I simply *hoped* there might be something more be in time. Everyone else at Edisto was pairing up, getting married. We were the only ones who didn't have anyone in our lives, so I thought, *Why not?*" She glared at Andrew and then at Suki. "You and Suki were only friends, too. How do you think it made me feel to hear you two suddenly got married? It really hurt me to learn about it after it was already done, too. I couldn't understand it." She sighed. "It didn't seem right."

Jane came over to link an arm around her sister's waist. "You've always been our dreamer, Emma, reading all the time, imagining stories. I kept telling you that Andrew didn't have any romantic feelings for you, but you wouldn't believe me. If you look back, you'll see it was always Suki that Andrew watched, tagged after, or listened to at the piano. They always had something special together, and finally realized it. That's not wrong, and you shouldn't make them feel bad for it. Especially tonight when Claire and Parker went to all this trouble to host a pretty reception for them."

Suki watched Emma wrestle with her feelings, not knowing what to say.

"I feel so bad you're upset, Emma," Suki said at last. "I'm really sorry."

"I'm sorry, too," Emma finally said, heaving a big sigh. "It's only that when I heard you two got married... and then saw you both come in tonight, so happy and everything, I just got mad."

"Well, quit being mad." Suki went over to hug her again. "You're my best friend since we were little girls. You know I love you, and so does Andrew."

"That's true." Andrew smiled at her. "I'm sort of flattered in a way to think you liked me. I was always the odd kid when we were all growing up together."

Jane reached out to pat his cheek. "Yes, but you certainly shaped up to be a handsome man. We're all so happy you bought the old Sandpiper house at Edisto, too, and fixed it up. That means we'll always get to see a lot of you and Suki down at the island."

She tucked Emma's arm into hers. "Let's go freshen up in the house and let Suki and Andrew talk to all their guests. I'm sure Claire and Parker will open up the buffet any minute, too. You and Suki can visit more later."

"Will you come over to the house one day so we can catch up?" Suki asked her.

"Sure." Emma answered, offering a somewhat feigned smile as she walked away with Jane.

Suki looked after her, worried, and then turned to Andrew as they made their way back across the lawn to talk with their guests. "Did you really have no idea Emma had a crush on you?"

"No, I didn't." He shook his head. "I didn't even believe J.T. and Chuck when they teased me about it once or twice." He grinned at her. "I did know Orin liked Emma though. He always instigated our threesome gatherings, hoping if he kept spending time around Emma she'd start to like him. He told me that whenever he asked her out, she'd say, 'Sure and let's ask Andrew, too,' so I always ended up going places with them as the third wheel so Orin could see Emma."

Suki giggled. "Maybe we can try to get them together more. Now that you're out of the picture, so to speak, Emma might notice Orin. He seems nice."

"He's a great guy, and he and Emma actually have a lot in common. Orin is really smitten with her, too. He's gotten frustrated trying to get her to notice him."

Inside the tent, Parker picked up a microphone to say a few words of welcome and then to encourage everyone to go through the buffet and enjoy dinner. Andrew and Suki, of course, started off the line and soon put thoughts of Emma and Orin aside to enjoy the beautiful reception and dinner Parker and Claire had orchestrated for them.

Later in the evening, Suki went into the house with Mary Helen so her sister could feed Bailey. Andrew suggested it would give Suki a few minutes to rest at the same time. Curled up on the bed in Mary Helen's old room now, Suki watched her sister settle into an easy chair, talking to little Bailey and starting to feed him.

"He is so precious," Suki said, watching.

Mary Helen stroked his head. "I can remember a time when I thought I only wanted to be a career woman and to never marry or have a family."

"I guess you're glad J.T. changed your mind." Suki leaned back on a pillow.

"Married life has been full of unexpected joys." She grinned. "J.T. is already asking how long it will be until we can sleep together again, and Bailey is only a week old today. " She arched an eyebrow at Suki. "Has Andrew made his move yet?"

Suki wrinkled her nose. "No, but like I told you I'm beginning to hope he will soon. Thanks for talking with me about all that."

Mary Helen laughed. "It's a little more natural and instinctive than playing the piano, little sister. Practice may make things better in that area—if not always perfect—but it isn't difficult. You know how Andrew is, though. He over-thinks and overanalyzes everything. If you wait on him to make the first move, you might be ninety-three before he ever does."

Suki sighed. "He did say in New York he'd let *me* decide when I wanted to move our relationship into more than friendship. Maybe he's waiting on me."

"Well, don't make him wait any longer." She laughed.

Suki thought of those words later that night after she and Andrew got home. While he was downstairs, she sneaked into his room to look around and saw one of those romance books she'd picked up at the library tucked under a magazine by the bed. One of the pages in the middle of the book was turned down. He'd obviously been reading it. She opened the book to the turned down page, read a little, and then smiled before tucking the book back under the magazine again.

In her room a short time later, after taking a shower, Suki studied her nightwear, trying to figure out what to wear. She decided at last on a filmy pale blue gown, mostly because she'd realized after buying it that it was all but transparent. She'd never taken it on the road with her after that. One time running out of a hotel in the middle of the night when a fire alarm went off made you think about those things.

She curled up in bed and read for a while, waiting to hear Andrew come up and get ready to settle down. Peeking around the corner later to see he'd gotten in bed with only the lamp by his bed on, Suki took a deep breath and then sprinted down the hall to rush into his room, racing over to jump on the end of his bed.

"I had a bad dream," she cried, wide-eyed. She crawled up the covers closer to him, glancing over onto the floor. "I dreamed there was a snake under my bed."

He chuckled, and pulled her up to curl beside him. "I used to dream that, too, when I was a kid. Scary, even when you know it's only a dream, isn't it?"

"Yes, it is." She scooted a little closer to him, glancing toward the floor again. "Could I stay here with you for a little while?"

He hesitated, and she wondered what he was thinking.

"Sure," he said after a minute or two.

She shivered then. "Maybe I can get under the covers with you, too."

He didn't answer for a few minutes and then lifted the covers.

She crawled under and sighed.

"What are you reading?" she asked, recognizing the book he'd quickly tucked under the bedding when she sprinted into the room. "It looked like one of those romances I picked up at the library."

Out of the corner of her eye, Suki saw his neck flush and he looked away.

She lowered her voice. "I hope it was one of those really *good* books, one of the sultry ones. You know. I've really been thinking about how fun it would be to try some of those things out."

Andrew tensed and Suki could actually feel his heartbeat kick up.

She turned over until she was all but lying on his chest then—on his bare chest. He wasn't wearing a pajama top. How nice, especially with her little nightgown so thin. She could feel the heat between them ramping up.

Suki smiled, tracing a finger across his chest. "You did say for me to tell you when I wanted to move our relationship into more than friendship. Do you want to try out some of the things we've been reading about?"

He groaned and closed his eyes. "You're killing me, Suki."

She kept her voice low and sultry. "Good. Would you like me to talk about what I'd like to try, what scenes in the book I think might be fun? I did read the whole book before you already. Twice, actually."

He opened his eyes then. "Are you sure about this?"

She moved closer, practically on top of him now, to trace her tongue around his mouth and then to kiss him. "Does that feel like a yes answer?" she whispered.

This time, finally, he wrapped his arms around her and kissed her back. Rather skillfully, too. Evidently kissing was one experience with women he had tried out often. Or his extra curricula reading had really paid off. He certainly did it very well.

"Ah, that's so nice," she whispered, as his lips wandered down her neck and then back to her mouth again.

As they kissed once more, Andrew's hands began to wander in lovely places. Their breathing escalated, their heartbeats kicked up and Suki decided they were figuring out what to do quite well. It felt wonderful.

Andrew shifted her position and began slipping her gown over her head.

"What are we going to do now?" she asked, suddenly eager to try more.

"Write a new chapter for the book and *not* talk anymore," he said, grinning at her in the dark. And she soon forgot about asking any more questions.

CHAPTER 8

Monday, March 29

Andrew, after a happy weekend learning about the pleasures of married life, whistled as he let himself into Westcott's Antiques early on Monday morning. As always, he'd arrived early but not as early as he usually did with Suki distracting him. He smiled at that memory as he checked through the pile of mail by the register. Sorting it quickly, he carried Parker's mail to put it on his office desk at the back of the store. He'd make another pot of coffee, too, in the store's break room. A second cup would be good today after so little sleep.

Pushing open the door to Parker's office and walking across the room to drop the mail on his desk, Andrew stopped in shock. A body lay sprawled on the floor behind Parker's desk. Stunned, his heart beating rapidly, and nearly hyperventilating at the sight, Andrew finally, after a few minutes, stepped past his fear to squat and put a hand on the man's pulse. No pulse. Nothing. And the body was already cold, stiff, and lifeless.

Andrew backed away then and pulled out his cell phone to call Drake, then Parker, and the police. Everything seemed to pass in a rush and a haze then as everyone showed up. Three officers and two paramedics came, one of the paramedics quickly determining the man dead. Andrew, still standing to one side of the large office beside Drake and Parker, could see the man's face as the paramedics turned him over.

"Do you know this man?" one of the police officers asked, identifying himself as Sergeant Metler while another officer took all their information—names, dates of birth, addresses, phone numbers.

"Yes, I recognize him," Parker said. "It's Marvin Donelson. He owns Bay Street Antiques, a couple of streets down from us."

"Does he have a key and access to your store?"

"No, he doesn't. I can't even recall the last time he stopped by our store."

One of the paramedics looked up from examining the body. "The man's been hit with a blunt object. Blow probably killed him. There isn't much blood though—only a little on the rug underneath him. He might have been moved."

Foul play confirmed, Sergeant Metler called a report in to the department and sent his officers to search the building inside and out and to look for evidence and a possible murder weapon.

"Did you know this man, also?" The Sergeant's glance moved to Andrew and Drake.

"Yes," Drake answered. "We're in the same kind of business, same town. Our paths cross, but I wasn't friends with Donelson."

The officer's eyes moved to Andrew. "And you?"

"I went to school with Sonny Donelson," Andrew answered. "Marvin is his grandfather. I saw Sonny's family sometimes at school events or at the ballfield." Andrew paused, wanting to be completely honest in his replies. "Now and then when I'm on Bay Street and have a minute I stop in to say hello to Sonny. A few times he's stopped by here."

"Can you give me the other Donelson family names?"

"Sonny's father is Walter Donelson, his mother AdaMae, his older sister Rowena. They all work in the business. Marvin did, too. Marvin's wife passed away some years ago. They were good people. I can't imagine any reason for someone to harm any of them."

"Thanks." The officer made notes as he asked questions and talked.

He looked up at Andrew again. "You say you were the one to find him?"

Andrew nodded. "Like I said earlier, I brought Parker's mail here after I arrived and unlocked the store. That's when I saw him."

"You didn't move him?"

"No, sir. I felt his pulse, then called Drake, Parker, and the police."

Andrew watched them begin to move the body now to take it to the morgue.

The officer sat down with them afterwards to ask an extensive number of other questions. Some disturbed Andrew—why the body was found in Parker's office, why anyone would bring a body to Westcott's if the man wasn't killed inside the building, how the body even got into Westcott's at night with the building locked. Sergeant Metler probed their relationships to Marvin Donelson, too, with subtle suggestions about the possible rivalry of the two businesses.

Andrew watched Drake's eyes narrow over those questions, and he could see Parker was visibly upset as the questions grew more personal. The other officers returned and Sergeant Metler stepped out of the room to speak to them.

When he came back and sat down again, he said, "No weapon has been found, no sign of forcible entry anywhere in the building or from outside the building. We took fingerprints at all entryways but I doubt we'll turn up any prints. We will need to attain fingerprints of all who work here to eliminate those." He looked down at his notes. "I'll also need to talk to everyone who works here, and to everyone who has, or was given in past, a key to the building."

"We changed the locks last year, so that would only be the three of us and Nora Cavanaugh, our other full-time employee," Parker answered.

"Are there other part-time staff who might have had access to a key?"

Parker frowned. "Our delivery man, Farris Bivens, has occasionally been given a key to bring in a delivery after hours but he returned it afterward. Our summer intern Janine Albert would also know where our extra keys are kept but she was never given a key since she didn't open or close. Both live in the area. I can give you their contact information."

"Good. We'll need to talk to everyone," the Sergeant said as he noted the new names. "This is a murder investigation now. Someone, for reasons known only to them, killed Marvin Donelson either here." He paused, lifting an eyebrow doubtfully. "Or they murdered him somewhere else and brought the body here."

Did they think one of them might have killed him? Andrew's shock at the idea must have been apparent because Drake shook his head at him to keep silent.

When the Sergeant looked up again, he finally said, "We'll probably have more questions for you as the investigation continues. Please contact me if you think of anything that might be relevant." He handed them cards as he stood and added, "And don't leave town without contacting our office." Then he left, the store finally silent again.

They both stared at the floor where the body had been, not saying anything at first.

"We'll need to call Nora," Drake finally said after a minute. "I don't want her hearing about this from a policeman knocking on her door."

Parker leaned his head back closing his eyes. "We'll need to call Farris and Janine for the same reasons." He glanced toward his desk. "I want to have this office thoroughly cleaned as well."

"I'll call our cleaning service and get them over here to take care of it before any news gets out," Drake said, running a hand through his hair. "You and I can roll up the rug and trash it if you like. I doubt you'll enjoy keeping it with a blood stain on it."

He glanced at Andrew. "How are you doing kid? It's a tough thing to walk in on a dead body first thing in the morning."

Andrew looked around the room and back toward the spot where he'd found Donelson. "This doesn't seem real. Why would anyone kill Marvin Donelson? And if they did, why bring him here?"

Drake crossed an ankle over his knee. "It seems obvious that whoever murdered Marvin hoped the police might think someone here at Westcott's was involved—or more specifically that someone here murdered the man himself."

Andrew's eyes widened.

"This isn't going to be good for business," Parker added. "You know the newspaper will pick up the story. It will probably hit front page."

"I'm sure you're right about that," Drake agreed. "The idea that Marvin was found here at our business, when he also had an antique business in town will get people talking and speculating. There were probably reporters outside snapping photos as the police and paramedics came and went."

"It's well known our stores are the two main antique businesses in town, even though our store is more high end and caters less to the tourist traffic than the Donelson's store on Bay Street," Parker said, shaking his head. "Some people might see our businesses as rivals, and I'm sure the press will put that spin on it in their reporting."

Drake gave a small laugh. "Eventually a few folks will remember, too, that Marvin and I had a running feud going. We bid against each other one too many times at estate sales. He got bitter over a few big losses he felt he had a right to."

"That's not reason for murder," Andrew put in. "And the fact that Marvin and his family owned another antique business isn't a reason for murder, either. Besides, I imagine few people know you and Marvin competed at estate sales."

Drake lifted an eyebrow. "The Donelson family will know and they'll talk. They'll be hurt and shocked, looking for answers, and wanting to blame someone. We'll be first in line, I can tell you that right now."

Parker stood. "Let's get this rug out of here through the back, Drake. We'd better roll it up and keep it in storage for a time before trashing it in case the police come back wanting a better look at it for some reason. I think you and I can probably clean the office rather than calling in our cleaning service, too. Having the service in today might give another opportunity for more speculation and gossip."

His eyes moved to meet Andrew's. "Can you open the store and keep things going out front, son? If any reporters come in, tell them the police told you not to discuss anything. Sound matter-of-fact and casual. Can you pull that off?"

"Yes, sir," he said, wanting to help in any way he could.

"We want to give a congenial appearance of 'business as usual' today and in the days to come. As news gets out, curious folks will stop by, perhaps some of our own customers. We'll all need to stay calm and collected and not get into any speculative talk with anyone."

"Good advice," Drake said, pushing Parker's desk back to pull the rug out from under it. "I picked up a great oriental that will look good in here, Parker. We'll go up to the storage room and get it after we get this place cleaned up."

Parker pulled his cell phone out of his pocket. "I'd better call Nora, too. She'll probably want to come in early. We need to fill her in on all this, and I'd say the store will be busy today. We'll probably need to take turns going to the Police Department for fingerprints around customers, too."

Taking a deep breath, Andrew walked back through the store to open the front door and turn the window sign from Closed to Open. He saw a few curious people standing across the street on the sidewalk, and he waved at them and smiled. Like Parker said, they needed everyone to see that it was 'business as usual' at Westcott's.

By the end of the day when Andrew headed home at last he felt exhausted. At the house, he filled Suki in on all the events that had occurred as they sat out on the back porch drinking cold glasses of iced tea.

Andrew, amid the turmoil of the day, hadn't even thought about dinner once, but Suki had gone to the store and picked up a few things to make a casserole for them. It was in the oven baking and she checked her watch every now and then, watching the time.

"How horrible for you to be the one to find that man's body. And how could the police even think any of you had anything to do with that man's death?" she asked.

"It's their job to consider every angle, I guess. We see that on television shows."

"I suppose. I'm sure Parker and Drake are upset, too. Like you said, this will probably impact Westcott's business."

"The curious will come to see where a murder happened. Others will avoid the site, worried that someone in our employ might be a murderer."

Her mouth dropped open. "I can't imagine anyone who knows Westcott's and its employees would think that for a minute."

"Well, I hope you're right."

"Let's go eat dinner," she said. "I'm glad I got restless today and decided to see if I could make something. You let me drop you off at work, so I could use the car if I needed it, so I drove to the Bi-Lo on Boundary."

She grinned at him as she headed to the kitchen. "I love that sporty little red Pontiac of yours."

"I probably thought of you when I bought it. I'll buy another car when I have time to look around so you can have that one." He caught up with her in the kitchen to pull her close and kiss her. "In all honesty, I think I bought a lot of things thinking of you and what you might like. Do you like the house?"

"I'm crazy about it. It's filled with things I'd have chosen myself. You being in antiques, we poked through a lot of stores together growing up, often talking about what we liked, what we'd put in our own homes someday." She went over to the stove to pull out the casserole she'd made. "I can't wait to see how you fixed up The Sandpiper, too. Since I'm feeling so much better now, could we go down for the weekend?"

"Sure. I worked last Saturday, so I'm off this weekend. I can get off early on Friday, too. Maybe we can make a reservation to eat at The Post Office on the way in."

"That would be great." She sat the casserole on a trivet on the round table by the window in the kitchen. Going back to the counter she got a side dish of tomatoes and avocadoes she'd chopped in a blue salad bowl, and a basket of French bread she'd heated.

"The casserole looks good," Andrew said, sitting down at the table with her after refilling their iced tea glasses again. "What is it?"

"A chicken and broccoli casserole. I called Mother for the recipe. It's made with chicken breasts, broccoli, a little cooked rice, cream of chicken soup, sour cream, some mayonnaise, and lots of cheese. You layer everything and bake it. It was always one of my favorite dishes growing up. Because it has the whole meal in the casserole recipe, I thought chopped tomatoes and avocadoes would be enough on the side along with bread."

She paused before picking up her fork. "Do you think we should say grace? We haven't been doing it, but I feel thankful I'm feeling better, that I can drive and do more things again. I'm also thankful you didn't run into a murderer this morning."

"I'll be happy to say grace," Andrew said. He sent her a suggestive look. "I have a lot to be thankful for, too."

"Oh, you." She swatted at him, but then leaned across the small table to kiss him. "We have had fun, haven't we?"

"Yes, we have," he said, kissing her back. And he meant it.

Later that evening they sat relaxing in the den with the cat, reading and listening to music. Andrew's musical library was primarily classical music, which Suki enjoyed, too.

He glanced across the room to see one of her fingers idly playing along with the melody on the arm of her chair. Holding her paperback book propped on a cushion with her other hand, she probably wasn't even aware she was playing. It saddened Andrew to watch her. She'd been here over a week now but hadn't touched the piano. In past he knew she practiced hours every day, got lost in her music. He wondered how she could walk away from it as she had?

He thought of saying something to her about it. Wondered if he should encourage her to talk about it or perhaps encourage her to play. But he kept quiet instead. No one had ever needed to encourage Suki to play since she was a small girl. The piano drew her like a magnet, wrapped her in its spell. Surely she would find her way back to it in time.

She looked up at him with a mischievous grin. "Married life is turning out to be nice, isn't it? I talked to Eito today and told him he'd made a good match. He seemed pleased." She hesitated. "I'd like to invite Eito, Ken, Marri, and Julianne down to the beach house later for a vacation. I think they'd love Edisto. Would that be all right with you?"

"That's a great idea."

"They've never visited in the South. I think we could introduce them to the beauty of South Carolina, and it would be wonderful to see them all again."

"The next time you talk to them, ask them to look ahead for a time when they can all come," he said. "They'll need to plan the trip around their work, and it might need to be after Julianne gets out of school. She's in kindergarten now. "

"I'll do that." Her eyes moved back to her book, but Andrew soon felt her watching him instead of reading and he looked up.

"What?'

"Sometimes it's nice to go to bed early, don't you think? You've had a pretty stressful day." He saw her lips twitch playfully over the words.

"That sounds like an excellent idea." He grinned at her. "You go on up and catch your shower first. I'll turn off the stereo and all the lights and be up soon."

She stood and started across the room. "You know," she said, pausing at the door to the hallway. "There's a very *big* shower in that master bedroom. I imagine two people could use it at once." She glanced away and then back at him with a little smile. "I think I remember reading something like that in one of those books."

"I think I remember the exact book you're talking about," Andrew said with a smirk as she headed down the hallway. He moved around the room quickly to turn off the lights and stereo and follow her upstairs.

CHAPTER 9

A week later Monday, April 5ᵗʰ

Suki padded down the stairs at Andrew's house on Point Street at Edisto a week later on Monday morning. Actually, she supposed it was her house now, too. That novel thought brought a smile despite the disturbing dream that woke her earlier.

As promised, she gave Andrew a call at the store. "I'm up and all is well," she told him. "Thanks for saying I could stay at the beach while you're at work this week. Mother needs to do some writing and she felt better going home to Beaufort knowing I'd be next door to Mary Helen and Bailey. After I fix breakfast I'm going to stay at Mary Helen's for the morning and help her with lunch. Kizzy is coming to our place to clean today and I want to come back after lunch before she leaves. Mary Helen usually takes a nap with Bailey in the afternoon anyway. She'll be okay by herself and she can phone if she needs me."

Suki walked over to open the curtains to the new day, already bright and sunny. "It looks like it's going to be a great sunny day."

"Relax and enjoy the beach and get some extra rest. I'm glad you called." He paused. "I may drive down to the island one night this week, if only to have supper with you."

"That would be fun. Thank Parker again for giving you a ride back so I could keep the car." She moved into the kitchen to start coffee. "Aren't you glad Drake helped you find that new Ford Explorer last week? I like having the Pontiac here with me, and your new Explorer will be great to use for hauling groceries, beach gear, or furniture you pick up for Westcott's."

"I'm sure Drake had that in mind, when he heard I was looking for another car." Andrew laughed. "The car drives like a dream, too. I really like it."

Suki heard voices in the background then.

"Drake and Parker are here and we need to have a meeting before we open the store. Mom's coming in for this one, too. I'll call you tonight. Okay?"

"Sure. Talk to you later." She laid her cell phone down on the kitchen table, trying not to let her eyes wander to the mahogany piano that dominated a corner of the open living, dining, and kitchen area of the beach house.

"I'd really hoped to escape looking at a piano every day while at the beach," she said to the instrument, scowling at it. "But here you are."

She'd been surprised to arrive at The Sandpiper and find yet *another* piano, this one not a big grand, like at Andrew's Beaufort house, but a smaller baby grand. Another Steinway, too, like the piano in Beaufort—the concert pianists' choice.

"Let's see," she'd asked Andrew almost sarcastically when she first toured the beach house. "You needed a second piano here for what reason?"

He shrugged. "I picked it up at an auction I attended with Drake. No one was biding much on it and I knew its value. I got it for an incredible bargain."

Andrew went over to sit down at the keyboard as if in justification. "I play a little, you know, and I enjoy it." He played some of a familiar Bach etude then. "Orin plays piano, too, as well as cello. Morgan comes down sometimes for a break, also. He loves having the piano here. He told me he'd composed a few pieces here—said it was an inspirational place, inducing lyrical song."

Suki didn't answer. After all, how could she be petty enough to deny others pleasure in playing simply because she couldn't bring herself to do it? And the piano was a beautiful one with a fabulous tone.

As she cooked a little breakfast, Suki couldn't help but remember the odd and disturbing dream she'd had shortly before dawn. She woke suddenly with the room almost lit with a soft glow, although it was still dark outside. She sat up at first, in surprise, but then pulled up the covers, turning to settle back down again. As she did so she seemed to hear a voice calling as if from a distance saying, "Play for me. Come and play for me."

Feeling frightened, she'd looked around the room and then got up to peek out the bedroom window. With the house above ground on stilts, like most beach homes, Suki knew she wouldn't see anyone looking directly in the window, but as clear as the voice was, she thought someone might be in the yard. Maybe even one of her old Edisto friends playing a trick on her. It was the kind of thing Chuck and J.T. used to do when younger. Both had been teases, laughing uproariously over their silly pranks, except when their parents caught them. But she saw no one—only a big moon in a dark sky.

After a little while she settled back down to sleep, but the memory lingered in her mind. It was an odd experience. Did fear prompt it? Was she mentally imagining Jonah calling to her, trying to pull her back on tour? How many times she remembered him cajoling and pushing her on and on when she felt worn out and tired, using the magic of his words and—as she now knew—the false pretenses of his feelings to pressure her. He always made her feel that everything he asked of her was only because he loved her and believed in her. What a lie. Even then a small side of her wondered about his feelings, often saw his selfishness assert itself. She wasn't stupid. She knew the more performances she gave, the more money he made. As a rising young agent and manager, he was building his name and future on the young stars he'd scouted out after joining the Greenwood Agency.

She read a quote somewhere saying the first step to living the life you really want to live is in leaving the old life you don't want behind. She certainly wanted to do that.

Shifting mental gears, Suki made an "egg in a hole" for her breakfast like her mother used to cook for her and Mary Helen as girls. She cut a hole in a slice of the thick homemade bread she'd bought at the market this weekend, dropped the bread into hot melted butter in a skillet, and then cracked an egg into the hole. After a few minutes, she flipped it over, cooked it a few minutes longer and then turned it onto her plate beside slices of fresh cantaloupe. Unlike Mary Helen she'd always liked to cook, especially fanciful and creative things. She probably picked up that trait from her mother.

Suki took her plate and coffee out onto the screened porch. The early April day was a little cool now but would quickly warm up. Suki settled at an old table on the porch where she could look out at the ocean. At Oleanders, her parents' home a block away, the screened porch extended all the way across the back of the house. But here at The Sandpiper the screened porch, an unusual one, curled in a hexagonal pattern around one the end of the house, with an open railed porch across the other side. A wide set of stairs led down between the porches to the yard and to a sandy pathway winding to the beach.

While eating, Suki looked around the house's property with interest. One of the islands many access roads lay to the left of the Sandpiper's side yard, shaded by oleanders and palms. Beyond that Suki could see J.T. and Mary Helen's more modern gray home and a glimpse of the Whaleys and her parents' places. To her right, beyond a cluster of oaks and pines, sat a sunny yellow house called The Treasure Chest. Andrew said the family who owned it now lived in Atlanta and seldom came to use it except during summer vacations and holidays. A lot of homes on the island were vacant much of the year or offered as rental homes with the island's realty companies. Families came and went in the rentals, in for a week or two to enjoy the beach, and then back to Wisconsin, Ohio, Tennessee, or Kentucky where they lived. It made Edisto a unique place, with many new people to meet and talk with year round. She'd always loved it.

Finishing her breakfast, she headed to Mary Helen's. Suki wore shorts and a t-shirt, with a favorite red sweatshirt decorated with white stars over it. Red had always been her favorite color, ever since she was a preschooler arguing with Mary Helen over who got the red glass at meals. Her new flip-flops were red, too. She'd picked them up this weekend at one of the local shops while exploring the island with Andrew.

Entering the back door of Mary Helen's big two-storied beach house now, Suki found her sister curled up on the sofa feeding Bailey.

"Hi, how are things going?" she asked.

Mary Helen laughed. "Other than the fact that I feel like an endless cow being milked at regular intervals, very good."

Suki settled into a chair beside her. "How many times did Bailey get you up last night?"

"Actually only twice after his last midnight feeding. Mother says its because he was a late baby and big at birth." She stroked his head. "I suppose there is some advantage to having a late baby. Jane's first, Elena—nearly three now—was premature, and Jane said she hardly got any sleep at first with her. Elena fed so often."

She shifted Bailey to her shoulder to pat his back. "Bailey feeds about every four hours and Mother really helped me to see the importance of a schedule and regularity. She's convinced that babies are creatures of habit. So whatever habits we establish become the ones they settle in to. She was a great help last week. I have to admit. I feel so much more confident with her teaching."

"Mother has always been smart," Suki said, propping her feet on a footstool.

"She gave me some great baby books, too, when I was pregnant." Mary Helen stood to walk around with Bailey, patting him on the back as she did. "Mother said God gave women nine months to get prepared for a new baby. She claimed it a shame not to use that time to learn as much as possible in order to be the best mother one could."

"I remember all those baby books you got at Christmas." Suki giggled.

"Yeah, and I read them all, too, and refer to them, as well. They really help."

"Does everything work by the book?"

Mary Helen laughed. "Of course not. Every baby is different, and every mother and every father is different. A lot of it is finding your own way, armed with the knowledge you've learned. But some things aren't in the books."

"What can I do to help you, Mary Helen?"

"Visit with me after I go put Bailey down in his crib. I'm used to working at the store and talking with people most all day. Being home and so quiet is wearing on me." She smiled at Suki. "You know we're different that way."

After a few minutes she came back to settle on the sofa again, carrying a baby monitor.

"Bailey will sleep for a while now, so tell me about what's happening with the murder. I still can't believe Andrew walked in on a dead body at Westcott's." Mary Helen shook her head. "I've imagined several times how I'd have reacted if that happened to me when I opened The Little Mermaid one morning. I doubt I'd have acted as calm as Andrew."

Suki walked into the kitchen to snag two bottles of cold water from the refrigerator, passing one to Mary Helen before she sat back down. "The publicity has been worse than expected. When Andrew, Drake, Nora, Parker, and Claire went to Marvin Donelson's funeral last week, the Donelson family all but snubbed them. People noticed. And with no leads on the murderer at all, it keeps a finger of doubt on the employees at Westcott's as possible suspects."

"I hate that for Parker and Mother and for everyone at the store."

"I'm sure talk and speculation will die down in time, but it's difficult for everyone right now. Even when Andrew and I went out to dinner one night, we could tell people were pointing and whispering, knowing Andrew found Marvin's body." She pulled off her sweatshirt to drape it over the chair beside her. "I know Andrew hasn't forgotten some of the talk that went around about his father years ago. He's worked so hard to be a different kind of man, one of character and integrity. I know this hurts his heart although he doesn't say so of course."

"Mother says everyone is hoping and praying for resolution. When they find the murderer everything will clear up."

"But the odd thing is, the police have virtually no clues. The coroner established that the body probably was moved, but no evidence shows where it was moved from. As the detective said, it could have been moved from another area of the store to Parker's office."

Mary Helen's mouth dropped open. "He said that?"

"Yes. Detective Dunnings, assigned to the case now, has made a lot of suggestive comments, as if employees are holding out on evidence related to the case. Drake said it's because he has no answers."

"Well, the whole thing is awful. Parker said it's affecting business, too—and not positively."

Mary Helen walked back to check on Bailey and then returned. "Have you seen Emma since she threw that petty fit at the reception? I still can't believe she acted like that."

"I haven't seen her. She didn't come to the Sandpiper on the weekend when Andrew and I invited everyone for dinner Saturday night."

Mary Helen smiled. "It was nice of you and Andrew to do that. I know J.T. and I usually host the gatherings for the gang at our place. But it was good for us to get away from the house for a little while, leaving Bailey with Mother and Parker—if only next door. Parenting is a pretty consuming task."

"It was fun. We did dinner the easy way, baked a beef tenderloin, a bunch of baked potatoes, made a giant salad, and bought two or three flavors of ice cream. We used plastic plates, cups and silver we could trash afterward, too.

"Well, it was great. I loved seeing everyone." She stuck her feet on the coffee table across from her. "Don't you like Chuck's new wife Toni?"

"I do and the more I get to know Barton, Jane's husband,

the more I like him, too. Only Emma is missing from our get-togethers." She sighed. "She must really believe in some way I stole Andrew from her."

Mary Helen wrinkled her nose. "Frankly, I think deep in her heart she knew Andrew wasn't interested in her. But Emma likes to dream, and she isn't always realistic."

"Jane and Andrew both claim Orin Jefferson really likes her."

"Then we need to work on doing a little matchmaking between them. I like Orin, don't you?"

"What I know of him." Suki considered the idea. "We talked about inviting Emma and Orin over to our place. I need to suggest to Andrew that we do it soon."

Mary Helen made a face. "You'd better invite a few other Beaufort friends, too, so Emma won't feel you're pushing Orin at her. Maybe invite a pretty girl Orin might find interesting." She grinned at the idea. "If Emma thought Orin was interested in someone else, she might decide to notice him more."

Suki laughed. "That's a great idea. I still know a few girls from back when I played with the Beaufort Symphony now and then. I'll work on that."

An hour or two later, after fixing lunch for herself and Mary Helen, Suki headed back to The Sandpiper, hoping to see Kizzy.

She came in the back door to find Kizzy working in the kitchen. The little woman soon enveloped her in a warm embrace. "There's my other little sweetheart," she said. "I was sorry to hear you've been so sick, but your mama told me the other day you're doing better now. I can see that for myself with that bloom in your cheek."

Kizzy Helton, a friend of all the family, had her own cleaning business on Edisto and had been cleaning all their homes for as long as Suki could remember. After Suki, Mary Helen, and their mother came to live at the island, they'd come to know Kizzy, her husband Lewis, and all her family well.

Suki asked about everyone now, and Kizzy was soon catching her up on all the news. "I'm tickled as can be you married that sweet

Andrew. He deserved a good woman. I'm so fond of him. Your marriage was a bit sudden, but I've prayed over it and I got a good witness about it."

Kizzy picked up a sponge to start wiping down the kitchen counters. "I'm sorry you had to leave your concert tour, but I'd love it if you'd play a piece for me while I finish cleaning this kitchen. You know how I love to hear you play."

Suki stood looking at the small black woman she loved so well, not knowing what to say. Glancing at the piano, she felt herself shiver.

"I'm not playing now, Kizzy," she said at last in a low voice.

"What do you mean you're not playing?"

Kizzy pointed to a chair at the kitchen table and indicated for Suki to sit down. "You need to be telling me what that's all about."

Suki sat down across from Kizzy and looked down at her hands in her lap. "After I collapsed, sick, at the Lincoln Center, I didn't want to play anymore. Just thinking about it upsets and panics me. I can't do it, Kizzy. I've left the tour and I don't know if I'll ever want to play again."

"Lord, Lord … what kind of fear have you allowed to get set up in you, and you a preacher's girl? You know fear and faith are bold-faced enemies. When you let the one in you're choosing to kick the other out."

Suki lifted her chin. "I haven't lost my faith, Kizzy."

"Well, when God gives you a gift and you decide not to use it, that's like throwing it back in God's face. A gift's a gift. The talents God gives us are expected to be used freely and used with gratitude. If I brought you one of my key lime pies, would you be throwing it back in my face? Certainly not." She shook her head.

She leaned forward. "You remember that story in the Bible about the talents don't you? The Lord said 'well done' to the ones who used their talents but He had no good thing to say to the one who hid his talent and didn't use it."

Suki started to cry. "I feel bad enough without you rebuking me Kizzy."

"Perhaps you need rebuking rather than folks pampering you and feeling sorry for you. Indulging your feelings. We're not to live by feelings but by faith and what's right."

"Well, I don't know what to do about it. Every time I even think about playing I freeze inside and feel sick and panicked." She sniffed. "The doctor said sometimes when people get sick physically it affects their emotions, too."

"Hmmph. So you gonna stay sick physically and emotionally after Jesus done paid to set you free from all that on the cross? Sure, the old devil comes stalking and attacking after our lives sometimes, but our job is to fight the good fight of faith, resist him and run him off, not put out the welcome mat and invite him in for iced tea and a piece of cake. You know that." She leaned forward. "You need to fight, girl. Whoever's been telling you just to lay down in this and accept it has been telling you wrong."

Suki crossed her arms, hugging herself. "You're not being very sympathetic, Kizzy."

"Sympathy ain't what you need. A bit of sound advice and a fighting spirit is what you need. Don't you feel your own spirit calling you to that piano, calling you to play and use your gift?"

Suki sighed. "Your words sound like that dream I had this morning that scared me."

Kizzy's eyes widened. "What dream, girl? Tell me about that."

She did.

Kizzy paused, thinking for a few minutes. "Do you remember the story in your Bible about little Samuel, how his mama took him to live with Eli the priest?"

"I always thought it was sad his mother finally had a child but then had to keep her promise and give him away to the church."

"You're missing the point, and it wasn't as though she never saw him again." Kizzy frowned. "The point was that the Lord called Samuel in the night. The boy heard it like an audible voice and he thought it was Eli, but it wasn't. It was God speaking a word to him. The Lord does that sometimes. All the wisdom God taught in His Word isn't some old story that's passed away. He's the same yesterday, today, and forevermore. If he can speak in the night to Samuel, He can speak in the night to you."

Suki put a hand to her heart. "You think that was God calling to me?"

"I sure do, girl, and you know God talks to me about things."

Suki well remembered that fact from her years growing up around Kizzy. She didn't always understand it but Kizzy seemed to have, as her mother said, her antenna tuned in to God a little more than most of us.

Suki glanced toward the piano. "But I simply can't play, Kizzy." She put a hand to her head. "Just thinking about it makes me feel sick."

Kizzy got up to come around the table to put a hand on Suki's head. "Well, we're sure going to pray about that fear that's tormenting you right here and right now. And child, the next time you hear God calling you in that way, like Samuel, you say 'Here I am, Lord,' and you ask Him to tell you what He wants you to do and ask Him to make you able to do it."

"I'll try," Suki said.

Kizzy closed her eyes. "Lord God," she prayed. "Sometimes the old enemy comes and really kicks up a mess in our lives, bringing in sickness, problems to attack us, but we know if we hold steadfast in our faith, resist the enemy, and seek after your knowledge and best will, that you'll help us."

She stroked Suki's hair. "Lord, I pray strength and health to this child in the name of Jesus. Touch her and make her whole and strong. Help her stand against fears that have tried to attack her life. I rebuke fear and tell it to leave her."

Kizzy sat down in the chair beside Suki's after a few minutes and reached out to take Suki's hands. "Lord you promised that you'd give us love, power, and a sound mind. I say by faith that this child's mind is sound and strong, and I speak your peace, love and power on her. You've given her a fine and blessed talent for music, and I pray in the days and weeks to come that You'll show her how you want her to use it now. A door never closes but that you don't open another. Satan may have tried to steal her song, but you'll give her another one and reawaken Your gift in her."

She looked right into Suki's eyes then. "Will you receive that prayer, child? If so, say, 'I receive that Lord and thank you for it.'"

Suki said the words with a wobbly voice, and then Kizzy hugged her tight. "You're going to be all right, girl. I've seen it. Give it time. Pray and seek after God and His best will every day. And don't you be saying no negative words about your life, you hear?"

"Yes, ma'am." Suki reached for a napkin on the table to blow her nose. "And thank you for praying for me."

"I love you, sweet child." She stood up. "But God loves you more. Always remember that. No one loves you more than God and He wants only good for you. There's no life on this earth He doesn't have a plan for. It's just that most folks won't seek after it and most aren't willing to do what it takes to walk in His best plan much of the time."

"I want God to help me with a new life and a new path."

"Then He will." Kizzy looked at her watch and then glanced around the kitchen. "Our praying took a bit of my time. Can you finish cleaning up the kitchen here so I can go on to the store to help Lewis out? You know we still own our grocery down near the McKinley Washington Bridge. The store gets busy this time in the afternoons."

"I'll be glad to."

Kizzy went over to put a hand on Suki's head again. "Close your eyes and tell me if you don't feel a new peace slipping in to your life."

Suki did and nodded as a soft, quiet feeling rolled over her.

"Fear hath a torment. You keep fighting it. Look for the root of it and dig it out." She looked into Suki's eyes again. "You know who's behind most any kind of fear. But only you can decide to let this one go. Do you understand?"

"Yes, ma'am, I do."

Kizzy went to get her purse from the counter, draping it over her shoulder. "I sure am glad to see you back at the island again, girl.

This place has a healing magic. You'll see. You marrying a sweet man to love will help, too. Remember to thank God every day for your blessings. We have so many and too often we only focus on our problems instead of our blessings." She started for the door. "I'll see you next Monday if you're down to the island again. You keep listening for your song. It'll come. It'll come."

After Kizzy left, Suki sat quietly on the porch for a time, thinking about Kizzy's words and her prayer. Then she decided to take a walk down the beach. In early April like this, she found the beaches quiet and almost deserted, so she prayed as she walked. She felt bad that she couldn't play for the little black woman she loved so much, but for the first time she felt hopeful that sometime, like Kizzy said, she'd get her song and her direction clear again.

CHAPTER 10

With Suki at the island, Andrew went over to have dinner with his mother on Monday night. He was overdue a visit with her. Andrew knew she'd been troubled about his sudden marriage and upset over the murder at the store. They needed to talk.

He turned into the driveway of the O'Connor House, a few blocks past Westcott's Antiques on Craven, and drove behind the house to park in his usual spot under a pair of giant oaks draped in moss. Somewhat like Parker's home, the O'Connor House was a gracious, historic downtown home, but situated on a less prestigious property. The old place was a beauty though—a red brick, two-storied house with wide, upper and lower front porches, embellished with white posts and railings. The windows were long, the ceilings high on both floors, and tall brick walls encased the back yard.

The house had been a single family dwelling at one time, but when Ira Dean and her husband Henry bought it forty years ago, the upper floor had already been converted into a full apartment. A covered entry on the back of the house, created for a servants' entrance, led upstairs to the spacious two-bedroom apartment Andrew grew up in.

Henry died when Andrew was only a boy, but Henry and Ira Dean O'Connor were probably two of the few who knew how much his mother's divorce from Hayden Cavanaugh had hurt Nora. A trusting young girl, enjoying a summer job in Beaufort and away from home for the first time, Nora had been swept off her feet by Hayden Cavanaugh, older than her, handsome, charming, and wealthy. Hayden ran the Beaufort branch of his family's realty business, headquartered in Savannah, and he and Andrew's mother fell madly in love. When summer ended they ran off and married so she wouldn't have to go home to Maine. That sudden marriage was the beginning of many grievances Hayden Cavanaugh's family held against Nora. And the beginning of many heartaches for Nora.

None of Hayden's family had never acknowledged that he had any problems to justify Nora divorcing him later. Instead, incensed at accusations that Hayden drank and was abusive, they ceased to acknowledge Nora and never reached out to get to know Andrew through all the years that followed, even though his father never married again or had other children. At twenty-one, when Andrew's father was tragically killed and he inherited his father's home—and his father's money—the family had been furious. Because of this painful past a part of Andrew understood why his mother didn't want to live in any house that had belonged to her former husband. But she'd insisted Andrew move there.

"You're twenty-one and it's time," she told him. "I never lived in that house with Hayden, but it's beautiful. You'd be foolish to turn it down." So he'd moved, at her urging, and Nora had stayed in her familiar place above Ira Dean's.

Although Nora worked with priceless antiques every day, her apartment leaned to the cozy, feminine side with soft chintz upholstery in the living areas and a fun, almost country kitchen with a colorful well-worn table and chairs in the center. Nora liked light colors, a contrast to the dark colors and furniture usually in Westcott's showrooms. Her bedroom furniture was white French provincial, and Andrew's old room bright and sunny, too, with the same sky blue twin spreads and striped wallpaper from his boyhood years.

"Is that you, Andrew?" his mother called as he unlocked the door and let himself into the apartment.

"Yeah," he answered, walking back to find her in the kitchen, putting the finishing touches on dinner. It hurt him sometimes that she'd wanted to stay here above Ira Dean's, living so simply when he could have bought her a fine home of her own.

Whenever he broached the subject, she argued. "Now why would I want all that space to putter around in by myself? I'm comfortable in my place. Ira Dean and I share meals now that you're gone. We watch movies together, laugh and gossip like women do."

"You did that before, too." He kidded her and laughed, because of course Ira Dean O'Connor was like family. He usually ran downstairs to visit her if she didn't come up to join them, but tonight he knew she'd gone to a church meeting.

Sniffing the air, he asked, "What did you cook for dinner?"

"Chicken and dumplings in the Crockpot because I remembered you liked it. I made some biscuits and a little fruit salad, too." She opened the Crockpot now to stir it. "I started most of the ingredients this morning before our meeting. After lunch, since I got off early today, I came home and finished it."

She came over to pat his cheek and kiss him. "You look wonderful son," she said, making him feel like a boy again. But with his mom it was okay.

She began to dish out two big bowls of chicken and dumplings, and Andrew moved into the familiar routine of pouring tea for them to drink, putting butter on the table, making sure they had napkins and silver.

When they sat down to eat at last, they both bowed their heads to offer a moment of silent grace, a custom Nora grew up with and brought to their home.

They settled in to eat then.

"I was glad to notice more color in Suki's cheeks Saturday at the reception than I saw on that first night when she came home with you." She gave Andrew a pointed look. "You do know coming home married like that was a shock to me. I always imagined I'd be there to see you wed when the time came."

He avoided her eyes. "The reception was almost like another wedding." Andrew reached for a biscuit. "Think of the expenses you saved. The groom's family usually pays for the reception, musical entertainment, the minister's fee, tuxedo rental, corsages, boutonnieres, groomsmen's gifts, and more. Weddings are costly."

"Are you purposely trying to provoke me, Andrew?"

"No, I'm only saying that in a lot of ways I'm glad I didn't have to go through all of that," he answered with honesty. "Suki was right. It was fun, for a change, doing something impulsive. I've watched other friends go through the stress of planning a big wedding. I wasn't sorry to miss that."

"Well, I was," she said buttering a biscuit. "But the reception was lovely, and the photographer made a lot of nice pictures. It will do."

He watched his mother as she ate, still a beautiful auburn haired woman with blue eyes like his, a peaches and cream complexion, and a sweet smile.

"I've been so lucky to have you for a mom," he said.

She offered him one of her smiles. "If you sweet talk your new wife like that, I imagine things will go well."

"Things are already going well." He grinned over several of his memories as he said the words.

"I can see you look like a well-contented cat," she replied, lifting an eyebrow. "I'm glad of that fact if she's being good to you."

"She is." Andrew didn't want to discuss this area further with his mother, so he changed the subject. "The detective came by the store again after you went home."

Nora made a face. "Detective Dunnings." She said the name with distaste. "He's certainly no favorite of mine, swinging his weight around and acting self-important when he hasn't discovered a single clue in all this to feel smug about."

"Drake dislikes him, too," Andrew said between bites of his mother's chicken and dumplings. "Parker and I aren't overly fond of him either, but we seem to keep our animosity more under lock and key than Drake."

She laughed. "Sometimes I admit I do love that 'in your face' aspect of Drake Hartwell Jenkins. He's such a typical Southern gentleman sometimes but always gets himself up in the air when everyone doesn't act with grace and gentile character."

"He talked to me the other day about why he's never married."

"Did he?" She looked surprised. "He's so secretive about his past, except to make jokes about it, I'm surprised you wormed anything out of him." She paused. "What did he tell you?"

"That he'd actually been engaged once. He said it was before he left the family business and came here to Beaufort."

Her eyes widened. "Really? He's never told me that, and I admit that Parker, Claire, and I have all wondered. And occasionally probed."

Andrew reached for another biscuit. "He said she broke the engagement when he didn't stay with the family business and with the wealth and social life that was a part of being a Jenkins."

"Ouch." She winced. "I hate that for him."

"He said it made him wary—like you are—about ever getting involved with anyone again. He claimed young hurts go deep or something like that."

"Wary. Hmmph." She spluttered. "I was a young pregnant girl when I had to leave your father. Working and raising a child doesn't leave much extra time."

"I suppose." He got up to get a second helping of the chicken and dumplings. "This is good, Mom."

"Is Suki cooking a little now that she's feeling better? Traveling the way she has these last years, I doubt she found much time to putter around the kitchen, but I remember as a girl she enjoyed helping her mother more than Mary Helen did."

"She still likes to putter in the kitchen. She's been getting some recipes from Claire to try. I help, too. Or sometimes I cook and she helps me." He smiled at his mother. "Don't worry that I'm not eating well."

"I think all mothers feel a little worried and possessive when their sons get married." She laughed. "After all, mothers are used to being the number one woman in their sons' lives until they marry. It's a change. However, you moved out on your own years ago to your own place. So things aren't so different for me."

"Good, because you'll always be my number one woman. You've sacrificed so much for me. I wish you'd let me do more for you now."

"Stop worrying over me. I'm very happy and content."

When his mother got up to fix dessert and coffee a little later, Andrew's thoughts slipped back to Drake. "What do you know about Drake's family and past?"

"Why?"she asked, starting the coffee.

He shrugged. "I guess him telling me about being engaged got me to thinking."

She grew quiet for a minute, cutting two pieces of a chocolate chip pie that was one of Andrew's favorites. "Here's what I know," she said at last. "Drake grew up in the prestigious Buckhead area of Atlanta in an old, monied family, one of four children. He had an older brother Mitchell and two younger sisters Gillis and Selena. Drake's father Conyer Jenkins was a governor's son and a Georgia attorney general. Jenkins County is named after Drake's family. Drake's father worked in the old family law firm and it was expected that Drake go into the firm as well."

She paused. "To put more pressure on the situation Drake's mother Taletha held a coveted social position in the community. Her father had been in the U.S. House of Representatives and her own family, as well as Conyer's, reached far back to a rich Georgia heritage. Taletha and Conyer expected all their children to make the family proud in the tradional way and each child had very defined expectations to fulfill."

Nora smiled as she placed a piece of pie and a cup of coffee in front of him. "Drake always joked that the first and last Jenkins children conformed and that the two middle children rebelled. Mitchell, the oldest, is an attorney with the family firm, as expected, and the younger daughter Selena married one of the partner's sons. Drake, as you know, studied law, started working in the business but hated it. When he confronted his father that he wanted to leave, it caused a huge family rift. He'd always loved antiques, poked through antiques stores as a kid. I know you remember him telling you that while he vacationed here in Beaufort he couldn't stay away from Westcott's. He says Vernon Westcott kidded him one day that he'd need to hire him if he kept hanging around. Drake jumped on the offer and the rest is history."

"What about the other sister?"

Nora sat down with her own plate. "I've met his sister Gillis. She shocked the family, too, by marrying a farmer, Daniel O'Neill. They own a flower farm called Belair. She and Drake stay in touch, and they come over to visit sometimes." Nora grinned. "You might say Gillis is a bit of a hippie, if you know the term."

Andrew nodded and then, after finishing another bite, said, "I know Drake walked away from everything to work at Westcott's, but I can see from his lifestyle that his Westcott salary alone can't be his only source of income." He glanced around, well aware that although his mother was relatively comfortable, Drake lived in a much higher fashion.

"Oh, Drake inherited money. I thought you knew that." She waved a hand. "All the Jenkins children did and all had trusts and such. Drake inherited more later, too, from a favorite uncle who never married."

"Well, that explains how he could afford his house down on the Harbor River, all the sharp clothes, cars, and his boat."

"I suppose." She cut into her pie.

He studied her. "Did it never bother you, working with Parker and Drake who always both had so much while we struggled?"

Her eyes met his. "We never struggled." She emphasized the last word. "I was blessed when Al Brimmer took me into his business and into his heart, when Ira Dean and Henry let us move into this apartment, and again when Parker and his wife Ann hired me at Westcott's Antiques when Al died. I consider my life a series of blessings. I hope you don't look at it differently. Our needs are met. I have no debts from living modestly. We have loved friends. You got a good education with scholarships and by working part time. You have a job you love. Like Drake you inherited money so you'll never have worries in that area unless you are careless or imprudent. You have a nice wife now, too. Do you have complaints about your life?" She scowled. "I don't think I raised you to be ungrateful or to be particularly money-conscious."

"You misunderstand." Andrew ran a hand through his hair in annoyance. "I just couldn't help being aware that you worked so hard when I was a child and didn't have many pleasures. I feel bad now, when I have an abundance of finances, that you won't let me do more for you."

She crossed her arms. "Honestly, sometimes I wonder if you really know me at all, son. I grew up in northern Maine in a small coastal town. The climate and isolation there breeds tough, independent individuals. My family, the Quinns, lived simply and appreciated simple pleasures. You've met your grandparents, my sister, her family, and others in the Quinn family on our visits to Maine. My father is a small town architect and works with his hands building furniture. You've seen some of his beautiful pieces. My mother, as you know, teaches math in the local high school. My sister Jillian married a local boy, still lives in town and is a nurse. She and her husband Ian have two children, now grown. Her husband Ian works with my grandparents and my Great Aunt Vesta running the Third Street Antique Mall, where I learned much of what I know about antiques before coming here. You've visited there as well."

She sent Andrew a stern look. "The point is Quinns work. We take gratitude in our days and remember to be thankful for what we have. A few times I wished things weren't so hard for us. A few times I admit I wished your father could have changed, straightened out." She sighed. "I hoped and believed for that for too many years. Even Quinns dream a little sometimes. But don't you feel sorry for me, or for yourself, or for our lives. Many people experience true trials. Ours have been few in comparison. Don't you remember enjoying a happy life growing up?"

"Yes." He ran a hand around his neck. "I didn't mean to sound ungrateful."

She chuckled. "As a little boy, you were always telling me someday you'd grow up, get a fine job, and make a lot of money for me so I could have beautiful things. I always told you I already had a beautiful life, but you never seemed to want to believe me."

Andrew couldn't help grinning at her words. "I always wished you might meet another man some day, too, a fine man who would be a good husband to you." He hesitated. "Drake says you don't put off vibes that tell men you might be interested in a relationship with them."

She snorted. "Is that right? I'm not sure when Drake Hartwell Jenkins became an expert on my love life. I've certainly kept my nose and opinions of him to myself, but I will say it always worried me that Drake might be a little too much of a ladies man like your father Hayden. However, I've revised that opinion over time. Drake is handsome and charming like your father but sensible and good, if a little outspoken sometimes."

"I shouldn't have told you he said that. He also said you deserved a good man, a beautiful woman like you."

She lifted an eyebrow. "And here I thought that man never noticed me. Isn't this a day for surprises?"

"Mother, will you let me know if you have need of anything? I'd like to share more with you, at least be there for you."

"I know you'll always be there for me, dear. That's the kind of man you are, and I'm so glad of it." She took their plates to the kitchen. "Take your coffee over to the living room and get more comfortable."

He moved to sit in his favorite seat, putting his coffee mug on a side table. His mother soon joined him, settling into a corner of the sofa.

"What brought on all these questions tonight, Andrew?"

He felt his neck flush. "Suki asks me a lot of questions, and I don't always have the answers. I realized when she asks me things that I should know how to reply, that I should have more answers and knowledge about friends and family."

"Women are, by and large, a more curious lot than men." Nora put her feet up on a footstool. "A woman will ask a man to tell her about an event and quickly find herself annoyed when all he says was that it was nice and that a big crowd attended." She laughed. "A woman wants to know who was there, what they wore, what food was served, how the room was decorated, and if anything interesting happened." She laughed. "You'll have to become more observant now that you're a married man, Andrew."

He laughed, too. "I've seen that."

"What else has Suki been asking you about that you couldn't answer well?"

He glanced away from her. "She's asked a lot of questions about my father's family, but I didn't want to ask you that."

"Why not? Your father's people are a piece of work and certainly have been a problem for me, but I can tell you about them. To most people the Cavanaugh family are beautiful, prosperous people. Hayden's father Raylon and his mother Verleen own Low Country Coastal Properties, a big realty firm in Savannah. You probably remember that."

She stopped to sip her coffee before it grew cold. "They had three daughters, Patricia, Winona, and Natalie, and one son, all beautiful and blond—as they were. From the first they all spoiled Hayden, doted on him, and could find no fault in him. Whatever wrongs he did they excuse to this day, and they still choose to live in denial about the problems he had with alcohol and with women. In a business sense your father was smart and crafty. He excelled in real estate and he did well in starting a new branch of the family company here in Beaufort. You can be proud of that about him."

"I always remember that everywhere we went, when I spent time with him, he seemed to know everyone, to be very popular."

"He was that and those very characteristics drew me." She hesitated, looking across the room at a photo of herself and Hayden still on the mantle among a group of family pictures. "When we married impulsively Hayden's family was furious. An unknown girl from northern Maine wasn't their idea of the perfect bride for their only son. Let's just say they never rolled out the red carpet for me. They were stunned when two years later I filed for divorce on causes of abuse and alcoholism. As you know, and to his sorrow, when your father drank too much he had anger issues and could use his tongue and his fists on anyone unlucky enough to get in his way. Too often that was me." Her voice dropped and she looked down at her lap.

"I'm sorry to make you remember that bad time, Mom."

"It was what it was Andrew. I should have left before, but when I became pregnant I had someone new to think about. That gave me the courage to finally leave, especially because your father did not want a child at that time. He made it clear what he expected me to do about the pregnancy. I chose differently." She smiled at him. "I've never regretted that decision. Later your father came to love you and to be proud of you, in his own way. He told me many times he'd been wrong in what he asked. He often tried to get me to come back to him. You may not know that. But I watched his life closely enough around town to know he hadn't really changed enough to be a good husband or a good father. Despite it all, though, he was a loveable, brilliant, charming man, and, in all honesty, I loved him until he died, foolish though that was."

This final admittance was a revelation to Andrew, although he didn't say so.

"Well, now that I've answered the questions Suki asked you about, I have one for you. Why does Suki not want to play the piano anymore? We all watched her star rise, her talents grow, and anyone who knew that girl realized how much she loved to play. In fact, keeping her away from a piano was often a challenge. If we visited an old house or a church with a piano in it, before we knew it that child was sitting dabbling on the keyboard."

Andrew picked at the last little crumbs of his pie. "I don't know the answer to that one, Mother. After she woke up in the hospital she said she didn't want to go back on tour and didn't want to play the piano anymore. I thought it was simply that she was sick, felt upset she'd collapsed on stage. But she was adamant. Didn't even want to ship her piano from New York when we married."

She lifted a brow at that last comment. "Not as though she'd *need* a piano, you having one at both your houses."

"Perhaps I was dreaming ahead, getting ready for her." He looked away as he said the words.

"Perhaps you were. Like Drake said to me, when we got to thinking about it, we weren't really surprised you said yes when Suki proposed marriage." She got up to take their plates and cups to the kitchen sink. "However, I'm sorry that Suki has been so deeply hurt in some way that she doesn't want to play the piano anymore. She has such a gift. I hope she will find her way back to music in time."

"Me, too," Andrew said. "I think something happened between Suki and her manager Jonah. They were dating, you know. Supposedly talking of a future. I feel sure that's a factor in all this somewhere, along with Suki being unhappy on tour. It's a hard life, even for a dedicated person."

Nora turned to look at him. "You don't think she's still in love with him, do you?"

"I don't think so. I remember how fondly she looked at Jonah last year when I spent an evening with them, attending one of her concerts in Raleigh. And I saw how she looked at him in the hospital. I saw no affection in her manner or words toward him then."

"Hmmm. Well I hope that's the case. I'd hate to think she married on the rebound, even if Eito did think it a good match." She grinned then. "By the way, that man sounds charming. I look forward to meeting him, his daughter and family, when they come down to Beaufort and to the beach house this summer."

"You'll like him." Andrew looked at his watch. "I'd better head home. Melville will be looking for me, and my work is stressful right now with all that's going on. I think I'll put my feet up, read a good book, and listen to some music to relax."

"Well, I'm glad you came for dinner," she said, getting up to give him a hug as he stood to leave. "And I'm glad for your happiness."

At home later, many of the words from his conversation with

his mother stayed in his mind, especially her comment wondering if Suki might still be in love with Jonah, if she'd married him on the rebound. She'd never told him yet what happened with Jonah, only that something occurred she didn't want to talk about yet. He knew the idea shouldn't bother him, but it did.

CHAPTER 11

About a week later, Suki was back in Beaufort getting ready to host a Friday evening dinner at her and Andrew's home for four of their friends. She'd stayed at the beach for a long, restful week, enjoyed time with Mary Helen, J.T., little Bailey and their friends. She explored familiar spots around the island, walked the beach, rode bikes, and found herself feeling stronger and healthier every day. She even had a nice tan to show for her week.

"This is our first time to entertain in our home since we got married," Suki said to Andrew as they put dinnerware around the table in the dining room. She paused in her job to glance around the room with pleasure. Andrew had decorated the sunny dining room in a more modern look, with deep crimson paint on the walls above the chair rail, a muted sage green below it. The colors set the scene for the beautiful antique table in the middle of the room, with six upholstered chairs in a fun cranberry and cream leopard print. The fanciful print led Andrew to hang a gold-framed zebra painting on one wall and an ornate round mirror on another. A fine breakfront sat to one side of the room, loaded with dishes, and a rich oak buffet balanced it on the other.

Andrew had put beaded placemats around the dining room table already, and Suki paused, studying the plate in her hand before putting it down. "I expected only antiques from you for the tableware, but these plain white plates with red rims look somewhat modern."

"They are modern. They're from William Sonoma." He laughed.

"It's hard to find a full set of antique dinnerware anymore or a set you'd want to use everyday, so I picked up this set because it matched the dining room décor well. I like to mix antique dishes and glassware with it though." He sat a lavishly patterned gold-trimmed bowl on each plate that she'd put out. "These bowls, for example, are a very old Limoge pattern. I thought they'd be nice for that fancy ice cream dessert we're serving after dinner."

"These bowls are gorgeous." She ran a finger over one. "I love the fun goblets you put out, too. Are they antiques?"

"Yes. The goblets are Red Sunset Carnival glass, gold-toned on the bottom, red on the top. They do have a fun look, don't they? When I go to estate sales and auctions with Drake, I try to pick up a few things I like."

She smiled at him. "You have a lot of red in your home decor, too. I like that."

"I must have been thinking of you when I decorated." He sat another bowl on the table and gave her a quick kiss. "But you should remember I like red, too."

"I do remember that, another thing we have in common." She studied the table now, lush in deep reds, gold, and white, with elegant gold flatware glowing beside each place setting. "Everything looks beautiful, doesn't it?"

"It does. What do you think about putting this vintage lazy Susan in the middle of the table?" Andrew retrieved it from a drawer in the buffet. "I picked it up at an estate sale. You can put bread, butter, sauces, or condiments on it to save passing things around." He moved a large ornate centerpiece from the middle of the table and put the turntable in place, flipping it around afterward.

"I like that," she said. "It would look even better if we put a pretty bread basket on it, and maybe some ornate salt and pepper shakers. If you have a small antique dish, too, I could put the herb butter in it that I made for the French bread."

He grinned. "Consider it done." He began to get things out to see how they looked on the lazy Susan.

Suki sat down in an extra dining room chair against the wall, watching him. "Tell me again who is coming besides Orin, Emma, and my friend Jules from school days. Remember I told you Jules played in the youth symphony with me, and she now plays violin with the Beaufort Symphony."

"I'm glad you invited Jules. I've met her—pretty dark-haired girl, works over at the Beaufort Inn at the desk and helps out with the events they cater."

"Yes, that's her. Her family owns that inn. Did you know that? I walked over to the Inn to see her this week to invite her tonight."

Andrew rolled cloth napkins and began slipping them inside a set of ornate napkin rings. "I asked Harris Briggs to be our sixth. I admire him. He teaches music at the Beaufort Middle School, works with orchestra, band, and chorus. He also helps with the Beaufort Youth Symphony. Harris loves to conduct and is so encouraging to the kids. Get him to talk about his work. You'll like his stories."

"That should be a nice group, and helps to deflect the idea that we're trying to match Emma up with Orin." She grinned. "I admit that I asked Jules to help us out a little by flirting some with Orin, too."

Andrew's eyes widened. "What if that backfires? What if Orin gets interested in Jules instead?"

She sent him an impatient look. "Then Orin is obviously not the right man for Emma if his interest will waver that quickly. However, if Emma sees that someone else finds Orin attractive and interesting, it might make her look his way with new eyes. As Mary Helen reminded me, Emma always seemed to want what someone else had, even when we were kids."

He frowned. "I hope she's not like Gracie Byrd in that."

Suki laughed. "Good gracious no. Emma has never been like that, and I hadn't thought about that girl and all the trouble she caused between Mary Helen and J.T. for a long time."

"Gracie almost broke J. T. and Mary Helen up."

"I remember. But I think, like Emma said herself, that she only got interested in you because you were the only two singles in the group and both lived here in Beaufort. She started imagining how nice it would be if you became a couple. Plus you were always kind to her. She just misinterpreted that as interest."

"Well, I hate that she did." He scowled, putting an ornate salt and pepper set on the turntable.

"Of course you are handsome, too." Suki got up to move closer to him, smoothing his shirt. "I love that blue shirt on you. It matches your eyes."

"You look good, too." He smoothed his hands over the loose, silky navy dress she wore with matching leggings underneath.

Suki glanced at the antique clock on the wall. "Everyone will be here soon. Is there anything else we need to do to finish dinner?"

"No. I've got the grill ready to put the flank steak on I've been marinating. The glazed carrots are wrapped in foil, ready to toss on the back of the grill." He started toward the kitchen. "You made the baked stuffed potatoes earlier today and only need to reheat them while I grill. Plus, we already made the sauce to drizzle over the asparagus you're planning to steam. We're going to have a great dinner."

He turned to grin at her as she followed him. "Everyone will love the Oreo ice cream cake we made, too. All we need to do is warm a little hot fudge sauce later to drizzle over it and maybe offer after-dinner coffee."

"We made iced tea to drink with dinner, too, and we picked up several bottles of sparkling water." Suki stopped in the kitchen to lean against the counter. "This is so much fun, Andrew. I never had time for gatherings like this, for cooking dinner for friends, or just sitting around in the evenings visiting when on tour so much."

"You shared get-togethers with others after your concerts," he reminded her. "I went to some with you and Jonah."

She frowned at the mention of Jonah's name. "Most of the people at those parties I never saw again. It isn't the same as time with friends."

The doorbell rang then and their evening began.

After a fun meal visiting, they all carried their coffee into the living room across the hall to relax. The décor there coordinated with the dining room with rich reds, golds, deep sage and celery greens. The room was large with space for two sofas, several comfortable chairs, sidepieces and the grand piano in one corner.

"That was a wonderful meal and a fabulous dessert," Harris said.

Harris Briggs had turned out to be a vibrant, interesting young man who obviously loved working with young people and music. Suki hadn't met him before and she really liked him. It had been good to see Jules again, too, wearing her dark hair coiled in a bun tonight like when performing. A poised and beautiful young woman, she seemed to enjoy flirting with Orin and with Harris over dinner. Suki had never been much of a flirt, her mind usually lost thinking about or playing music.

Orin seemed to enjoy the special attention directed his way tonight, too, and acted relaxed and happy. In addition to playing the cello, Orin taught computer graphics and website design at the community college, which Suki hadn't known about him. Emma, after a little initial awkwardness with Andrew—and with her—began to relax and to have a good time. As an English teacher, Emma had a lot of tales of her own to add to Orin and Harris's stories of working with students and she was comfortable with all their other topics of conversation as well.

"I loved the dinner you two fixed," she said now, smiling with more ease at Suki and Andrew, sitting together on one of the sofas.

"Thanks. I'm so glad you could come tonight," Suki said.

"How's Mary Helen's baby?"

Suki began to catch Emma up on a few recent stories about Bailey.

Orin got up as they talked and wandered to the piano, sitting down to start playing a small melody and then a Bach piece.

"That's lovely," Jules exclaimed. "I didn't realize you played piano as well as cello."

"I played piano from my toddler years since my mother taught piano at our home—still does—and then I started the cello later."

"A multi-talented man," Jules said, getting up to stand closer to the piano.

Orin moved into Mozart's *Sonata in D Major* then. Suki recognized it.

"Come and play with me Suki," he said. "This piece is made for two, great for a duet. I'm sure you know it, and I'd be thrilled if you'd play with me. I could tell all my friends I played with the angel."

Suki felt herself tense all over, and she clenched her hands tight in her lap. For a few minutes, panic swept over her and she didn't answer.

"I haven't played since New York, Orin," she said finally after the silence lengthened.

He glanced toward her with shock. "What? I didn't know that. Did you hurt yourself when you collapsed? I knew you'd been in the hospital but I thought you were better."

"Suki is better," Andrew intervened when she couldn't seem to find any words. "She got seriously overtaxed and overworked on tour and she's taking a break from playing."

They all looked stunned at his words.

"But you have such a gift." Jules' mouth dropped open. "I've heard you play, watched you play, and I saw you get better and better in our school days and then get that fabulous contract to go on concert tour. You're incredibly well known now for your talent."

"Oh, Suki, I can't believe you're not playing either," Emma said, learning forward with concern. "I know Jane and Mary Helen said you weren't going back on tour but I never imagined you wouldn't still be playing piano. Or practicing every day like you always did. It's always been your life, a part of who you are. Surely you can't just walk away from it. You're so gifted."

Suki felt tears begin to gather behind her eyes. Panic slid over her in waves and every muscle felt tense. She thought of getting up to run out of the room but found herself almost frozen in place.

Harris, who knew her less well than the others, glanced her way in sympathy. "She'll play again if and when she's ready," he said matter-of-factly. "But for now, I'll play with you, Orin. Like you, I learned my early love for music by taking piano lessons as a kid. If you'll play something more on my level, we'll do a duet."

He got up and walked to the piano, scooting onto the bench beside Orin. "How about this?" Harris began to play the old Hoagy Carmichael classic *Heart and Soul* that every kid learns to play in duet when young.

Orin laughed and joined in, and Suki sighed with relief as everyone giggled and began to talk at once, remembering the first time they'd played or heard that old tune.

Harris and Orin embellished the little melody and then moved into a rendition of the Beatles classic *Let It Be*, which Suki knew was an easy piece for less experienced pianists because it held so many repeating chords. Everyone began to sing along with the familiar Beatles song, lightening the atmosphere even more. After its finale, Orin and Harris began playing other popular tunes they knew with everyone singing and joining in.

Deapite the shift in the group's direction, it took Suki a little while to relax enough to join in on the conversation again after being put on the spot and asked to play. Harris didn't know much of her past, but she knew Emma, Jules, and Orin had been upset to learn she wasn't playing. It created an awkward, embarrassing moment.

While Orin and Harris played and sang, Suki slipped out of the room for a minute, supposedly to get more coffee, but she really simply needed a change of scene for a moment and a chance to collect herself, as well. When she returned, everyone continued to make an effort to move on as usual, but Suki saw how they all continued to glance at her from time to time throughout the rest of the evening, wondering at her response earlier. Probably wondering about her mental health, too. What a mess.

As Andrew saw the last of their guests out of the door a little later, he turned to Suki and smiled. "Everyone had a good time, don't you think?"

In response, Suki sat down on the nearest chair and burst into tears.

Andrew moved to sit beside her. "Hey. It's all right. Surely you knew people would be surprised you didn't want to play anymore. It's always been such a part of you."

"I was so embarrassed." She sniffed and wiped at her tears. "Especially because I simply froze over Orin's question to me. I'd actually been sort of enjoying his playing and felt proud it wasn't bothering me, and then he asked me to play. So sweetly too. I couldn't even find my voice at first to answer and then everyone acted so shocked at what I said. So disappointed in me." She hugged herself. "Will it always be like this? Everyone judging me, thinking I'm wasting my talent. Thinking I'm acting crazy."

"They just didn't know, Suki, so they were surprised to learn you aren't playing now," Andrew said in a soothing voice. "I'm sure you'd have been equally surprised if Jules suddenly announced she wasn't playing the violin anymore. You know how much she's enjoyed performing for so many years, how she's grown in her talent."

"I guess you're right," she admitted.

Andrew looked back, remembering. "Harris was nice stepping in like he did, don't you think? Offering to play with Orin, defusing the situation? He's a fine man, sensitive to others. I'll bet he's a great teacher."

"I like him, too." Suki lifted her eyes to look at Andrew now. "I'm sorry I ruined our nice evening."

"That little moment didn't ruin our evening." He put an arm around her. "Our dinner was a great hit. Everybody got along and enjoyed a good time." He grinned. "I saw Emma's eyes watching Orin more thoughtfully several times, too."

"So did I." Suki wiped her eyes and sighed.

Andrew chuckled. "Do you know what else I noticed? Jules seemed really taken with Orin and he seemed to really like her. Also Harris and Emma had many more things in common than I realized. Their passion for teaching, their love for books. Did you see how animated they got talking to each other? I think Harris was attracted to Emma."

Suki looked up, picking up on his conversation. "What?"

"I'm serious. I heard Harris suggest to Emma in the hall, before they left, that they go to the symphony together next weekend to hear Orin and Jules play." He reached down to pet Melville who'd come into the room. "She said yes and looked sort of starry eyed, too. They swapped phone numbers and I'm guessing Harris will be calling her before then."

She shook her head. "I totally missed all that." She giggled. "But I do remember worrying over how Orin lit up like a Christmas tree over Jules's flattery. I'd asked her to flirt with him a little, but I thought she was moving in rather strongly."

Andrew picked up the cat and sat back to stroke him. "You never know about people, do you?"

Suki got up from her chair after a few minutes. "I'm going to finish cleaning up the kitchen so we can head to bed. There are a few cups and glasses in the living and dining room. You go relax in the den and I'll go get them."

In the living room a few minutes later, Suki stared at the piano again remembering the scene earlier. She remembered, too, Kizzy's words that fear carried a torment and that she needed to look for the root of it and dig it out so she could move on. What had Kizzy said next to her? That only she knew what and who lay behind most of that fear, that only she could decide to let it go? Suki hadn't fully registered until now the word "who" in that statement, and realized the "who" had to be Jonah. It was, in part, Jonah's face Suki saw tonight when Orin asked her to play before she started to freeze and panic. She'd kept all that locked inside, what she saw before her concert at the Lincoln Center in New York. She'd never told anyone about it. Was that part of her problem?

She thought about this as she loaded the last of the cups, glasses, and a few small plates and silverware into the dishwasher. Andrew, tired, had gone upstairs to start his shower and get ready for bed. Suki sat for a few minutes in the quiet before turning off the light to start after him.

In the darkened bedroom, after they'd climbed into bed and turned off the light, she asked, "Andrew, are you still awake?"

"Yes." He rolled over to move closer.

"I need to tell you about something."

"Did you break an antique glass? Step on Melville's tail?" he teased.

She closed her eyes. "I'm trying to be serious."

"Okay." He stroked her hair.

She tried to find a way to begin. "Remember back in New York when you asked me if anything had happened with Jonah, and I said I didn't want to talk about it?"

He nodded.

"Well, something did happen." She closed her eyes, searching for the words. "That afternoon before the concert, Eito came over. I'd fallen asleep while Julianne was playing a little piece for me on the piano. When she saw me asleep, she slipped back across the hall, and Eito came over to check on me. He made me tea and worried about me being sick. He told me he thought I should take a break from tour to rest and get better. My cough was really bad then; I felt feverish and unsteady on my feet. I was so tired, too."

Suki paused for a moment, thinking back to that night. "I worried Jonah would be disappointed in me, but Eito said I should go talk with him. He assured me that if Jonah cared for me, he'd want me to get better above all. He suggested Jonah might not even realize how sick I was, that maybe I hadn't told him."

She hesitated. "I decided he might be right. As Eito said, if I could skip the next event or two, have a few weeks to totally rest. I could get my energy back, get a chance to heal. It sounded blissful, so I left early and went over to the Lincoln Center to look for Jonah to talk with him. I knew he'd scheduled a meeting and would be going to the Center early. I almost fainted just getting there and I got woozy and dizzy walking down the steps to the offices where I thought I'd find him."

Suki closed her eyes on the scene that roared back into her consciousness now. Upset, she started to cough and cry.

Andrew stroked her cheek. "Tell me what happened."

"The hallway was dark, but I could see a light at one of the offices at the end of the hall. I made my way there and, seeing the door cracked, pushed it open a little bit to see if it was Jonah." She felt the tears start again. "It was. He lay on a couch with his clothes partly off on top of this woman. I knew her. It was one of the other young artists he managed who'd flown into New York for a show with the Brooklyn Philharmonic. They didn't see me." She felt her breath coming in spurts, felt like she was back there again. "I backed out, leaned against the wall in the hallway. I could hear them, hear their words, their sounds."

She felt Andrew take her hands.

"Somehow I got down the hallway and up the stairs again. I just wanted to get away and find a place to be quiet and alone, to try to think. But one of the managers spotted me, whisked me off to an interview with a member of the press, then I was taken on to costume. My make-up artist helped me dress, fussed over the dark circles under my eyes. Before I knew it I stood in the wings on the stage, waiting for my cue to go on. You know the rest."

She leaned her head into his chest and cried. "I'm sorry I didn't tell you before. But I was so humiliated."

Andrew kissed her forehead. "When you sat down at the piano, you looked across the stage and saw Jonah standing in the wings," he remembered. "I was sitting on the front row so I could see that. I remember you just stared at him, almost frozen."

"He was smiling, sending me that special nod and wink like he always did, but Nita stood right behind him, with a hand on his shoulder. She was smiling, too, but with a smug smile I'd seen before. I knew then it wasn't the first time between them."

"I remember seeing a woman behind him," Andrew said.

"That was Nita. It all hit me then. I froze and suddenly I fainted or something."

"I wish I'd known." Andrew tensed. "I'd have hit Jonah and never let him in your room at the hospital. I would have never let him push on you like he did either, try to make you feel guilty when you were sick."

"I was too humiliated to tell anyone." She wiped at her tears. "I realized how foolish I'd been, how naïve and trusting. I knew, too, that I'd pushed on and on with the concert tour, unhappy, only because of my love for Jonah—or what I thought was love."

"It hurts to be betrayed by someone you care about." Andrew smoothed back her hair. "I still remember how hurt you, your mother, and Mary Helen were over what happened with Miles Lawrence when you were little. How you all believed he'd started to love each of you, that he might become your new father. Then you saw him in a compromising situation. Did you think of that when you saw Jonah?"

"No," she admitted. "Not consciously anyway. It was Mother and Mary Helen who were hurt most by that. I was too little to develop the strong feelings they did. But I remember it, of course. I remember a lot of times over the last year, too, when I dismissed so many things. Allowed myself to be lied to, exploited. I've always been so trusting, so eager to please in many ways. I felt so monumentally stupid."

"It's not a bad thing to trust, to hope for the best in others, to look for the best. It's a better way to make your way through life, even if you get hurt sometimes, I think. If you're always suspicious, rigid, and untrusting as you walk through life, that makes for a miserable life. I've known people like that. Always angry, bitter, unsmiling, and assuming the worst. We need to be as wise as we can be in life, to try to be discerning about people, but when we trust—and love—we always risk getting hurt."

She took the tissue he handed her from the bedside table and blew her nose. "An old proverb says 'better to have loved and lost than never to have loved at all' but I don't know if I believe that."

"I don't think that old proverb was talking about betrayal. I think it meant to have loved and lost someone to a death or a hurtful break up."

She lay back on her pillow. "Do you feel bad that I told you this?"

"No. I wondered what happened, hoped you'd share with me

some day. I like to think we can share anything with each other." He was quiet for a minute. "Do you still love him?"

"I don't think so. How could I?" She sighed. "I guess I still love some of the good memories. Does that sound awful?"

"No. Perhaps those are the memories you should hold on to. Even if Jonah pushed you too hard, perhaps lied to you about how much he cared, and wasn't faithful, he did recognize your talent back in college the first time he heard you. He presented you to his agency, got you a contract. Set up some fantastic opportunities for you. He was smart, and he did a lot for you career wise. Even I saw that."

"That's the other thing that's been troubling me. I feel so guilty I didn't love being on the concert tour. Even before I saw Jonah cheating, I carried that guilt around. I loved to play but I hated all that travel, pressure, people always pushing, talking, making demands all the time. It should have been my 'dream come true,' and I felt so guilty I didn't love it. I knew, too, that I would let so many people down if I didn't continue. I started to feel I didn't deserve anything that came my way because I wasn't truly grateful down inside."

"Listen, Suki, there are many ways to use the talents we're given. People in all areas of life often try several careers, many different jobs, and fail at many of them because something went wrong. But they keep seeking and looking for the right path and eventually they find it. Like Drake did. He could have chosen to feel guilty about how he walked away from the family business or that many in his family still haven't forgiven him for that, but he knows within himself he made the right choice for himself." He kissed her on the forehead. "You're a smart, talented, gifted woman in many ways. You'll find your way, find what you want to do, what you're meant to do in the way you're meant to do it."

"Mother always said God has a right plan for each of us."

"She's right." He leaned over to kiss her more deeply. "I should feel guilty that the sad time with your career and what you saw with Jonah made you decide to marry me, but I can't. I'm too happy with you, still so tickled and thrilled you wanted me."

She put a hand fondly on his cheek. "That did turn out to be a happy part of all of this, didn't it?"

"Yes, it did." He kissed her neck letting his lips slide lower. "Do you want to talk anymore?"

Suki smiled in the dark. "No, I think there might be some other things we could do that would be more fun."

He chuckled and pulled her closer.

She'd figure out later when the house was quiet, while Andrew worked at Westcott's, if all this talk made things any better. She hoped it had helped to banish some of her fears and shame. She yearned to move on.

CHAPTER 12

Three days later on Monday morning before the store opened, Andrew sat in Parker's office at one of Westcott's weekly staff meetings. They all tried to meet together about once a month, but this past month since the murder they'd met a little more often.

"I can't believe it's been almost a month now since Marvin Donelson was murdered," Nora said. "And the police still haven't found so much as one good lead." She glanced toward a calendar hanging on Parker's wall. "It's April nineteenth now. Why haven't they uncovered any clues? It keeps the speculative gossip going with the murder unresolved."

"You're right, Nora." Drake took a sip of the hot coffee he'd just poured. "A couple browsing in the store yesterday actually asked me if they could see where the dead body was found."

"Great." Parker rolled his eyes. "I hope you didn't show them."

Drake laughed one of his low, slow laughs. "No. I suggested they play detective around Beaufort to see if they could uncover a clue about the murderer. Told them the police didn't seem able to come up with a single clue. They went off tittering about that."

Nora crossed her leg, and Andrew noticed how Drake's eyes moved to study the movement and the expanse of bare leg revealed below his mother's fitted skirt today. She noticed as well and yanked down her skirt, glaring at him. Drake only grinned.

Funny how, since being married for a time, Andrew had begun to notice these little interactions between Drake and his mother. Or had they only begun recently? He didn't know, but they interested him.

Parker drummed his fingers on the desk, pulling Andrew's attention away. "It does seem difficult to imagine that neither the police or the detective assigned to the case have turned up any leads," he said. "At least none they've told us about. I admit I'd certainly like to see the end of Detective Dunnings' visits and the end to his questions to all of us. He has questioned Farris, Janine, our neighbor businesses, and even antiques store associates we do business with in other cities. It seems so intrusive."

"That little Dunnings detective ferret gets on my nerves, too, with his supercilious attitude," Drake put in. "Always acting like we're hiding something from him."

Nora sighed. "Granted, I don't like him either, but I'm sure he feels frustrated he hasn't uncovered any helpful evidence. After all, someone killed that man."

"The Donelsons are still snubbing us, too," Andrew put in. "I hate that. Sonny and I used to be good friends before this."

"AdaMae, Sonny's mother, is the worst among them." Nora pursed her mouth. "She sticks her nose up and won't speak to me when we pass on the street now."

"It's a bad situation." Parker's fingers drummed a little impatiently on the desk again. "I think we've talked about all the business we need to this morning. We talked about the shipment coming in later today, a couple of estate sales we want to catch in the next weeks. Is there anything else?"

No one responded, so they each began to gather up coffee cups and papers. Each of them held their areas of expertise at Westcott's Antiques. Parker carried the overall management role, Drake did most of the buying and attended the majority of the auctions and antique sales. Nora did the books, handled the day-to-day administrative tasks, and watched the upstairs store area from the glass front window of her office while she worked. If anyone needed help upstairs she stopped to move out onto the floor to talk with them. Downstairs, Andrew handled all the walk-in business and sales most days, did Internet searches for sales and auctions, and scrolled through online sites to look for items of interest when business in the store was slow.

Parker and Drake alternated in working the store with him and Nora, filling in as needed on busy days or when they held store sales. In summer, their busiest time for walk-in traffic with the mass of tourists that visited the coast, they hired an intern to work. Janine had done a great job for them this summer. They'd probably hire her again next summer since she was still a student and lived in the area. She occasionally worked part-time for them now when needed. Ira Dean O'Connor occasionally filled in, too. She didn't know the business well but she was sociable with the customers.

"I'm going to head out," Parker said. "I have a meeting with the Houstons in Summerville who are selling their old family plantation. Since I know them, I told them I'd buy what pieces I could and advise them about selling the rest."

"I'll go with you if you like," Drake offered. "Andrew and Nora can cover the store."

"That would be good." Parker closed the file on his desk and put it away in a drawer. "You have a better eye sometimes for what will sell at Westcott's than I do."

They left and Nora headed upstairs to get some paperwork done while Andrew opened the store for the day. Most days Andrew and his mother brought a sandwich or something for lunch—an old habit established when money was tight. Drake, more sociable and restless, preferred to go out for lunch, while Parker usually went home to share lunch with Claire when he worked the store. Claire always liked someone to talk with to break her day between writing on her books.

Andrew occasionally went home to eat with Suki now or he met her for lunch downtown, but she didn't seem to mind her days alone. He'd watched with pleasure how she'd grown stronger since early March when they married. She read, walked or biked around Beaufort now, explored the shops, met with old friends occasionally for lunch, and often drove down to the island to spend the day with Mary Helen. Sometimes Mary Helen and Bailey came up to spend the day with her and they shopped together. Suki seemed more peaceful since talking with him about Jonah. He was glad she'd finally felt led to do that. But she still wasn't playing, or practicing, the piano that he knew of. He felt sad watching her fingers play along with a song without her awareness many evenings. One night he'd even watched her fingers moving while she slept. With her gift and calling, he hoped she'd find her way back to playing soon.

At about two in the afternoon, Andrew looked up to see Coralee Jefferson let herself in the front door. As usual, she had her hair neatly coifed, her glasses around her neck on a sparkly chain, and wore one of her typical floral dresses. But she didn't look happy.

"Andrew," she said briskly coming up to the counter. "My husband Bertram wanted me to go straight to the police about this matter, but I decided to come here first. I've been doing business with Westcott's Antiques for over forty years, after all. I've never had a problem before and Ann Westcott was a dear friend. God rest her soul."

"What's the problem Mrs. Jefferson? I'm sure we can resolve it."

She plunked her large handbag on the counter and dug into it to bring out a velvet ring box. "This is the problem." She opened the box to pull out an emerald ring Andrew remembered her buying at the store in the summer and dropped it into Andrew's hand.

It was an impressive 14k white gold ring, with a square cut emerald framed in small diamonds—a big sale for the store. "I remember you buying this ring," he said. "A beautiful piece of estate jewelry."

"The emerald is a fake," she stated flatly. "I took it to be cleaned over in Charleston, along with some other pieces, and they tested it."

Andrew knew his eyes flew open.

"I took my jewelry to Carlson's because I buy most of my jewelry pieces from them. Their gemologist, Mr. Holbert, examined this ring and told me it wasn't a genuine stone. I'm sure you know the man. He isn't wrong about these things. He even had another expert look at it, knowing I'd bought the ring from Westcott's." She handed him a card. "Mr. Holbert said to give you his card so you could call him if you wanted."

"I don't know what to say." Andrew shook his head, studying the ring in his hand. "When we purchased this ring it came with a certificate of authenticity and then we had our own appraiser here in Beaufort examine it before putting it out in the store for sale. You might recall I gave you copies of that paperwork."

She sniffed. "I still have them, but they don't mean much when the ring is not genuine. This is not what I expect of Westcott's."

"Be assured, Mrs. Jefferson, I will advise Parker of this, and Westcott's will cut a check and return your money. I'll also take the ring again to our appraiser and contact Mr. Holbert who examined the ring in Charleston. I'm not sure what occurred, but we will make this right. Nothing like this has ever happened at Westcott's before, and this is a serious matter we will look into immediately."

"I should hope so." She stuck up her chin.

"Let me ask you this," Andrew said, glancing at the ring, which looked to him just as he remembered. "Did you find any problems with the other pieces you bought from us? I recall you purchased several other items in the last year, too."

She put a hand on one hip. "You may be sure I gathered up all the jewelry I'd bought from you and took it over to be examined. However, this was the only one that was fake. That fact also made me decide to come to you directly rather than to the police."

"I want you to know we will look into this to learn what happened, Mrs. Jefferson. Believe me, I am as concerned as you are. Westcott's reputation is important to us." He pulled out his cell phone to call his mother upstairs. "I will have Nora write you a check today, while you are here, if you'd like."

"Indeed I would like that. Thank you, and I'm glad to see you aren't trying to blame me in some way," she said. "Bertram suggested you might. I'll be pleased to go home and show him you dealt reputably with us. However, the entire matter is upsetting, especially with all this murder business associated with your store, as well."

Andrew briefly acquainted his mother with the matter on the phone and she soon whisked downstairs to hug and commiserate with Mrs. Jefferson. Evidently they were friends through Ira Dean Connor and a social group they all attended.

"This is simply terrible," Nora said. "Undoubtedly, someone has found a way to access our store, Coralee. We will need to have all our jewelry carefully examined. Andrew and I are so grateful you came to bring this to our attention. Westcott's prides itself on being a store of the highest integrity. We're just dreadfully upset over this."

She led Mrs. Jefferson to her office upstairs to cut her a check, working her magic to sooth the woman's ruffled feathers.

Andrew studied the ring again after she left. How could this have happened? He knew their appraiser examined this ring before they put it out for sale. They always had every piece of jewelry appraised after purchase, even when bought with certificates of authenticity.

With the store quiet for a moment, Andrew called the store in Charleston that Mrs. Jefferson had visited. He knew the jeweler Ewing Holbert and Ewing quickly appraised Andrew of the situation on his end.

"I thought I discerned a problem as soon as I started to clean the ring," he said. "I did a careful appraisal before speaking to Mrs. Jefferson, too."

"We're simply stunned over this," Andrew told him. "The ring came with a certificate of authenticity and we had our appraiser here, Brewer Addison, examine it, too. You know his reputation."

"Yes I do. You'd better see what's behind this," Ewing advised. "Obviously someone has access to your store. I don't think the problem is with the Jeffersons and you know you had the ring examined and authenticated before you put it out for sale."

"So you think someone exchanged the ring while it was in the store?"

"Not entirely," Ewing answered. "The gold setting and the small square of diamonds around the emerald were true and authentic. The ring base is the genuine thing. We checked it carefully. But the stone had been exchanged." He paused."My father used to see this a lot with old jewelry from the depression era and in earlier times when the wealthy got stressed financially for money. They'd replace the stones. Large, simply shaped stones are the easiest to swap out. It takes a clever person to do it, though, and a good eye to tell the difference when the old settings are left in place."

Stunned at all this might mean for the store, Andrew hung up and then turned to flash a warm smile to Mrs. Jefferson coming back down the steps with Nora now.

"Nora has assured me that these kinds of things simply don't happen at Westcott's and she is as shocked as I was." Mrs Jefferson lifted an eyebrow. "I hope, for your store's sake, this was an isolated incident and that you won't have further problems. Your store has enough gossip already going around with that dead man found here. Murdered too. A business can only stand so much scandal, you know."

"Yes ma'am," he said, walking to open the front door for her. "And thank you again for coming directly to us about this problem."

She offered him a smug smile. "Nora gave me a little gift certificate, too, along with my check. I'll look forward to coming back one day to buy something with it."

Andrew turned back into the store to find his mother coming down the stairs.

"What a mess," she said. "I called Parker. He and Drake, finished with the clients in Summerville, are on their way back to the store. We're lucky Mrs. Jefferson came to us directly about this problem and not to the police. I can only imagine what that Detective Dunnings would have done with this. I gave Coralee a very big gift certificate with the understanding she would keep this little matter to herself."

Andrew's eyes widened. "You bribed her?"

"That's an unkind way to look at it. I'd rather say, after Coralee and I discussed how important keeping this matter quiet could be, that I rewarded her for promising she wouldn't mention it to a soul. She might be a bit of a snob, but I've always known Coralee

Jefferson to be honorable. Let's hope she meant what she said. She also assured me she'd insist Bertram keep the matter quiet, too."

Andrew leaned against the counter by the register. "How much did you give her?"

"What I thought it would take to keep her good will. I'm sure Parker won't fault me. It's a serious matter for an antiques store's reputation to be questioned. We'll need to do everything we can to head this off before any other problems occur. You do realize how bad this could be for the store if we find other jewelry has been compromised?"

Andrew told her then about his talk with Ewing Holbert.

She shook her head. "I know Ewing well. If he says the stone was replaced, you can be sure it was. That man is an expert with antique and estate jewelry."

Andrew looked at the ring again, passing it to his mother to examine. "You just wrote a refund check to Coralee Jefferson for this ring, so you know the ring was worth nearly six thousand dollars."

"I do. And you need to take this ring, along with all our antique jewelry in the case, to our appraiser here in Beaufort to examine. Parker and Drake don't think the problem could possibly be with Brewer Addison who does our authenticity checks. His family has owned that jewelry store on Port Republic for three generations. But we need to know if any other pieces have been tampered with. When Parker gets in we're going to examine all other sales made anywhere around the same time as the ring sale to Coralee." She sighed. "Depending on what we learn, we may need to check back with all our customers who made large purchases this year. I don't look forward to that, but it might have to be done."

Andrew put the emerald ring back in its box, then got the key out to open the jewelry cabinet to take out the cases holding their other jewelry. "Should I take everything, Mother?" he asked, studying the two locked display cases of jewelry.

They'd only recently started carrying fine antique jewelry since Andrew began working at the store. He'd encouraged it as a new store sales item. That thought certainly didn't make him feel better today.

"We'll want Brewer to look at every item as he can," Nora said, answering his question, "but for today take Coralee's ring and all the other rings of value. Also take those highend bracelets that only have one main stone. If Ewing Holbert is right, the thieves probably targeted only pieces with single stones easy to exchange."

Andrew stopped as a new thought hit him. "Mother, if thieves took the stones out of the jewelry and replaced them, they also had to return the jewelry to our stock with the replacement stones in them. Ewing said the setting and small diamonds around the stone of Mrs. Jefferson's ring were authentic. To a casual observer, it was the same ring."

"Yes." She frowned, pushing a strand of hair behind her ear. "Which means we have yet another serious problem to deal with at Westcott's. I hope we can keep this discreet. Thieves or not, I hold little confidence that the police can help us very much after what I've seen lately. We may need to play detective on our own with this case. At least for as long as we can."

Andrew called Brewer Addison to tell them about their situation and to learn if he could make time to see him in this emergency. Luckily, Brewer was in town and had extra help in the store so he could examine some of the pieces this afternoon.

Nora went upstairs to begin pulling the records she and Parker would need on past sales and Andrew found a box and began to pack up the jewelry.

About the time Andrew got the jewelry pieces ready to transport, Parker and Drake returned. Nora shooed him out the door to meet Brewer and said she would fill Parker and Drake in on the situation. Between the three of them, they'd cover the store while he was gone, too.

In the back room of Addison Jewelers & Co., Brewer began his examinations. He saw right away after only a quick study that the stone in Coralee Jefferson's ring had been replaced. "I remember this ring well. The emerald was an old one and valuable. Replacing that stone was a quick and clever criminal move, however they could not have done an intricate work like that in your store. My guess is they took the ring to another location, replaced the stone, and then returned the ring in some way. Looking at the ring without instruments, no one would realize it had been exchanged. The stone is a well made replacement."

Brewer began to look through the other rings Andrew had brought then. "My guess is that only standard cuts were targeted for the exchanges—square, round, rectangular, and oval shapes—and that any stones replaced were primary gemstones easier to duplicate—emeralds, rubies, diamonds, and sapphires. These stones would be the simplest synthetic stones to locate or create. The original stones, in most cases, would be the most valuable to remarket, too. Other types of gemstones vary so much in color, like opals, jades, or even alexandrites, that it would be difficult to find or keep comparable replacements of those stones on hand to exchange."

Brewer began to put different rings under the special binocular microscope he used in his lab for examinations. Andrew knew from coming to his lab before that he had a variety of tools here to help in identification, including a refractometer, jemeter, dichroscope, battery operated probe, and many other precision instruments he'd forgotten the names of. Just like in a doctor's office, a row of credentialed appraisal diplomas hung on Brewer's wall, too.

"To really analyze these, I'll need to keep the jewelry for a day or two and possibly remove some of the stones to examine them more carefully. For now I'm just trying to discern any that are suspicious. If any rings have been replaced with stones like the emerald I first looked at, my job will be easier. A trained eye and a few examinations will tell the tale."

Andrew sat down on a stool to watch him. Brewer studied several rings, setting one after the other aside, and then he held up a ruby ring. "Here's another fake, this ruby ring in the intricate gold setting. Pretty thing, the original probably dating back to the 1800s. I remember looking at this ring when you brought it this summer.

Notice this stone is a simple oval shape." He pointed at the ring with a tool. "A clever expert would only have to lift these four prongs holding the gemstone in place and then make the switch. I'll study this one more carefully later, but I can say right now with surety this is not the stone I looked at this summer."

Andrew groaned.

Before Brewer finished, he had spotted a fake diamond ring, another emerald, and a rectangular shaped sapphire. "I'm seeing the pattern here I expected to find, but so far only these three rings seem to have been substituted of all the rings, brooches, and bracelets you brought in. Rings are simpler to pocket and return." He looked across at Andrew after laying down a tool. "You do realize the profit for a good thief in this, don't you? Just adding up the value of these stones alone should show you why a jewelry thief would attempt these exchanges."

"Yes," Andrew answered. "I've been adding up the costs in my mind. At least we haven't sold these rings yet. Insurance will cover for the loss, but it's the other items we might have sold that worry me even more. If we need to contact some of our customers who purchased items similar to these in the last year, could you examine them to see if there is a problem?"

"Of course." Brewer tapped his chin. "Why don't you tell them you're offering a special cleaning on valuable pieces purchased in the last year, that you'll even provide pick up and delivery? It might keep you from having to explain your concerns to most of your customers. People know those checks and cleanings of old pieces are pricey. I'd say they'd be delighted to say yes."

Andrew brightened. "That's a good idea."

Brewer looked at his watch. "Both of us need to call it a day now. I need to go and help Rachel close the store and you need to head back to Westcott's to give them your report. Take pictures of these rings I identified with your cell phone if you wish, but I need to keep them to study them more closely. I might find some clues to help with this problem." He began to pack up the other jewelry. "I can look through this lot more carefully tomorrow, but for now it seems that only the stones in these three rings have been swapped out, plus Coralee Jefferson's ring of course."

Andrew snapped a few shots of each ring. "I have paperwork and photos of these rings in our files, too."

"So do I. It's important to keep good documentation in our businesses."

"I guess it could have been worse," Andrew added, helping to pack up the jewelry. "Westcott's sells primarily high end furniture and other large home items. We keep a little china, silver, glassware, statuary, and a few unique items for decoration and show. But we've only started carrying some antique jewelry in the last few years." He paused. "Do you think thieves would target the lesser priced pieces we have?"

"I wouldn't think so," he answered. "For now, just to be safe though, I'd pack away all your jewelry until we can give it a check. I'll work some exam times into my schedule in the next week for you."

Andrew considered Brewer's words. "That's good advice. We only have two cases of jewelry, and we can put some other antique items in those display cases from the storage room upstairs—old snuff boxes, paperweights, things like that."

Brewer grinned at Andrew then. "Be glad you're not a jewelry store like we are. I'd need to examine our entire inventory." He paused, a frown crossing his brow then. "I may do a check on all our more expensive pieces, now that I think on it. Especially our older, antique ones. We do carry some antique jewelry, although not much in our stock." He picked up one of the rings to study it. "I don't like the idea of a clever jewelry thief working around the Beaufort area."

Andrew sighed. "I hope you won't say anything to anyone about this, Brewer. You know the situation we're in at Westcott's Antiques with Marvin Donelson's body found there. We really hope this won't come to the police's attention right now unless we decide to take it to them. Parker is changing all the store locks again, updating store security. By the time I get back, he'll probably have more ideas going."

Brewer Addison walked him out of the lab to the door. "My guess is that whoever pulled off these switches is long gone now. They usually target an area, do a little work, make a sweet little profit, and then pack up and move on to greener pastures before someone notices their exchanges."

"Well, I really hate it's happened to us right now at Westcott's. The timing is bad."

"That's true. I hope some better luck comes your way soon, and especially that whoever murdered Marvin Donelson is found. I know the Donelson family well and hate they've experienced such a tragedy."

"Me, too," Andrew said, heading back to the store. Life certainly had gotten complicated lately.

CHAPTER 13

With all the problems going on at the store, Suki knew Andrew had been preoccupied and worried. He'd told her several times, since they discovered the thefts on Monday, that he felt especially bad because he'd been the one to encourage Westcott's to begin carrying a line of antique jewelry. Often he'd been the one to locate the pieces or purchase them at auctions or estate sales he attended with Drake.

"Honestly, Andrew," she said over breakfast later in the week as he voiced worries about the issue again. "No one is faulting you in this. You wouldn't fault Drake if someone found a way to thieve items he bought for the store."

"Mother said the same thing," he admitted. "But I still remember Parker's concerns about carrying any items in the store small enough to fit in a pocket. Shoplifting can always be a problem in a retail store, especially in a tourist destination like Beaufort. It's never been a problem at Westcott's before in all its history. Everything was too large to carry out of the store." He finished off the last bite of his bacon. "I just wish now I hadn't pushed it."

"Well, I'm glad it's Thursday," she said. "You need a break. Going to the symphony tonight will take your mind off things. I like it that we're going out afterward with Orin, Emma, Harris, and Jules, too. I'm so excited the orchestra is playing songs from Walt Disney's *Fantasia*. Orin and a group of students in his graphics department created movie clips to be shown on a screen above the orchestra. Won't that be fun? I loved that fanciful film and the classical pieces Disney spotlighted in it."

"I'm glad you're looking forward to this performance," he said, finally smiling.

After he left for the store, Suki took a second cup of coffee out on the screened porch to think about her own problems. She'd experienced another of those odd dreams ... but hesitated to worry Andrew about it. He didn't need anything else to be concerned about. She hardly wanted to tell anyone else about her dreams either. Most of her family and friends already knew she'd battled emotional as well as physical problems since her collapse. The last thing she needed to do was feed that image about herself.

On an impulse, she picked up her phone and called Kizzy Helton at Edisto. "Hi, Kizzy, it's Suki. Did I catch you cleaning?"

"It's my day at Isabel and Ezra Compton's, but I can sit down for a minute. Is anything wrong? Has there been a problem in your family?"

"No ma'am." She hesitated. "I had another of those dreams."

"Hmmm. Have you been praying since to understand them? To get past some of those locked up fears?"

"Yes, ma'am, and I thought I'd made some good steps forward. Moved past some things and a lot of bad memories. You know."

"Are you playing the piano again?"

"No, but I'm more comfortable listening to others play. I'm less panicked walking by the piano in our house." She offered a small laugh.

"Was the dream the same?" Kizzy asked.

Suki hesitated. "No. The words I heard were the same but this time I saw a scene clearly in my mind."

"What did you see, girl?"

"I saw the piano in the church we attend here in Beaufort, the one where Morgan Dillon always gave me my lessons growing up."

"Were the words still the same as you heard before?"

"Yes. I seemed to hear several times, 'Come and play for me.'"

Kizzy chuckled a little then. "Well, honey that's easy to discern. I told you before God was speaking to you. He's showing you

He wants you to come play for Him in the church. Being as its daytime, there won't be no one there, I don't suppose, except you and Him. So he knows you won't have no pressure. He just wants to hear your gift. Your song. Get on over there and play for Him. Surely you don't want to disrespect the Lord? You might not feel you want to play for me or anyone else yet but you can play for God. He'll help you, too. You get on over there and do that."

"I can't just walk in and play."

"Why not? You used to always do that whenever you visited around here in other churches. Homes, too. I never recall you having hesitancy to sit down to any piano. They sort of called your name and you walked on over and sat down and played." She paused. "That big old church you go to will be open during the mornings. A friend of my boy Harlan takes care of the grounds and cemetery there. If the sanctuary isn't open—and it often is being historic and all—tell them you want to go in and look around. They won't mind. Then when it's just you and God, you can play."

Suki thought about it, not answering.

"Honey, if God gave you that dream this morning, He knows it's the right time for the church and for you. Myself, I've got enough righteous respect for God not to be disobeying Him in things. I hope you have that, too." She paused. "I've got to get on back to cleaning this house now. You know I work at the store in the afternoons, too."

"Yes. Thank you, Kizzy."

"Any time, child, any time. You mind God now. Don't let no grass grow under your feet doing what the Lord asks."

Suki hung up and thought about the conversation. Then she laughed. Kizzy always seemed to have the simplest answers to things.

She closed her eyes for a moment. "Well, Lord, if those dreams are from You, as Kizzy says, and if You want me to play for You, I'll try. I guess. I don't know if I can. You know how I freeze up, how my hands get all stiff and everything." A small laugh slipped out. "If you want to hear me play, you may have to swirl some miracle dust in that sanctuary or do something supernatural in me."

Getting up from the couch on the porch, she took her coffee cup into the kitchen and then started upstairs to get ready. "At least if I have one of those awful panic attacks and get humiliated, no one will see but You."

With the old Baptist church on Charles Street only about a few blocks from Westcott's, Suki decided to park near the store and then walk to the church instead of driving. She'd be less noticeable walking, could slip into and out of the church more quietly. The day, in mid April, was warm but not too hot. She slipped on a pair of blue capris and a feminine white chiffon top in a soft knit, pulled on a pair of socks, and then laced up her favorite canvas walking shoes. She plaited her hair in a French braid to keep it off her neck, draped the long strap of a leather purse across her shoulder and headed out of the house.

Walking through the historic streets of Beaufort was always a pleasure. Suki loved the gracious old homes, flowering shrubs, and the beds of spring flowers she spotted along her way. She prayed under her breath as she walked, but as she grew closer to the big white steepled church, with its tall white pillars in front, she felt more and more anxious. To gain courage, she walked around the shady cemetery beside the church first, remembering the first time she'd heard piano music coming from the church when at the cemetery with Parker and Mary Helen as a girl. She'd begged to go inside, and found Morgan Dillon playing the piano. Before then she'd only had unpleasant experiences with piano lessons, except in working with her own mother, but she liked Morgan. And when he offered to teach her she agreed to try it. How wonderful he'd been to her through the years afterward, how patient and wise, supportive and encouraging.

Gaining courage from the memory, Suki walked up the long sweep of front steps to the church's door. She found it open, pushed the door ajar to slip inside, and then walked through the narthex and into the old historic church sanctuary. Long rows of sectioned pews flanked either side of a wide center aisle with balconies above on both sides and in back. Elegant chandeliers hung from the ceiling above and Suki could see the silver pipes of the church organ behind the altar. Across the dark hardwood floor in front of the chancel sat the old grand piano she remembered so well. It almost seemed to smile at her in welcome.

The church was empty, and Suki moved from the end of the aisle across the floor to put her hand on the piano—almost like greeting an old friend. She moved closer to the keyboard and slid onto the piano bench. She needed to sit down as her knees felt shaky.

Suki closed her eyes. "You asked me to come and play for you, God, so here I am. I'm scared, but You said in your Word you'd strengthen me when I needed it and that nothing is impossible to you. If You'll strengthen me and help me, I'll play."

She waited for a moment and then put her hands on the keyboard. As she did a sweet peace swept over her, seeming to relax her, and her fingers began to play. She hadn't consciously decided about what play but she soon recognized the tune, "Tis So Sweet To Trust in Jesus," an old hymn and one of Kizzy Helton's favorites. She smiled at the thought. How appropriate. Hymns seemed to be what her hands wanted to play then—"Great Is Thy Faithfulness," "What A Friend We Have in Jesus," "Here I Am Lord," and "It Is Well With My Soul." The words seemed to echo the thoughts in her heart. Even though it had been a month, her fingers remembered exactly what to do, and her heart and soul soared to return to what she had always so loved.

Suki played for a long time, mostly with her eyes closed, before she paused, feeling a sense that someone was there in the room. Glancing around her she saw Morgan Dillon sitting in one of the pews against the wall under the balcony, weeping.

"I didn't see you," she said.

"I know." He didn't wipe at the tears, and she felt some of her own begin at the back of her eyes.

"How long have you been playing again?"

She turned her eyes back to the keyboard. "This is the first time I've played since I collapsed."

He came to sit beside her on the piano bench, hugging her as he did, and she found herself telling him about the dream that brought her here, about Kizzy's encouragement.

"With her faith, Kizzy always sees things so simply," she told him. "To her, if God says to do a thing, you will be able to do it. No questions or worries. And, as she said, who would want to disrespect the Lord and not do what He asks?"

"Who indeed?" Morgan mopped his eyes again.

Suki's eyes slid over him for a minute. His dark hair had become touched with silver over the years and his face had a few more wrinkles, but he was as dear as ever. This kind man, who'd always understood her need to play not only her own songs from out of her heart, had helped her grow in her talents through years of lessons and training. He'd enabled her to share her love of music with others, helped her bring bring joy through her playing.

"You're not asking me what next?" She bit her lip. "You're not asking if I want to perform again or what I'll do now that I'm playing again."

"Considering the greatest Teacher sent you here today, I'll trust He has the answers you need in the right timing." Putting his hands on the keyboard he began to play the hymn "Trust and Obey." After listening to a few lines, Suki joined in, and the two of them played in harmony, Morgan on the lower keys, she on the upper.

As she played, she heard the words to the hymn in her mind. Was it really that simple, the way to live life, the best way to happiness? To simply listen to God, to walk by His side, to trust and obey? To do whatever he asked, to go where he asked?

Morgan began to sing some of the lines then in his rich baritone voice, reminding her of more of the words to the old hymn—that doubts and fears just can't abide when we walk by God's side.

"Is that true?" she asked, interrupting him.

He smiled and continued playing. "That God banishes doubts and fears? I've always seen it to be true."

"I was so afraid to come today, so full of doubts and fears, but I feel so good now. So at peace. So right again." She began to play with him once more. "I think God will show me the next steps, too, don't you?"

"I have no doubt of it."

After a joyous time of playing together, Morgan turned to her. "Play the piece for me you were meant to play when you collapsed."

Suki knew her eyes widened and felt her hands clench at the thought.

Morgan put a hand over hers. "The idea rose up out of my spirit, Suki. I doubt I'd have asked you otherwise. But if fears and doubts are gone and if you're walking on in your life now, following after His way and design, playing that piece is a simple thing."

Suki considered his words and offered a little prayer in her mind. "Okay. Go sit in the pew and be my audience then." She pointed to the front pew closest to the piano.

He got up to move to the pew and sat down. "What will you play?"

"The orchestra was doing Tchaikovsky pieces that night and I was to play the *Sleeping Beauty Waltz* with them," she told him. "Funny that I was the one to go to sleep before playing it, like the princess with the spell put on her by the wicked witch."

Morgan chuckled. "I never thought Jonah was totally wicked, but I definitely saw he pushed you too hard. It worried me. I also saw that he played on your innocence, letting you think he was in love with you."

"You knew?" her eyes widened.

"I suspected it. Jonah was very ambitious. That ambition came above many things for him, and he was not a man of faith."

"That really matters doesn't it?"

"I think so. Don't you? Especially after today?"

She smiled. "I realize I haven't given faith and trust in God as much importance as I should or let it be a guide for my life. I guess I didn't realize, or wasn't taught, that God is interested in every little thing in our lives."

"And that He wants to be Lord of every little thing, too?"

"You and Kizzy—how did you both get to be so wise?"

"In the same way you're becoming wise, with God's help, leading, teaching, and guidance. Faith is a growth process like all other things."

She paused, looking down at the keyboard. "Jonah was using me emotionally. I unfortunately saw firsthand, in the worst possible way, that I wasn't Jonah's only love interest. I saw him in a compromising situation right before the New York performance, when I was so desperately sick, and not long before I collapsed."

"That explains many things I've wondered about. I knew it would take a lot for you to collapse and walk away from the piano."

"I was unhappy on tour, sick, and then betrayed. I guess I just broke."

"I'd say at the Lincoln Center you just passed out from being sick. You should never have been asked to perform when so ill—especially over and over again when you weren't getting better. You shared with me earlier how long you'd been ill on the tour. Jonah should have pulled you off. Your recovery should have come first."

"Well, as I learned, putting me first wasn't exactly at the top of Jonah's list."

"That was then Suki; this is now," he said matter-of-factly. "You have no contract to fulfill any longer. No agent or manager to please. You can do anything you want." He smiled. "Or actually, I'd say you should do whatever He says you should do, go where He says you should go. It seems you've acquired a new agent."

She giggled. "I think you're right. And since He nudged you to ask me to play the *Sleeping Beauty Waltz* then I will. My first solo appearance under my new manager."

Suki began to play the classical piece then, her hands rippling up and down the keys and then moving into the rolling, lyrical melody that led into the familiar, well-known waltz movement. How easy it was to play again. How right. It felt wonderful.

She smiled as she played, soon lost in the music, and as she finished she turned to see Morgan crying again.

"I never realized I was such an emotional man," he said. "But it's such a joy to see my sleeping beauty wake again, to hear you play once more. And so flawlessly. You've lost little in your month of rest."

Suki turned to him. "By the way, what were you doing here today?"

"Planning to practice. I still play for the church."

"That's good of you."

"Just giving back of what's been given to me. I still play with the symphony, too. I planned to practice for that, as well, while here. Will you and Andrew be coming tonight? I know he bought season tickets. He often takes someone with him. I assumed it would be you now."

"It will definitely be me," she said, grinning at him. "I am thrilled the orchestra is doing this special spring show linked to the college students' project to show segments of *Fantasia*. That will be so fun. Orin teaches in the Visual Arts and Design department and he told us all about it at a little dinner gathering we had at our house last Friday."

"It should be entertaining," Morgan agreed.

"I'm looking forward to seeing you play again tonight with the symphony, Morgan, and to see Jules and Orin play, too. I haven't seen them perform with the symphony yet."

"Both are good musicians." He paused. "Will you practice more at home now? I can give you some homework."

She laughed. "I would guess the piano and I will become good friends again, and I will keep your offer in mind. Maybe I'll come to play here with you again one day."

"I'd like that. We used to play for each other and play together many times."

"Those were the best of times."

"We'll share them again." He stroked a hand over his chin, which Suki knew usually meant he was thinking. "Would you consider playing with me here at the church one Sunday? We could play together, do a duet, during service or you could play piano while I play organ. Many here at the church have watched you grow up, heard you play when you were younger. It would be a nice low key way for you to share a little."

She smiled. "Let me think about it. I need to find my own way. Okay?"

"Of course." Morgan stood and came over to kiss her cheek. "You come back to play here anytime you want though."

"I will." She stood, slipping her purse back over her shoulder. Suki knew he'd come to practice himself so she needed to yield the piano to him now, to give him time to practice for the concert tonight and for church on Sunday.

As she left, she realized for the first time that she liked the thought that a piano waited for her when she got back home. She could play more today. And tonight after she and Andrew got home from the symphony, maybe she'd play for him.

CHAPTER 14

All week, Andrew, Drake, Parker, and Nora worked to get to the bottom of the jewelry thefts occurring at Westcott's. In addition, Parker scheduled a locksmith to come and change every lock in the store, had the security system inspected, and considered seriously for the first time installing a security camera. They'd never had the latter in all the history of the store but were giving thought to it now with the events occurring recently.

The four met in Parker's office on Thursday morning to catch up.

Andrew glanced down at his notes. "Brewer Addison finished examining the store jewelry," he told them. "Besides the five rings you know about—including Coralee Jefferson's—Brewer only found one more ring with a stone exchanged. All the bracelets, brooches, and pendants were fine. Evidently, this exchange artist favors rings."

"What was the other ring?" Parker asked.

"A round blue-gray sapphire, surrounded with small diamonds, worth nearly seven thousand because the sapphire had a strong six-ray star in it. It was a gorgeous piece."

Nora leaned forward to offer her report. "In examining our inventory records against the jewelry in stock, I also found one additional piece missing. Last spring we purchased a man's ring, a cat's-eye alexandrite in an 18 karat yellow gold setting. There's no bill of sale for it that I can find so I can only assume it was also stolen. The ring is no longer in our inventory."

"Dang," Drake interrupted. "I remember that ring. I picked it up at an estate sale in Georgia last May. It was one of those cat's-eyes where the color would change. Interesting ring. I really liked it and thought of keeping it for myself. It was worth about four thousand, if I remember right."

Parker glanced at the notes he'd been taking. "So, that's a total of seven rings. Six with exchanged stones, including Coralee's, in our store stock now, and the seventh evidently stolen without an exchange brought back." He glanced at Nora. "Do you think any other rings have been sold from the store and may turn up to cause problems later?"

"I'm not sure." She glanced at the printout in her lap. "On a good note in answer to that, of all the jewelry sales in the last two years, since we began selling antique pieces of any great value, I've only found two other sales that fit the profile of the pieces we've discovered this jewelry thief targets. One was an antique opal ring. Brewer said he believed thefts like this seldom involve opals because the color varies so much, but I have the woman's name and address that bought the ring. She lives at Hilton Head."

"Have you contacted her yet?" Parker asked.

"No, not yet, because, like I said, the ring was an opal," she answered. "I did contact Reeva Marsden who purchased a ruby ring set in white gold two years ago. I used the idea Brewer suggested, letting her know we were providing a free cleaning and examination last week, and she took me up on it. She lives on Fripp Island and said she'd love to have it done while she shopped in town and had lunch with a friend. I set an appointment with Brewer, took the ring to him to examine and clean. He said there was no problem with that ring and she took it home again, feeling very happy our store was so thoughtful."

"Well, that's a relief," Drake put in. "Parker, do you think we ought to follow up and have more jewelry that we sold examined? Pendants or bracelets or anything?"

"No," Parker said. "From talking with Brewer I feel pretty confident this operation only goes after rings. We've followed up on those well now and also locked all our jewelry in the safe for a time. What I do want to do now is to talk with anyone who has worked in the store part-time with us." He paused. "Nora has agreed to talk to Ira Dean. She only fills in here occasionally, but she might have seen or noticed something."

"You all know," Nora put in, "that we keep extra keys to all our locks, doors, and such in the break room on a key rack behind the door inside a closed cabinet. Those extra keys have come in handy many times when someone lost a key, forget their keys, or couldn't get into a display case, locked cabinet, or such when needed. Parker and I realized that besides the keys we each carry, this might be a place where someone could attain a key to a jewelry case or to the store. Only our employees would know about this cabinet or know that we keep a key to this locked cabinet on a little hook under the sink."

Parker came in to the conversation then. "I've talked to Farris carefully. He has no idea we even keep other keys in the store." He looked at Andrew. "I'd like you to track down Janine Albert between classes over at the college today. Nora keeps a copy of her class schedule, so we know when she might sub or fill in at the store for us. When she worked this summer, I showed her where we keep the extra keys."

"I don't think that sweet girl had anything to do with this mess," Nora added, handing Andrew the copy of Janine's schedule. "But we need to check out everything possible. Would you mind going to talk to her?"

"No, not at all." Andrew answered. "She'll wonder at the questions, though."

"You'll probably need to tell her about the thefts," Parker said. "She works here often enough that she needs to know, and I believe we can count on her to be discreet."

"I'll cover the store," Drake put in. "I hadn't planned to travel today anyway with the symphony tonight. Nora and I always attend with Parker and Claire; we all hold season tickets."

"I really look forward to going tonight." Nora smiled. "This should be a good performance."

Parker glanced at Andrew. "Is Suki going with you?"

"Yes, and she said this morning she's looking forward to it."

"Good," Parker said. "Claire and I hope that by being around music and performances she'll soon want to return to playing. Her health seems much improved. We're both very happy about that."

"Yes, sir. I am, too," Andrew answered.

Seeing it was nearly time to open the store, Andrew said, "I think I'll head on over to the campus since we're finished. After I've talked to Janine, I'll come back and let you know if she offered any ideas to help with this. She worked all of last summer when a lot of traffic came in and out of the store."

"We'll see you later then," his mother said, as she started back to her office.

Knowing it never easy to find a parking spot near the campus, Andrew decided to walk the few blocks to the college. The University of South Carolina Beaufort (USCB) began long ago out of the roots of the historic Beaufort College and had now grown to cover an eight-acre campus on the waterfront in Beaufort's historic district. Andrew knew from Orin that the school was expanding yearly and offering more and more programs all the time.

Emma had gone to work at USCB teaching English after getting her masters. Orin, a whiz with computers, worked in the college's Visual Arts and Design department teaching courses like Graphic Design, Broadcast Design, Web Design, and more. He loved the creative link of media to fine arts, and had a creative hand in the production tonight of *Fantasia* with its mix of film clips and orchestra numbers. Janine, now in her junior year at USCB, was majoring in Retail Management and wanted to work in an antiquities business after graduation if possible. She interned last summer with Westcott's and Andrew knew that Parker hoped to hire her again this summer before she graduated next spring.

After stopping at the main office to pick up a map, to pinpoint the building where Janine was finishing a class, Andrew headed across campus to look for her as she came out after class.

Spotting her, Andrew waved and walked over to talk to her, explaining that he needed a short meeting with her if she had time.

"I'm sorry, but I can't meet right now, Andrew," she said. "I have an appointment with my advisor, but I can meet in about thirty minutes if that's okay."

"That's fine. I'll drop by my friend Orin's office and visit with him while I wait." He glanced at his watch. "I'll meet you at eleven-thirty at one of the nice outside tables at the Magnolia Bakery Café across the street."

"That sounds great," she said, waving at him before she walked away.

Andrew walked over to Orin's office then and found him grading papers. "Got a minute?" he asked, sticking his head in the door.

"Sure. Come in." Orin moved a stack of papers off the chair by his desk so Andrew could sit down. "What brings you over to campus?"

"I needed to meet with Janine for a few minutes. We hope she'll intern again with us this summer."

Orin seemed satisfied with that answer and it was the truth.

"Is Suki coming to the symphony with you tonight?" Orin asked. "I hate that I embarrassed her Friday at your place. I'm so sorry." He ran a hand through his sweep of dark hair. "Honestly, Andrew, I didn't know she'd walked away from the piano. Jules, Emma, and I were simply shocked. I'm sure we made her feel bad."

"I probably should have mentioned it to all of you before you came over," Andrew replied. "Don't worry about it."

"Jules and I were talking later about it at symphony practice. We hope Suki will be all right in time and that she'll return to playing again. She's so gifted."

"Yeah, I do, too. We both loved having you guys over."

"I had a great time." Orin leaned toward him. "You know, I'd never really gotten to know Jules before that night. We play in the symphony together, go to practice at the same times, run into each other now and then. But we'd never talked before."

Andrew watched his friend's face flush a little.

"I really like Jules," he said. "I think she likes me, too. We hung out after practice the other night. Had fun, forgot the time." He grinned at Andrew. "You know."

"Jules is a talented and beautiful girl," Andrew said, not sure what else to say.

Orin shuffled a stack of papers on his desk. "Jules told me that Suki asked her to flirt with me a little, to maybe get Emma to notice me more. Don't get mad about Jules telling me that. She said she needed to know if I was serious about Emma. I told her I liked Emma and had tried often to get her to go out with me, but that Emma didn't have much interest in me." He wiggled his eyebrows. "Jules said she couldn't understand that at all."

"So, you and Jules really hit it off?" Andrew smiled.

"Oh, yeah," Orin said with enthusiasm. "We have so much in common and the chemistry is great if you know what I mean." He hesitated. "What worries me is if you think Emma will be upset about it. I did sort of pursue her for a while."

"As you said, you got no encouragement back for that, either." Andrew sat back in the chair and crossed his legs. "It seemed obvious to me Emma just wasn't 'in to you,' if you know what I mean. I wondered why you kept trying at all."

Orin twisted one of his rings. "She's a pretty woman, smart, interesting. Whenever I crossed paths with her around campus I liked her. I suppose I kept thinking that if we ever got together something might click." He looked across at Andrew and frowned. "When we all go out tonight after the symphony, do you think Emma will be upset if she notices Jules and I are interested in each other?"

Andrew laughed. "No. And I think Harris and Emma will both be relieved to see your interest refocused."

"What?" Orin's eyes blinked open. "Emma likes Harris?"

"Actually I think Harris started it, but it appears the attraction is mutual."

Orin shook his head. "Well, isn't that the dangdest thing! Looks like your and Suki's dinner party started two new matches!"

"Well, I'm simply glad Emma has her eye now on anyone else but me," Andrew said with relief. "I was really embarrassed at the wedding when she went after Suki."

Orin shook his head. "Yeah. I wasn't exactly thrilled when Jane announced I was interested in Emma, either, right in front of everyone. I thought I was being discreet."

"Believe me, Orin, no one thought you were being discreet. You are one of those guys whose emotions are pretty evident to all."

They talked a little more after that, caught up on a few things, and then Andrew headed across the street from the campus to meet with Janine at the café.

"Hi, Andrew." She waved at him from one of the café's tables outside. "Did you get to visit with Orin?"

"I did. Let's go in the café, order a coffee and one of their pastries, and then we'll bring them back outside to talk. Okay?"

"Sure. It's a nice day."

A few minutes later, settled back at their table, Andrew told Janine candidly about all that had happened at Westcott's.

"Oh, my," she said when he finished. "First Mr. Donelson found dead and now this."

"Parker wanted me to ask you, Janine, to think back to see if you could remember seeing or hearing anything that might have happened this summer that seemed odd. Anyone suspicious coming into the store, anyone coming out of the back room where we keep our extra keys, anything that might have a link to this."

Janine bit her lip thinking.

Attractive with dark curly hair, brown eyes and black-rimmed glasses, Janine was serious natured but good with people in the store. She'd been an asset to Westcott's.

She sighed after a time. "So many people came in and out of the store last summer. Honestly, it's been so long since then that I can hardly remember anyone I met or talked to in particular. I really can't remember anything odd occurring. I'm sorry."

"Don't worry about it," he said. "But if anything comes to mind. Anything at all, will you call me?"

"Sure. With all that's happened, do you think Parker will still want me to work at the store this summer?"

Andrew smiled then. "We all hope you'll still intern with us this summer. You're one of the best interns we've had."

She flushed with pleasure. "Thanks. I really hope I can work in a store like Westcott Antiques after I graduate."

"Drake and Parker have a lot of contacts. I'm sure they'll help you find something."

Her eyes lit. "Oh, that would be great!"

They visited and talked a few minutes longer, finishing their coffee and pastries, before Andrew glanced at his watch. "I'd better get back to the store."

"I have another class soon, too. Please tell everyone I'm so sorry about the problems." Janine stood, picking up her books and purse from a side chair. "I'll stop by to talk to Parker or Nora about a work schedule soon and I'll call you if I think of anything that might help with this problem at the store."

Heading back to Westcott's, Andrew's mind turned over and over trying to think how anyone could have gotten access to the antique rings in the store, locked securely in Westcott's glass topped cases at all times. And even if someone had pocketed a ring while in the store, how did they return it and then continue getting rings and returning them multiple times? Store policy demanded employees only take one piece of jewelry at a time out of the case, returning it before taking out another, to reduce the likelihood of theft. No one could pocket a handful of rings at once. Nora or Parker would have noticed a hit like that on their inventory, too. It just didn't make sense to Andrew. Neither did the murder.

He arrived home later than usual, after staying past the regular store hours for a delayed shipment. "Sorry I'm so late," he apologized to Suki, grabbing a quick bite to eat in the kitchen before heading upstairs to dress for the symphony. "That shipment coming in from Virginia was four hours behind schedule. The delivery truck got caught in a big traffic pile up coming through North Carolina where a bad wreck closed the highway."

"It's okay, Andrew." Suki had already dressed for the evening. She wore a sleeveless dress with a white beaded top and a full black skirt below it, dropping to her knees.

"You look gorgeous." Andrew said. He started to add that he missed the red cummerbund and shoes she usually wore with dressy outfits like this when she performed, but then he bit his tongue before he said it. She was looking forward to this evening and he didn't want to spoil it for her.

"Go get dressed," she told him, seeing that he'd finished eating. "I'll put these things away here in the kitchen. I don't want to be late."

A short time later, after parking, Andrew and Suki made their way to their seats in the Performance Art Theatre where the symphony played at the college's Center for the Arts. They both waved at Emma and Harris as they headed down the aisle to Andrew's seats and spoke to several other people they knew. Andrew's seats were on the left side of the theatre, Parker's, Claire's, Drake's, and Nora's on the right. Suki waved at them across the room, too, as they settled into their own cushioned theater chairs.

The orchestra began to tune up then, the lights dimming in warning, even as they settled into their seats and got comfortable.

"There's Orin on stage to the right," Andrew pointed him out to Suki. "And there's Jules on the left with the violinists."

"Yes, and I see Morgan at the piano to the left with the percussion section, looking very sharp tonight." She smiled.

A big screen hung from the ceiling behind the orchestra on stage, and Andrew knew they'd see film clips from the Disney movie *Fantasia* on the big screen to accompany the orchestra's pieces tonight.

"I've seen this done with Bugs Bunny cartoons, too," Suki said. "You know how many of them have classical pieces to accompany them."

Andrew grinned. "Like *The Barber of Seville* where Bugs is getting a haircut from Elmer Fudd?"

"Exactly." She studied her program. "Ah, look. They're

performing the *Chinese Dance* where all the little mushrooms dance around to the music. I love that piece."

Andrew looked down at his program, too. "They're also playing Stravinsky's *Russian Dance*. I like that *Fantasia* piece, too, and they're performing *Waltz of the Flowers*, one of your favorites and a piece you've played many times since you were a girl."

"It is one of my favorites," she said as the lights dropped and the first violinist came out followed by the Maestro.

The conductor had been with the orchestra for years and he recognized Suki as soon as he saw her. She'd performed here with the orchestra many times in past, this being her hometown. He nodded to her as he took his place and the performance began.

The concert, as expected, was fun and entertaining. The pieces from Disney's old classic movie were familiar to most attending and everyone seemed to enjoy seeing the film clips, related to each musical piece, dance across the screen, just as in the movie.

At the intermission, they mingled with friends and family in the vestibule before returning to their seats. After a long, stressful day Andrew was finally beginning to relax. He felt pleased, too, to see what a good time Suki seemed to be having tonight, how comfortable and easy she acted, often swaying a little to familiar tunes. A good sign.

When the Maestro came back on stage after the intermission, he offered a few words of thanks to different people and to the USCB Visual Arts Department for their work in putting together the video portion of the show. He recognized different individuals and had them stand for applause. Then he said, "I see we have a special guest visiting with us tonight, pianist Sarah Katherine Avery, who grew up here in Beaufort and has performed with us many times."

He smiled at Suki. "Our first number as we start this part of the program is Tchaikovsky's *Waltz of the Flowers*. I recall you've performed that piece with our orchestra in past and wondered if you might be willing to do so tonight. I'm sure Morgan Dillon would relinquish the piano to you, as your proud teacher for many years."

Oh, no, Andrew thought. He hated for Suki's evening to be ruined with another embarrassing moment. He knew she'd be upset over this. He tried to think if he should say something, turning to look at Suki to see her reaction. To his astonishment, she stood and began to make her way to the stage.

Walking up the steps and then across the stage, to applause, she took the conductor's hand and said, "I would be honored to play but only if you let Morgan play with me. The *Waltz of the Flowers* is a lovely duet piece and it would be my joy to play it with my long time teacher and your orchestra pianist."

Amazingly, as Suki made her way to the piano Andrew saw Morgan wink at her. What was going on? Had Morgan planned this? Andrew glanced across the room and saw Parker and Claire raise their eyebrows at him and he shrugged, letting them know he'd certainly known nothing about this in advance. Had Suki? Surely she would have told him if this had been planned.

He studied her as she sat down at the piano with Morgan. She seemed so comfortable, so at peace, so professional. What had happened to bring so much change? He had a lot of questions he wanted to ask her.

Then as she began to play he forgot all his questions, so joyously glad to hear her playing again. As she and Morgan played with the orchestra, the Disney video of hundreds of little fairies filled the screen to accompany them, the fanciful sprites flitting from flower to flower and skating across the frozen pond to the melody. It was more than a magical moment. Andrew had a difficult time keeping his overload of emotions in check. His angel was playing again. Beautifully, smoothly, and gracefully. And smiling as she played.

CHAPTER 15

When the Maestro asked her to play, Suki felt simply stunned. *What should she do?* Her eyes flew to Morgan's at the piano on the stage, wondering if he'd instigated it. The worried shake of his head convinced her the answer was no.

Looking around, she saw Jules bite her lip in concern and pass an ill at ease look across the stage to Orin, who rolled his eyes. Several rows away, Emma gasped and put a hand to her mouth in dismay. Even Suki's parents glanced her way in alarm, expecting to be embarrassed as she declined the Maestro's gracious offer. Glancing toward the warm and natural smile on the conductor's face, Suki felt sure he knew nothing of her past troubles and was unaware she hadn't played in public since her collapse on stage. She could tell, too, from Andrew's stiffening posture and shocked face that he knew nothing of this in advance, either. *Great. What an awkward situation.*

Realizing a few minutes had passed and that a response was necessary, Suki made a quick decision. She stood, nodding at the conductor as she moved out of her seat toward the aisle. Somehow she would find a way to play and not endure another time of humiliation tonight. She'd play tonight—somehow—for the people here who loved her, who'd supported her since her girlhood days.

Under her breath, she said a prayer asking God to help her, as she walked up on the stage. As the applause began, and as she saw an encouraging smile cross Morgan's face, she knew what she'd ask the conductor, too. She'd ask to play with Morgan like she had earlier today, knowing his presence would give her the extra boost of confidence she needed.

The conductor inclined his head with pleasure at her request, turning back to the orchestra as she made her way to the piano. Morgan winked at her as she grew closer, scooting over on the piano bench so she could join him. Surprisingly, her legs weren't shaking at all, her body not tensing up. What a wonderful relief.

When the music began and their prompt came, she and Morgan began to play. A joyous calm came over her the minute that her hands moved across the keyboard and the sweet pleasure of making music swept through her.

She and Morgan played in lovely unison as if they'd practiced and readied to perform tonight, which was no surprise since they'd played this piece so many times together in past. She'd also performed the *Waltz of the Flowers* hundreds of times on her own and knew it by heart. It had always been a favorite since her childhood. She smiled, remembering this was the piece she'd wanted to play as a little girl at her first recital with this orchestra many, many years ago, but Morgan had thought it too hard for her. She wondered if he was remembering that now, or recalling the first time she performed here on this stage when she froze and couldn't play a note. She'd seen Miles Lawrence in the audience that night and it upset her. But Andrew had come and rescued her. She looked toward him now and saw his surprised but happy face. Sweet man.

The applause thundered when she and Morgan finished. The Maestro held out a hand for her to come to the front to take a bow, and more applause followed as she did. Camera lights flashed as the ovation continued. The press was here. Suki should have expected that. They always covered the symphony's concerts.

She returned to her seat and the concert moved on, the orchestra beginning their next piece, Ponchielli's lively *Dance of the Hours*, while *Fantasia's* alligators and hippos danced light-heartedly, and sometimes frantically, across the screen behind them, making everyone laugh.

Beside her Andrew took her hand and squeezed it. "I didn't know they would ask you to play," he whispered in her ear.

She gave him a small kiss in the dark. "I know. It's okay."

"You were wonderful," he added. "Are you all right?"

She smiled at him. "I'm more than all right," she said softly. "Don't worry. We'll talk about it later."

He nodded and they turned their attention back to the screen, soon laughing at the pink hippo dancing across the stage pursued by her alligator suitor. How did the staff at Disney ever think of all these fun animated cartoons to accompany pieces like this one by Strauss, she thought? They were incredible.

After the show, Suki was overwhelmed with congratulations for her performance. She and Andrew stayed swamped with kind words from friends and acquaintances from the audience for some time, many also congratulating them on their marriage. Her mother wept and hugged her. Parker, Nora, and Drake were equally thrilled she'd begun to play again. It took forever to get out of the theatre to meet with Jules, Orin, Emma, and Harris at a nearby bistro for dessert and coffee. There her friends added their joyous hugs, all wanting to know what had happened and what led her to perform.

Not ready to share yet about her dream, Suki said instead she'd gone walking to the cemetery and church, stepped inside the sanctuary, and decided to play. "It's where I always took my lessons with Morgan," she explained. "I suppose I felt comfortable to play there. And, of course, that opened the floodgates."

"I'd say God had a hand in that, too," Harris said wisely.

"You'd be right in that," she agreed, not adding more, but she knew from Andrew's eyes watching her he would want to know more later on.

Orin changed the subject then, for which Suki was glad. "Did you know that Disney employed one thousand artists and technicians in making *Fantasia* and that the film included over five-hundred animated characters? Just the creation of an animated film like *Fantasia* was nothing short of a miracle in 1940. With all the classical music included, many people expected the show to bomb when it first opened on Broadway but it became the longest running show of its time."

"Didn't Leopold Stokowski, with the Philadelphia Orchestra, conduct the film's score? " Jules asked. "I think I remember reading that."

"Yes." Orin leaned toward her. "They both really saw the vision of this new style of motion picture presentation. It's an incredible story of how they created the film."

The conversation shifted to music and drama and memories of the evening's show. Suki was glad to see the focus of their conversation shift.

Later when they came home, she and Andrew changed into old clothes and slipped out onto the screened porch to rest and talk, drinking one of the spritzer recipes Suki had learned to make from Parker.

"Umm," Andrew said, sipping his drink and putting his feet up on a wicker ottoman. "This is a new recipe. What is it?"

"It's a cherry vanilla soda, with a few crushed cherries, a little vanilla bean and sugar, all mixed with seltzer and lemon-lime soda." She smiled at him. "I got Parker to copy off several of his spritzer recipes for me. His wife Ann used to make all sorts of different varieties." She pointed to a gold swizzle stick in her drink. "Parker gave me this cute set of antique swizzle sticks, too. I love the pineapples on the tops, don't you?"

"I do. I'll watch for more swizzle sticks at the estate sales with Drake."

Suki saw him watching her thoughtfully then.

"Are you going to tell me what really happened and why you suddenly started playing the paino again?" he asked. "I know the struggles you were having."

She sighed."I planned to tell you everything after we got home tonight. Then at the symphony the Maestro surprised me and asked me to play. I looked around at everyone's faces and decided I simply wasn't going to endure another humiliation—and a highly public one that everyone would talk about. You saw the press snapping pictures. I can only imagine what they'd have said if I refused and hadn't played."

Andrew reached for one of the shortbread cookies they'd put on a plate and brought to the porch. "What made things different tonight? Besides that you played with Morgan earlier in the church? And what made you decide to go to the church today anyway?"

Suki told him everything then. About the dreams, about her talks with Kizzy and Kizzy's counsel, about her personal battles within herself to try to work past her fears. She even told him about her prayers and her studies spiritually to try to find deeper answers. Everything she could remember.

He chuckled over her stories about Kizzy. "That woman surely has a close relationship with the Lord. I respect that."

"So do I. She was right, too. She was right about everything." Suki pulled her legs up under her on the porch sofa. "She prayed for me and that helped, but she said I had to find my own way past my fears. She reminded me, too, that fear and faith don't mix. Fears and doubts cancel out faith. They're like opposites." She searched her mind for an illustrative example. "Like when you try to push two magnets together using the wrong ends. They repel rather than attract."

"Some of your fears were linked to Jonah."

"Yes." She looked down at her hands. "The piano kept reminding me of those scenes I witnessed with him, of betrayal and hurt. I associated the two. I know that now."

He considered her words. "You said earlier you worried that if you played again Jonah would hear of it, come and find you, persuade you in some way to go back on tour. Does that still worry you?"

She thought about the question carefully. "Mary Helen and I ran into Miles Lawrence one day when we were walking up the beach together. He tried to talk with us, acted charming—you know how he is—but Mary Helen wasn't friendly in return. She cut off his conversation and we walked on. Even after all these years she still gets uncomfortable around Miles. I might be like that around Jonah for a time. Maybe even for a long time. I lost a sort of trusting innocence with Jonah. You know that belief that people are basically good, that people who say they care about you really do. It's painful. You feel leery any time you're with someone that you know exploited and used you, was emotionally dishonest."

Andrew sipped at his spritzer. "I think I know what you mean. My father hurt my mother and me like that. He acted like he cared, and we know he really did in a way, but it hurt to always get drawn in with his charisma, his words, and then realize that the person he always put first was himself." He paused. "As a small boy, I kept wanting him and my mother to get back together in some way, but then when I was around eight or nine I woke up late at night one of those times mother let me spend the night at his place. I padded downstairs—not here but in his house before—and found him with a woman. I didn't know much about stuff like that so I was shocked as well as disappointed. I never wanted to spend the night with him again, and mother never made me after she learned what happened. You carry those young hurts a long time. They impact you."

"Thanks for understanding that. I'm not sure why I fell so heavily under Jonah's spell." She sighed.

"I know why," he said. "He saw your talent and possibilities like no one else had. That's very enticing and alluring when someone believes in you beyond how you see yourself. They seem to pull you up to a better self, a higher place. It's hard not to be attracted and grateful to anyone who helps you reach higher. Even if they push you a little too much. Sometimes we don't push ourselves enough. We stay in the valley of mediocrity because it's comfortable. We seem to be waiting for someone to tell us it's okay to reach for something higher, to dream of something bigger. When they see us as larger than we see ourselves, we love them for it."

She smiled at him. "That's very wise and sounds like experience talking."

"Drake and Parker did that for me. I'm grateful for it." He ran a hand over one arm. "My father had a reputation around town. People often looked at me and expected me to be like him. We looked alike. I sometimes feared I would become like him. Drake and Parker wisely counseled me that I could chart my own course. They seemed to recognize the best in me as a boy when I didn't see much of any merit in myself. They helped to pattern a healthy image I could follow after, too. They were strong men, good mentors, and both had stepped away from what others expected of them to follow their own star, so to speak."

"You did really love your father though," Suki said on a sudden realization.

"Yes, very much. He, like Jonah, was a strong powerful, charismatic personality. Just being around him was exciting. He radiated life. His business sense was remarkable, and he had a gift for persuading people and for making money. He also offered an alluring role model but, as you recall about Jonah, his affection had a hook in it."

"We share a nice love, I think," she said then. "We both want the best for each other but we don't lie, exploit, or use each other in an unkind way. Your heart can safely rest with that kind of love. Eito was right about us being a good match."

"He was." Andrew smiled at her. "Will I get to hear the lovely sounds of the piano every day now in my home?"

She waved a hand. "You know how I am about the piano. It draws me like a lover. I doubt I can stay away."

"That's good news."

"Tell me more about what's happening in uncovering the thefts at the store," she said then. "I heard Drake say something to you related to your meeting today."

He filled her in on the situation, soon scowling. "What worries me is that I don't know if we'll ever find out who changed out the stones in the rings or who killed Marvin Donelson and dumped him in our store. It keeps me uncomfortable and it hurts the store's image. It makes us feel like we never know when the next shoe will drop either. It's changed the atmosphere at Westcott's."

"Even your love for your work there?" She saw his surprise to her question. "Perhaps." He made a face. "Not that I would ever leave, but it's stolen some of the joy, the ease. I don't know how to explain it."

"It's like a subtle fear. An uncertainty and unease you carry around all the time."

"I suppose it is. I hate that."

She smiled. "Kizzy would tell you to realize that those fears and doubts don't come from God, that you need to work on getting rid of them." She crossed her arms thinking. "We may not know who stole those rings or who killed Mr. Donelson, but God does. Have you really prayed and asked Him to help you uncover the answers? Have you really believed He would?"

A worried crease crossed his brow. "I guess I just thought God had given me a good mind and if I used it I'd figure things out."

She teased him then. "How's that working out for you?"

He laughed. "Not so good."

"Maybe you ought to spend a little time in the church tomorrow yourself," she suggested with a small smirk.

"You have a point." He stood and walked over to pull her to her feet and kiss her. "I think I'd like my beautiful wife to play for me and then take her to bed."

"I think that can be arranged. What do you want to hear?"

"What you played in the church today, since I missed that performance."

She picked up their empty glasses to carry to the kitchen. "My new Heavenly Agent had me play beautiful old hymns today. You might prefer classics."

"No, play the hymns for me," he said, following her. "I'm sure I need to hear them. As Kizzy said all fears have torment, big or small, and they keep faith from rising up. You're right that I need to give the problems at work to God and believe, with faith, that He'll bring in the answers."

"Well, then." She laughed. "The first song I'm playing is 'Great Is Thy Faithfulness.'"

CHAPTER 16

Remembering his conversation with Suki from the night before, Andrew left the house a little early the next morning on Friday so he could stop by the church to pray. It wasn't as though he needed to go to a church to pray, but he thought stopping by the church might help him focus. His mind stayed in such a turmoil these days since all the problems at Westcott's started, and Suki was right that his own efforts to resolve them had met with no good results.

Andrew slipped into the old sanctuary and into one of the back pews. Closing his eyes and bowing his head, he prayed, "God, I want to thank you first for helping Suki past her fears so she could play again. I'm so grateful. I hope you'll help her find a way to share her talents in future with others."

He paused, searching for words. "I'm sorry I've tried to handle all these problems at work without praying for Your help and answers. I hope you'll forgive that and help the answers come in that we need. I looked up some scriptures last night to help me not to lean to my own wisdom and understanding so much, and I found the promise in I John that says 'if I ask anything according to Your will and with confidence, that you'll always hear me' and in John 14 that 'whatever I ask in Your name you'll do it.' That last one is a pretty huge promise but I got to thinking about all the mountains You moved in the Bible so Your people could march on and get past their troubles. Mine seem small in comparison to some of those. But despite that, I'm trusting them into Your care this morning, purposed to put my fears and doubts aside. After all,

'all things are possible to You.'"

Andrew spent a little more time praying until he felt better, felt like he'd given all his worries to God. With a lighter heart and mind, he went to work to start his day.

Around noon, while Andrew worked to arrange a group of Faberge jeweled eggs in one of the display cases, Janine came into the store wearing a troubled look.

"Hi," she said. "Do you have time to talk?"

"Sure." He looked around the store. "Its quiet now. If it's okay, we can sit and talk behind the register. If someone comes in needing help, Mom can come down. She's upstairs."

With a sigh she followed him behind the register, sitting down beside him on one of the old stools they kept there.

"What's the matter?" Andrew asked.

"I've thought of something I need to tell you from this summer, but I hate to. It's really embarrassing, and it probably doesn't have anything to do with anything." Janine twisted her hands in her lap.

Andrew waited.

"I had a boyfriend who came into the store a lot this summer. You may not remember him—a little taller than me, dark hair tied in a ponytail behind, real cute. We dated a lot through the summer. He was studying photography, working on a summer project. He always had his camera with him. He took pictures of buildings, statues, trees, all sorts of things. One of his assignments was to learn to take good pictures of small items so he took photos of little things in the store. He took pictures of antique spoons, miniature figurines, and jewelry."

She looked down at her hands. "He came around the store a lot near time to close, when things were quiet. Sometimes we planned going out after. I let him get cokes for us out of the break room and I let him use the restroom back there."

"Did you always go in the back with him?"

"No." She frowned. "I did at first but then when I got to know him really well, it seemed sort of stupid to follow him to the bathroom and stuff." She twisted her hands again. "Sometimes, because he was hanging out with me, he covered while I ran back to the bathroom or to the break room, too."

Janine looked at him with anguished eyes. "It's probably nothing that he hung around at the store. It was only while we were dating. I thought about not telling you at all."

"What was his name? Are you still dating him?"

"His name was Bruce Steele, and no I'm not dating him anymore." She rolled her eyes. "He dumped me after the summer."

"Does he still live around here?"

"He did. I think he lived over near Charleston, though. He said he was in the photography department at the Art Institute of Charleston. They have a Commercial Photography degree."

"Do you have his address and phone?"

"I had his phone number, but he changed it later. I never had his address, just knew he lived on Rittenburg Avenue near the school. He said it was only a one bedroom place, sort of a dump, so we usually hung out down here where he worked on his projects."

Andrew picked up a note pad from beside the register to write down the details Janine offered. "Did you ever see him afterward in our store or around town?"

She sighed. "This is the part I hate to admit. I introduced him to this other girl I know and he dumped me for her. She was real pretty, blond, thin, dressed sharp. Bruce ran into us eating lunch together at a little restaurant near campus and he went after her big time as soon as they met. I guess I could tell he really liked her right off, but I still didn't expect he would dump me flat like he did."

Andrew wondered if any of this mattered. "Do you think he's still dating this other girl, still around town so we might talk to him? We could see if he noticed anything while hanging around here so much."

She picked at her blue jeans. "I think they dated until the last month or two, so I guess he was still hanging around here then. But I ran into Carly a couple of weeks ago and she said he dumped her, too. She sort of apologized to me then for snaking him. She said we neither one lost much. I gathered, from what she said, he put a big rush on her, too."

None of this seemed to make any difference to Andrew in all that had occurred at Westcott's. "Do you think this Carly might have a current phone number for the boy?"

"She might. You could ask her." She pushed her glasses up on her nose. "She works part-time for the Donelsons at Bay Street Antiques, has for about two years, I think. Their store is open longer hours than Westcott's, being on the main street and carrying more items that tourists buy. She works mostly afternoons and evenings around her school schedule."

Andrew sat up straighter, this new information catching his full attention. "She works with the Donelsons?"

"Yeah, that's what I said."

Not wanting to say more until he could think about all this, Andrew said instead, "I'm really glad you came by to share this with me, Janine. We're trying to follow up on anyone who spent time in the store, who might have seen or heard something. If we can locate Bruce, he might remember something to help us, being here as much as he was this summer."

"Okay." She twisted her hands. "Do you think Parker will still hire me, knowing I broke some of the store rules? I know we're not supposed to let the public into the back of the store, that there are restrooms people can use down the street at The Arsenal."

Andrew stood. "I don't think Parker will avoid hiring you for that, but you should be more careful in future. Don't let anyone into 'off' areas of the store or allow them to take photos of our merchandise without getting an okay from Parker."

Janine draped her purse over her shoulder, standing. "I'm sorry about anything I did that wasn't okay while working." She shook her head. "I'm also sorry I was such an idiot about Bruce. He was older, charming, and he made a real fool of me. I regret that, too."

"So do I." He grinned at her. "Do you have Carly's phone number?"

"No. But someone at the Donelson's store will have it."

"Maybe I'll drop by there," he remarked casually. "I know Sonny;

we went to school together."

"Good," she said heading for the door. "You call me if you need to ask me anything else, okay?"

After she left, Andrew sat back down on the bench, his mind popping. It seemed odd that this young photographer put the dating rush on two girls who worked at Beaufort antiques stores. Or was it a coincidence?

Andrew phoned his mom upstairs. "Do you think you could come downstairs and cover the store for me until Drake comes in at around one? There's something I need to take care of."

She came downstairs after talking to him. "You sounded upset. Is anything wrong?"

"Nothing for you to worry about. Just something important I need to check out and I don't want to wait to do it." He grinned at her. "I'll tell you about it when I get back."

"All right. Get some lunch, too, while you're out."

It was only a few blocks to Bay Street from Westcott's on Craven, so Andrew walked to the Donelsons' Bay Street Antiques store instead of driving. When he stepped into the store, he saw Sonny behind the register.

His old friend frowned. "Andrew. What can I do for you?" The words weren't welcoming.

"I may have a lead to help in relation to your grandfather." With customers nearby, he didn't want to add any more details.

Sonny opened the door to the office behind him at the register. "Rowena? Are you finished with your lunch? I could use someone to cover the store."

She came out, her natural smile freezing at the sight of Andrew.

"Andrew says he might have a lead to help in relation to Grandad. We're going to walk around the corner to Blackstone's Café to talk for a minute. I need to grab lunch anyway. I'm sure I won't be long."

Sonny led the way out of the store. "I wanted us to get out of the store before my mom or dad wandered in. They're still pretty upset about Grandad's murder, especially with no resolution found yet. It leaves things hanging. You know."

"I do." Andrew followed his friend. "Lunch is a good idea, too. I haven't eaten and Blackstone's makes great burgers."

Sonny actually smiled then. "You're right. They do."

The two of them had often shared lunch at Blackstone's in past.

After they ordered, they settled down at a table on the restaurant's back patio where they could have some privacy. Andrew studied his old friend as they ordered, a relatively tall man about his own height with dark hair, a square, honest face, and brown eyes. He'd always liked Sonny and missed their friendship.

"Do they still ring the ship's bell here at eight in the morning and stand together for the Pledge of Allegiance?" Andrew asked, making casual conversation.

"Yeah," Sonny grinned. "I often catch that when I stop by to pick up coffee to take to the store." His expression turned serious then. "What did you mean about possibly knowing something about what happened to my granddad?"

Andrew told him then about the thefts that had been occurring at Westcott's. He hadn't asked permission from Parker to tell Sonny about this, but he needed Sonny to know these facts for any of the rest of the story to make sense.

"Do you think there's some link between those thefts and my granddad being found murdered in your store?"

"I didn't before," Andrew admitted. "But today our summer intern Janine Albert came in to tell me about a boyfriend of hers who hung around the store a little more than occasionally this summer." He told Sonny about Janine's story then and about how the man, Bruce Steele, dumped Janine to start dating Carly, who worked at their store.

'That's Carly Ryker. She's worked with us about two years now."

Andrew ran a hand through his hair. "It seemed almost too much of a coincidence to me that this man, Bruce Steele, would date Janine, hang around Westcott's at all hours, then after meeting Carly and learning she worked at your store, dump Janine, and put the rush on Carly. Janine said a couple of weeks ago Bruce suddenly dumped Carly. About the time your grandfather was killed. All of it started to make me wonder."

Sonny looked confused. "Do you think this man might have had something to do with the murder?"

"It's possible. If Bruce was involved in exchanging the stones in rings at Westcott's, he might have dumped Janine and started to date Carly to get access to your store. I remember Brewer Addison telling me an exchange artist like this usually hits more than one store in an area, then moving on before the thefts become apparent." Andrew leaned forward, putting an elbow on the table. "What if Bruce Steele was swapping out rings at your store, too? And what if your granddad caught him?"

Sonny's eyes widened. "You're assuming we've had stones exchanged in our jewelry. No one has come in to suggest that to us."

"It wouldn't take long to get Brewer Addison to check your antique rings of value. This particular exchange artist seems to focus on rings. Or at least he did at Westcott's. Wouldn't you like to be sure he hadn't targeted some of your pieces?"

"I would." Sonny crossed his arms. "But I'd like to do this quietly without talking to my parents about it at first. They've had so much to deal with already." He paused, thinking. "Do you think Brewer might look at the pieces today? Maybe you could go with me to take them over. I'm open to check into this out with you Andrew. But you do realize there may be no links at all between the two stores in this."

"I know that, and I hope you'll be discreet about Westcott's losses, whatever we learn. Our reputation is compromised enough with your grandfather's body found at our store."

Their lunch arrived, and they stopped talking to eat for a time.

Sonny rubbed his chin thoughtfully after finishing most of his burger. "This boyfriend of Janine's obviously had access to your store's back rooms, to the keys to your store, as well as to your locked jewelry cases."

"That seemed obvious to me after I listened to Janine's story,"

Andrew admitted. "It's the first lead we've found to anyone able to gain access into our jewelry stock or our store since the investigation began."

"I know you'll want to talk to Carly as you did to Janine right away, with what you've learned, but would you mind waiting until I see if Brewer would take a look at our antique ring stock? If we've had exchanges, too, I'll have questions for Carly myself."

Andrew glanced at his watch. "If you want I can call Brewer Addison, fill him in on the situation, and ask if he could make time to look at your jewelry this afternoon. Would that work for you?"

Sonny nodded. "Yes. I'd like to know before one of our clients comes in, irate and waving a fake ring like what happened to you." He rubbed his neck. "Man, if we've had thefts, too, we'll need to do all the same things you've done, change locks, check security, go through inventory lists, contact past customers. I sure don't look forward to that."

"Well, like you said, it could be only a coincidence. Carly Ryker is a striking girl. Bruce Steele might simply be a player, moving from girlfriend to girlfriend."

"I guess we'll know soon enough." Sonny smiled at Andrew. "Deep down, I could never believe anyone at Westcott's had anything to do with grandad's death, but you must admit, his body found at your store seemed suspicious. We all know your store's security, and we couldn't see any way Grandad could get into your store, dead or alive, except through an employee."

"You can be sure the police have pointed this out to us time and again." Andrew reached for the check on their table. "Let's pay for our lunch and call Brewer."

Later that afternoon, appraiser Brewer Addison looked across at the two young men seated in his back laboratory and shook his head. He pushed three rings toward them. "I've found these three so far—a ruby, a diamond, an emerald—and I'm not finished looking through the rings you brought me yet. These three have definitely had the stones replaced. Looks like our replacement artist hit both your stores. I'm sorry."

Sonny groaned as he added up in his mind the values of the antique gemstones replaced with synthetics only an expert would recognize as fake. As Brewer went back to work on his examinations, Sonny asked, "Would you mind if Andrew and I go to the store to talk to Carly? It seems likely the boyfriend she and Janine shared may be a key to these thefts, and I'd like to talk with her as soon as possible to see what she knows. She's working four to close tonight. I can call her and ask her to come in early to talk with us."

Brewer looked up from his work. "Go on. See if you can't track down a lead. I'd like to see this thief caught before any more stores are hit. It won't do the reputations of any of the stores around here any good if this gets out."

Sonny was able to reach Carly, who agreed to come in early to the store to meet with them. About thirty minutes later, Sonny led Carly to his office upstairs where they could talk quietly. On the way to meet with her, Sonny decided he would only tell her they'd found a few rings with stones replaced in his store, to see what she knew.

After hearing Sonny's story, Carly began to cry. "That sneaky snake." She sniffed. "I wondered why he always turned up at the store late at night to see me when it was mostly dead of traffic. He hung around the store, asked questions, took pictures all the time. He really had me fooled that he was crazy about me."

She crossed one long, model-slim leg over another.

Andrew had forgotten what a strikingly beautiful girl she was, her tousled platinum blond hair framing a pretty face with cat-green eyes.

Carly sighed. "Bruce was a really good looking man in a bad boy way." She rolled her eyes. "I don't know why I always find that type so attractive. He came on to me right away when I met him with Janine, especially after he learned I worked at your store. I guess I'm looking back and seeing that link for the first time now. He really went after me right off. I was stupid enough to think it was all about me. We dated all fall and until this spring. It was really good with us. You know." She rolled her eyes suggestively. "I thought we might even get married when we both got out of school."

She shrugged. "He took a lot of trips he said had to do with a job he had that helped to pay for his school. Some kind of delivery job that took him out of state. He never really explained it. He'd be gone for a while and then show up again, sweet and smooth, and telling me how much he missed me."

She crossed her arms, looking down at her lap. "But one night about a month ago in March, I came around the corner in the store from the bathroom and saw him with his hands in the jewelry case, getting a ring out. Then I saw him stick it in his pocket."

She sighed. "I waited in the back hall for a few minutes, then came out and didn't say anything. Later, though, I decided to tell your granddad. He'd always been so sweet to me, like my own granddaddy. I like my job here at Bay Street and I didn't want to get fired if someone realized a ring had been swiped on my shift."

"You told my granddad?" Sonny's eyes popped open.

"He said not to worry about it. Told me he'd look into it, do some security checks." She closed her eyes. "But I didn't feel the same about Bruce after that. I know he picked up on it. I sort of discouraged him from coming around the store, too, and watched him more carefully when he did. Maybe he figured out I knew something because I didn't see him much after that."

She looked up, tears in her eyes. "Your granddad got killed not long after that so I never got to ask him about what he found out about Bruce. I guess he never had time to look into it. I saw Bruce take that one ring in the store, but I don't know if he took any of the other rings in the store. Honest, Sonny. That's all I know."

Andrew lifted an eyebrow toward Sonny and rolled his eyes. Obviously Carly did not see a possible link in any way between Bruce's theft and Marvin Donelson's death. But facts were adding up that the thefts and Marvin's murder might be linked.

"Thanks for talking with us," Sonny said to Carly. "Do you have a phone number and address for Bruce?"

She sniffed, tears starting in her eyes again. "I never had his address, just knew he lived over near the Art Institute in Charleston.

He said it was kind of a crummy place, never wanted to take me there. I have his old phone number, but he's changed it. I haven't seen him at all since March. I was thinking about going over to the school to look for him but thought that might be kind of pathetic. Now that I've talked to you, I think he might have only been using me to get into the store or something." She wiped at her face. "But I don't know for sure. What do you think?"

Andrew handed her a tissue from a box on a side table. "I think you can find someone who cares more about you, Carly. And considering Bruce might have been involved in some criminal activity, I don't think it would be wise for you to try contact him or look for him. It might implicate you."

Her eyes widened. "Oh I never thought of that." She turned to Sonny. "I didn't have anything to do with Bruce taking that ring Mr. Donelson, and if he took more stuff, I swear I didn't know anything about it."

"I believe you, Carly." Sonny steepled his fingers, thinking for a moment. "It's possible the police might need to get involved in this. If they do, they might ask you more questions. Don't panic if they do. Just tell them everything you told us, okay?"

She bit her lip. "Okay. I'm really sorry about Bruce."

Sonny glanced at his watch. "You'd better go on down to work. Rowena is covering for you and I know she could use some help."

"Sure." She mopped at her face again and then picked up her purse to head out.

Sonny snorted as soon as she was out of hearing range. "I always knew that girl wasn't a rocket scientist, but honestly, I saw a new side of 'dumb blond' today."

Andrew kicked at him. "Watch the blond jokes. You know I'm married to a smart, gifted blond woman. It isn't hair color that determines intelligence."

"Sorry, I just got frustrated listening to her. Do you think she'll look back later and realize she might have set my granddad up to be murdered, telling him about the theft of that ring?"

"I don't know," Andrew said. He leaned his head back against the big chair he sat in. "Do you think it's possible your grandfather looked into the situation more and decided to talk to Bruce, to confront him?"

Sonny scowled. "I don't know, Andrew. But I can tell you my grandfather had excellent appraisal skills. He learned those skills from his dad back when there weren't many experts to rely on. Grandad had some tools, too. He might have started checking some of our jewelry. But if he did, I don't know why he didn't say anything to any of us."

Andrew tried to think what might have happened. "Maybe he was looking into things after hours when Bruce came back to return the ring Carly saw him take. Bruce's usual method might have been to pocket a ring and then return it in the next day or two with the gemstone swapped out. Maybe your grandad caught him."

"It's possible. I don't know if we'll ever know for sure unless Bruce is caught and the police get him to talk." Sonny looked across at Andrew. "Knowing what we do about Bruce and that he was probably operating the same racket at Westcott's, we can also assume he had a key to Westcott's. It's easy to duplicate keys. If he did murder Grandad, meaning to or not, he might have taken him to Westcott's so no one would suspect him. He'd been sniffing after Carly for nearly a year and hadn't dated Janine since last summer, so no one would make the link between him and Westcott's Antiques after all this time."

"If that's true, he's more of an operator and a professional than we imagined. It takes intelligence to think things out with that much detail, to change his phone, and all but disappear."

Sonny sat up and put his hands on his desk. "We need to go to the police with this, Andrew, and now. They might be able to track this man down, and he needs to be stopped before he harms someone else. If he took my grandfather's life, he won't hesitate to kill again." He shook his head. "I hate for the news to get out that we've had thefts at both our stores, but we need to do the right thing and report this. The police and that detective working on the case have found no clues. With this information, they might be able to do more. Also, this will help clear Westcott's name as related to the murder. Will you go with me? I'd like to go now."

"Yes, let me call Suki to tell her I might be late. And, like you, we'll both need to talk with all our employees and our family after we meet with the police."

The rest of the afternoon and evening proved to be stressful, full of questions at the police department and questions from the press—who seemed to hang around the police station waiting for something to happen. Later, Andrew faced a second sweep of questions at Westcott's when he met with Parker, Drake, and Nora to tell his story to them.

"You're the hero of the day," Suki said to him later when he finally got home, "for putting all those facts together and then going to see Sonny."

"Maybe. But I'm glad to finally see some answers to all this surfacing at last. Now if the police can only catch Bruce Steele we might learn for sure all that really happened."

CHAPTER 17

A week had passed since Andrew and Sonny Donelson went to the police to tell them all they'd learned about Marvin Donelson's death and the store thefts undoubtedly related to it. Andrew had been too busy to even consider going to the beach house for the weekend afterward, but he encouraged Suki to go anyway.

"Why don't you go down to the beach and spend some time with Mary Helen and Bailey?" he suggested. "It's going to be nuts around here—phones ringing, long hours, meetings. I'd be happier knowing you're out of it."

Suki felt guilty to comply, but her mother encouraged her to do the same. "If you could go down to stay at the beach house, I'd be so grateful. I'm speaking at that children's book festival in Texas and will be gone for most of the week. Little Bailey is barely a month old and Mary Helen is determined to start back to work part-time at the Mermaid. It might be a help to her if you could go down this week while I'm gone and keep Bailey sometimes if that becomes a problem. I know Andrew and Parker will be covered up with work, calls, interviews, and all the media about Marvin's death and the ongoing investigation. I can't ask Parker to go."

Worrying a little herself about Mary Helen going back to work so soon, Suki headed down to the Sandpiper and to Edisto on Friday as everyone suggested. Almost a week later now, she sat in a rocking chair at The Little Mermaid holding Bailey while Mary Helen worked. She was looking through catalogs and planning items to order for the store for the upcoming tourist traffic soon to hit the island as summer arrived.

"I am so glad to get back to work," Mary Helen said. "I don't know why Mother thought I couldn't manage here with Bailey. I've done great this week. Everyone who comes in loves goo-ing and coo-ing over the baby. You've seen it. And with his crib in the back and the monitor, I can listen for him and check on him often. The Mermaid isn't exactly a New York gift shop on Broadway teeming with traffic all the time."

"No, and I still remember that traffic. I'm not sure Bailey would have been safe in a New York shop." Suki smiled and shifted the baby in her arms. "Still I'm glad Isabel insisted on limiting your hours, and it's good of her and Nancy to cover the busiest days. That helps."

"It does. Parenting is time consuming, but it's rewarding in a new way, too. Bailey grows and changes every day. It's fun watching that."

Suki envied a little the loving expression she saw Mary Helen give to her baby. "You know you're crazy about him."

Mary Helen grinned. "Nothing prepares you for the way you will feel about a child. I don't know quite how to explain it. No book has words for it." She walked around the counter. "He's fast asleep now. Let me go put him in the crib. I don't want him to get in the habit of wanting to be rocked and held all the time."

Suki gave him up reluctantly.

"Watch the store for a minute. I'll bring you a bottle of water when I come back."

Suki got up to walk around the familiar children's gift shop. She and Mary Helen had fallen in love with the store as little girls—especially Mary Helen. Their mother had worked here for a number of years with Isabel Compton and when Mary Helen grew older she worked in the store with Isabel every summer and loved it. The work fanned her dream to get into retail as a career. A disappointment brought her back to the island several years ago, and Isabel talked her in to working at the Mermaid again. Mary Helen meant that time to be temporary but the beauty of Edisto, and a rekindled love for J.T. Mikell, worked their dual magic on her heart. She stayed, married J.T., and entered into a partnership at the store with Isabel. From what Suki could see all those decisions had turned out to be happy ones.

Stopping at a store display, Suki picked up a snow globe with a mermaid sitting on a rock inside it. She turned it over to let the silvery sparkles fall across the scene in the globe.

"You always loved those snow globes as a girl," Mary Helen said, coming back into the room.

"Yes, and you sent me a grand piano in a snow globe for my birthday earlier this year. It plays *Fur Elise* while silvery little flakes drift down over the piano. I love it." She sat the mermaid globe back on the shelf.

"I'm glad you liked it, and I'm thrilled you've started playing the piano again. It's so wonderful to listen to you." She grinned. "Bailey loves it, too."

"I think we all carry an inborn love for beautiful music."

"You're probably right." She gestured to the little table in the front window. "Come sit down and visit with me for a minute while we drink these waters. I'm supposed to drink a lot of water while nursing. Mother picked up all these flavored waters to encourage me to drink more. These are kiwi strawberry, I think."

Suki followed Mary Helen over to the table at the window. It had always been their place to sit and visit. The window looked out over the sidewalk leading up to the shop, so they could see when any customers arrived. They could also enjoy the landscaped yard with a riot of flowers in bloom in the beds around the trees and clustered in a circle around a mermaid birdbath.

Suki smiled at the scene. "The daffodils and azaleas are pretty right now."

"They are. I take no credit for them, though. Isabel hires a wonderful landscaper to take care of the property. She says it helps to draw traffic, and of course we have yard art and statuary for sale around the yard, as well."

Suki changed the subject. "You've been happy back at Edisto

and at the Mermaid, haven't you?"

"I have," she admitted readily. "Are you happy being back?"

"Mostly yes. I'm still working myself through some issues and still not as strong as I'd like to be even after so long now."

"Healing takes time." Mary Helen unscrewed the cap of her water and drank about a third of it. "What did Andrew tell you this morning about the ongoing investigation? I saw his and Sonny's picture in the paper last weekend, snapped when they were coming out of the police station on Friday. Mother said the new discoveries about the thefts at both stores, and Carly Ryder prattling to the press that she told Marvin about seeing that man steal from the Donelson's store, moved suspicion about Marvin's murder to the jewelry thief rather than continuing to focus it on Parker or anyone at Westcott's. That's a relief."

"It is, but the police can't find a single trace of that man Bruce Steele. He seems to have totally vanished. Andrew says that leaves things hanging and unresolved."

"Maybe they'll track him down."

"I hope so. Andrew, Parker, and everyone at Westcott's are really tired of the questions from Sergeant Metler and Detective Dunnings. The news coverage of the murder and thefts hasn't helped business either. I hate all of this has happened."

"Me, too." Mary Helen changed the subject. "I saved the article from the paper about you playing at the symphony last week, in case you need a second copy. You might send it to your Japanese friends. I can't wait to meet them."

"They're flying down in May to see me play at the church and to enjoy some time at the beach. I want to host a little dinner party for them, too. I'm inviting all our family, and Nora and Drake, to our house in Beaufort on Sunday afternoon. That's the day after the concert at the church. Can you and J.T. come? Bailey, too?"

"Sure. What time on Sunday?"

"With the concert Saturday evening on May the eighth, I planned the dinner the next evening on the ninth at five."

"Sounds good to me." Mary Helen finished off her water and set the bottle aside. "It's good of you to give a concert to make money for renovations at the church. You do realize publicity will get out that you're giving a solo performance again—even for charity. Does it worry you that Jonah may try to get in touch with you? You shared with me what happened with him and about him calling and screaming at Andrew. Parker told Mother he threatened to find a way to come and talk with you. He probably won't be happy to learn you're performing again without potentially contacting him to agent you."

Suki scowled and lifted her chin. "Jonah Dobrowski will *never* agent me again. Nothing he can say or offer will change my mind about that."

"Good. I'm glad to hear it. Sometimes you can be too tender-hearted and forgiving about things."

"Not about things like this." Suki snapped out the words.

"Well, keep that attitude." Mary Helen gave her a thumbs-up sign. "I never liked that man anyway. I always thought him a little smarmy and full of himself."

Suki laughed. "I wish I'd had your discernment earlier."

"Well, we all make mistakes about people, and people disappoint us sometimes. I've decided that's just a part of life." Mary Helen got up and took their empty water bottles to drop in the trash. "I see a group of tourists heading up the sidewalk. With the morning moving along, it will get busier in the store now. Why don't you head on home? I can take care of things here, and Isabel will be in soon. I know you told me Emma is driving down to have lunch with you today and spend the afternoon."

Suki glanced at her watch. "I would like to stop by the store to pick up a few things for our lunch. Are you sure you'll be okay? What if Bailey starts crying?"

She pointed out the window. "See that gaggle of middle-aged women? They'll probably fight to get their hands on him if he decides to cry. But he should sleep until Isabel comes. I'll feed him again then, help Isabel a little longer in the store, and then head on home. J.T. is grilling burgers tonight if you want to pop over to eat with us instead of eating by yourself."

"I'd like that," she said, walking over to get her purse from under the register.

Suki listened to Mary Helen greet the women as she made her way out to her car a few minutes later. Mary Helen had such a gifted, easy way with people and her love for the store showed in her eyes and actions.

Suki climbed in her little red Pontiac and drove the few blocks down the street to the Piggly Wiggly. She planned to make fresh tuna salad stuffed in tomatoes for lunch, a favorite of Emma's, with fresh strawberries on the side. At the store, she picked up chips and dessert as extras. Suki was so glad her friendship with Emma Whaley was returning to the easy camaraderie of their past. They'd been best friends since early childhood.

Back at the beach house, she put her groceries up, made their tuna salad and popped it in the refrigerator. On the screened porch she set the glass-topped table with silverware, cute placemats and napkins, adding a colorful pot of silk tulips as a centerpiece. With time to spare, she headed to the piano to practice.

Emma found her there an hour later as she let herself in the back door of the house. "Don't stop playing," she said. "I want to sit and listen for a few minutes."

She settled into a spot on the sofa and Suki played on until she finished her piece.

"It's good to see you," Suki said then, turning on the piano stool to face Emma.

"You, too." Emma sent her a warm smile. "While I sat here listening to you, I was swamped with a zillion memories of listening to you play like this at Oleanders when we were girls."

Suki traced a hand over the piano keys. "We had a happy childhood didn't we?"

"We did. It seems funny sometimes to realize we're all grown up."

Suki laughed. "None of us seemed very grown up a few weeks ago when Chuck, J.T., Jane and Mary Helen battled it out in a water fight in the ocean. Even Barton and Toni got into it. Then we all played night tag later, even Andrew and me. It didn't seem so different from times in our childhood."

"I wish I'd been able to come that night."

"We missed you," Suki said, getting up to head to the kitchen to put lunch together.

Emma followed her and perched on a stool at the bar.

"I'm making tuna salad in tomatoes because I remembered you like it." Suki got out the tuna salad and two big tomatoes, and then began to cut and section the tomatoes, scooping mounds of tuna into each. "If you want you can put those chips in a bowl." She pointed toward the bag on the counter. "Get that dish of strawberries I chopped up earlier out of the refriegerator, too, if you would."

Emma began to help get their lunch ready. "I'm so glad I didn't have classes this afternoon so I could drive over," she said. "On Tuesdays and Thurdays, my classes are in the morning and both let out by noon. But on Monday, Wednesday, and Friday they're scattered throughout the day."

"How many classes are you teaching right now?"

"This semester I'm teaching five, an English composition and a literature class on Tuesday and Thursday mornings, and another comp class, a second lit class, and a creative writing class on Monday, Wednesday, and Fridays." She hesitated. "I've been thinking about starting to work on my doctorate. It would really enhance my status on faculty and increase my salary. There's a PhD program in Columbia at the main campus in English and American Literature, and I think my department would work with me so I can study and teach. It would be a little demanding, but it's a good time for me to think about doing it while I'm single. It's about a two-and-a-half hour drive to Columbia to the main campus from Beaufort, not too far for me to attend. Chuck and Tom both commuted to Columbia to get their undergrad degrees. They managed. I'm sure I can, too."

"You always made such good grades and were smarter than all

of us in English. I remember you helping us with our papers in high school."

She laughed. "I love reminding Jane and Chuck of that, when they were both older than me. J.T., too."

"Everyone says you're a fabulous teacher. I don't doubt it for a minute. Even when we played school as kids, you were a good teacher."

Emma laughed. "Your mother was better, always so creative and encouraging. I think she made me want to teach. My parents were both in real estate, but it never drew me like it did Tom, Chuck, and Jane."

Suki finished fixing their lunch plates. "Take your plate and this glass of tea out to the table on the porch. I'll bring mine out and then run back in for the chips and fruit."

They settled down after a few minutes on the Sandpiper's shady screened porch. Suki had turned on the paddle fan to keep them cool, but a light breeze from off the ocean wafted through the porch every few minutes, too.

Emma leaned her head back. "I miss living down at the beach and listening to the ocean, the gulls, and all the sea sounds every day. I miss walking on the beach, too."

"You come down often," Suki reminded her.

She smiled. "Not often enough when you have the sea in your soul."

"Ah, I love that thought."

They both ate their lunch then, chatting and enjoying the ocean sounds.

"I played for Kizzy on Monday while she was cleaning," Suki said when they were nearly finished with lunch. "You remember I told you how she helped me get past the issues and fears that kept me from the piano. She said on Monday I'd found my song." She smiled remembering the words. "Kizzy encouraged me to walk the beach, listen to the songs of the ocean, the gulls, and the wind and to let them tell me what to play."

"That woman has the sweetest spirit," Emma said. "Did you

walk down the beach like she asked?"

"I did," Suki answered. "That song I was playing when you came in earlier was one I wrote, one I heard in my mind while walking up the beach and praying. Does that sound silly?"

"No. You were being inspired. Most all great compositions, symphonies, and literature grew out of inspirational moments. I love telling my students stories about the writers we study. Many sacrificed a lot to write, to follow their callings. Following any art as a career is often difficult. In times past, there were patrons of the arts who subsidized artists, but those times are gone. Many writers, artists, and musicians struggle and aren't recognized or celebrated until they pass on. That's sad, isn't it?"

"Yes. It is. And the world isn't an easy place for artists. They're different."

"Will you play your new composition at your concert?"

"I'm thinking about it. I call it *Edisto Song,* from Kizzy's words."

Emma drank some of her tea, considering that. "I like that title, Suki. I love that you're creating your own pieces again, too. Many artists can play well but not many can also write their own songs or compositions. I know you've made recordings in past. I have several of your CDs. You could make more. You don't have to be on tour to record. I remember you used to drive to Nashville with Morgan or Parker to record at a studio there. In fact, you don't need an agent or an agency contract to share your work or to do performances of any kind. I'm sure many orchestras would welcome having you come to play with them again, and other venues would open where you can share, too."

"Thanks." Suki smiled at her. "I've actually had an offer to play with the Atlanta Symphony Orchestra. They saw that I'd performed with the symphony here. Knowing I was living in the south now, they called to invite me. They tracked me down through the Maestro at the Beaufort Symphony."

Emma clapped her hands. "That's wonderful!"

Suki put a finger to her lips. "I haven't told very many people yet, but I will soon. So keep this to yourself for now, okay?"

"I will. Harris will be so excited about this for you!"

"Hmmm. Let's take these plates into the house and get a piece of cheesecake for dessert and then I want to hear more about Harris," Suki said, watching Emma blush.

Back on the porch again, Emma looked out toward the ocean thoughtfully. "It seems like I've had crushes on so many boys and men who didn't like me in return or who dated me for a while and then dumped me. Being really smart isn't always an attribute that makes you popular with the opposite sex or with a lot of people. But what is so extraordinary to me is that Harris came after me. He really liked me from the first, and even when he's really gotten to know me better he still likes me."

She put a hand to her heart. "He thinks I am so special and he makes me feel...." She stopped to search for the right word. "Cherished. That's the perfect word. It means cared for beyond measure and treasured in the heart. I've never had anyone feel like that about me. And he's so smart and caring and good. I feel so lucky I met him, Suki."

"I am *so* happy for you, Emma. I really like Harris, too. I loved hearing about all that he does working with the kids at his school in the music program. I promised him I'd come and talk to some of his classes."

She smiled. "He told me. His kids are already excited about that. He wants them to meet musicians so they can begin to get vision for what they might do with music."

Suki forked up another bite of cheesecake. "It doesn't hurt that he's tall and good-looking, too, and so personable. I still remember how kind he was when I froze that night and couldn't play at our house."

Emma looked down at her plate. "I'm sorry I was ugly to you about marrying Andrew. I just let a nasty jealous spirit get into me. I hope you've forgiven me for all my hateful words. I feel so ashamed to think back on them."

"Stop beating yourself up over that. Andrew and I married very impulsively. It made his mother mad, my parents unhappy, and shocked a lot of our friends. But it was the right thing for us to do." She paused to sip her tea. "I rarely do very impulsive things. Developing my abilities with the piano has been such a focused, planned, and disciplined regime. It sort of shaped the rest of my life to match. It was entirely out of character for either Andrew or me to suddenly do something without thinking first about the consequences, our families, and a thousand other things." She grinned. "But I love that we married that way. It's the happiest and most fun memory. If we'd given ourselves too much time to think about it or analyze it, we might not have done it at all. And oh my, what we would have missed!"

They both giggled.

"I brought my bathing suit with me," Emma said. "Can we go down to the beach for the afternoon before I need to head back to Beaufort? I'd love to get some sun, take a walk up around the Point, and play in the ocean."

"I'd love that, too. Let's clean up these dishes and then I'll get some chairs and an umbrella for us to take to the beach. Like you, I want to savor these days before the island gets more crowded with summer tourists."

CHAPTER 18

A week or so later on a busy Saturday, Andrew worked to pack a collection of six antique thimbles for a tourist while Drake chatted with the customer and rang up the sale. Now that May had arrived, with visitors streaming in from the nearby beach islands, business had picked up in the store.

"I am so pleased to find these beautiful thimbles to add to my collection," the customer, a Mrs. Farber, said. "I don't have any just like these." She sent Drake a charming smile.

Not surprising. All women smiled at Drake.

Andrew finished packing all the thimbles in bubble wrap inside a small box, and then tucked the box into a forest green bag with the words Westcott's Antiques in gold scrolled lettering across the front.

Drake took the bag to hand to Mrs. Farber. "These particular thimbles are porcelain cloisonné, originally made in Germany. I found them at an estate sale several months ago. I liked that each one is so unique in shape and design."

"So do I, and thank you so much for talking with me today. I learned many interesting facts about my own collection I didn't know from you."

Her friend waved at her from the door, ready to leave, so the woman reached for her purchase, also nodding at Andrew before starting across the store toward her friend.

Drake leaned against the counter watching her. "That was one classy and beautiful woman."

Lifting his eyebrows, Andrew's eyes moved in question toward the woman as she and her friend left.

Drake laughed at his expression. "Just because she isn't a young girl any more doesn't mean she isn't beautiful. I love the way women age when they do it gracefully and well. Notice how she walked with ease and confidence and dressed with class to suit her figure. So many women just throw on anything today and go out the door in some of the most abominable outfits, too tight, the colors mismatched, their feet in plastic flip flops or heinously bright tennis shoes in a garish clashing color."

He sighed, shaking his head in thought. "It worries me that style seems to have vanished from the world today. That middle-aged woman you waited on in the store earlier had Hello Kitty tattoos on her arms. Can you believe that? My opinion about tattoos in general is better not spoken, but you would think—even if someone chose to put permanent graphics on their bodies—that they would at least choose a tasteful design." He tucked the sales receipt in the bottom drawer of the register.

Andrew's eyes moved to study a group of tourists walking by the store, many stopping to look in Westcott's windows.

Drake, now on one of his rants, pointed at the two younger women. "Look at those two girls standing at the window, dressed in ratty torn jeans and tight revealing T-shirts with trashy invitational sayings across the front. Despite the fact that they're dressed like streetwalkers, those girls would probably get all huffed up if a man gave them the eye or tried to proposition them. What should they expect though?" He snorted. "That's probably their mother with them, too. Her clothes look like she slept in them. Don't people iron anymore today? And I'll bet that man with them is the dad— gaudy, floral print shirt and shorts hanging below his belly, nearly falling off."

Andrew chuckled. "The fashion policeman is out again, I see."

"You may laugh, but I think clothes tell the world who you are and about your character. Many people seem to forget that." Drake lifted his chin. "Yet they'll come in here and look at every antique piece we have trying to find a little scratch or a small flaw on it, hoping to point it out. It's hypocritical."

"The world is full of all different kinds of people, Drake. If everyone was like you, the world would be a boring place, don't you think?"

"I'm not so sure about that," he said, straightening his tie.

Nora came out from the back of the store then. "When Parker comes in, would one of you tell him I put those letters on his desk for him to sign?" She paused before starting back up the stairs to her office. "I think I'll run over to the Magnolia Bakery Café for a shrimp salad for lunch today. Do either of you want me to bring you back anything?"

Andrew smiled at his mother. "I brought a roast beef and cheese sandwich from home. I'll just eat that. But you can bring me one of the café's homemade cinnamon rolls for dessert."

"I'll do that." She smiled back at him. "How about you, Drake?"

"Actually, I'll go with you if Andrew thinks he can cover the store by himself for a little while. They serve an excellent crab crepe at the Magnolia."

"Go with mother, Drake. I'll be fine," Andrew said.

"Well." Nora hesitated. "I suppose that would be all right."

Drake straightened his collar. "Fine. You go upstairs and get your purse. I'll drive."

She headed up the wide hardwood stairs to Westcott's upper level. Drake watched her. "Now that is another example of a classy, beautiful woman."

"That's my mother, Drake." Andrew frowned.

"My comment was purely in appreciation and related to the subject we were discussing earlier. Surely you recognize your mother is lovely, always tastefully dressed, and, mercy, watch her walk. She has that poise and quiet confidence I was talking about. Just oozes Southern charm and grace."

Andrew's eyes widened.

Drake shook his head at him. "For a man as in tune to the beauty of things, antique furniture, fine jewelry, and collectibles, surely you've also developed an appreciation for a beautiful woman when you see one. I should hope you're aware of your wife's appeal. It's dangerous when a man doesn't appreciate his fine possessions."

Andrew snorted. "I doubt Suki would appreciate being thought of as a possession."

"Nonsense, son. Both men and women think of each other that way. That's why you'll see them bristle if someone shows their partner too much interest in the wrong way." He shook his head as he got out his keys. "You really need to smarten up more about people, especially about men and woman and their ways. It's wise to be discerning."

Andrew snorted at that comment, too. "Spoken by the man who still isn't married at middle age."

"Perhaps it's because I'm discerning that I'm not married, and perhaps I'm waiting for a chance at the perfect item. I've seen you do the same at an estate sale—shop carefully, knowing what you have in mind and knowing what you want."

"Again, women are not items." Andrew scowled.

"But they can be beautiful accompaniments to a man's life. Don't you agree?" Drake smiled and then left with Nora as she came back down the stairs, leaving Andrew to try and make sense of that last comment. Sometimes he thought Drake should have been a psychologist instead of an antiques dealer. Those types always talked in psychological circles.

A hum of tourists and a few regular clients came in the store then, keeping Andrew busy. He loved telling them about the furniture and antiques in Westcott's, adding in special stories he'd learned while purchasing different items in the store. He found people liked knowing the history of old pieces.

After Drake and Nora returned to cover the store, he went back to the break room to eat his sandwich and the cinnamon roll his mother brought him. When he was almost finished Ira Dean O'Connor stuck her head in the door.

"How's my boy?" she asked, coming in the room to lean over to kiss him on the cheek.

Andrew could hardly be embarrassed over affection from this woman who'd kept him as a baby and helped to raise him while his mother worked. "I'm good Ira Dean. What are you doing here?" He smiled with warmth at the older woman, dressed in one of her bright outfits, her short, curly, white hair framing her face, her million dollar smile aimed at him with obvious pleasure.

"I popped by to say hello and to bring someone to meet you." She gestured then toward an elderly woman behind her in the doorway, probably in her eighties but still gracious in bearing, dressed in a long, soft blue summer dress, her silvery white hair in a sleek bun.

"This is my friend Lydia," Ira Dean said in introduction. "We're in the DAR, the Daughters of the American Revolution, together. She was my roommate at state conference in Columbia, back in March, and we got to be good friends. Lydia lives in one of those old, historic homes in downtown Savannah, a lot like O'Connor House. She loves antiques, as I do, so of course I wanted her to see Westcott's."

"Nice to meet you Lydia," Andrew said, offering a hand.

She nodded. "I am pleased to meet you, too."

The woman looked familiar in some way but Andrew couldn't place it. "Have we met before here at the store?" he asked.

"Not here. No." She smiled in a misty way. "We met when you were very small, but I haven't seen you since you've grown up. I'm Lydia Cavanaugh. Your great grandmother."

Andrew jerked back his hand, his eyes moving with anger to Ira Dean.

"Settle down, Andrew." Ira Dean shook her head. "I've already told Lydia all about both you and Nora and about your past with her grandson Hayden. Let's just say she had no idea of any of the truth about anything, and knowing differently now, she wanted to meet you. She hopes to go upstairs and talk to your mother, too."

"I don't think Mother would like being interrupted at work to speak to anyone in the Cavanaugh family. Surely you would know that."

Ira Dean put a hand on one hip. "It's not like you to be rude,

Andrew. Neither your mother or I encouraged that kind of behavior in you."

Andrew reined in his emotions. "I'm sorry, Mrs. Cavanaugh. My experiences in past with my father's family have not been positive ones. They threatened to sue me and my mother over my father's will and they acted particularly nasty as well. I hated that time for my mother's sake, and I have only bad memories of the Cavanaugh family's unkindness to us through the years."

Ira Dean gestured to Lydia to take a seat at the table in the break room, ignoring his words. She sat down in another chair, smiling as though she hadn't pulled a fast one on Andrew. So much for getting rid of them quickly, he thought

Lydia Cavanaugh clasped her hands together nervously and then looked across the table at Andrew with a clear gaze from blue eyes so like his own. "I can't say I blame you for your harsh feelings, Andrew, after what I learned from Ira Dean. I didn't come to stay long today. I know you're at work, but I wanted to come to say I'm sorry for what your mother and you suffered at the hands of my grandson Hayden and at the hands of my son Russell, his wife, and girls."

She paused to collect her thoughts, and Andrew couldn't help but note she was a handsome woman, even at her age.

She cleared her throat then. "I always knew my son Russell and his family could see no wrong in Hayden and, perhaps, in a way, I realized there was a possibility Hayden had been abusive. I did know he drank too much. However, he denied all of the allegations, and my son Russell and his wife Verleen seemed certain Hayden had been wronged in the divorce claims. In my husband Franklin's and my heart, I'm sure you can see why we wanted to believe better of Hayden, although that doesn't make it right we obviously believed a lie. We should have been broad-minded enough to have at least met and talked with your mother to hear her side of things. But of course we were all shocked and hurt and advised by our attorney not to meet or discuss issues with your mother. With all of us living in Savannah, too, we weren't privy to see more of

Hayden than what he presented to us on family visits. It's hard to believe ill about your children or your grandchildren. Perhaps you'll understand that some day."

Andrew stood, hoping to make it clear he wanted them to leave. "I don't like to look back on those times nor do I really care to discuss them at length. However, I thank you for coming by to offer your apologies today Mrs. Cavanaugh. It's the first time anyone in your family has ever said a kind word to me or my mother."

Lydia Cavanaugh stood and so did Ira Dean.

Ira Dean made a tsk-tsking noise. "I know it's hard for you to receive this apology, Andrew, but it is an apology—and a sincere one. People often do wrong things, judge unwisely without enough facts. However, it takes a person with integrity and strength of character to say they are sorry when they learn the truth. When you think about this later, you'll realize Lydia meant only kindness in coming to see you today."

Andrew felt little remorse listening to Ira Dean's words. He turned to Lydia. "How does the rest of your family feel about this?" He couldn't resist asking.

"We've held several family meetings to discuss this." She made a face. "Let's just say I haven't been on the top of the family popularity list lately with the facts I've brought to everyone's attention. You may be assured I'm gathering more facts, as well. I am not finished with this situation by a long shot. I hope, after you think about it more, you might be willing to allow me a small space in your life. Perhaps your mother will, as well. You are family, even though we've treated you shabbily. In all honesty and sincerity, I'd like you to know that I'd like to treat you more honorably in future and to get to know you better."

Ira Dean started toward the door, Lydia Cavanaugh behind her. "I'm taking Lydia upstairs to talk to Nora just as she did to you. You stay here Andrew and don't intervene, you hear? Lydia deserves a chance to make her apologies."

Lydia turned as they left, putting a hand to her mouth, tears in her eyes. "You look so much like your father. The resemblance is striking. It's almost like seeing Hayden again."

Andrew waited to scowl until after she left. She could have left off that last remark for sure. It didn't endear her to him at all.

After cleaning up from lunch, Andrew went back out front in the store to work, keeping busy with customers or cleaning around the store until Ira Dean and Lydia Cavanaugh came down the stairs from his mother's office and finally left the building.

"You can quit hiding now," Drake said. "They're gone."

"I didn't realize I'd been that obvious." Andrew came over to the register where Drake was working. "I gather you knew who that was?"

"I did, even before Ira Dean introduced me. I've met the Cavanaugh family at a few events here and there. Mostly avoided them if I could."

Nora came down the stairs then, too. "Are you all right, Andrew?" she asked. "Ira Dean said you were upset."

"Aren't *you* upset?" He crossed his arms, annoyed all over again.

She sent him a rather smug smile. "Actually it felt rather nice to have one of the high and mighty Cavanaughs come to apologize to us today. The act is long overdue, if you ask me."

"I'd agree with that," Drake put in. "Is that why Lydia Alizay Cavanaugh was here today? To apologize? She's the big power head behind the Cavanaugh machine now that her husband Franklin is gone, she and her son Russell Cavanaugh."

"Pardon me if I'm not impressed." Andrew made a face.

Nora shook a finger at him. "It took a lot for a woman like Lydia Cavanaugh to do what she did today. You should respect that, even if you don't want to form a late life friendship with her. Besides, the woman is your blood relative. She indicated to me she was gathering information to form a more true picture of what your father was like and of the reasons that forced me to divorce him." She took a deep breath. "I, for one, would be glad to have cordial relations with your father's family, to be able to run into one of them without getting snubbed or insulted in some way. I'd like that for you and Suki, too."

"I can't see why you would want to forgive them after the way they acted."

"Can't you?" She lifted an eyebrow. "I seem to recall raising you in the church and in the Christian faith, reading Bible stories to you and teaching you the importance of forgiveness. Everyone deserves forgiveness, not necessarily open trust again, but certainly forgiveness. To not give it, especially when asked for, is unbiblical."

"Uh, oh. Watch out for the preacher." Drake wiggled his eyebrows.

Nora turned on him, irritated. "I know you have issues with your family as well, Drake Hartwell Jenkins, but I hope you would be forgiving to them if the opportunity ever presented itself. They are your family after all." She leaned closer toward him. "And don't be teaching my son disrespect for his faith."

Drake put up his hands. "I stand corrected. Your mother is right, Andrew. Even research has proved that harboring unforgiveness is unhealthy for you—in physical as well as emotional ways. Give some thought to your reactions today and consider working on your attitude. I'd avoid taking this issue to Suki until you think it through a little more, too." He glanced toward the clock. "She's giving her first solo performance at the church tonight. She doesn't need you acting sour and emotionally upset when you go home after work."

"That's a good point, Andrew," his mother added. "You know this is an important evening for Suki." She gave Drake an appreciative smile. "I'm glad Drake reminded me of her performance tonight."

"I'd hardly go home and dump on her when I know she's performing," Andrew said in a sullen voice.

"I know, but you are upset," his mother said. "Suki will pick up on it. You know how sensitive she is. Why don't you come upstairs where you and I can talk about this issue some more? I might be able to help you understand a little more about Lydia Cavanaugh and about your father's family and that time when we divorced. Remember you weren't even born when it happened. I'd like you to go home feeling more peaceful."

"Okay," he replied with some reluctance, thinking of Suki. "Maybe if I talk some things out with you, it might help. Even if only to vent. I don't want the Cavanaughs causing any more problems in my life than they have already."

"That's the spirit," his mother said, starting toward the stairs. "This is a special time for Suki. She's giving her first solo performance after being sick, and her New York neighbors flew in yesterday so they could attend. Mary Helen and J.T. are bringing them over to the church tonight and then back to Beaufort tomorrow for the little dinner at your house. Like Drake said, you don't need to dump your feelings from meeting with your great grandmother on Suki tonight except with a positive spin."

Andrew started after her. "She can read me pretty well, Mom."

"Then we'll need to get your attitude turned around so she can read something positive," Nora said, pausing on the stairs. "The positive is that your great grandmother came to see you today and expressed her regrets over her family's behavior in the past. Isn't that nice, when you think of it in the right way, stepping outside your own feelings?"

"I love a brilliant woman," Drake added with a grin. "You listen to her, Andrew."

Nora turned to Drake. "You can cover for a bit while Andrew and I talk, can't you?"

"I can," he replied. "You can pay me back by letting me take you out to a late dinner after the concert tonight. With it starting at six we'll be finished by eight. I can pick you up a little after five thirty to drive you to the church, too. I know Ira Dean isn't going tonight because of another commitment. She suggested I might take you with me."

"Did she?" Nora raised her eyebrows. "And how will treating me to dinner benefit you as a return favor?"

"I'd enjoy some more of your engaging company." Drake offered her one of his charismatic smiles. "Besides, I have to drive back into town for the concert tonight and you know I hate to eat alone." He paused. "We also need to make plans for that estate sale we're going to next week. I forgot to bring it up at lunch today. We can talk about it tonight over dinner."

"Oh, my, I'd forgotten that," she said. "Do you think we should leave the store for an entire day right now with all that's going on with the investigation?"

"We definitely should, Nora. This is a big, big sale at that plantation outside of Columbia. I can look at all the major items and furniture while you scout through all the china and small items. We sold all those antique thimbles from our last estate sale this morning."

"Really?"

"Yes, and we need more small collectibles like that to fill our display cases until we decide to put the jewelry back out."

"All right. All right," she said, waving a hand.

Drake grinned and turned to greet a customer coming in the door.

Andrew followed his mother up the stairs wondering again about his mother and Drake's odd friendship. It seemed like Drake just asked his mother out for a date but then they went so many places together it was hard to tell.

CHAPTER 19

On Sunday afternoon, Suki walked with her arm in Eito Masako's through the landscaped back yard of her home, pointing out flowers and shrubs to him.

"That gorgeous tree is a magnolia," she told him. "Come and see how wonderful the white blossoms smell."

He tucked his head close to the bloom she held down. "Ah, that is a heady fragrance. I do not see many of these trees in New York."

She smiled at him. "It's a true Southern tree. It likes a warmer climate than New York to best thrive."

"It is lovely here Sarah Katherine." He looked around in admiration. "A fine garden with much beauty and peace."

"We tend to think of it as a back yard rather than a garden." She paused to sit on a bench under a shady tree, patting the space beside her to encourage him to stop and sit down with her.

He sat with his usual careful poise. "In Japan this back yard area would be called a *uriniwa,* which means a rear garden."

She looked around, thinking of the term, and then said, "I'm so pleased you, Marri, Ken, and Julianne could come down to visit us."

He nodded. "It is our honor and pleasure. You were most gracious, as well, to offer us your lovely beach home at Edisto. Julianne has not spent much time at the ocean and she has been enchanted exploring and discovering a whole new world of beauty."

Suki smiled. "Julianne has also been enchanted with little Bailey."

He shook his head in agreement. "Your sister Mary Helen has been most kind to let Julianne hold him and help care for him." He turned to look at Suki. "It is good practice, as Marri and Ken are expecting another baby before Christmas."

"Oh! Marri hasn't told me." Suki put her hands together in pleasure.

"Well, I have that joy then. I know she intended to tell you in a quiet moment with Julianne not present. She and Ken want to wait to tell Julianne the news after the first months are past and all is well."

He crossed his hands in his lap, a familiar gesture. "It is convenient that I was able to move to your apartment in March. My little room at Marri and Ken's will be needed for the new baby now. And I will still be close at hand." He paused. "You were most kind and generous to leave me your furnishings as you did, and the lovely piano for Julianne. I feel as though I moved into a place already familiar and loved."

"Good. I'm happy for that."

"And are you happy, Sarah Katherine, you and Andrew?"

"Very much so." She smiled at him.

"Ah, then I have made another successful match."

"Yes, that is certainly true. We thank you. I don't think I saw Andrew as a potential husband until you suggested the idea."

"A good *nakado* has a way of knowing and sensing these things, but we are always pleased to learn our matches are bringing happiness to the couples we help."

"You are such a special man Eito. I'm glad God brought you into my life."

He turned to look at her. "I see a new element of faith emerging in your speech."

"Yes, I've grown closer to God since coming back home. Andrew and I both."

"That is good. A strong faith has been shown to strengthen a marriage and to enhance the quality of life and longevity."

"I'm glad we've had these few quiet moments together before

dinner. Mother, Nora, and Mary Helen all but shooed me out of the kitchen, saying this meal was in my honor for performing again and helping the church. They insisted on bringing all the food, too." She reached out to pick a white gardenia blossom from the shrub by their bench and tucked it in the pocket of Eito's lightweight summer jacket, worn loose over a white shirt.

Eito sniffed the air. "That is another pleasing fragrance. The gardenia is native to Japan and China. Did you know that? The bloom was always a favorite of my wife's."

"I've heard you speak of her often, and Marri showed me pictures of her. I know you must miss her."

"I do. We were matched through a *nakado*. One does not procure one's own matches, even when in the profession. The self clouds the vision. But a *nakodo* friend of my father's introduced us, and we made a strong and good match."

"There is much to be said for matchmaking, although I'm not sure if our culture ever will fully embrace it as much as yours."

He laughed. "Yes, that is true. Your culture is very individualistic, not as collectivist as the Japanese culture. Individualistic cultures are oriented around the self, being independent, putting the welfare of the individual as a priority, rather than identifying with a group mentality. In Japan, one thinks more of the good of others, the family and the group, as equally important to the needs and desires of the self. It changes the values and actions."

"I can see that."

Marri and Ken came across the yard then, both with their sleek, black hair and dark brown eyes, and both smiling. Ken was a holistic therapist, specializing in East Asian Medicine. He and a colleague, Ryan Sato, had a clinic in New York. Suki had often benefited from Ken's Sotai therapies and Shiatsu massage. Marri worked as an International Student Advisor for Columbia University's International House on Riverside.

"Your mother sent us to get you both for dinner," Marri said. "I see you've been showing my father the garden. We looked at it earlier with Julianne, who was eager to see and explore everything the minute we arrived. It is very different from New York here. Ken says he can hardly get used to looking up and not seeing buildings all around."

Ken laughed. "Here there is so much open space and so much green. So many rich flowers and shrubs." He gestured around him. "You have a beautiful home both here and at the beach Sarah." None of her New York friends had picked up on her nickname yet.

"I feel very blessed." She turned to Marri as they all started back toward the house. "I hear from Eito congratulations are in order with a new baby coming."

"Yes." Marri smiled at her father. "I planned to tell you later outside Julianne's hearing, but I am glad my father shared with you. We are very excited. I've enjoyed time with your sister's baby to get me in practice again."

"So has Julianne." Ken laughed. "I hope she has not made a pest of herself playing with Bailey so much. She is very taken with him."

"It is hard not to love little Bailey," Suki replied. "He's such a joyful baby."

Back inside, everyone gathered to start through the buffet set up on the kitchen island. Parker had brought a honey-baked ham and Nora and Claire had fixed an assortment of sides—a corn casserole, green beans, a macaroni salad, fruit salad, sliced tomatoes, and yeast rolls. Mary Helen brought several of Kizzy's pies for dessert, picked up at the Helton Grocery, and she had made fruit tca for all.

"I may not be the cook Mother and Nora are," Mary Helen announced. "But I do make fabulous fruit tea."

Parker offered thanks and they all made their way through the buffet to fill their plates, carrying them out to the screened porch, where Andrew had set up two tables end to end, covered with colorful cloths. The paddle fan whirled gently overhead as they ate and they could hear the birds in the trees and smell the magnolias and gardenias wafting on the breeze.

Eito, as the eldest, had been given the seat of honor at one end of the long table, Parker at the other, with Suki, Andrew, Marri, Julianne, and Claire to Eito's left, and Drake, Nora, Ken, Mary Helen, and J.T. to Eito's right, a lovely party of twelve in total. Bailey, already fed, slept in a crib inside the house, with a monitor on the table beside Mary Helen so she could hear if he woke and cried.

They all caught up on news and got better acquainted as they ate, also talking, of course, about the concert the night before.

"Everything was so lovely," Claire said. "I am so proud of you, Suki, for giving this concert and donating the money from it to the church for needed renovations. Historic churches are costly to maintain."

"I agree it was a wonderful concert," Marri added, her eyes sparkling. "And such a beautiful church. We loved how Suki talked about each piece before she played, too."

Mary Helen smiled. "Kizzy Helton cried when you dedicated the song you wrote at Edisto to her and acknowledged her help in bringing your joy and love for the piano back."

Claire put a hand to her heart. "I cried over that, too. There weren't many dry eyes in the church of any of the people who know and love you, dear."

Parker smiled down the table at Suki. "I liked that you played that fun piece from Ferde Grofe's *Grand Canyon Suite* "On the Trail" and how you told everyone before you played it to listen for the donkeys walking and swaying down the trail, even braying. "He laughed. "The children in the audience loved that piece!"

"That was my favorite, too," Julianne added.

Suki smiled with pleasure. "I tried to pick a variety of pieces everyone would enjoy. I like people to realize music can be fun, that it can make you see scenes, feel like you're in a particular setting, capture the vision of a place, a moment, or a feeling."

"When you talk to your audience before you play, it helps them see those things, too," Andrew said. "That's so special and personal. I hope you'll continue to do more of that."

She looked down at her plate. "Jonah never wanted me to do that at any performance and he fussed at me the one time I did. He thought it unprofessional."

Eito made a rude noise. "Another reason to think less of that small-minded man."

"I agree with that." Parker chuckled. "And Eito, I think Claire and I owe you thanks for seeing that Andrew and our daughter would make a good match. Perhaps there is more merit to matchmaking than I might have thought."

Eito nodded. "It is an honored custom in our country."

Drake leaned forward, putting his chin on his hand. "I imagine it's difficult matchmaking for some people."

Eito tilted his head. "You mean for someone like yourself?"

Drake sat back, grinning. "I doubt that you'd be able to find a good match for me. Everyone seems to say I'm difficult."

"Is that so?" Eito looked surprised. "A true Southern gentleman such as yourself and fine to look at, too? I can't imagine that would be a problem."

Drake laughed. "Well, perhaps sometime I'll talk with you more to see who you might have in mind for me."

Eito raised his eyebrows, realizing Drake was teasing him. "I see no reason for us to schedule a session. I have met you on several occasions when you, Parker, Claire, Andrew, and his mother came to Suki's concerts and when you stayed over to visit in New York. You shared much about yourself in those visits and I observed you."

"You observed me?"

"Oh, yes. Not to be rude, of course, but it is a part of who I am to observe and watch people and life. I do believe I know you quite well already."

"So you have someone in mind for me?" Drake asked with a bit of a smirk.

Suki bit her lip, somewhat concerned that Drake was being rude to Eito. He did tend to be somewhat outspoken and opinionated.

A small silence fell, as if everyone was trying to decide whether to change the subject or not.

Eito put his hands together, lacing his fingers as he often did and looking around the table with a smile. "Often the best matches are right under our noses, only we have not acknowledged the suitabilites. Like with Andrew and Suki, they thought of themselves as only friends, but of course I saw more. As they considered it, they also began to see more clearly how compatible they were as a match. It is often that way with many couples." He paused for a moment. "It is very obvious to me that you, Drake, and Nora are a perfect match. Have you never considered it?"

Nora gasped and then laughed. "Oh, I think you have missed that one."

"Oh, no, I do not think so," Eito said, with that calm certainty Suki recognized in him.

She looked at Andrew with an uh-oh expression.

Andrew shook his head. "Mother and Drake are long time friends, Eito. They work together and they do know each other well, but there are not romantic feelings between them."

"Not any that we've seen." Mary Helen giggled.

Claire gave her a rebuking look. "Perhaps this isn't the best time for this discussion," she said in a sweet way.

Eito nodded. "I would not have introduced the subject if Drake had not initiated the topic."

Drake rolled his eyes. "You may be sure I wish I had not Mr. Masako."

Eito looked directly at Drake then. "This is not a thought that is new to you, only one unacknowledged. Your admiration for Miss Nora has not been noticed only by me. Nor is Nora unaware of it. It is simply that you have both tucked away the thoughts, and it has never been spoken of. That is a shame when you are both so suitable."

Ken leaned forward to catch his father-in-law's eye. "Maybe you should let this one go for now. You know we talked before about times when it is best not to mix work and pleasure."

"You could be right. I wouldn't want anyone to feel

uncomfortable." Eito smiled broadly around the table then. "I have been told we have homemade pies for dessert made by that charming woman I met on the island and at the concert. What is her name again?" He turned to Mary Helen in question.

"It's Kizzy Helton, Eito. And she makes incredible key lime and lemon pies. I bought two of each and you may have your pick." Mary Helen stood to start toward the kitchen.

"I'll help you cut the pie," Nora said, obviously glad to have a reason to leave the table and the conversation.

"Perhaps we could all take our pie into the living room," Claire suggested. "It would make a nice change, and if we are lucky Suki will play a piece or two on the piano for us." She smiled at Suki in that suggestive way of hers, asking for her support to move them all out of this awkward moment.

"I would count it a pleasure," Suki agreed, getting up from the table. "You and Andrew can help me gather up these supper dishes to take to the kitchen." She looked around with a smile. "Everything was simply wonderful. I so appreciate all of you bringing dinner. I know everyone enjoyed it."

"I certainly did," J.T. said, standing. "I'll help gather up the plates to take inside, too. This has been a great evening. Mary Helen and I have really loved getting to know Eito, Marri, Ken, and little Julianne since they arrived. We're tickled they plan to stay at the beach until next weekend, too. Jane plans to come to the beach tomorrow and bring her little girl Elena, who is nearly five now. She and Julianne will enjoy playing together."

"How old is their baby, John Jared, now?" Suki asked.

"Two and beginning to toddle around," J.T. answered. "Haven't you seen him since you've been home?"

"No, although I've seen Jane and Barton several times," Suki replied. "I'll look forward to seeing the children again soon. Mother and I are coming down to Oleanders for a few days so I can have more time with Marri, Ken, Julianne, and Eito before they leave. One day we plan to take them to Charleston and another day to see other sights around the area. I want them to go home with a lot of wonderful memories."

"I am so excited to see everything," Marri added. "Here, let me gather up glasses to help."

Happily, the mood changed to a congenial, less strained atmosphere once again. But Suki couldn't help wondering about Eito's words.

Later that evening when everyone had gone home, she and Andrew relaxed in the den with their feet up.

"Are you thinking about what Eito said about your mother and Drake?" she asked.

"How could I not be thinking about it? You know how certain Eito is about anything he sees in his professional mode." He made a face. "I hope this doesn't make things awkward for Mother and Drake at work."

She shrugged. "Oh, you know Drake. He'll find some sarcastic, joking way to set it all aside and make everyone laugh about it."

"Maybe," Andrew said, petting Melville absently who was curled up on his lap.

Suki leaned forward, picking up on his unspoken words. "What are you thinking?"

"I just keep remembering a lot of little things, times Drake has looked at my mother not as a friend, made complimentary comments, found excuses to take her places, seemed to contrive ways to spend time with her."

"Really? I guess I hadn't noticed that. I only thought of them as work friends."

"Perhaps that's all there is to it, but I can't discount Eito's words or discernment entirely. You know he sees things others don't see. Kind of like Kizzy does, but in a different way."

Suki giggled. "He is an odd little man in some ways, but I truly love him."

Andrew shrugged. "Maybe there is a little something between Mother and Drake. That's probably all Eito saw. But if they were going to get together surely they would have done so by now."

"I'm sure you're right." She changed the subject. "How are things going with the investigation?"

He shifted Melville on his lap so he could cross his legs. "Things are going nowhere in the investigation. I got so excited when Janine told me about Bruce Steele, after Sonny found his store had also experienced thefts, and when Carly shared that she'd made Sonny's grandfather aware of a store theft she saw. The police kicked into high gear looking for Steele but he seems to have vanished. Simply disappeared without a trace."

She bit her lip. "What does that mean?"

"It means there is still no real proof Bruce Steele murdered Marvin Donelson. Thousands of questions have been asked of all the staff at Bay Street Antiques, but no one saw anything or heard anything. They've found no blood or evidence in the store of a murder committed there. They found no other evidence to prove that Bruce Steele replaced the gemstones in any of the rings in our store or Sonny's. It's discouraging."

He closed his eyes, leaning his head back against the chair. "We really have no sure way of knowing if either the thief or the murderer really was Steele. As Detective Dunnings said in that sanctimonious tone of his Bruce Steele might have only stolen the one ring. He was young. The young are often foolish and do foolish things."

She put her hands on her hips. "Surely he doesn't really believe that's all there is to it this with all the evidence now uncovered?"

"Whether he does or doesn't isn't a factor in the case. It's only here-say evidence with nothing proven or solid."

"Couldn't they trace Bruce through his school in Charleston or through his address?"

"A Bruce Steele did become a student and register for classes. He only took a course or two each semester. He did live in an apartment down the street from the school. According to his landlady, he paid his bills, lived quietly but skipped out on his lease in March. Evidently he used falsified identification, or so the police said."

"What does that mean?"

"There really is no Bruce Steele. It was a created identity, the name and social security taken from nursing home records in another state. It's a common method for identity theft now." He frowned. "As another oddity, the landlady at the apartment said a woman lived with Steele—or at least stayed there a lot. However, she didn't know her name or anything about her. Probably another reason Steele didn't want to take Janine or Carly back to his apartment. He told them it was a dump, but it was actually a nice apartment, according to Detective Dunnings. So everything about Steele was basically a lie. That's the way professional thieves operate."

"Yet, knowing all that, the detective still doubts that Bruce Steele is guilty of the thefts and possibly the murder?"

Andrew rubbed his neck. "Dunnings has to say professionally only what proof he's found and it's scanty. Which leaves everything still hanging in the investigation."

"I hate that." Suki bit at one of her nails. "Do you think they will find him eventually?"

"Everyone certainly hopes so. No one likes an open case. That means whoever stole and replaced the stones in the rings and whoever killed Marvin Donelson is still out there somewhere, where he can continue the same crimes."

She sighed. "Well, at least everyone in Beaufort believes this man was the thief and the murderer and not you, Parker, or anyone else at Westcott's. You and Sonny Donelson are friends again, too, and his family has apologized for their behavior."

"That's the one plus in all this."

She yawned. "I'm tired. Let's go to bed." She slipped her feet into her slippers, straightened the cushions on the sofa, and came over to kiss him. "You know Eito, Marri, Ken, and Julianne are staying at the Sandpiper, at our house. But would you mind if I go down to the island with Mother to stay at Oleanders for the rest of the time while they are are visiting? I want to spend time with them, take them to some tourist attractions."

"That's a wonderful idea. You should go, and staying at Oleanders with your mother will continue to give them some privacy at our place." He got up and shifted Melville back into the chair, still asleep. "I want them to have a good time. They've all been such a blessing to us."

"I agree." She smiled at him.

He put his arm around her as they started for the stairs, switching off the downstairs lights as they left. "I hope you'll practice at Oleanders while staying with your mother, too. Your old piano is still there. The concert in Atlanta is next month. I know you got word from them about the exact pieces they want you to play."

"I did. I'm doing all Beethoven Piano Sonatas, because the orchestra is doing a Beethoven tribute night. I know most all the pieces on the list already; I've played them before. But I will need to practice a lot before then. Will you come to Atlanta with me?"

He kissed her. "I wouldn't miss it for the world. I'm so glad you're playing again."

CHAPTER 20

Saturday, May 21ˢᵗ, the following week

"**D**id Suki's friends have a good time visiting at Edisto and seeing the sights last week?" Parker asked Andrew over a week later. They were working the store together this Friday since Drake and Nora had driven to Columbia to attend the big estate sale.

"Eito, Marri, Ken, and Julianne all had a wonderful time and they hope to come back next summer," he answered.

"I'm glad," Parker said, walking over to wipe fringerprints off an antique table.

Changing the subject, Andrew asked, "Have you heard from Drake and Nora?"

"I got a text from Nora earlier that they'd arrived and that the sale looked like an excellent one. I imagine they'll find some good pieces for the store." He walked back behind the register to sit on one of the stools beside Andrew.

"Drake said the sale was at an old plantation house in Richland County outside Columbia," Andrew said. "The owners, both elderly, had tried to keep the place going by conducting tours, but now wanted to sell out. Drake heard some business is purchasing the entire property and may incorporate the old house and grounds into its plan for a golf resort. At this estate sale, the family is selling out a houseful of antique furniture and a wide array of china, glassware, crystal, collectibles, and jewelry. Nora is good at sorting through small items to know what to buy and Drake has an eye for what furniture to bid on. I'm sure they'll come home with our store truck crammed with new items for the store."

Parker took a sip from his big coffee mug on the store counter. "I think I read Kyle Richardson's big auction house in Columbia, a business we've worked with before, is handling the auction."

"Yes, that's right. With the weather fair, Drake said they were bringing many items out of the house to display in big tents."

Parker nodded. "I've been to events like that before. Of course, the auction house will have its people everywhere to watch over the goods and answer questions." He sorted through a pile of circulars on the counter by the register as they talked. "Some of these big estate sales last several days, but this sale is a one-day event. Drake says there will be a crowd of buyers and dealers there."

"Drake loves those events though." Andrew smiled. "It's good he could drive the truck so Farris wouldn't have to follow them with it."

"Yes. Drake and Nora drove up early so they could have plenty of time to see all the items to be sold before the auction begins."

"The actual auction starts at two, doesn't it, after giving everyone ample time to look around?" Andrew asked. "Even if the auction lasts several hours, I guess they should both be back by the time we close or shortly after."

Parker nodded and then went to talk to a group of customers milling around in the store. It was Friday, always a busy day at Westcott's.

That evening after work, when Andrew and Suki were fixing salad to go with the enchiladas baking in the oven, Parker called.

"Andrew, have you heard from your mother?" he asked.

"No, but you can call or text her." He grinned. "I've been teaching her to text and she's getting pretty good at it."

"I *have* tried to call and text both her and Drake. I'm not getting any answer. I haven't heard from either of them since this morning."

Andrew sat down on the stool at the kitchen counter. "Maybe they've just been really busy, Parker. Those big estate sales are often hectic."

"That's true," he agreed. "However, I spoke with the auction house and the sale ended some time ago. Most of the buyers and dealers have left the grounds."

"You're worried about this, aren't you? Why?"

Parker hesitated. "I'm not sure, but something doesn't feel right. Drake always calls me, excited to tell me about things he's bid on and purchased, and he always calls to keep me in touch with when he'll be back to unload at the store. If he buys a lot of merchandise, I call Farris to come help unload."

"Do you want me to try to contact Mother? To call or text her?"

"It wouldn't hurt. Maybe if they see we're both worried, they'll check in."

"What else can I do?"

"Nothing for now, but I'm going to make a few other calls from the house here. I have a private phone number for the owner of the auction house in Columbia. I think I'll call him, see if he went over to the auction or talked to Drake. He knows him well."

Suki took the enchiladas out of the oven and sat the dish on top of the stove.

"I'll text Mom before Suki and I sit down to eat dinner. Will you call me if you hear anything?"

"I will. They probably just got busy, like you said, or stopped for dinner somewhere on the way back from Columbia. Enjoy your supper and give Suki my love," he added and then hung up.

"Was that Parker?" Suki asked, putting enchiladas and some big dollops of sour cream and guacamole on their plates. "Is everything all right?"

"Parker hasn't heard anything from Drake or Mother since this morning and it worries him."

They carried their plates over to the table by the kitchen window to eat, a pleasant spot where they could look out over the back yard. Suki had already put a big bowl of salad on the table, some chopped watermelon, and glasses of iced tea.

"Are they just late getting back?" she asked.

"Yes, I guess so. They might have stopped to eat or gotten caught up in traffic. What bothers Parker is that they didn't check in like they usually do, and he's tried calling and texting them with no answer." Andrew paused to call and text his mother and Drake, too.

"Funny. I'm not getting any answer from them either," he said after a few minutes.

"There's probably some good explanation," she said.

He agreed but he felt a little troubled about it through dinner.

At around eight, Parker called him back. "Have you heard anything from either Drake or your mother?" he asked.

"No, are they not back yet?"

He heaved an audible sigh. "No, and I'm really concerned, Andrew. Kyle Richardson, who owns the auction company that conducted the estate sale, did go out to the site today to help with the event. He saw Drake and Nora earlier today, spoke to them, but said they neither one placed any bids at the auction. He checked his records. He didn't see either of them at the auction in the afternoon, either. Kyle told me he assumed they hadn't found pieces or merchandise they wanted to bid on and went home."

"What?" Andrew asked, a prickle of alarm sliding over him. "If that's so, they would have been back to the store long before we closed at five."

"Yes." Parker hesitated. "I don't mean to overly alarm you, but I've contacted the police department in Eastover in Richland County, the closest town to the estate sale plantation site to report them missing. I sent the department descriptive information, the license plate of the truck, and photos. Since they don't believe Drake and Nora may be in danger, they probably won't start a search for them, at least until tomorrow, but they are now noted as missing. I admit Claire and I are seriously worried about this. I've worked with Drake and Nora for a very long time. It is not like either of them to cut out of an auction they'd looked forward to for months. It isn't like them, either, to not check in with me if they decided to explore another venue or event and it isn't like either of them to not let me know if they would return late."

Andrew got up from his chair to pace. "What can we do, Parker?"

"I don't know, but I think I'll drive up to Columbia and over to the plantation in Eastover early tomorrow morning, if Drake and Nora haven't returned or we haven't heard from them. I want to stop by the police department, check out the area, talk to people near the estate sale site and at the auction house in Columbia."

Andrew's mind swirled then with lurid possibilities. "Do you think there's been foul play, that something's happened to them?"

"I don't know," Parked replied. "There's no need to get more alarmed than needed right now. One of them might have gotten sick, cutting their trip short unexpectedly or their truck might have broken down. A lot of things can change plans and cause people to be late getting home."

"Maybe I should drive up tonight?"

Parker cleared his throat. "There's little you could do in the dark, Andrew, and it would be pitch dark by the time you arrived. The morning will be soon enough. I'll head to Columbia then."

"I want to go with you," Andrew said.

"I'll need someone to cover the store," Parker answered with a practical tone.

"I'll call Janine or Ira Dean. If either of them can cover, can I go with you?"

He sighed. "I suppose so. I know you're as concerned as I am, maybe more so since your mother is missing, as is Drake."

Andrew filled Suki in on the situation when he hung up, then sat down in his chair to call Janine first about covering at the store.

"Tomorrow is Saturday. I don't have any classes," Janine told him. "I can come to open and close the store if I can pick up a key. I'm down on Bay Street right now with some friends. We had dinner and we're just hanging out. I can swing by your house to get a key if you want, save you bringing one over to me." She paused. "I really hope Drake and Nora are okay. I know you and Parker must be horribly worried."

"We are concerned," he said, downplaying the situation. "I really appreciate you giving up your Saturday to come work at the store for us."

"No problem," she assured him.

When he hung up, Suki said, "I'll go over to the store at mid morning before things get busy to help Janine, too. Saturdays can be hectic at Westcott's. I learned as a girl, hanging out in the store with Parker, to run a cash register and I can talk to customers and keep an eye on the upstairs if anyone goes up there to look around. It will be easier for Janine if I help."

"Thank you," Andrew said, seeing the wisdom of her suggestion.

"This is so awful. What if something has happened to them?" Tears began to trickle down her face.

"Let's try not to get overly concerned yet. They'll probably call or show up before the night's over with a good explanation."

But they didn't.

Having slept little, Andrew got up, dressed, and made breakfast really early. Parker called at six to see if he was ready to leave, and they soon hit the road. They'd arrive in Eastover in a little over two hours.

Eastover was a small town, east of Columbia, an old historic town settled in the 1700s, with a number of gracious old plantations, the Magnolia Plantation, Wavering Place, Beulah and Minerva Plantations, all built by early families on the Congaree and Wateree rivers. Most of these old homes had been lost to time but some had been saved and preserved, often as bed and breakfasts. With the town only having about eight hundred in population, the small police department downtown on Henry Street wasn't hard to find.

Parker and Andrew talked to one of the officers there, who agreed to go with them to look around the old plantation grounds. The Richwoods Plantation, where the estate sale had been held, lay on a big expanse of land along the Wateree River off McCords Ferry Road. A caretaker lived in a small house near the fenced entrance to the property and he agreed to let them in to explore.

"This here was a fine, fine plantation in its day," Sergeant Bivens said to them as they parked their cars to get out. He'd gotten keys from the caretaker to get into the house and any locked outbuildings around the grounds. "The McCord family kept the place up real nice. Most of these old places didn't fare as well as this." He walked them toward the big house. "Gregor McCord was a judge, a real respected man. His wife Lola Ray did a lot of good philanthropic things to benefit the town."

Andrew and Parker hardly cared about the history of the estate but they didn't want to alienate the sergeant to say so. Parker had experienced enough trouble getting him to come and look around the estate.

The sergeant waved a hand. "You can see all the tent holes out there in the yard where the auction house set things up. I didn't come out yesterday for the sale but one of the deputies did. These big auction houses like extra security on hand. It's not likely much can happen with so many security eyes around."

He turned to them as they started up the row of steps to the wide, stately home and grinned. "I saw in the information you submitted that both this man and woman missing was single. Are you sure they didn't just run off together?" He laughed at his own words.

Parker lifted an eyebrow, not laughing. "Drake Jenkins and Nora Cavanaugh are responsible, middle-aged, professionals, not young kids. So, no, that isn't a possibility."

"That love bug can bite all ages." He chuckled again, opening the door to the big house to them.

With the sergeant's escort they walked through the house, virtually empty now, watching for anything that might offer them a clue to Nora and Drake's disappearance, but found nothing. Outside, they walked the grounds but didn't find any clues or pieces of evidence to tell them Nora and Drake had ever been there.

"Don't know what you expected to find here," the sergeant said, patiently following them around or leaning against his car to watch them. "Wherever these folks might be, I'm certain it wouldn't be here. We've done talked to a few locals around the area, showed some pictures in the diner and to the deputy that came out to help with the sale. Nobody seems to recall seeing or talking to them."

"Well, I appreciate you bringing us out here," Parker said. "We feel better for looking around where they were last seen."

"Yeah, Kyle Richardson from over at the auction house called and he said for us to be nice and helpful to you. I reckon you'll be heading over to his place in Columbia next?"

Parker glanced at his watch. "Yes. The auction house should be open now. Kyle said we could talk with some of his people who were here yesterday at the sale."

After leaving the plantation house, they cut over to one of the main highways into Columbia and soon made their way to Richardson's big auction house.

"Nice place," Andrew said as they drove up. "I hope we'll learn something here when talking to Richardson's people. We certainly didn't find a clue at the plantation house or around the grounds. I don't know what I thought we might find there, but I hoped we might find something."

"So did I," Parker agreed.

Parker and Andrew had walked around downtown in Eastover themselves before leaving, showing photos of Drake and Nora. Nobody recalled seeing them, just as the sergeant had said.

Kyle Richardson, a portly but distinguished middle-years man with a nearly bald head and a welcoming smile, led them back to his office to talk. He took them to the break room for coffee before they settled down in chairs in his office.

"I sure can't understand this," Kyle said, leaning back in the chair behind his desk. "I talked to Drake yesterday morning when all the dealers and buyers were milling around. He seemed excited about a number of items. I saw Nora, too, looking through china and an array of collectibles on tables under the tents, taking notes, obviously interested. It sure surprised me when I didn't see them bidding later at the auction. I actually looked around for them but never saw them. I don't know what else I can tell you."

Andrew leaned forward. "Did any of your people see them later? Notice that they were upset? See either of them get injured or anything?" He looked at Parker. "We haven't checked at the closest hospital to the auction house. Perhaps we should."

Parker nodded. "We can do that. But I can't imagine if either got sick or injured, and taken to the hospital, that we wouldn't have also been contacted. I know Drake would have called if something happened to Nora, or vice versa."

"I guess you're right," Andrew admitted.

Kyle Richardson scratched his head. "There are a few other auctions and sales going on around the southeast area right now, some only an hour or so away, but like you, I wouldn't imagine Drake would take off and go to any of them without contacting you." He shook his head. "I sure do hope nothing bad has happened, but I can't imagine anything happened at the sale. We keep a lot of security working at these big events, our own people, a deputy or officer from the local police station, extra help we hire through an agency. There are a couple of small companies that have trained people to come in and help with these larger events. They help man the tent areas, station themselves around the house and property, assist with parking cars and such. We get several hundred or more dealers, buyers, and visitors at these big sales. You can't be too careful."

Parker smiled at him. "I know you run a highly professional auction company, Kyle. I've been to many of your events. You, your staff, and extra help do a great job with everything. Including security. I didn't mean to imply your company is in any way responsible for Drake and Nora being missing."

"No, and I don't blame you for coming to ask questions." He shook his head. "You must both be about worried sick over this. I sure do hope you or the police get some answers soon. I've asked a couple of my people to talk with you that saw Drake and Nora yesterday. Several know them from past events. Do you want to speak with them now? We're glad to do anything we can to help you with this."

Andrew and Parker talked with three other staff members but learned no new information to help them. While at Richardson's, they also called to check the hospitals near Eastover and even several hospitals off the interstate heading back to Beaufort, but found no further clues.

"This doesn't make sense," Andrew said as they got back in the car. "People don't simply disappear."

Parker scowled. "Evidently they do. I sure can't think what else to do. Kyle recommended a private detective in this area that he knows. The man's name is Hiram Landers."

"Are we going to go see him now?"

"Not right now, but I called and made an appointment for later. The man's office is actually in Cayce, southeast of Columbia and practically on our way back home, so I told him we'd come there. It's in Richland County, too, not far from Eastover. If we need to go back to Eastover with him, its only about thirty miles. For now, we have time to grab some lunch."

Parker pulled out his phone to hunt for a restaurant nearby. After a few minutes he said, "There's a Cracker Barrel not far from Cayce. How about that? We have time to get a decent meal, and we can talk there."

"Sounds good to me."

At the Cracker Barrel, they actually said very little at first, both mulling over their own thoughts, frustrated at so little progress. Worried, too. They ordered and ate, mostly reviewing what they'd already learned while eating lunch, trying to think what might have happened to Drake and Nora.

"If I let my mind run free with this, I feel sick," Andrew finally admitted.

"Well, don't go there. Claire and I prayed last night. You and I prayed on the way up here." He grinned at Andrew. "By the way, I'm glad to know you're a praying man."

"Yes, sir. I believe God is working on this, even if we don't see results yet. I want to stand in that. I'm sure if Mother is in trouble in some way, she's been praying."

They finished their lunch. And then Parker's phone rang.

He pulled it out of his back pocket. "Parker Avery here," he answered.

Andrew couldn't hear the caller's words but he watched a smile of relief cross Parker's face.

"Yes, Sergeant Bivens. We're still in the area, only about thirty miles from you. We can be there in in about twenty minutes."

Andrew heard a little muffled conversation in the background and then heard Parker chuckle. "Yes, sir, I know Drake Hartwell can be stubborn and outspoken. Let's just go along with him for now."

He hung up and waved at their waitress for their ticket. "They've found Drake and Nora. Come on, let me pay our bill and I'll tell you the rest on the way."

"Thank God," Andrew said with relief. "Are they all right?"

Parker laughed, heading to the register. "Sounds like it. Drake felt well enough to argue. That's a good sign."

After they paid their bill and headed out of the parking lot, Parker continued, "Sergeant Bivens said someone locked them in the back of the Westcott's truck after driving the truck down a remote backroad on the plantation to a swampy spot along the river. The plantation caretaker was fishing on the river in an old boat a little while ago, saw the vehicle on the bank, recognized it from the pictures we showed him earlier today, and called Sergeant Bivens. The sergeant headed out there with another deputy and they found Drake and Nora locked in the back of the truck. They'd been there since yesterday around noon, but Drake stubbornly refused to be taken to the hospital to be checked out."

"Was Mother all right, too?"

"I gather they're both good, considering. I'm sure we'll get the whole story when we get there."

The next hour went by in a whirl. The caretaker met them at the gate to the old plantation and drove them down to the river in his truck.

"You don't want to take that nice car of yours down that old muddy road," he said. "A truck can get down there, but you wouldn't want to be getting stuck there. Bad swampy area back there. Snakes around the river, too. Best you drive with me."

They arrived to find Drake and Nora waiting with Sergeant Bivens. His mother had already insisted on getting her purse out of the car to freshen up and she looked surprisingly good for someone who'd spent the night in the back of a delivery truck. Drake seemed positively perky.

Andrew hugged both his mother and Drake with relief, and wiped away a few tears when no one was looking. "We're so glad you're okay," he said. "What happened?"

Drake answered for her. "Let's go down to the police station with the sergeant, and we'll tell it once to everyone. Nora and I would like to head home, as you'd imagine, and neither of us wants to stand around here in this swamp visiting. We've already been swatting mosquitoes while waiting on you two to arrive."

Sergeant Bivens suggested again that Drake and Nora go to the local hospital to be checked, but they both refused.

"I've told you we're both fine," Drake insisted, frowning. "I don't care what your protocol is."

The sergeant sent him a narrowed gaze. "Maybe not, but you're still required to come downtown to the police station to fill out paperwork on all that occurred. That's not arguable." He insisted Drake and Nora both ride into town in the back of his car, too, determined neither would give him the slip and take off.

"Dang stubborn man," the sergeant muttered to Parker. "You'd think the man would be more grateful we even found him out here. As remote and isolated as this backwater place is, they could have ended up here for days before somebody spotted the truck."

"We are grateful," Nora said, smiling at him. "If we acted less than gracious, I hope you'll overlook it. It's been a somewhat stressful and eventful night." She sent Drake a pointed look and surprisingly he winked and grinned at her.

She rolled her eyes at him before climbing into the sergeant's car.

Andrew and Parker rode with the caretaker back to their car and then transferred to Parker's car to follow the sergeant into town.

At the police station Drake and Nora got a chance to freshen up in the bathroom before questioning, and one of the officers went around the corner to a local diner to buy them sandwiches and soup.

After eating a little, Drake looked around at them and began his account. "Yesterday after I finished looking through all the furniture and large items to be auctioned in the afternoon, I went to find Nora. She was looking through china, collectibles, and jewelry in one of the tents. While waiting for her, I wandered over to a nearby table loaded with estate jewelry that a young man was handling. As I asked him about a few pieces of interest, I happened to glance at his hand and noticed he was wearing a striking cat's eye ring—the very same cat's eye ring missing from our store to be exact. I studied the young man then, noticing he matched the description Janine and Carly gave of Bruce Steele as well as the school photo the police found that I also saw."

He took a long drink of water before continuing. "I began to study the jewelry on his table then. I picked up several of the rings to look at them more carefully. Having talked to Brimer several times while he examined more of our jewelry inventory, I knew more what to look for in order to tell if stones might have been replaced."

Drake crossed an ankle over his knee. "Nora came over to join me, and while I finished talking with the young man, she glanced at his hand and saw the ring, too."

"I acted foolish then," Nora interrupted. "Without thinking, I said, 'that ring looks just like one we used to have in our store at Westcott's.'"

"I'm sure I must have rolled my eyes at her over the remark, an equally dumb move," Drake put in. "I saw the young man tense and go on alert. I grabbed Nora's arm and directed her away from the table, but in looking back I could see he was watching us."

Drake paused. "By asking a few questions discreetly from staff working at the sale, we learned his name, Cameron Rembert, and that he was working with the Hartung Agency. That's one of the security agencies hired to work at various estate sales. I'd seen the Hartung truck parked to the side of the parking lot when we came in, so I came up with the bright idea of going over to get the truck's license plate number before we spoke to the deputy or any of Richardson's security men on the property."

"It wasn't a totally bad idea," Nora said, defending him. "We both feared he might bolt after seeing us. If he did, having a license plate number for the police to trace would really help."

Drake continued. "The man must have been discreetly following us, because he slipped up behind us with a gun when we moved out of sight of the crowd to head around the side of the truck." He sighed. "I knew the man had killed before, so when he told us to walk casually to our truck parked nearby, I went along. He insisted we get into the back of our truck and then he locked us in. I thought he'd done that to make time to get in his own truck and flee."

"Instead, we heard our truck start up and realized he was taking us somewhere," Nora said. "I got scared then, thinking he might be planning to murder us somewhere away from the crowds. That thought grew stronger when I could feel the truck soon driving down a rutted, back road."

Drake interrupted. "I looked around for a possible weapon, trying to get prepared for whatever was to come, but the man didn't open the back of the truck after it stopped. Instead, all we could hear was continuing silence as the minutes ticked by and the sound of the river. He must have walked back to the plantation."

"Yeah, he only took you about a mile and a half away," the sergeant added. "But down that old road no one would have seen your truck or heard you if you hollered for help as loud as you could. Like you said, he evidently left you and walked back out."

"We figured that out after a time," Nora said. "We also realized that Cameron Rembert, aka Bruce Steele, probably left the sale after returning. Of course he might have had to wait for a ride back in the Hartung Agency truck after the auction completed since he probably didn't come to the estate sale alone."

Drake handed a slip of paper to the sergeant. "Here's the license plate number. He took our cellphones and keys away from us before locking us in the truck, but this scrap of paper was in my shirt pocket."

The sergeant pulled his belt up over his belly. "This will help, but the man may have fled again by now, like you told me he did in Beaufort." He looked toward Parker and Andrew. "Drake filled me in on all that story while we waited for you two, but I needed to get it all official you understand."

"I can't think of anything else to tell you," Drake said. "Can you, Nora?"

She sighed. "I do remember one more thing, what he said to Drake and me when he held that gun on us and told us to get in the back of the truck. He said, 'You know I killed before; be smart and don't tempt me to do it again.'"

"That was a little telling," Parker said. "I hope you will pass those words that Nora heard and this report along to Detective Dunnings and Sergeant Metler in Beaufort. This will link directly to their investigation."

Drake finished off the last bite of his sandwich and asked, "When can we get our truck, sergeant?"

"I had some men pick it up while we talked. We dusted it for prints everywhere we could. You said your prints, Nora's prints, and others on staff at Westcott's were on file in Beaufort, so we'll look to see if any new ones turn up. You also said the man didn't have gloves on. We might get lucky over that." He patted the file on his desk. "I think that's all I need from you folks. If I think of something to ask further, I'll get in touch with you."

As they headed out the door, Nora said. "I surely am looking forward to getting home again." She hugged Andrew. "How wonderful that you and Parker came looking for us. We heard that because the caretaker, Mr. Owen, had seen the pictures of the Westcott's delivery truck you showed him earlier, he recognized it on the riverbank when he saw it while fishing, and called the sergeant. Who knows how long we might have waited in the back of that truck if you hadn't come to look for us as you did."

"We do owe you thanks for that," Drake said. "I also intend to do something fine for Mr. Owen, the caretaker, for reporting the truck. He could have just motored on his way down the river and chosen not to get involved."

"How did you manage in the truck overnight?" Parker asked, curious.

Drake grinned. "We keep old moving-blankets and buckets in that old truck, if you remember. It was a bit primitive, but we did all right. I'd stuck a case of bottled waters in the back as well, in case we needed them while at the estate sale, so we did have water."

"But no food," Nora added. "We got a little hungry and that's a fact."

As they neared the parking area, Andrew said, "I can drive the truck back, Mother, so you and Drake can ride back more comfortably with Parker."

Drake turned to give them an odd smile then. "Actually I think I'd like to drive the truck back and Nora may want to ride with me. We have a lot to talk about."

Andrew saw Parker's eyebrows lift.

Drake smiled at Andrew. "You see I compromised your mother, spending the night with her unchaperoned. So as a good Southern gentleman, I offered marriage and we're going to get married. We need to talk about plans for that."

"What?" Andrew knew his mouth dropped open. "That's ridiculous. This is the twenty-first century. No one goes by those old rules anymore, and it's not as though anything happened in that old truck overnight."

His mother blushed and looked down at her shoes.

Parker's lips twitched, as he tried not to smile. "Well, considering everything that's happened, perhaps a marriage *is* in order. Standing in stead for Nora's father and as her employer, I should probably insist on it. Unless Nora has an objection."

She crossed her arms nervously, avoiding Andrew's eyes. Finally, with a small smile, she said, "Well, Eito did say we'd be a good match. Drake and I discussed that and decided we agreed with him."

"What? You can't just up and get married over something like that." Andrew all but hollered.

Nora raised her chin to look at him directly. "I don't see why not, Andrew. You certainly did. And things seemed to work out rather well for you, didn't they?"

Flabbergasted, Andrew could hardly argue with her challenge.

Parker laughed out loud. "Well, this has certainly been an eventful two days. But if you all don't mind I'd like to head home. Personally I am worn out. You know everyone at home is worried and waiting for more news, too, even though I called Claire and asked her to tell everyone you were both safe."

Still feeling surly, Andrew mumbled, "They'll have another shock when you come home with this marriage news."

Drake walked closer to him, fixing him with a steely glance. "At least we're choosing to let our friends and family know *beforehand* about our wedding plans and we're inviting them to attend. Unless, of course, you don't want to come to your own mother's wedding."

"I didn't say that," Andrew replied, looking away from him.

"Good, because I want to make it perfectly clear that you and I both want the same thing, your mother's best happiness. Do you understand me?"

Andrew nodded.

"Well, perhaps you might offer us your congratulations."

"Yeah, sure." Shamed now by Drake's comments, Andrew moved to give his mother a hug. "I didn't mean to be ugly, Mom. You know I've always wanted you to marry again and to marry someone who would love and cherish you."

She smiled. "I think I discovered that man was nearby all along. We simply needed a little time together and a chance to see each other in a new way."

Drake put an arm around her. "And we certainly have done that." He grinned at Parker and Andrew. "Expect a wedding soon. Having wasted quite a number of years hoping your mother would notice me, I don't want to waste any more time."

His comments surprised Andrew again.

"Let's go home," Parker said, draping an arm over Andrew's shoulder as Drake and Nora walked over to climb into the delivery truck. "They'll be all right. And you'll be tickled about this once you get to thinking about it. The man has practically been a father to you all your life already. Keep that in mind."

"Yes, I suppose he has," Andrew said, watching with amazement as Drake kissed his mother before helping her into the truck.

CHAPTER 21

On Saturday while Parker and Andrew were away from Westcott's Antiques, Suki enjoyed getting to know Janine Albert better as they worked covering the store. She recognized the same love for antiques, beautiful old furniture and collectibles in Janine that she saw in Parker and Andrew. They had fun talking between customers.

"I still feel *so* bad about falling for Bruce Steele last summer and him turning out to be a thief and probably a murderer," Janine confessed. "That sure doesn't say much about my discernment with men, does it?"

"We all make mistakes with men," Suki said, as they sat on stools behind the register taking a break between customers. "I certainly made some, too. I fell hard for the agent managing my career, Jonah Dobrowski, and then saw him with someone else in a compromising situation. It made me feel like a real fool."

Janine looked up from the sales catalog she'd been browsing through. "Oh, that's awful. I'm sorry. I felt stupid when Bruce dropped me flat and started seeing Carly, too. I've had that happen often, I'm sorry to say." She paused, looking thoughtful. "It makes me remember a saying my Grandma used to make: You have to kiss a lot of toads to find a prince."

Suki laughed.

"I think you found yours already," Janine added, laughing, too. "I hope I meet someone nice someday myself."

"I'm sure you will."

Janine drummed her fingers on the table. She looked around and then dropped her voice, "It seems like all the boys I go out with want more on a date than I want to give, too. Do you know what I mean?"

"I think that's been a problem for women since the beginning of time." Suki smiled.

"Well I think it's a worse problem today with our society so permissive. Everyone says I'm old fashioned, but when I talked to my Grandma about it she snorted and said, 'Why buy the cow when you can get the milk for free?' It made me laugh, but I still think some things are better in marriage."

"My mother taught Mary Helen and me that no healthy, long-lasting relationship is built around sex. She also taught us there are benefits to both men and women in a committed relationship of marriage." She made a face, pausing. "I don't like to think of marriage in terms of either a man or woman 'buying' the other, but I do think, in anything, we feel better with a committed, contractual legal agreement. It sort of says, 'I'm serious about this relationship and I mean to commit to it and to you for life.'"

"I agree with that, too. I wish more people did." Janine got up to go talk with a group of customers coming in the store.

A little after noon, Suki walked down Craven Street and then cut south on Cataret to the Lowcountry Produce Market & Café to pick up lunch for herself and Janine. They'd both decided on Salad Samplers with a trio of egg, tuna, and chicken salad over mixed greens. Suki enjoyed the walk in the May sunshine and when she came back with their lunch, she and Janine settled down at the counter to eat between customers. Janine, with a high level of energy, had been dusting the store all day and adjusting various displays to make them more attractive.

"You have a very artful eye." Suki complimented her, noticing the way Janine had hung a cute wire bird cage in the front window and added other items to make the window display more appealing.

"Thanks." She smiled as she dug into her salad. "Nora taught me a lot about decorating and arrangement, and she gives me liberty to try out new things if I want to." She paused. "I hope she and Drake are okay. I've worried about them all day."

"Me, too," Suki said, getting up to help a couple from Missouri find the store's display of antique spoons. The lady, a Mrs. Reynolds, collected them and always tried to find new ones to take home whenever she and her husband traveled.

"That lady loved that old spoon with the South Carolina scene painted at the top," Janine said as the couple left. "You can buy newer ones like that just about anywhere at the little gift shops, but that one dated back to the 1800s. It was a treasure."

Suki's phone rang then and she snatched it up from the counter, glancing down at her phone to see her mother's number.

"Hi, Mother," she answered. "Have you heard anything from Parker and Andrew?"

"Yes, Parker just called," she replied, her voice excited. "Thank God, Drake and Nora are both safe. Parker said they recognized Bruce Steele working at the estate sale, tried to get a driver's license number before talking to a police officer, but Bruce followed them and pulled a gun on them. He locked them in the Westcott's truck, after taking away their phones and keys, drove the truck down some backwoods road on the plantation grounds and abandoned them. Thankfully they are both all right."

"Oh, how awful," Suki said. "Where are they now?"

"Heading to the police station to make a report. After that Parker says they can all head home. I know they'll tell us all more later, but Parker and Andrew wanted us all to know they are safe and well. I'm going to call Ira Dean, Mary Helen, and a few others who've been worried, too. Parker said he and Andrew should be back before the store closes."

"Did she say Drake and Nora are all right?" Janine asked as soon as Suki hung up.

"Yes. The call was good news." Suki repeated what Claire had said.

"What a relief." Janine fanned herself. "But how creepy for them to get locked in that old delivery truck overnight. It would have been dark and scary in there. Who found them?"

"Claire didn't say, but at least they're safe now. I know Andrew and Parker are glad they drove to Columbia so they could be a help, too. Everyone's been so worried. Anything could have happened."

A big group of customers came in the front door then, so both Janine and Suki moved out on the floor to greet and talk to them.

At about four-thirty after a long busy Saturday, the door opened again. Suki looked up from checking her cell phone for messages with shock to see Jonah Dobrowski walking into Westcott's. He was dressed in a neat pinstriped shirt tucked into khaki slacks, and he looked exactly as Suki remembered.

She tensed, grabbing Janine's hand without realizing it.

"What's wrong?" Janine whispered, glancing toward the man at the door.

"That's Jonah Dobrowski, the agent I was telling you about."

"Oh no." Janine turned to Suki. "Do you want to go hide in the back room and let me get rid of him?"

While she considered the idea, Jonah spotted her, a wide charming smile spreading across his face.

"No. He's seen me now," Suki said with resignation, watching him stride across the store. "I can talk to him. It will be all right."

"I'll stay right here with you," Janine promised.

"Actually, it might be better if you busy yourself cleaning or waiting on customers who come in and let me talk to him alone. It's an overdue conversation." She stood, taking a deep breath.

"Okay, but I won't go far." Janine whispered, hopping off the stool behind the register as Jonah came closer.

"Can I help you with something?" she asked, moving out from behind the counter.

"I'm here to see Sarah Katherine." His eyes moved past Janine's to hers.

Janine gave him a syrupy smile. "Well, I'm sure *Mrs. Cavanaugh* will be glad to speak with you."

Ignoring her, Jonah walked behind the counter to wrap Suki in a hug. "What a joy to find you here, Sarah. I drove all the way here from Charleston, where one of my artists has a performance tonight, just to see you. I planned to ask in the store for your phone or address. But here you are!"

Suki pushed him away. "What do you want, Jonah?"

He looked surprised at her tone. "I wanted to see you. I admit I still don't understand at all why you married suddenly and moved away without talking with me, why you cancelled your contract with Greenwood and with me." He gave her a wounded look. "I wasn't only your mangager, after all. We had a special personal relationship."

She made no comment as he hesitated, watching her.

He sighed then. "It hurt me, too, when you didn't want to see me at the hospital. I thought it because you were upset over fainting at the show and upset about being sick."

Jonah leaned against the counter, giving her all of his attention with those concerned eyes of his, that charming manner. What a snake.

He feigned a distressed look, stroking his short beard in a familiar gesture. "How could my Sarah treat me like that? Even if your affections had changed, why would you leave town without talking with me? Surely you know I would still want to represent you and your talent even if you married someone else? I don't understand any of this. Give me one reason to try to help me understand. Then maybe we can talk about it."

Suki watched him while he talked, seeing how artfully he worked to make a person feel special to him. Not at all concerned if he lied or if anything he said was true. How naïve she'd been before.

Jonah paused as if waiting for an answer.

"You asked me for one reason," she said finally. "Here is one reason: Nita."

"My little violinist?" He looked confused.

"Don't play stupid." She glared at him. "I saw you with her the night of the concert."

She saw his eyes widen and, could practically see the wheels in his head turning now looking for a smooth reply. "That was nothing, and little Nita is not like you, Sarah. She is somewhat of an opportunist, eager to try anything to boost her career."

"That description sounds like you as well. I imagine you'll make a perfect couple."

"Ouch, you are harsh." He put a hand to his heart, feigning hurt.

When she didn't reply he crossed his arms and gave her a smug look. "So you decided to get even with me by marrying your gay friend and running off?"

Suki laughed. "I can assure you Andrew is not gay, and the reasons why I chose to marry Andrew are my own. We've known each other since childhood, and surely even you realized the long-time affection between us."

He waved a hand. "Well, obviously I viewed the relationship as only a friendship. It must have bloomed into something more behind my back. Perhaps you had been being unfaithful to me, too?"

She felt like slapping him.

"No, that's your area of expertise."

He studied her as if deciding what approach to take next. "Well, despite any romantic problems, Sarah, you didn't need to walk out on your contract with me," he said at last. "I have been a good agent to you. I recognized the larger opportunity for your talent before anyone else did, signing you to Greenwood, and I managed your career for the last two years so that you attained an excellent reputation as a concert pianist. Despite your sarcastic remarks and obvious antagonism, you owe me thanks for that."

She considered his words. "Perhaps I do owe you some thanks. I offer that now, but I did decide in the hospital I didn't want to be on the concert tour any longer."

"Even if you don't want to tour as extensively, I can still manage you, Sarah. I have contacts that can help you. I know you've started to play again. You played here for the Beaufort Symphony and I know you are performing in Atlanta with the symphony next month. I can work with you to add more shows to your schedule, to be sure everything is set up as it should be for each performance, and to attain good media coverage for you and better recognition. You know I can do that."

Suki tried to think how to answer. Jonah always had a hard time taking no for an answer. In the past he'd used so many artful techniques to bulldoze her into doing what he wanted, making her think his plans were the best for her, when they were really more about what was best for him. "Jonah, I'd hoped not to be this direct, but I simply do not want you for an agent anymore. In any capacity."

"Why?" he interrupted.

"For many reasons, none you will probably like," she replied. "An agent should be someone you can trust not to exploit you for his gain by overscheduling you. An agent shouldn't be someone who would send you on stage sick again and again, endangering your health and future. An agent should also be someone who does not use his position to convince you he holds more interest in you than he does."

He shrugged. "That is the industry, Sarah. The way things are. A good agent knows he needs to heavily schedule a new talent to move them into the public's view, to gain recognition for them. All musicians push their clients to perform, often when tired and sick. That's the way it is in the professional world. As for the latter accusation, I wasn't insincere. I fell a little in love with you. Who knows where those affections would have gone in time."

She shook her head. "People in love don't cheat with others, Jonah."

He ran a hand through his hair. "Constancy is not a common trait in the entertainment field. It's naïve of you to expect to see that."

Annoyed at his condescending tone, she said, "Then I am naïve. I want constancy in a relationship and I expect it."

He smirked. "You expect your Andrew to be constant?"

"Yes. She does and he will," said a menacing voice.

Suki's eyes widened to see Andrew walking toward them. He'd obviously come in the back entrance.

To her amazement, Andrew snatched Jonah up from the stool by his shirt. Glaring down at him, he said, "I've had a really bad day and coming home to find you here insulting Suki and me doesn't make it any better."

Jonah jerked away from him. "I told you earlier I had a right to talk with Sarah Katherine myself about her contract."

"She has *no* contract, and you are not her agent anymore. I think I overheard her telling you some of the reasons why."

Jonah actually shook a fist at Andrew then. "Don't be a fool. I *made* her. She was just a little college performer before I signed her. A few shows here and there will hardly take her back to a true concert pianist level now without a good agent and a solid agency behind her. If you cared about Sarah at all, you'd encourage her to sign with me. She needs me and I can take her to greatness."

"No, I disagree. You almost killed her, pushing her until she collapsed, exploiting her in her career and with her emotions."

Jonah clenched his other fist. "You have no right to talk to me like that."

"I have every right. I'm her husband and protector. If I'd known all you'd done to hurt her before, I'd have done this in the hospital." Andrew's fist plowed neatly into Jonah's nose then, knocking him to the floor.

"Are you crazy?" Jonah said, putting a hand to his nose, which had started to bleed profusely.

Andrew stayed in a poised position, practically daring Jonah to get up. "No, I am not crazy, and I want you to get up and get out of my store. Parker and I told you before that Suki didn't want to see you or talk to you. Her attorney also told your agency the same, after telling them about your rude and angry call here. I doubt the Greenwood Agency would like to learn you had been here harassing my wife in my place of business in front of my employees."

Janine walked over with a little smile. "Here's a tissue," she said, offering one to Jonah. "Would you like a hand up?"

He snorted, but took the tissue to begin mopping at his nose.

Suki, her knees starting to shake, sat back down on the stool behind the counter.

"Are all of you crazy?" Jonah asked, pushing himself up from the floor. "If I never see any of you again, it will be too soon." He strode across the room toward the door then, slamming the front door hard behind him as he passed through.

Janine put both hands together and clapped. "Oh, you were wonderful Andrew! I'm so glad you came when you did. I hated listening to all those hateful things that man had started to say to Suki."

Andrew walked over to put his hands on Suki's face. "Are you all right?"

"Yes," she said and then began to cry a little. "I'm glad you came when you did, though. Jonah started out with his usual charm, but then he started to get a little nasty."

"You didn't have to talk to him at all," Andrew said, hugging her.

"I suppose it was overdue that I did. Now I don't have to battle fear about running into him again, wondering what I'd say." She pulled away to look at him. "Did you hurt your fist?"

He flexed it. "If I did, it was worth it."

Janine heaved a dramatic sigh. "Andrew, I never imagined you the fighting, chivalrous sort at all. But you were awesome, just like in a movie."

He laughed. "It wasn't exactly a romantic scene, Janine, but the last two days have been so stressful and full of emotion that I guess I'd just run out of my usual patience and diplomacy."

"You *were* romantic, though," Suki added.

He smiled back at her.

"Since that awful man is gone, sit down and tell us how Drake and Nora are doing," Janine asked, "Are they with Parker?"

Andrew dropped down on the stool beside Suki, while Janine leaned on the counter near by. "Parker dropped me off here and then drove on home to see Claire." His eyes moved to Suki's. "I encouraged him to go on home, told him I'd close the store and ride home with you, Suki. Drake and Nora drove the truck back.

I don't think they're home yet, but I'm sure they won't come here when they get back. They're both exhausted and still wearing the clothes they wore yesterday."

"Tell us what happened," Suki said. "You know we want to know."

Andrew related the whole story to them of Drake and Nora seeing Bruce Steele and how they ended up in the truck after. He did leave off the latter part of his story about Drake and Nora getting married. He'd tell Suki that later.

"I'm so glad Nora and Drake are okay," Suki said when he finished.

"What a story," Janine added, shaking her head. "Looking back, I'm really lucky I didn't get further involved with Bruce Steele either." She shivered. "It gives me the creeps just thinking about it now. I wonder if Cameron Reichert is really Bruce Steele's's real name anyway. He surely is a con artist."

"And probably more than just a con artist if he murdered Marvin Donelson." Andrew glanced at the clock. "It's nearly six now Janine. You go on home. Suki and I will lock up." He reached out a hand to take hers. "Thanks again for giving up your Saturday to come in and help us. Parker said to expect double pay for pitching in for an emergency."

"Oh, you don't need to do that," she said, reaching under the counter to get her purse. "I was happy to help."

"Well, think of the extra money as a little perk. And we look forward to having you work for us again this summer, too."

"I'll stop by to talk to Nora about my hours before the month is out," she said.

Andrew saw Janine out, locked the door behind her and turned the sign in the window to Closed. The he walked back across the store and pulled Suki up from her seat to wrap her in his arms and kiss her. "Gosh I'm glad to see you."

"I'm glad to see you, too." She gave him a teasing smile. "You were my big hero this afternoon. As Janine said, just like in a romance movie."

"I don't regret hitting him." Andrew scowled. "That little weasel had it coming. I still can't believe he came in here at the store to bother you like he did." He moved over to the counter to begin closing out the register. "What was he doing in Beaufort?"

"He said one of his artists was performing in Charleston tonight, probably with the Charleston Symphony. I don't keep up with the artists he manages anymore." She leaned against the counter watching him, weary from the stress of the day. "Why don't I take you out to dinner tonight? We're both tired. It would be nice to just relax and look out over the river. Let's go to Saltus River Grill on the waterfront. I'm in the mood for their sea scallops, gnocchi, and sugar snap peas. What do you say? You like that restaurant, too."

"That sounds like a great idea. Let me call ahead and get them to put us on the waiting list for a table outside." He pulled his phone out of his back pocket. "It's only six now. The big dinner crowd won't start to arrive until six-thirty and after."

They locked up the store, turned out the lights, and drove down to find a parking spot near the restaurant on Bay Street. After arriving the waiter took them to a shaded outdoor table looking across the Beaufort River and the Henry Chambers Waterfront Park. Beaufort offered many urban seafood grills like this along the riverfront.

After they ordered Suki told Andrew more about her encounter with Jonah and candidly related the details of their conversation.

"Perhaps we won't see any more of Jonah after this," Andrew commented.

She stirred her tea thoughtfully, looking out to watch a sailboat glide toward the marina. "Do you think Jonah is right, that by not choosing to work with an agent and an agency that I'm throwing away my chances for any real success as a pianist?"

"I don't know. There are different types of success," he replied. "I suppose it depends on what you want. You could go back on tour with another agent and another agency if you like. I'll support you in anything you want to do. I hope you know that."

Their food arrived, and they talked to the waiter for a few minutes before Suki added more. "I don't want that heavy life of travel all over the United States and abroad right now. But I do hope I can continue to get opportunities to perform. Maybe Morgan would help to manage my schedule. He did before when I was in high school and college. He has a lot of connections."

"You could talk to him. You know Parker, Claire, and I will help in any way we can, too. Your gift will make a way for itself."

"I hope so. For now, I'm just happy to be playing again and to be free from Jonah."

They ate dinner, Andrew catching Suki up on more facts of the day. As he spoke of leaving the police station in Eastover to head home, she noticed he grew quiet, picking at the remaining food on his plate.

"Something's bothering you, Andrew. Tell me what it is."

He sighed. "Drake and Nora are getting married."

She knew her mouth dropped open. "What?"

"It's true." He filled her in on what Drake had said and how Nora responded.

She giggled, stopping when she saw Andrew frown. "How could you be upset over this? You love Drake. Surely you know he'll be good to your mother. You've wanted her to find someone. And she has."

"It's just so sudden."

She thought about it. "No more sudden than our marriage, and maybe less so, remembering what Drake said to you. Besides, Eito said they were a perfect match, and you know he has a great track record."

"I suppose."

"Well, I think it's lovely," she added. "I'm crazy about them both and the more I think about it, the more I like the idea of them together. Drake has that nice house over at Habersham, too. You and I have been there many times. So has Nora. Drake's house looks out over the river in back, and that whole Habersham area is beautiful with walking trails, a town center, and parks throughout. It's perfect for them, and it's marvelous they're going to be sharing their lives now."

Andrew frowned. "Will I have to call Drake Dad now?"

"No, silly. Mary Helen and I have always called Parker simply Parker, like we always did before he and Mother married." She laughed. "Besides I think Drake would wet his pants if you called him Dad!"

Andrew laughed. "Yeah, he probably would."

She smiled at him. "Be happy for them. This is good news." She lifted her tea glass. "Here's to Drake and Nora. May they know as much happiness as we've found."

He clinked his own glass with hers, and then laughed again. "We'll have to invite Eito to the wedding. I'll pay for his flight down if he will come."

"That's a wonderful idea," she said. "Isn't it great how everything is working out? Now if the police can just catch that awful thief, everything will be simply perfect."

CHAPTER 22

Andrew and Suki drove to Atlanta on Saturday, June twelfth, three weeks later. Her concert performance with the Atlanta Symphony was not until 8:00 pm, giving them time to drive over early from Beaufort before the event. When they arrived they planned to check in at their hotel, then go to the Atlanta Symphony Hall nearby on Peachtree so Suki could remind herself of the stage and play the orchestra's piano to be comfortable with it later. Not all performers did this, but Suki liked to familiarize herself with the stage and piano when she could.

Their conversation since leaving Beaufort had centered on the police's capture of the jewelry thief.

"We keep calling him Bruce Steele but what was his real name?" Suki asked. "Did Detective Dunnings tell you when he came in to talk to everyone at the store?"

"Yes, he did. Despite how unpleasant Detective Dunnings has been in past, he seemed eager to share details about the police capture with us. Drake said he saw it as a personal coup, even if not directly involved." He pulled the Pontiac out around a slow moving truck on the highway before continuing his thought. "Bruce Steele, aka Cameron Rembert and other aliases he used, was actually born Jeremy Butler in a small town outside Raleigh, North Carolina, called Clayton. Detective Dunnings said he came from a nice home and spent time working in his grandparents' jewelry store in Clayton when younger. Evidently he was one of those kids never content with staying in the straight and narrow, always bucking against the norms, disrespecting his family and their values."

"That's sad."

"It is. The detective said Jeremy spent a little time in college in Asheville, North Carolina, but soon dropped out. He stayed around the Asheville area afterward, working retail in a jewelry store, since it was the work he knew best. The store owner, like Brewer Addison, was also an appraiser, often refitting and replacing stones and he began to teach Jeremy his skills." Andrew shrugged. "The rest you can guess."

"I know you said the police picked him up based on a license plate number," Suki said, sipping from a bottle of spring water. "Was that the truck license number Drake wrote down?"

"No. It was a car license number that one of the employees with Richardson's security team wrote down," he explained. "Kyle Richardson remembered later that his security team always notes the license plate numbers of employees at their estate sales—you know, dealers, helpers, staff, and others allowed in before the event opens to the public. One of Kyle Richardson's men recalled that Rembert, the name Jeremy was using then, came in his own car, following the other employees in the Hartung Agency truck. And, of course, he noted the license plate number."

Andrew shifted lanes on the highway, smiling at a dog with his head hanging out the window. "Richardson called it in to the Eastover police. They sent the information through the system, listing the car as associated with a crime. Rembert, aka Bruce Steele, left the auction site in his car, probably right after driving Drake and Nora down that back road. He didn't realize anyone had noted his license plate. That's where the police got lucky. Jeremy fled the state immediately, but a police officer stopped him for speeding near Myrtle Beach early this week, then took him in after seeing the license number in the system."

"I guess they took him first to the police office at Myrtle Beach and then sent him back to Beaufort."

"Yeah. I don't know all the details of that but I know Detective Dunnings got involved then."

"Did Bruce, Rembert, Jeremy or whatever his name is, confess to the thefts and to Marvin Donelson's murder?"

Andrew grinned. "No, but Jeremy's girlfriend ratted him out—Freda something, I can't remember her last name. Do you remember the police learned a woman was seen at his apartment in Charleston?"

"I do. Was that her?"

"Yes. Evidently, they'd been together for years. She was a Certified Nursing Assistant (CNA), who worked in nursing homes and helped Jeremy attain false identification material. But despite her living with him and working with him all those years, he hadn't told her all the details about his business."

"That wasn't smart."

"No. Detective Dunnings said she got especially upset learning Jeremy had gotten emotionally involved with Janine and all but lived with Carly. When she learned Marvin Donelson had been murdered, too, she really freaked. Jeremy had only told her he hit Marvin and knocked him out before they fled town. He didn't tell her the blow killed the old man. Freda wanted nothing to do with a murder charge, so she folded and told everything she knew. She'll face charges for her part in things, but giving witness against Jeremy might help things go lighter for her."

"It's tragic to think that smart young people like Jeremy and Freda would use their talents for criminal activities when there is so much they could have done with their lives. And now look—they'll both spend time in prison, Jeremy probably a long time."

Andrew turned to glance at her a minute. "This couple had been stealing identities, thieving from stores, and involved in murder. Justice has to occur for that."

"I know." She made a face at him. "I just hate to see wasted lives, people drifting into crime, drugs, excessive gambling, alcoholism, abuse, and other awful things."

"Drake told me once he thought a million little compromising decisions occur before people decide to walk totally down a wrong path. He explained that people commit a small wrong, get away with it, and then decide to commit another. Eventually they silence their consciences to all the wrong that they do and begin to justify it. Wrong habits take root and wrong lifestles are settled into."

She offered him one of her sunny smiles. "Drake's such a smart man. I'm so glad he and Nora are getting married. I can't wait for their wedding later this month."

Andrew laughed. "Drake wanted to have a small, quick wedding, but Mother insisted on waiting a month so her family in Maine could make plans to come down. She said since she and my father ran off to marry, that she was going to start this marriage the right way, in church with friends and family. She also wants her father to walk her down the aisle and give her away this time."

"Looking back I'm glad Marri pushed me to invite a few more people to our wedding in New York." She wrapped a strand of hair behind her ear. "I loved that Eito gave me away, too. It might hurt Parker's feelings to know that, though, so don't tell him."

"I won't."Andrew grinned at her. "I'm glad Eito, Marri, and Ken are coming for Drake and Mother's wedding. Surprisingly, Drake contacted them to invite them before I could and insisted on paying their travel expenses. As he told Eito, it was his matchmaking nudge that pushed them both to think of each other more seriously, like with us."

Suki straightened her seatbelt. "I'll call Eito when we get home to tell him how happy I am that they're coming, and of course they're welcome to stay at our place at the beach again."

"Be sure to tell Eito you're playing at the wedding, too." He slowed as traffic picked up coming in to Atlanta. "It was good of you to offer to do that for Mother and Drake."

"It's my pleasure. I look forward to it and I talked Harris into singing, too. He has the best tenor voice, and I found out through Emma he sings in the choir at his church and that he sometimes does solos at weddings and events."

"Drake is grumbling at every new plan Mother adds but when the time comes he'll be gracious and a good Southern gentleman through it all to please her." Andrew hesitated. "He does really love her. I can see that now that he's not trying to hide it anymore. It shines out of his eyes when he's with her. He told me he'd carried feelings for Mother for years, ever since I was small, but felt she wasn't totally over my dad." He paused. "Mother said as much to me one time, too, surprising me."

Suki changed the subject. "On another thought about family, I'm glad you agreed to let your great grandmother Lydia take us out to lunch on your day off last week. I really liked her, and even if the rest of your father's family hasn't come around and is ready to apologize, at least one member of the family has turned out to be nice."

Andrew glanced out the window at the increasing traffic before answering. "Yeah, you're right. She is a nice lady, I admit. I always hated having such bad family relations on my dad's side. This does help a little."

"Maybe the others will come around in time."

He made a face. "I doubt it. Parker said families can be funny about holding on to old grudges, lies, and bitterness. He's dealt with it in his family, with their resentment about him not loving the farm and moving away from East Tennessee. Your mother, Claire, dealt with it with her parents, too, especially with her mother."

She nodded. "Yes, my Grandmother Verna Hampton is still, after all these years, a snobby, sharp-tongued woman. I'll never forget how ugly she acted to Mother, Mary Helen, and me when we went to live with her after my daddy died. Grandad Hampton has mellowed out nicely and is a right sweet man now, but not our grandmother." Suki glanced out the window at the streams of cars. "I hate Atlanta traffic, don't you?"

"Yes," he answered honestly. "But I'm happy you got this opportunity to play with the symphony."

"So am I, and I know they only asked me because they were caught in a bind when their June pianist cancelled. He was in a wreck or something. The conductor saw some media about me performing in Beaufort in my hometown. He already knew me and knew I'd stepped off tour after being ill, so he tracked me down."

"He won't regret it." Andrew smiled at her.

She smiled back at him. "I'm tickled Morgan Dillon is driving up for the performance, too. I forgot to tell you an old college friend of his is in town, also. He asked if he could bring her to an early dinner with us before the show. He suggested four thirty. By the time our food arrives, it should be about five, so I'll still have plenty of time to eat, rest, and get to the symphony hall before the performance."

"That sounds good. We'd need to catch a bite to eat before the concert anyway and I always enjoy time with Morgan."

About twenty minutes later they pulled into the Marriott Residence Inn, a tall brick hotel at the corner of 11th and Peachtree. Their room was a studio suite, clean and modern, with a small balcony looking out over a cityscape. After settling in, they drove the short distance to the Atlanta Symphony Hall. Suki practiced briefly and then they headed over to the Pasta Da Pulcinella, a cozy Italian restaurant on Peachtree Walk.

Morgan rose from a table to wave at them as they came in the door, walking over to shake Andrew's hand and to hug Suki. He led them through the restaurant to their table, a small cozy one set for four with a white tablecloth and candles, and with the typical ambience of fine Italian restaurants. Morgan gestured to an elegant older woman seated at the table, who rose as they walked over.

"This is my old and dear friend Ellen Madeleine Rettenbaum."

She stood to shake both their hands, offering greetings in a rich, cultured voice, before they all sat down at the table. Andrew studied her as Morgan asked Suki about their trip and their hotel. The woman was beautiful and refined in appearance with keen, intelligent blue-gray eyes, sleek white hair in a stylish cut, and impeccable make-up. She wore a black finely tailored dress, ready for the symphony, and a long string of gold beads. From Andrew's observations, everything about Ellen Madeleine Rettenbaum reeked of money, breeding, assurance, and power.

"How did you two meet?" he heard Suki ask her. Morgan had never married and Andrew knew Suki was curious about this woman he'd brought to meet them.

She smiled. "Morgan and I attended college together at Berklee College of Music in Boston. Morgan, a gifted musician, went on a four-year full tuition scholarship, in love with the piano and organ. I went on my family's money, gifted enough in piano to get in and sent there by my parents to learn about music and musicians to manage our family business." She laughed a deep, mellow laugh at her own words.

She reached across the table to lay a hand over Morgan's. "I will admit Morgan and I fell madly in love but we had very different ambitions. In addition, I was a Yankee to my toes and Morgan despaired of the north and its cruel winters. He whined with homesickness all his years at school for the south and returned after he graduated. I know he hoped I might go with him, but I had my own little world and responsibilities to return to. As an only child, I was expected to work in and eventually take over the business my parents had worked so hard to develop. And frankly, I wanted that role and that life."

Suki looked between Ellen Rettenbaum and Morgan, not quite sure what to say.

Morgan winked at her. "Don't feel sad for us. We remained staunch friends all these years. I didn't marry—and not from a broken heart—but Ellen did, and I was fond of her husband Maxwell, and deeply saddened when he died two years ago. I am also fond of her grown children, her son Frederick and her daughter Regina."

Ellen looked up from studying her menu. "Fortunately, my son Frederick has taken to the business now that he's grown, giving me a little more time to travel, and Regina, recently out of college, is beginning to work with us, also."

The waiter came, demanding that they attend to their menus for a few moments. After perusing the posh listings, Andrew chose an entrée that seemed at least somewhat familiar, a chicken milanese dish, said to be a breaded chicken cutlet with roasted potatoes, field greens and more."

"There's wine in that sauce, Andrew," Suki prompted.

"Oh." He frowned at the menu.

"Order the grilled lamp chop with risotto and broccoli," Morgan suggested. "You'll like it. I'll take what Andrew planned to order," he told the waiter.

Ellen ordered a shrimp linguine in cream garlic sauce and Suki crepes stuffed with chicken and spinach. Ellen and Morgan ordered wine, but Suki and Andrew orderd water and a café latte to sip on.

"Do you avoid alcohol?" Ellen asked Andrew as the waiter left.

"My father, now deceased, had a problem with it so I've always avoided it," he answered candidly. "Suki avoids it, too, because it negatively impacts her playing."

"Alcohol can dull and impact many things, but I occasionally enjoy a small glass of wine with friends." Ellen smiled, lifting her glass to Morgan.

"Remind me what you are playing tonight?" Morgan asked Suki.

"The orchestra is doing a Beethoven tribute tonight, and I'm doing two Beethoven sonatas, the *Sonata No 21 in C Major* first and the *Sonata No 14 Moonlight* after the intermission."

"Ah, *The Moonlight Sonata,* one of my favorites," Ellen put in. "Calm, slow, deep and more than merely music. That piece is particularly in your best style, too."

Andrew saw Suki lift her brows in surprise.

"I do know music, my dear. I manage Rettenbaum Associates, one of the top agencies representing classical musicians in America."

Suki sent a wary, questioning look to Morgan.

He took a sip of his wine. "I set up this meeting for you to meet Ellen," he said.

Seeing Suki tense, Andrew frowned. "Morgan, you know it isn't in Suki's best interest to deal with issues that might be stressful before she performs."

"Well, this is not stressful," Ellen put in, offering a congenial smile. "I would think, in fact, it might give Suki confidence and poise to know that two of her admirers want to see her enjoy a new opportunity, performing in a more limited way, that would bring her joy and give her the chance to share her gift with others more."

"Let me explain," Morgan interrupted, his eyes moving to Suki's. "I promise this won't be upsetting, dear. It's simply something for you to think about."

The waiter brought Caesar and argula salads, passing them around, before Morgan continued. "Suki, you came to meet with me recently and asked me to help agent you so that you could continue to do some performances. I knew that you didn't want the type of grueling schedule Jonah set for you again, but I also knew I didn't have the contacts to help you effectively. So I called Ellen Madeleine for advice." He smiled. "I may be a little biased, but I agree she is the best in the industry."

"I always knew I liked you." Ellen smiled at him.

Morgan smiled back. "Originally, I thought Ellen might simply steer me to some contacts I could use, but after we talked, she came back with a better idea."

"I told Morgan I would be willing to represent you in a smaller way," Ellen put in as Morgan paused. "I know you asked Morgan for help and not me but as much as I love Morgan, and as much as you do, he simply doesn't know the business or have the contacts I do. You need an agency as a pianist, mostly so you can play and do what you do best. My idea is that Morgan and I will work together to see you get some fine opportunities and a chance to grow further as a pianist. With the concert following that you have established, we can build on that without overtaxing you or keeping you on the road all the time. Your star might not rise as fast with a limited schedule, but it will rise in a quieter way."

Trying to be fair, Andrew asked, "What do you propose?"

She looked at Suki in answer. "Morgan and I have talked, and he thinks you could manage a ten concert a year schedule, one each month with December and June off. In between, you wouldn't have the continued bookings for small performances, colleges, competitions, and little solo venues Jonah kept your time consumed with. I studied the schedule he had you on and, admittedly, it was grueling." She fingered the beads around her neck. "Morgan says your favorite performances are those with orchestras and actually they are the easiest to book, as well. Their only demand of you, like tonight, is playing a few pieces mixed in with the orchestra's concert rather than putting you on stage alone for an entire solo performance. Those solo concerts are very demanding, and frankly, only the best known pianists can draw enough crowd to support events like that."

"I don't like solo events as much as performing with an orchestra," Suki confirmed. "I enjoy being a part of an evening with an orchestra much better than playing alone. It's less stressful and I like seeing other musicians spotlighted. I also enjoy events where several perform, a cellist, a violinist, or a singer." She shrugged. "You know."

"Yes, I do, and I'm glad you like to share the stage. Many temperamental artists don't like doing that and are frequently difficult to work with." She smiled. "I made many calls and heard only the most gracious comments from conductors and directors about you. You seem to have made friends and admirers wherever you've gone."

Suki laughed. "Except perhaps admirers with the New York Philharmonic and at the Lincoln Center in New York where I fainted on stage in the middle of a show."

Ellen shook her head. "Actually that Maestro was as concerned as a sweet father about you when I contacted him. He is eager to have you return in the future."

"Really?" Suki seemed pleased.

Andrew frowned. "Would you be all right about traveling again, Suki? Navigating your way through busy airports? Staying alone in unfamiliar cities?"

She sighed. "That was the part I hated the most. I got so lonely on the road."

Ellen leaned forward, pushing her salad aside. "First, you traveled entirely too much. We've already established that. Second, I have a lovely answer to that. I told you my daughter Regina, about your age, is coming into the business. She needs a performer to help manage, to travel with and learn with. Morgan thinks you would suit and enjoy each others company, so I propose sending Regina with you. When she cannot go, I may pop in myself or send Morgan. He wants to be very involved in your career, and I am delighted to have him do so."

Ellen sent Morgan a warm smile. "Besides, any time Suki needs to fly to New York for meetings perhaps I can persuade you to come with her. It will allow me some delightful time with you while you are in the city."

Suki scowled. "I definitely don't want to move back to New York."

Ellen put a hand to her chest. "And heavens, who suggested it? You have a lovely home in Beaufort, from what Morgan tells me, a fine family and friends. I think he told me you own two homes, one a vacation place at the ocean." She laughed. "I also heard you own two fantastic Steinways, one in each house. Morgan raved so much about the one at the beach, and about the atmosphere there, it makes we want to see it."

Andrew looked up from his salad. "Perhaps you could fly down for needed meetings and stay at the beach house."

"What a gracious idea." Ellen beamed at him.

The waiter came, bringing their food and they all stopped to chat with him for a minute and then began tasting their entrees.

"Everything is good," Andrew said. "Thanks for suggesting this restaurant, Morgan."

"It's a favorite place of mine, and I knew Ellen Madeleine loved Italian."

"I do." She smiled at him and then turned to Suki again. "I so look forward to hearing you play tonight. I have greatly enjoyed several of your other performances and, admittedly, envied the Greenwood Agency your contract. You have a fabulous gift. As you know, the musician becomes a performer in a concert. Playing a concert is much like theatre. Special clothes, costume, role, and more make a performer memorable. Morgan says you have created much of your own persona to make your performances memorable already."

Morgan steepled his fingers. "At each show when the house lights dim and the audience falls silent, an expectancy fills the air. When Suki comes out, she casts a touch of magic over the stage with her. She seems to take the audience into her spell, weaving a story with her playing, taking them to other places and times, making people forget themselves and transcend the normal everyday aspects of their lives."

Suki blushed. "How kind of you, Morgan."

Morgan turned to Ellen. "If she can be allowed to share with her audience some of the thoughts that flow through her mind while playing, it adds even more magic."

"Some orchestras might allow that. We can ask." Ellen looked thoughtful. "What would you tell them that you see when you play the sonatas you're doing tonight?"

A little smile curled across Suki's mouth. "When I play the twenty-first sonata, I see it as sparkling, playful and imaginative. I often envision fireflies flitting around in parts of the music, rising and falling. In *The Moonlight Sonata,* I see a boat gently gliding across the water. It is, as you said, a deep and slow piece, more than merely music. It paints a mood like a painter would a canvas, taking you to another place, to a peaceful, beautiful, almost hypnotic place."

Ellen put a hand to her chin in thought. "Ah, you do have a gift for words. It is rare for a pianist to engage the audience in both words and music, but I can see that would add something special to your performances."

They finished their dinner, talking of music and performances, of family, and of memories Morgan had of Suki in her early years. He made her giggle and laugh many times, lightening the mood of their evening.

Suki ate lightly, as she always did before a show, only adding a lemon sorbetto for dessert, while Andrew, Ellen, and Morgan enjoyed tiramisu or cheesecake. Andrew could tell she enjoyed her meal though. And he was pleased to see Ellen Rettenbaum place no further pressure on her after putting forth her offer.

As they finished dinner, Ellen smiled at him and then turned to Suki. "You and Andrew think about this offer for a contract. I drew up a three-year contract with the usual agency rates. I put in easy opportunities for the artist and the agency to back away if things aren't working out well. I know other agencies are less indulgent, but my view is who wants an unhappy performer?"

She paused, blotting her mouth with her napkin. "An artist needs to put their heart and time into practicing and perfecting their art and performing it for others. I feel an agent's role is to manage their career in such a way that an artist can do exactly that—focus on their art. In your case—focus on the piano, performing as you love but still having time to write and create some of your own work. Morgan tells me you compose as he does. Some of those pieces will fit beautifully on recordings, which we can time to come out around your shows when we have the media's attention already. I don't mind saying I've developed excellent skills in sales, marketing, and publicity. We should all know our strengths. As I see it, I have gifts to offer you and you have gifts to offer me."

To Andrew's surprise, Suki reached her hands across the table to take Ellen's. "I like you and feel a sense of harmony with you. I didn't think I wanted to work with any other agency again, so hurt and exploited before, but I feel I can trust you and I greatly trust Morgan and his judgment. I see no reason to say no to the contract you are offering. There may be some details to talk about, but I can tell you right now my answer is yes. And thank you for a second opportunity. I feel like that is exactly what this is."

She withdrew her hands from Ellen's and smiled at Andrew. "I keep hearing Kizzy's words that all things work for good, even when it looks like everything has gone wrong. Do you think it's a mistake for us to say yes to Ellen and this opportunity she's offering us? We are a team now. What you think matters deeply to me. I would hope you might travel to my performances with me when you can, too."

"It would be hard to keep me from one of your performances if I could possibly be there, Suki, and I can think of no reason to

say no to Ellen, either." He smiled at her. "I'm remembering that
your impulsive decisions for what feels right always seem to work
out beautifully."

Suki laughed, turning to Ellen. "Andrew is referring to the fact
that we married very impulsively in New York, pushed by me."

"For which I'm glad." Andrew winked at her.

Morgan put his hands together in delight, looking from Ellen to
Suki. "I knew you two would like each other. I just felt it. But after
all Suki had gone through I didn't want to even suggest the idea of
another contract until you could both meet and talk."

"I thank you for your help," Suki said to Morgan.

As they left, Ellen wrapped an arm around Suki. "I look forward
even more now to hearing you play tonight since we're going to
be working together. If you're sure of your commitment, I could
hint to the press that I'm here finalizing a contract agreement with
you for our agency. It should stir interest and start to bring people
knocking on my door. What do you think?"

Suki wrinkled her nose in pleasure. "It's a lovely idea. You and
Morgan hang around after the show and we'll let the photographers
snap some photos, too."

"Excellent idea." They walked out of the restaurant still talking.

Andrew, walking a few paces behind them with Morgan, said,
"Well, that worked out well."

He sighed. "Yes it did, and I'm glad for it. I know Suki came to
me for help, but I knew I couldn't do for her what Ellen could."

"Well, thank you for making this special contact for her."

Morgan's eyes twinkled. "It gave me the opportunity to see Ellen
Madeleine again, too. After loving a woman like that, most other
women never seem to measure up."

"You still love her?" Andrew asked, as the women strolled
beyond their hearing.

"Oh, perhaps not in the old way, but well enough. Admittedly,
too, it's delightful to spend time with her again. She's such a smart,
brilliant woman."

"Rather good looking, too," Andrew said, watching her from the back.

He saw Morgan flush a little. "Well, yes, of course. That, too."

Later at the Atlanta Symphony Hall, as the lights dimmed and the orchestra tuned up to play, Andrew had a few quiet moments to think over all that had occurred. It seemed God had decided Suki deserved another chance, but on more gracious terms. As he and Suki had discussed later, resting in their room before she needed to head to the hall, they could think of no reason not to sign with Rettenbaum. In the classical music arena, it was difficult to impossible for a concert pianist to book her own shows and even if Suki decided to slow down later and perform in more quiet ways, Andrew felt glad for her to receive this second chance to broaden her name and reputation now.

After several opening orchestral numbers, Suki walked across the stage to play. She was dressed in one of her white silky dresses tonight, her trademark red cummerbund back in place along with her lucky red shoes. The audience loved these unique little things in all her performances and the sparkling glow she cast, with her warm smiles toward the audience, and the lights flickering over her fair hair. She often did look like an angel with a halo.

Suki winked at Andrew before she sat down at the piano, and then she paused and closed her eyes before playing, building expectancy. But Andrew knew the pause was because she always prayed before she played. He prayed, too, that she would give her best. And she did, her fingers scampering over the keyboard in the fast, playful sonata. Then later, after the intermission, Andrew saw many in the audience swaying to the deep, calm rhythmic strains of *The Moonlight Sonata* as she played again.

As Suki took her bows to thundering applause afterward, Andrew felt a deeper pride well within him than before. Because they were one now, her success was his success, her joy his. And somehow he wasn't surprised when she threw him one of the red roses she'd been given.

CHAPTER 23

The next weekend after the concert in Atlanta, Suki and Andrew went down to the island for the weekend. J.T. and Mary Helen had invited all the old Edisto gang for one of their potluck cookout parties. Suki was thrilled that all the former kids who'd played so happily together on the island were coming with their spouses or dates— J.T. and Mary Helen, Barton and Jane, Chuck and his new wife Toni, and Emma, bringing Harris Briggs. Even the older boys, Tom Whaley and his wife Nola, and Ryder from Savannah with his wife Jennifer were coming tonight. The event was a special occasion for all to celebrate Emma and Harris's engagement.

"You're the last of us to marry little sister." Tom teased Emma after everyone arrived and gathered on the open deck of J.T. and Mary Helen's house.

"I'm so happy for you both," Suki said, hugging Emma. "When is the wedding?"

"We're getting married the last Saturday in July. I know it seems soon, but we wanted time to snag a honeymoon before both our school years start in August."

Andrew laughed. "It doesn't seem soon to us."

"That's the truth." Suki grinned, before turning back to Emma. "Didn't Harris tell me you'd found a house to buy that you like, too?"

"We did," Harris answered, moving to join them. "It's a great little rancher in the Mossy Oaks neighborhood not far from my school and not far, either, from downtown Beaufort and the college where Emma teaches." He pulled out his cell phone to show everyone photos of the house.

"Oh, it's really nice," Jane said, catching their conversation about the new house and coming over to see the photos. "It has a wonderful yard, too. I can't wait to see it."

"It's on Battery Creek Road off the Ribault Road, not far from Suki and Andrew's place," Emma told them. "It has three bedrooms, two baths, two spacious living areas and a big open kitchen, and a nice screened room across the back. The house is close to the Spanish Moss Bicycle Trail, too, and near a park the city is developing."

Everybody looked at the pictures of the house and admired Emma's engagement ring. They all liked Harris and he already fit into their group comfortably.

"Hey, Chuck," J.T. called from the door that led into the house. "You need to come help me throw shrimp into these two pots of water bubbling on my stove if we're going to eat dinner anytime soon."

"Heading your way," Chuck answered.

"Jane, maybe you and Toni can put put plates, silver and napkins on those two long tables we pushed together to eat on," Mary Helen said.

"And Nola and I will start taking the covers off of the other dishes everyone brought," Jennifer added. "We sure have a lot of food here to enjoy tonight."

Mary Helen waved at Tom and Ryder. "Would you guys go down to the freezer in the storage room and bring up a couple of bags of ice to put in those two coolers?" She pointed at two coolers at the end of the buffet table where colas, jugs of tea, and lemonade waited, along with stacks of plastic glasses.

"Sure. We'll take care of it," Tom said as the two started down the deck stairs.

Everyone soon pitched in to do something to help out.

Little formal planning went into their cookouts. After J.T. and Mary Helen let everyone know the main meat course, somehow the rest worked out that an ample variety of sides and desserts showed up to sample.

"I used to try to plan things more thoroughly when J.T. and I first got married," Mary Helen admitted to Suki. "But I gave up after a time or two and just let it happen naturally. I learned the looser way to host these events is the best."

"Who's keeping Bailey tonight?" Suki asked.

Mary Helen grinned. "Isabel and Ezra Compton have him. They've gotten really attached to him, living close to us and with Bailey at the store so much." She placed candles down the long table they planned to eat on.

"Everyone farmed their babies and kids out tonight with either grandparents, friends, or sitters," Nola said, smiling.

"Don't worry about Bailey," Ryder's wife Jennifer added. "Everyone deserves a parents' night out now and then. Bailey will be fine." She laughed. "I soon learned to take any free night out I could get with mine."

Mary Helen grinned. "Well, I'm ony three houses away if they need me."

They all laughed and talked as they got ready for dinner.

The Mikell house porch had become the gathering spot for their group events the year after J. T. bought his parents beach house. The porch had ample room for two long outdoor tables pushed together that easily seated fourteen or more. Against the house, J.T. always set up two more long tables to hold the food, drinks, and desserts everyone brought. Parking was never a problem either, with one of the beach's access parking areas right beside the house.

Suki looked around at all her old friends, remembering happy times from their early years. She smiled at Mary Helen as she lit candles that she'd placed down the tables. The candles, in colorful containers, had a little citronella in them to help ward off mosquitoes.

"With the sea breezes this close to the ocean, insects are less of a problem, but the candles still help," Mary Helen said, lighting the last one. "They smell nice, too."

"They do." Suki scanned her eyes over the tables. "Everything looks great. Now we just have to wait for the guys to bring out the shrimp."

Mary Helen hugged her sister impulsively. "I'm so proud about your new contract. Mother and Parker said you really like the woman who owns the agency."

Suki leaned against the deck rail. "Yes, I do. Ellen Madeleine Rettenbaum is a peach, a sophisticated, smart, and savvy woman, but a genuinely nice person, too. I'd started to wonder whether the classical music world held any of that type of individual anymore. Especially among the agencies managing the artists."

"You had a nasty experience with Jonah." Mary Helen wrinkled her nose and then grinned. "I hope he heard you signed with another agency and, from what Andrew said, a better one than Greenwood anyway. Morgan said Rettenbaum Associates is one of the top agencies for musicians."

"Well, Morgan is probably a little biased, but Rettenbaum is good, and I'm glad Ellen was willing to work out a limited contract for me so I could continue to perform. I'd like a few more years of touring before I step back and start a family."

"I'd wondered about that." Mary Helen smiled.

"I know many professional artists forego family for their career, but I don't want to do that. I'm aware that the industry frowns on women who try to do both. I may have to look at new life options in the years to come, but as Kizzy would say, God will make a way for me to continue to share and use my gifts."

"Gosh, I love that little woman. She so helped me when my life fell apart."

"Me, too. I'd like to live as close to the heart of God as she does."

"That's a sweet way of putting it." Mary Helen smiled. "I heard you went to play at her church one Sunday recently."

"I did, and I had a blast. I could really let loose there and play with more enthusiasm than I can at most other church performances." She giggled. "I admit I love to go to Kizzy's church. You almost hate to leave; the Lord is so present in the services and the people."

"J.T. and I have visited there often, too. I know what you mean." She frowned. "Shouldn't all churches be like that?"

"Probably, but you know they aren't. Most churches get caught up in patterns, traditions, and rituals, and, frankly, most people in church don't spend much time with God during the week. Kizzy told me the level of the anointing in church services on Sunday is equal to the amount of time during the week that the people in the church spend in prayer and studying the Word. She also said it was linked to the people's expectancy. She said, 'Folks should ask themselves: Do they expect and want God to show up in their services to do whatever He sees fit or would they rather He stay up in heaven and just look down now and again on the service and nod?'"

Mary Helen burst out laughing. "I can just hear Kizzy saying that, and she's probably right."

J.T. and Chuck came out of the house carrying two big bowls filled with boiled shrimp. "Time to eat," they called.

Everyone quieted for J.T. to offer a quick blessing and then they all began to fill their plates with shrimp, corn and lima beans, broccoli salad, macaroni and cheese, green beans, potato casserole, sliced tomatoes, pickled beets, snap peas, strawberry jello salad, bread, and more. A coconut cake, brownies, lemon squares, and an apple cobbler waited on a side table for dessert later. It seemed obvious no one would go home hungry tonight.

Later after the party ended, Suki and Andrew took a walk up the beach in the dark. A nearly full moon cast enough light across the beach for them to enjoy a late night stroll. It was restful and peaceful listening to the ocean washing up quietly on the beach, the busy sounds of the day absent.

"I was thinking back, remembering everyone as kids tonight," Suki said. "I don't think I ever thought much back then about what we all would do when we grew up. I suppose when I did think about it, I imagined most of us would move far away, discover other lives and places." She gave a small laugh. "But no one went very far, and those of us who did seemed to find their way back home again. Even Ryder, who lives the farthest of all of us from Edisto, is only two hours away in Savannah."

"This place has a magic that gets into your soul if you stay here long." Andrew reached for her hand. "I'm glad that magic drew you back."

She shook her head. "I'm glad I found you in a more special way. You drew me back more than anything, Andrew."

He stopped to look at her. "If yearning and loving could draw a person back, I worked hard at that in my mind, dreaming, wishing, and hoping life might bring us together. I doubted it would ever happen, that we'd ever get together any time in our future. You had your dreams, your talents to develop. I knew you would travel, go other places, and I knew my heart was here and in Beaufort. I never said anything to you about feeling anything more than friendship, partly for that reason and partly because I couldn't imagine you might ever care for me in a deeper way. But I was crazy about you inside for years. I don't know if I ever told you that."

"No, I don't think you did." She kissed him. "I also don't think I tell you often enough how much I love you, how my love for you keeps growing and deepening every day. I didn't love you in that strong a way when we married, but Eito was right that love would grow. It took root, developed, and flourished, like that flowering vine that covers the arbor in our back yard now, the one that keeps spreading and growing so much we have to cut the thing back all the time."

"I'm glad you love me; I love you, too." He kissed her there in the moonlight, a sweet, meaningful, tender kiss that seemed to speak its own language.

She looked at him with affection and then glanced out to sea where the moon trailed a sparkling path of light across the water. It was a beautiful summer night.

"Let's go skinny-dipping," she said, glancing up and down the beach. "There's nobody out tonight. It will be fun."

Andrew looked alarmed. "We're not ten and twelve years old now, Suki. Someone may come along and see us."

"So?" she replied. "Once we scamper down to the water we'll be covered by the ocean. No one will know we don't have any clothes on."

He shook his head, obviously troubled at her idea. "They'll know if they see a pile of our clothes on the beach."

She looked around. "We'll put our clothes in that old broken beach chair someone left behind. No one walking by will know whose clothes they are. They'll just think someone left some things down at the beach." She grinned at him. "Come on. Be impulsive."

Andrew rolled his eyes. "What if someone we know sees us?"

She giggled. "Then they'll think we're crazy in love. And aren't we?"

He smiled at her then. "I suppose we are." He started unbuttoning his shirt.

After getting mostly undressed, they looked up and down the beach before pulling off the last layers of their clothes quickly and then racing with laughter into the water. They splashed each other once out in the ocean, enjoying the warm water, which hadn't totally cooled from the day.

"I married a crazy woman," Andrew said, swimming over to pull her against him to kiss her.

She wrapped her legs around him, kissing him back. "Have you noticed this is a lot more exciting than when we were kids?"

"I did notice that," he agreed, and they didn't talk for a while then, enjoying that new wonder.

Dressed again later, they sat in partially damp clothes on the sand, looking out across the ocean, enjoying the sounds of the waves and the quiet of the night.

"I do admit that was fun," Andrew said, winking at her.

She grinned at him, hugging her knees. "I remember when we used to sit on the sand late at night like this and play Secrets in the Dark."

"I remember that, too."

"We'd tell each other secrets no one else knew, like we did in the hospital in New York." She smiled at him.

"Married now, we don't have secrets from each other anymore, do we?"

"Everyone has secret thoughts, secret dreams they don't always share, even with the ones they love most."

He looked doubtful.

"Do you want us to have a baby?" she asked him.

His eyes widened. "Is that a secret you need to tell me? I thought you wanted to stay on the pill for a while."

"I do, but I do want to have a baby in future, even though I know it will change my career, put touring on hold, and change my status as a musician in the industry. That's just the way things are. Will you feel bad if I do wait a few years to have babies though?"

"Of course not." He traced a hand over her arm. "You should know by now I only want you to be happy."

She wrinkled her nose. "I'd hardly want to decide to have a baby without discussing it with you though. I'm twenty-four now. If we wait until my contract is almost out, I'll be nearly twenty-seven. We could wait until then. It would give me three more years to build my status as a pianist. Would you mind to wait until then?"

"No, and I think that's a good, wise plan."

She sighed. "I'd worried that you would be disappointed I wanted to wait."

"I'm good at waiting." He grinned at her, his words teasing.

Suki smiled at his words. "Did you really know you loved me, more than as a friend, when we were only kids?"

"Yes." He brushed a strand of wet hair behind her ear. "I knew when we went skinny-dipping before, too. I'm sure the event was much more exciting to me at that time than you. I was starting puberty at that point. Young boys in those years get some pretty racy thoughts."

"Hmmm," she answered, deciding not to ask more about that.

She decided to change the subject. "Tell me a secret you haven't shared with anyone."

He looked out to sea, thinking. "Okay. I felt angry at first when I learned Mother and Drake were getting married. I realize now it was because I'd basically been the only man in my mother's life since only a baby. Even though I respected Drake, I think I resented that he'd be the number one man for mother when they married."

"You know that no one can take your place in your mother's affections, Andrew."

"I know." He shrugged. "My thoughts were immature, but I felt them for several days until I figured out why I got so upset."

"But you're happy now that they're getting married next weekend, aren't you? I know Parker and Mother are excited about it. They're letting relatives of Nora's stay in their beach house just like we're hosting Eito and his family. I heard that some of Drake's family might come to the wedding, too. Your mother insisted on inviting them."

"Drake wasn't surprised the sister he's close to and her family plan to come, but I think he was shocked that his parents decided to come, along with his older brother Mitchell and his younger sister Selena and their families. Nora helped them make arrangements to stay at the Beaufort Inn, not far from Westcott's and the church. Drake's mother Taletha huffily told Nora that Drake had never bothered to invite them to visit before."

Suki laughed. "Well, this will be an event to remember for Drake, for sure."

"Drake's sister Gillis says she's glad an event is drawing the family back together. She said Southern families, despite their disputes, tend to show up in force for weddings and funerals."

"Well, I'll look forward to meeting them," Suki added. "It's a good thing Nora insisted the wedding would be held at the big Baptist church. It sounds like a lot of people will attend."

Andrew brushed sand off his leg. "I'm looking forward to it and to seeing family I haven't seen for a long time. I think all of Mother's close family are coming from Maine. We've made many trips there, but their trips to see us have been rare."

Suki picked up a shell from the sand to study it. "Your mother wouldn't let Parker and my mother host a reception for them at their house, like they did for us. Instead, she and Ira Dean decided to host a simple reception in the fellowship hall of the church, with only cake, mints, nuts, and punch."

Andrew's lips twitched. "But as the groom, Drake is hosting a huge sit-down dinner for family and those in the wedding the night before at the Beaufort Inn. Jules is the caterer in charge of it and she said Drake has gone all out."

Suki giggled. "I imagine that money is one area Drake and your mother will have small arguments about in future. Drake likes fine things and doesn't mind to spend money on them, and your mother is thrifty and prudent and likes to keep things simple."

"It should be interesting," he said.

Suki got up to grab a large seashell she saw washing up in the surf and brought it back with her, sitting down again.

"Listen," she said, putting the shell against her ear and then handing it to him. "You can hear the sea in it."

Andrew put it against his ear to listen. "Yes, I can hear it." He studied the big conch shell then. "Nice shell, too."

"We can take it back to the house to put on the deck rail." Suki traced a finger over it. "It doesn't even have any broken places, and it's a pretty white color, too."

"Conch shells and knobbed welks look a lot alike. Many people don't know the difference." He turned to her then. "Do you want to share another Secret in the Dark with me?"

She looked down and traced some patterns in the sand before answering. "Okay. I'll admit I didn't think I wanted another agency contract until Ellen Madeleine Rettenbaum offered me one. I think I secretly told myself I didn't want that life again because I couldn't imagine a way might open to enjoy the best of both worlds, to have a sweet husband, a home, and to also be a concert pianist in a limited but satisfying way." She smiled at him. "Sometimes it takes us a little time, I think, to sort out our feelings when unexpected events and changes happen in our lives."

"I agree." Andrew draped an arm around her shoulders and pulled her closer. "In looking back I see how God worked the hard times your mother passed through, losing your dad, to open new doors to create a career for her and to connect her with Parker. I see that with Mary Helen, too. When her dreams crashed and she came back to the island to lick her wounds, a new life opened for her. I do believe, if we keep faith, that all things work for good in our lives, don't you?"

"I really do." She kissed him again. "We'd better head back to the house. My underwear is wet and sticking to me."

He laughed and then stood, reaching a hand down to help her up.

They walked back up the beach then, thinking their own thoughts.

"I was remembering Kizzy telling Mary Helen how she believed God lived strong at Edisto," Andrew said, taking her hand in his after a while. "She seemed so sure God would give you back your song here. And I think He did."

"Yes, and I can compose here so easily. I've already started working on several new pieces. I often hear them walking down the beach like this."

"Like you heard *Edisto Song?*"

"Just like that."

He swung her hand. "Well, here's to many more songs and wonderful memories at Edisto. I'm so glad I'll be discovering them with you."

She looked around her at the broad beach, at the darkened homes on The Point around her, and then out over the sea and the night sky. "I hope other people will come here and realize what a special place this is."

"Well, let's hope not too many people discover it," Andrew added. "We want Edisto to stay quiet and less commercial. And always special."

She squeezed his hand. "Then we'll believe for that. I want our children to walk here some day, just as we're doing, and to see some of the same wonders and share some of the same thoughts."

As they started up the beach path to their house, Andrew looked back across the ocean wistfully and said, "Then long live Edisto."

Recipes from Edisto Song

Nora's Chicken and Dumplings

1 lg onion, diced	1 tsp poultry seasoning
4 skinless chicken breasts	1 sprinkle black pepper
1 can cr of celery soup	2 cups low sodium chicken broth
1 can cr of chicken soup	2 cups frozen peas-and-carrots
1 Tbsp fresh parsley	1 can (8 pcs) refrigerated biscuits

Directions:
In electric slow cooker lay diced onions and top with chicken breasts. Mix soups and seasonings in side dish and spread over chicken breasts. Top with broth and cook on high for 5 hours. At appx four hours, add vegetables to the slow cooker. Roll out the biscuits thin and cut each into 4 strips. Lay the biscuit strips on top. Replace the lid and cook remaining hour. At five hours, remove chicken breasts and slightly shred. Add back into the cooker and stir a little. This may break up the biscuit dumplings some but that's okay. Let all cook an additional ten minutes and serve.

Suki's Broccoli Apple Salad

2-3 cups broccoli pieces	1 cup pecans, chopped
1 cup shredded carrots	1 cup mayonnaise
2 cups apples, chopped	1 cup plain Greek yogurt
1 cup golden raisins	1 tsp sugar; dash salt & pepper
1 cup dried cranberries	1 tsp lemon juice

Directions:
Combine broccoli, carrots, apples, raisins, cranberries, and pecans in a large bowl. In a small side bowl, combine mayo, yogurt, lemon juice, sugar, and a touch of salt and pepper. Stir mayo mix into broccoli mix. Can serve immediately or chill and serve.

Nora's Chocolate Chip Pie

1 cup sugar   1 cup chopped pecans
½ cup flour   1 cup chocolate chips
1 stick butter, melted   1 tsp vanilla
2 eggs, beaten   1 frozen pie crust

Directions:
Mix sugar, flour, egg, and melted, slightly cooled butter. Work in vanilla, and then add nuts and chips. Pour all into the unbaked pie crust. Bake 30 minutes at 350 degrees. Test with toothpick. Should be chewy, not runny. Serve with whipped topping, if desired.

Suki and Andrew's Beaufort Enchilada Skillet

1 small box corn muffin mix   1 tsp cumin, chili power, cayenne
1 egg   ½ lb jalapenos, chpd
½ cup sour cream   ½ cup green chilis, diced
½ cup creamed corn   1 cup cheddar sheese, shredded
1 onion, chopped   1 cup jack cheese, shredded
2 cloves garlic, minced   1/3 cup red enchilada sauce
1 lb ground chuck   ½ bunch cilantro

Directions:
Preheat oven to 400 degrees. Prepare cornbread base by combining boxed corn muffin mix, sour cream, creamed corn, and one egg. Pour into a large cast iron skillet. Bake for 20 minutes or until golden brown on top. While baked muffin mixture cools, sauté onions over medium heat in another skillet; when translucent, add garlic and cook til fragrant. Add ground chuck, cumin, chili power, cayenne and a little salt and pepper if desired. Then add jalapenos and green chilis and cook until enchilada meat mixture is done. Drain excess fat. Next add ½ cup of each of the cheeses and stir in. Poke the cornbread mixture with the handle of a wooden spoon to make holes and then pour the enchilada mixture over it in

skillet. Top with leftover ½ cup of the cheeses and bake for about 20 minutes. Sprinkle with chopped cilantro. Serve with guacamole and sour cream on the side.

Mary Helen's Easy Edisto Fudge

2 cups sugar	5-oz can evaporated milk
4 Tbsp cocoa	1 tsp vanilla
1 stick salted butter	½ chopped pecans if desired

Directions:
Mix sugar and cocoa in saucepan, then add a stick of butter and the can of evaporated milk. Stir well until the mixture starts boiling. Stir continuously for 7 minutes. Then remove from heat and add vanilla, stirring again for 3 minutes. Work in nuts if desired. Pour mixture into a buttered 9x13 or square baking dish to set.

Claire Avery's Chicken and Broccoli Casserole

4 chicken breasts, cooked and chopped	1 cup sour cream
2 cups cooked white rice	½ cup mayonnaise
1 can cream of chicken soup	1 Tbsp lemon juice
2 ½ cups shredded cheddar cheese	1 med head broccoli

Directions:
Preheat oven to 350 degrees and grease a 9x13x2-baking dish with cooking spray. Cut up broccoli to use small florets and set aside. Spread cooked rice in the baking dish. Layer the broccoli over it. In a side dish mix the chicken soup, sour cream mayo, lemon juice, shredded or cut up chicken, half the cheese, and a little salt and pepper to taste. Pour this mixture over the broccoli and rice. Bake for 40 minutes.

Suki's Corn Casserole

2 pkg frozen yellow corn
1 can creamed corn
½ sleve crushed crackers

1 cream of celery soup
1 onion, chopped fine
3 eggs, beaten

Directions:
Put frozen yellow corn and creamed corn in a square baking dish. Saute onion. Add to the corn mixture. Beat eggs in a side dish and stir in soups, mixing well. Add to corn mixture. Season with salt and pepper, if desired. Mix in crushed crackers. Bake at 350 degrees for 35-40 minutes.

Emma's Strawberry Pretzel Salad

3 cups crushed pretzels
3 Tbsp + ¾ cup sugar
¾ cup melted butter
2 3-oz pkg cream cheese

1 6-oz pkg strawberry gelatin
2 cups boiling water
2 10-oz pkg frozen strawberries
1 8-oz cool whip

Directions:
Mix pretzels, butter and 3 Tbsp sugar and put in 9x13 baking dish sprayed with cooking spray. Bake at 350 degrees for 15 minutes and cool. Combine softened cream cheese and ¾ cup sugar and beat with beater until smooth. Fold in the whipped topping and refrigerate about 30 minutes. Dissolve strawberry gelatin in 2 cups boiling water; stir in frozen strawberries. Chill until thick and spreadable. Layer cream cheese and whipped topping mix over pretzel mix. Layer strawberry gelatin mixture over cream cheese layer. Refrigerate until completed chilled, at least an hour or overnite.

A Reading Group Guide

EDISTO SONG

Lin Stepp

About This Guide

The questions on the following pages are included
to enhance your group's reading of
Lin Stepp's *Edisto Song*

DISCUSSION QUESTIONS

1. As this book begins Suki, or Sarah Katherine Avery, is living in New York City. Now grown and finished with her education, what is Suki's occupation? What orchestra is she getting ready to play with as the story starts? Why is her neighbor Eito concerned about her playing? Have you ever pushed on to work when sick? Why do you think we push ourselves when we shouldn't?

2. Heeding Eito's advice, Suki decides to go early to the Lincoln Center to talk with her agent and manager Jonah Dobrowksi about taking a break after her performance that night. What happens when she seeks out Jonah? Why is this especially shocking to Suki? How did you feel about Jonah after this event? What happens when Suki comes out on stage to perform?

3. Andrew Cavanaugh has been a friend of Suki's since their childhood years. What is Andrew doing with his life now that he's grown? Where does he work? Why did he come to New York to see Suki perform rather than her parents? At the hospital, what does he find out about Suki's health situation? What does he hear Suki telling her agent about continuing on the concert tour? What do you remember about Andrew from past books?

4. Eito Masako, Suki's neighbor, an older Japanese gentlemen who lives with his daughter Mari, son-in-law Ken, and granddaughter Julianne, across the hall from Suki's apartment in New York was a professional nakodo for much of his life in Japan. What is a nakodo? With a strong success rate in matching couples, how does Eito view Suki's relationship with her agent Jonah Dabrowski? At the hospital he seems glad to see that relationship changing. What does he say to Suki and Andrew about their relationship that surprises them both?

5. As Suki and Andrew talk in the hospital late one night when she

is felling better and getting ready to be released, what suggestion does she make to Andrew as they talk about her future? Is Andrew surprised? Were you? What reasons does Suki give for wanting to take this action impulsively rather than waiting? After a discussion what do the two of them decide to do, how and when? Do you think they made a wise decision?

6. Who meets Andrew and Suki at the airport when they return? Drake suggests a meeting of Suki and Andrew's family at Andrew's home in Beaufort. Who gathers at that meeting and what is their reaction to learning Andrew and Suki are married? What event happens for Mary Helen there, adding a new surprise? Andrew and Suki agree to sleep in separate rooms while Suki heals and while the two settle in together. What do you soon learn about their feelings for each other that they don't share with one another? How do they soon resolve these issues and settle in to being a traditionally married couple?

7. Many people don't understand Suki giving up her career but especially her reluctance to play the piano again at all. How does Jonah respond to this news and to Suki and Andrew's marriage? Both their parents are partly appeased by giving a reception later at Claire and Parker's home. How does Suki's best friend from girlhood, Emma, let them know of her disapproval of their marriage at this event and why is she so upset? What plot do Suki, Mary Helen, and Andrew hatch later to try to orchestrate a new relationship for Emma with Orin? How does that backfire, and yet work out for good – for Emma, Orin, Jules, and Harris? Have you ever tried to play matchmaker for any of your friends? How did it work out?

8. What upsetting event happens as Andrew goes in to work to Westcott's Antiques one Monday morning? Who was murdered? Why did the murder reflect badly on Westcott's and its employees? Why did the investigation drag on and on with no resolution as

the book continues? How did Coralee Jefferson's angry visit later to Westcott's reveal a new problem for the store? In what way did Ewing Holbert and Brewer Addison aid in explaining the jewelry thefts? What remembrances, that Janine shared with Andrew, helped to turn the tide in revealing a motive for the murder? What did Andrew learn was going on in his store and in Sonny Donelson's store? Why didn't these new understandings resolve the thefts and murder at that time? Do you think Andrew's prayers in the church helped these situations to come to light?

9. While Andrew was embroiled with the investigation at Westcott's, Suki was dealing with her fears and disturbing dreams about the piano. How does Kizzy Helton help Suki in understanding these dreams? How does she counsel Suki about not allowing fear into her life and not using her talents? Suki, upset, replies, "I feel bad enough without you rebuking me," Kizzy answers, "Perhaps you need rebuking rather than folks pampering you and feeling sorry for you." What did you think about her counsel and prayers for Suki? How did Kizzy later help Suki again when Suki phones her about yet another dream? Did she follow Suki's advice to go to the church? What happened there? Why was this a hard thing for Suki to do? Have you ever experienced a strong fear that negatively impacted your life?

10. Who is Morgan Dillon and what part has he played in Suki's life? When Suki goes to play in the church, why is Morgan there and how does he react to hearing her play? What type of music does Suki feel led to play this first time again at the piano? How does Morgan not only show support for Suki but also give her good Godly counsel about her life and talents? What hymn do they play together? What piece do they later play together at the concert, bringing Suki another victory over her fears? Have you ever known anyone in your life who has given you good, wise, and loving counsel when you needed it?

11. In this book you learn a lot about Andrew's and his mother

Nora's past. What broke up his mother and father Hayden Cavanaugh's marriage? Where did Nora move when she left Andrew's father? How did she end up working at Westcott's? How did Andrew's father's family respond to Nora and to Andrew over the divorce? Do you think it is sometimes difficult for families to see wrong in their children, even when they are grown? How does Andrew's grandmother Lydia Cavanaugh later reach out and try to restore peace with Andrew and Nora?

12. Andrew grew up with a single mother, living very modestly. Now he is well to do with two homes—one in Beaufort and one at Edisto. How did he end up with the house in Beaufort? Do you remember from the earlier book *Return to Edisto* how Andrew learned The Sandpiper was for sale at Edisto and how he was able to buy it? While Andrew worries that his mother has had to struggle, she maintains "We never struggled … I consider my life a series of blessings." What did you think about her attitude about her life and how she raised Andrew?

13. Mary Helen and Suki have always been close as sisters, even if different in age and interests. How is Mary Helen a help to Suki in this book with advice she gives and love and acceptance she offers? How is Suki also a help to Mary Helen with her new baby? Did you enjoy watching how these two sisters grew and changed over the three books in this series? Do you have a sister or sisters you are close to? What is your relationship like with them?

14. Andrew has always hoped his mother might meet a good man and remarry. After he marries Suki, he begins to notice some subtle differences in the interactions between his mother and Drake Jenkins. When Eito Masoko comes to Edisto for a visit, he suggests that Drake and Andrew's mother would be a good match. How do Nora and Drake respond to Eito's idea? What do Andrew and Suki think about it?

15. When Drake and Nora go to an estate sale on a buying trip for the store, they seem to disappear. Parker and Andrew go looking for them, anxious and upset. Where are Drake and Nora found? What happened to them? How does this event begin to further resolve the thefts and murder that have been going on in Beaufort? Additionally, what announcement does Drake make about his and Nora's relationship after they are found? What did Andrew think about this?

16. Bruce Steele, with multiple aliases, who seems to have been behind both the murder of Marvin Donelson and the thefts and murder at the Donelson's store and at Westcott's totally disappears once again after the estate sale. How is he later captured? What do you learn about him and about his background? What part did his girlfriend play in the crimes? Have you ever thought, like Suki, that it's a shame clever criminals don't employ their talents to something useful?

17. When Suki goes to perform at the Atlanta Symphony, she and Andrew have dinner before the show with Morgan Dillon and a friend. Who does the friend turn out to be professionally? What offer does she make to Suki? What does Suki think about Ellen Rettenbaum and does she take Ellen up on her offer to represent her? How is this a good second chance for Suki with her career at this time?

18. In the final chapter all the old friends from Edisto get together on the Mikells' porch for one of their cookouts. Who is there? What announcement are they celebrating? What things do Suki and Andrew share with each other afterward as they walk up the beach? What impulsive thing do they do, reminiscent of a younger time in their lives? Did you enjoy how this story and this trilogy, following the lives of Claire and her daughters, ended? What did you most enjoy about this book?

About the Author

Lin Stepp

Dr. Lin Stepp is a *New York Times*, *USA Today*, and *Publishers Weekly* Best-Selling international author. A native Tenessean, she has also worked as a businesswoman and educator. A previous faculty member at Tusculum College, Stepp taught research and a variety of psychology and counseling courses for almost twenty years. Her business background includes over twenty-five years in marketing, sales, production art, and regional publishing.

Stepp writes engaging, heart-warming contemporary Southern fiction with a strong sense of place and has sixteen published novels set in different locations around the Smoky Mountains and the South Carolina coast. Her coastal novels in the Edisto Trilogy are *Edisto Song* (2021), *Return to Edisto* (2020), and *Claire at Edisto* (2019). The latest Tennessee and North Carolina mountain novels are *Downsizing* (2021), *Happy Valley* (2020), *The Interlude* (2019), *Lost Inheritance* (2018) and *Daddy's Girl* (2017), with previous novels including *Welcome Back* (2016), *Saving Laurel Springs* (2015), *Makin' Miracles* (2015), *Down by the River* (2014) and a novella *A Smoky Mountain Gift* in the Christmas anthology *When The Snow Falls* (2014) published by Kensington of New York. Other earlier titles include: *Second Hand Rose* (2013), *Delia's Place* (2012), *For Six Good Reasons* (2011), *Tell Me About Orchard Hollow* (2010), and *The Foster Girls* (2009). In addition Stepp and her husband J.L. Stepp have co-authored a Smoky Mountains hiking guidebook titled *The Afternoon Hiker* (2014) and two state parks guidebook, *Discovering Tennessee State Parks* (2018) and *Exploring South Carolina State.Parks* (2021).

For more about Stepp's work and to keep up with her monthly blog, newsletter, and ongoing appearances and signing events, see: *www.linstepp.com*.

CPSIA information can be obtained
at www.ICGtesting.com
Printed in the USA
BVHW031656220321
603177BV00003B/61